Praise for *Paper Roses*

"*Paper Roses* is a delightful start to Amanda's Texas Dreams series and will satisfy the longings of many readers."

Relz Reviews

"Memorable characters and beautiful prose makes this an unforgettable work of Christian fiction."

Libraries Alive!

Praise for *Scattered Petals*

"Cabot weaves a powerful story of healing."

RT Book Reviews

"*Scattered Petals* is an exceptional book!"

Elaine Barbieri, *New York Times* bestselling author

"I highly recommend this poignant novel."

Vickie McDonough, award-winning author,
Texas Boardinghouse Brides series

"Crafting characters rich with emotion, Amanda Cabot pens a compelling story of devastation and loss, of healing and second chances. But most of all, of transcending faith."

Tamera Alexander, bestselling author, *From a Distance*

"*Scattered Petals* combines memorable imagery and likable characters in a story that illustrates both the redemptive power of forgiveness and the beauty of unselfish love in ways readers will not soon forget."

Stephanie Grace Whitson, author, *A Claim of Her Own*

Praise for *Tomorrow's Garden*

"Amanda Cabot's characters and storytelling create the extraordinary out of this Texas tale. I'm in love with her books."

Laurie Alice Eakes, author, *Lady in the Mist*

TOMORROW'S GARDEN

BOOKS BY AMANDA CABOT

TOMORROW'S GARDEN

A NOVEL

TEXAS DREAMS • 3

Amanda Cabot

Revell

a division of Baker Publishing Group
Grand Rapids, Michigan

© 2011 by Amanda Cabot

Published by Revell
a division of Baker Publishing Group
P.O. Box 6287, Grand Rapids, MI 49516-6287
www.revellbooks.com

Printed in the United States of America

Library of Congress Cataloging-in-Publication Data
Cabot, Amanda, 1948–
    Tomorrow's garden : a novel / Amanda Cabot.
      p.   cm. — (Texas dreams ; 3)
    ISBN 978-0-8007-3326-1 (pbk.)
    1. Women teachers—Fiction. 2. Texas Rangers—Fiction. 3. Texas Hill Country (Tex.)—Fiction. 4. Texas—History—1846–1950—Fiction. I. Title.
PS3603.A35T66 2011
813'.6—dc22
                                      2010043467

11 12 13 14 15 16 17   7 6 5 4 3 2 1

For Miranda Lynn Marzahn,
the first of a new generation.
May your life be filled with love.

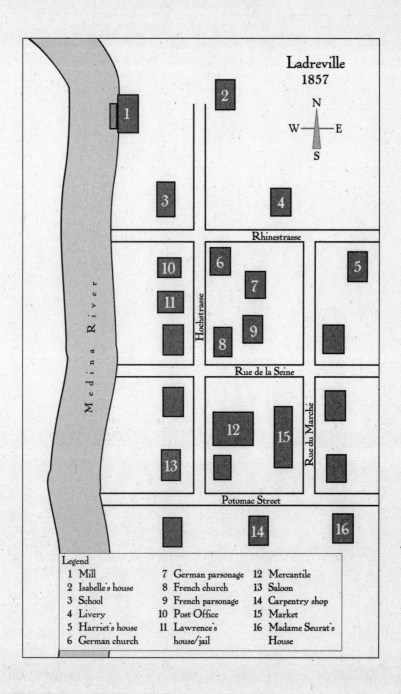

Ladreville
1857

N
W — E
S

Medina River

Rhinestrasse

Hochstrasse

Rue de la Seine

Rue du Marché

Potomac Street

Legend
1 Mill
2 Isabelle's house
3 School
4 Livery
5 Harriet's house
6 German church
7 German parsonage
8 French church
9 French parsonage
10 Post Office
11 Lawrence's
   house/jail
12 Mercantile
13 Saloon
14 Carpentry shop
15 Market
16 Madame Seurat's
   House

1

"Trouble's coming."

Harriet Kirk looked up from the crate of dishes she was packing. Though Jake's words were ominous, her brother's voice held a note of glee, as if he welcomed the visitor. What he probably welcomed was the break from carrying boxes and crates to the wagon. Even though it was only midmorning, the Texas sun was hot, a fact that Jake announced each time Harriet gave him a new load.

"It's the parson." Mary scurried from the window and buried her face in Harriet's skirts. Harriet's eight-year-old sister wasn't normally so shy, but visitors to the Kirk home were rare. "Why's he here?"

Why indeed? The Kirk children had lived in this small Texas town their whole lives, in this house for the past seven years. Not once in those seven years had the town's minister paid a call on them, though there had certainly been events that would have warranted a visit from the clergy. But today, when they were less than twenty-four hours from leaving Fortune forever, he had decided to visit.

"Good morning, Reverend Bruckner." Reluctantly summoning the manners her grandmother had instilled in her, Harriet ushered the minister into the family's tiny parlor and offered him one of the two chairs that held no boxes. The tall man whose dark hair was only lightly threaded with gray appeared uneasy, perhaps because of the chaos that surrounded him. Though she wished otherwise, the house looked as if a band of ruffians had ransacked it. There were no ruffians, of course, simply Harriet's five sisters and brothers who, now that she was engaged in polite conversation with Reverend Bruckner, had fled the house and were, judging by their muffled shouts, attempting to load the wagon. Harriet tried not to sigh at the realization that she would have to rearrange the crates as soon as the minister left.

"May I get you a cup of coffee?" she asked, hoping he would refuse. The sooner he left, the sooner she could get back to work. Harriet didn't want to think about the scene unfolding in the front yard. Though Ruth would try her best to control the younger children, she was no match for the three boys. With Jake as ringleader, there was no telling what mischief they were wreaking.

As if he'd read her thoughts, the minister shook his head. "I cannot stay long, but I would be remiss if I did not try to persuade you to remain in Fortune. The town needs you."

If it wouldn't have been unspeakably rude, Harriet would have laughed. Though the town needed a schoolteacher, she was not the one they wanted. The residents had made that abundantly clear. She might be Miss Kirk of the Fortune

Kirks, but once Jake's shenanigans had become public knowledge, few parents trusted her ability to maintain discipline in the school.

"I appreciate your concern, Reverend, but I've given my word." Joyfully, gratefully, irrevocably. Mr. Ladre's correspondence had been the one bright spot in an otherwise troubling spring.

The minister leaned forward, pursing his lips as he was wont to do when he reached the end of his sermon. "I wish there were some way I could dissuade you. The truth is, my concern is not simply for the town. It distresses me to think you're leaving because of my nephew. Perhaps if I had . . ."

So that was why he had come. Thomas. Though she had no kind words for his nephew, Harriet couldn't let Reverend Bruckner harbor guilt. "Thomas is not the reason we're going to Ladreville. I was intrigued from the moment I saw Mr. Ladre's advertisement for a schoolteacher." And that had been posted weeks before Thomas Bruckner had made her an object of the town's pity, telling everyone she was too hoity-toity for him to marry. "Did you know that Ladreville was founded by emigrants from Alsace? Most of them speak French and German with only a smattering of English." She was talking quickly now, trying to avoid thinking of the reasons she had decided her family should leave Fortune and travel more than a hundred miles to the Hill Country. "Living there will give my brothers and sisters a real-life education they could never get from books." That was true, but more importantly, they could start anew, for no one in Ladreville would know what had happened here.

The minister inclined his head, as if accepting Harriet's reasoning. "I've heard the Hill Country is beautiful. I must

13

confess, though, that I worry about you traveling all that way alone. Texas is a big state, you know. Dangerous too."

She nodded. "We won't be traveling alone. A family from Haven is going to San Antonio, and they've agreed to let us accompany them."

"That's prudent."

Harriet was always prudent. Or at least she tried to be. "Mr. Ladre thought it would be a three-day journey on horseback. I'm allowing six because we'll be pulling a wagon." A wagon that even now was being loaded by her five enthusiastic but inexperienced siblings. She managed a bright smile. "Just think. By this time next week, my family will be in our new home."

Once again the minister's expression sobered. "I pray you're not making a mistake, leaving this home."

"I'm not." Grandma always said that home is where your heart is. That was why Harriet knew Fortune was not her home and hadn't been for a long time.

ॐ

"There must be a mistake." Blood drained from the petite blonde's face, and her eyes darkened with what appeared to be horror.

Lawrence Wood gritted his teeth. There was a mistake, all right, and he was the one who'd made it. He must have been plumb loco to have come to Ladreville. It was one thing to agree to be the town's sheriff. No one could deny that the years he'd spent with the Texas Rangers qualified him to catch cattle rustlers and deal with petty crimes. But mayor? He'd had no way of knowing that mayoral duties included dealing with a woman who regarded a perfectly fine house as if it were a crumbling shack. She had seemed reasonable, if a bit brusque, when they'd met in his office, and she'd been almost cordial as they'd walked the two blocks to the house, her family trailing in their wagon. All that had changed when he pointed to the two-story house. What had she expected—a castle? There were none of those in Ladreville, Texas.

Lawrence gritted his teeth again as he forced his tone to remain civil. "I'm sorry, ma'am, but this is the only vacant building in Ladreville. It must be the one Michel Ladre intended for you." He should never have agreed to pick up the pieces when the town's founder left with no warning. That had been a mistake, a definite mistake.

The woman drew herself up to her full height, which couldn't have been more than five feet, and gave the house another appraising glance. Surely he was imagining apprehension in her expression. "It's unsuitable," she announced in a voice that was surprisingly melodic even though laced with asperity. "I specifically told Mr. Ladre that I required stone or brick accommodations for my family."

If that stipulation had been in the correspondence she'd sent Michel Ladre, Lawrence hadn't seen it. He'd read everything about the town's new schoolmarm, including the fact that Michel had promised her a furnished home suitable for her and her five siblings. Unfortunately, it appeared that Miss Harriet Kirk's definition of suitable differed from the previous mayor's.

Lawrence looked down the street, trying to marshal his annoyance. Michel Ladre had chosen well when he'd laid out the town that now bore his name. Though the buildings were only a dozen years old, the ancient trees gave them an air of permanence, making it easy to believe that Ladreville had been here far longer than a decade.

"This house is stone," he said as civilly as he could. He sure as shooting didn't want to rile Miss Kirk, not when the town needed her so badly, but for the life of him, he couldn't picture this woman in front of a classroom. Oh, it was true she looked as prim and proper as the teachers who had drummed learning into his head, with her silver blonde hair pulled back into a no-nonsense knot and spectacles perched in front of those gray eyes. The problem was, she was so tiny that her most difficult students would tower over her. How would she maintain discipline? If her pupils were as cantankerous as Lawrence and his classmates had been, she would have a tough row to hoe.

"It is only part stone," she said in a voice that brooked no disagreement. "The second story is timber."

Lawrence couldn't dispute that. The building in question resembled many of the others in Ladreville and reflected the distinctly European architecture the town's Alsatian emigrants preferred. When they'd left the Old Country, Ladreville's French- and German-speaking residents had brought centuries of tradition with them. Though Lawrence deplored the enmity that occasionally divided the town, he admired the settlers' fanciful house designs and their ability to farm even the rocky ground of the Hill Country. But, while he liked the half-timbered buildings and the ones like this that were a combination of stone and timber, it was clear that Miss Harriet Kirk did not.

"Ma'am . . ."

"Please do not address me as ma'am. I've already told you that my name is Harriet Kirk."

It wasn't his imagination. The slight tremor in her voice told him she was distressed about something, and he would bet it wasn't his form of address. What could have bothered her? Lawrence gentled his tone as he said, "And you know my name is Lawrence Wood, but that doesn't change the situation. This is the sole place in town large enough for you and your siblings."

He looked at the wagon that held the five younger Kirks. Though their hair was golden, not silver, blond and their eyes blue rather than gray, they bore an unmistakable resemblance to Miss Kirk. Lawrence was no expert on children's ages, but he guessed the three boys were between ten and sixteen, while the youngest girl couldn't be more than seven or eight. She flashed him a sweet smile that turned his stomach inside out as he wondered if that was how Lizbeth would have looked at that age.

Tamping back the unwelcome thought, Lawrence focused on the other occupants of the wagon. The older girl, who ducked her head rather than meet his gaze, appeared to be full grown, maybe seventeen or eighteen. Miss Kirk, he knew from her correspondence with Michel, was twenty-three. Lizbeth would have been older than that. Lawrence took a deep breath as he tried to ease the pain that had lingered far too long. The sooner he got the Kirk family settled, the better. Once they were out of sight, the memories would fade.

He turned to the new schoolteacher. "If you don't like this house, the only alternative would be to board some of the children with other families. Perhaps the boys—"

"Absolutely not." The flash in her eyes underscored Miss Kirk's disapproval.

"Then, ma'am, er, Miss Kirk," Lawrence corrected himself

quickly, "I'm afraid this is where you'll be living. May I assist you in unloading the wagon?" Even though it was only mid-morning, the day promised to be another scorcher. Lawrence glanced down the street. Klaus could leave the livery for a few minutes. If he enlisted his help, they'd make short work of getting the Kirks settled.

Miss Kirk shook her head. The almost regal gesture appeared incongruous coming from a woman clothed in the ugliest dress Lawrence had ever seen. He gave the younger Kirks a quick glance. Their garb was unexceptional, but Miss Kirk's could only be described as deplorable. It wasn't simply that the mousy brown color failed to flatter her, but the design itself made her look dumpy. Lawrence's sister Lottie would be horrified.

Apparently oblivious to his assessment of her traveling suit, Miss Kirk shook her head. "No, thank you, Mr. Wood. My family and I can manage quite well."

He doubted that. Judging from the size of several of the crates in the back of the wagon, it would take more than three young boys to carry them. "If you say so."

"I do." Her eyes sparkled, and for the first time Lawrence thought he saw amusement in them, although he couldn't for the life of him figure out what she found amusing, any more than he could figure out what might have frightened her. "Are you an only child?"

It was absurd to feel as if he'd been ambushed. Miss Kirk had no way of knowing that her question deepened the pain that the sight of her youngest sister had revived. "I have an older sister named Lottie," he replied. That was the truth. If it wasn't the whole truth, well . . . Miss Kirk had no reason to know that. "Why did you think I was an only child?"

18

"Because if you were part of a family, you would recognize the power of sibling rivalry. You'd be amazed at how much my brothers and sisters can do. Size is not an indication of ability or strength." The firmness in her voice left no doubt that she was a schoolmarm, accustomed to her word being law.

"If you say so."

"I do."

"Very well, then. I'll return at half past four to escort you to the Bar C. Sarah and Clay Canfield have arranged a supper for you to meet their neighbors." When she said nothing, Lawrence added, "Sarah was the town's last teacher."

Miss Kirk nodded as if she knew that. "I'm sure we can find our way alone. After all, we came from Fortune without your assistance."

He ought to be glad to be rid of her. It was only foolish pride that made him resent her dismissal. "That may be true," Lawrence admitted, "but Sarah was most particular that I escort you. My experience has been that Sarah Canfield is not a woman to cross."

"Neither am I, Mr. Wood. Neither am I."

"Oh, I can see that, Miss Kirk." He touched his fingers to his hat brim as he nodded in farewell. "Until later."

Lawrence spun on his heel and strode back toward his office, his long legs covering the distance in half the time it had taken to travel the opposite direction. Then he had tried to match his stride to Miss Kirk's. There was no need for that now. What he needed was to put distance between himself and the town's new teacher.

What on earth was wrong with the woman? Surely there was no reason for her to be so prickly. Miss Harriet Kirk might be a good teacher, and for the sake of Ladreville's children Lawrence hoped she was, but not even the most charitable person would describe her as friendly. Cold, aloof, possibly frightened. Those were the words he would have used, and the last surprised him.

Though he would have expected her to be apprehensive over moving to a new town, it appeared that what concerned Miss Kirk was the house, and that was a puzzlement. For his part, Lawrence couldn't imagine why anyone would object to the building. It was one of the largest and most attractive in Ladreville, situated on a quiet block of Rhinestrasse, only two blocks from the school. Miss Kirk didn't seem to notice that. All she noticed was the partially wooden exterior. For some reason that was enough to condemn the house.

Lawrence paused in front of the structure the town had designated as the mayor's residence and office, the one that was now his home. Undoubtedly Miss Kirk would approve of it, for all three stories were constructed of stone. Although he'd been aware of that, Lawrence had placed no significance on the building material, nor had he cared that it was considerably larger than he needed.

It was true that he hadn't been pleased with the house's proximity to the river. Though others, including Clay Canfield, who had pointed to it with pride, claimed the Medina was one of the most beautiful rivers in Texas, to Lawrence it was nothing more than water, and water was dangerous. Admittedly, after spending more nights than not sleeping under stars with a saddle for a pillow, anything that had four walls and a roof looked mighty good, but Lawrence would have been happier—a whole lot happier—if those four walls and roof had been located anywhere else. It wasn't simply the Medina, either. The last place on earth Lawrence Wood wanted to be was Ladreville, Texas.

"You didn't have to be so mean to the mayor. He was only trying to help. Honestly, Harriet, sometimes I think you just don't understand people."

Harriet sighed as her sister's words registered. She didn't need more aggravation, but it appeared she was going to get it. Though Ruth was invariably shy around strangers, she rarely hesitated to voice her opinion when she disapproved of something Harriet had done. Right now it was clear Ruth disapproved of the way her sister had handled the housing situation and the man who had pitied her. Oh, he'd tried to hide it, but Harriet recognized pity when she saw it. Pity was what the townspeople had displayed when they'd stood in the Fortune cemetery as two coffins were lowered into the ground. Pity was what she had heard in their voices when she had moved herself and the younger children into a house that was far too small for six people. And pity was what Mr. Lawrence Wood had shown when he'd seen her reaction to this house. Harriet didn't want pity. She wanted a place where her siblings would be safe.

"You weren't supposed to be listening." She tipped her head up ever so slightly as she chided her sister. Though five years younger, Ruth was a couple inches taller than Harriet and had inherited their mother's beauty along with her golden hair and blue eyes. Harriet alone among the Kirk children had their father's silvery hair and gray eyes. "I told you to keep the others occupied."

Ruth shrugged. "That's hard to do when you get riled. You both raised your voices."

Grandma would have been appalled. When Harriet had been a child, her grandmother had insisted that a lady never raised her voice and that she never, ever made a spectacle of herself outdoors. "The Kirk name is a proud one," she had announced, her eyes steely with disapproval when she had discovered Harriet climbing a tree. "You must never let it be disgraced." Harriet, it appeared, had done exactly that this morning. So much for setting positive examples for the younger children.

"I can't undo the damage," she said with another sigh, wondering whether the handsome blond man's pity had been caused by her unmaidenly behavior. That had been one of Thomas's complaints the day she refused his offer of marriage. He had claimed that, no matter how wealthy she was, Harriet would never catch a husband unless she adopted a more feminine demeanor. He had been wrong, of course. Not only was Harriet not wealthy, but she had no desire for a husband, if it meant one who turned out to be like Thomas Bruckner. Beauty, Grandma had claimed, was only skin deep. That had certainly been true of Thomas.

"Let's see what the inside of the house looks like." Harriet turned toward the wagon. As she'd expected, her brothers were slouched against the back, refusing to let Mary climb down. "Enough of that. Boys, you can start unloading our trunks. Leave them on the front porch until Ruth and I decide where they're going. But first, help Mary down and give her the food basket." Harriet smiled at her youngest sister, knowing how much the eight-year-old craved feeling useful. "I'm trusting you to keep the basket safe. It's very important you make sure no one sneaks any of our dinner."

Mary grasped the basket handle firmly before she flashed a warning look at her brothers. Though they wouldn't be quiet, at least the four youngest children were occupied.

That would give Harriet and Ruth a chance to explore the house's interior.

Five minutes later, Harriet was back on the first floor, studying the parlor. Considerably more spacious than the one where she and her siblings had spent the last seven years, it boasted two wing chairs, a horsehair settee, and half a dozen upholstered chairs, all clustered around a brightly colored floral rug. Chintz curtains hung at the windows, their green pattern coordinating with the rug. It was an attractive room, large enough to accommodate all of them but not so fussy that Harriet would worry if the boys began to tussle. They could use a gathering room like this. Unfortunately, it was not possible.

"It'll be a bit cramped," she said with another sigh, "but if we move all the furniture out, there'll be room for three beds. Daniel won't be happy about sharing with Mary again, but it can't be helped."

Ruth pursed her lips. "I think you're being unreasonable. There are three perfectly good bedrooms on the second floor."

"And you know why we can't use them." It was a shame. If the exterior had been stone, the house would have been perfect. The first floor held a well-appointed kitchen along with a spacious dining room and the parlor. The second story, as Ruth had pointed out, boasted three large bedrooms. But nothing changed the fact that the second story was timber.

The sounds of raucous laughter followed by an ominous splintering of wood drifted in from the porch. When Harriet turned to learn what her brothers had broken, Ruth laid a hand on her arm. "There's no reason to think this house will burn," she said. "Besides, you saw the second stairway."

Harriet hadn't expected that. In addition to the interior

stairway in the back of the house, there was another set of stairs, this one on the exterior of the house. Because it was outside, it would provide a faster and safer egress from the second floor than relying on the main staircase.

"If something happened," Ruth continued, "we could get out easily. I know you're going to be busy getting everything ready for school, but I'll make sure we all practice leaving. I'll even wake the children up in the middle of the night the way you used to do."

Everyone had hated that, but Harriet had had no choice. She had to ensure that her family knew what to do if their house caught fire. She couldn't let them die the way Mother and Father had.

"I still don't like the idea." But, she admitted, it would be more comfortable for everyone if they used both the bedrooms and the parlor for their normally designated purposes.

"Please, Harriet." Ruth tightened her grip on Harriet's arm, keeping her from investigating the boys' activity, despite Daniel's nervous laugh and Jake's clearly audible shushing. Whatever was happening on the porch was not good, and yet Ruth believed their sleeping arrangements to be more important than the damage the boys were wreaking. "I'll share the back room with Mary," she volunteered. "You can have the one in front for yourself."

That was a major concession, for shy Ruth hated having others around her, even her younger sister. When they'd been crowded into the small house that had once been their grandparents', she had slept on the floor in the dining room because it was the only place where she had had even a modicum of privacy.

Ignoring the boys' hoots and the ominous silence that

followed them, Harriet considered her sister's proposition. If Ruth was willing to make what was for her a huge sacrifice, she must feel strongly about the safety of the second story. Perhaps it wasn't as dangerous as Harriet feared. The family would be less inclined to complain if they had more room, and there was no doubt about it: Harriet would enjoy having a room of her own. She knew from experience that it would be a welcome refuge after a day of teaching.

"All right, but we'll practice our exit before we go to supper today."

Ruth had the good sense to merely nod rather than grin triumphantly.

An hour later, the trunks had been dragged upstairs and everyone was gathered around the dining room table, acting as if it had been weeks rather than hours since their last meal. Mary preened over the fact that she'd kept the food safe, while the boys feigned ignorance of the broken crates. Fortunately, though the wood had been splintered, Harriet's precious books had suffered no damage, and so she had not scolded her brothers for their carelessness.

"I like this town," Mary said between bites of hard-boiled egg. "It's pretty."

Indeed it was. The half-timbered houses with flower-filled window boxes made it look like a scene from a storybook. That had been a pleasant surprise. Though Michel Ladre had touted the virtues of the town he'd founded, pointing out that it had French settlers as well as the Germans who were common in this part of Texas, he had neglected to mention Ladreville's charming architecture.

"The settlers came from Alsace. That's the area on the French and German border," Harriet said in her best schoolmarm manner. "That's why the houses are so different from the ones in Fortune." With the exception of the house that her grandparents had constructed of stone to remind them of their home in England, Fortune's other buildings were timber. "That's also why the streets have unusual names."

The settlers, apparently paying tribute to both their past and their present, had named the east-west streets after rivers: Rhinestrasse, rue de la Seine, and Potomac Street, while the north-south streets were called Hochstrasse and rue du Marché. As they'd ridden down Hochstrasse, the German version of High Street, on their entry into Ladreville, Harriet had been impressed with the cleanliness and prosperity of the town as well as the fanciful buildings that made her heart sing with joy. Looking at them, she felt as if she'd been transported inside the pages of one of her favorite books. That was more than she'd expected when she'd accepted the offer to teach here, for she had sought nothing more than a chance to start over in a town that knew nothing of the Kirk family history.

Ladreville was larger than Fortune, and, if Michel Ladre, the former mayor who had left so suddenly that he had not taken the time to notify her, had not exaggerated, was a more progressive community. Why, he had announced with pride in one of his letters, Ladreville had two churches, and as the town's teacher, Harriet was expected to attend services at both, alternating between them. Though she would have preferred that her family have only one congregation, she had not told the mayor that lest it influence his decision. There were some things he did not need to know. Now that mayor was gone, replaced by Lawrence Wood, the big man who did not understand why this house was less than perfect.

"I don't like the town," Jake announced. It was a predictable reaction. At fourteen, Jake was convinced he was an adult and did not require Harriet in his life. That meant that anything his oldest sister did was wrong. "I don't see why we had to leave Fortune."

"You already know why. We had no future there. Besides," she said with a stern look at Jake, "I'll earn more money teaching here." Ladreville offered its schoolteacher more than twice what she had been paid in Fortune. Perhaps more importantly, Jake would be away from the boys she had considered a pernicious influence.

"Money isn't everything."

"It is if you want to eat and have a roof over your head." Though she had planned to wait a day or two before making her announcement, Jake's belligerence goaded her into saying, "That's the reason everyone's going to work until school starts."

Twelve-year-old Sam grinned. "I like to work."

"Well, I don't." Once again, Jake's response was predictable.

Ruth laid down her fork and looked at Harriet, a question in her eyes. "It depends on what you mean by work."

"It's simple. Everyone is going to contribute to this family." No one would grow up like Father, believing that work was beneath his dignity. Harriet gave Jake a stern look before turning her attention to Sam and Daniel. "I imagine one of the farmers will hire you boys. There's plenty to do in the fields." And, unlike the people in Fortune, no one would look askance if the Kirk children took jobs. No one in Ladreville believed they were wealthy. Fortunately, there were no expectations—false or otherwise—here.

When Jake groaned, Daniel grinned as he said, "Maybe we can play with the animals. I liked those goats we saw."

His brother shot him a scornful look. "Dummy. You don't know anything. No one pays you to play with goats."

Though Harriet had been refilling the children's glasses, she plunked the pitcher on the table and fixed her gaze on Jake. "That's quite enough, Jake. There's no reason to upset your brother." At ten, Daniel idolized his oldest brother, and the harsh words had brought a flush to his cheeks.

Harriet tried not to sigh. This was one of the problems she hoped their new home would resolve. Surely here Jake would revert to his former amiable self. The transformation, it appeared, would not be immediate.

"Why shouldn't I upset him?" Jake demanded. "You upset me. First you drag me away from my friends, then you announce you're selling me into slavery."

On another day she might have been more patient, but today Harriet was tired and frustrated. It was one thing for Jake to be discontented, quite another for him to poison the others' minds. "Not one more word out of you. Do you hear?"

Though his expression was sullen, Jake nodded. "Yes, ma'am."

"What about me?" Mary asked, her little face contorted with confusion. "What am I going to do?"

"You and Ruth will take care of the house and cook the meals."

The frown vanished, replaced by a brilliant smile. "Goody. Ruth can teach me to cook."

It appeared that Mary was the only member of the Kirk family who liked Harriet's plan, for worry lines appeared between Ruth's eyes. "You mean I have to go to the market?"

Harriet had coddled Ruth, coddled all of them, for that matter, but it had to stop. "It's about time you did. Staying inside isn't good for you." Or for the rest of the family. Though Harriet knew her sister was only shy, someone in Fortune had started the rumor that Ruth was touched in the head, the result of which had been that the majority of Fortune's youngsters would no longer play with the Kirk children, lest they contract some unspeakable disease.

Ruth's lips tightened. "I wish we hadn't come here."

"Me too." Jake seconded his sister's declaration.

Though the others said nothing, Harriet sensed they were siding with Jake and Ruth. Had she made a mistake in believing they could start over here? It couldn't be a mistake. She wouldn't let it be, for there was no turning back.

2

"The big man's here." Though Harriet was just inside the door, Mary shouted as if she needed to be heard at the far end of the house.

"His name is Mr. Wood," Harriet explained as she shooed the rest of the family outside. He was indeed big, although it was rude of Mary to say so. Harriet studied the man who stood next to his palomino, noticing how the horse's coat was almost the same shade as the mayor's hair and wondering if that was the reason he'd chosen this particular stallion.

"Good afternoon, Mr. Wood," Harriet said, continuing her appraisal as she approached him. Her first impressions had not been wrong. He was tall—at least a foot taller than she—and the muscles of his arms and shoulders were scarcely hidden by his chambray shirt and loose-fitting jacket. From his freshly polished boots to the top of his hat, this was a man who demanded attention. It wasn't anything he said or even his expression; it was simply the way he stood, the almost imperious angle of his head combined with the seemingly casual way his hand remained close to his hip, ready to draw the six-shooter at the slightest provocation. Every inch of this man announced that he was a formidable force.

He wasn't only formidable. He was also handsome. Harriet didn't claim to be an expert on men, and her experience with Thomas had taught her to look beyond a pretty face, but there was no doubt that Lawrence Wood was handsome. While many men adorned themselves with facial hair, at least a moustache if not a full beard, Ladreville's mayor was clean-shaven, leaving no doubt that his features were finely chiseled. His jaw was firm and square, his cheekbones were well sculpted, and his nose was perfectly straight. But the dominant feature in the close-to-perfect face was his deep blue eyes. Right now those eyes were fixed on her. Thank goodness she saw no sign of pity in them.

"Good afternoon, Miss Kirk. I see that you believe in punctuality."

Had he thought she'd keep him waiting? Though Harriet had heard of women doing that, she had always considered it the height of rudeness. "Does that surprise you?"

"No, ma'am. Not at all."

Though his words were polite, his eyes were sparkling with something . . . could it be laughter? That was absurd. There was nothing humorous about punctuality. Biting back the tart response that tickled the tip of her tongue, Harriet climbed into the wagon with her siblings. Though she normally drove the team, she had agreed that Jake could take the reins this afternoon. Perhaps that would improve his mood.

"We're going to the other side of the river," Mr. Wood said as he mounted his horse. "Follow me."

"Say, mister, that's a nice horse you've got," Sam called out.

The mayor slowed his pace to come alongside the wagon. "His name is Snip," he told Sam. "When I saw the white mark between his nostrils, I knew that would be his name."

"How come?" Mary appeared fascinated by either the horse or the story.

"That kind of marking is called a snip," Mr. Wood explained. Oddly, though Mary had asked the question, he directed his words to Sam. "If it extended all the way up his face, it would be a blaze."

"I see." Sam nodded solemnly.

Harriet bit back a smile as she realized Lawrence Wood had given her siblings a short lesson on equine terminology. Though they complained when she took the opportunity to teach them something, they appeared to relish the mayor's tutelage. Only Jake remained sullen.

When they reached the end of Rhinestrasse and approached the Medina River, Jake scowled. "This town's so backward it doesn't have a bridge."

Surely it was Harriet's imagination that the mayor, who'd been riding next to them, cringed, just as it must have been her imagination that, although he looked at the others, he had averted his eyes from Mary. Harriet looked at the water, assessing the level. "There's no need for a bridge. The water's not very deep."

Lawrence Wood shook his head. "That's true most of the time, but summer rain can swell the river by more than a foot in the space of an hour. There's no crossing it then."

"Then it's fortunate everything is on this bank." As they'd driven into town, she had noted that the primary business establishments were on Hochstrasse, and Jake had reported that the open-air market was located on rue du Marché, the

French name for Market Street, only a block away from their house. As far as Harriet could see, the far side of the river was pastoral.

"Most everything is here," Mr. Wood said, "but the doctor and the new midwife are on the other bank. That's why I've been trying to convince the townspeople to build a bridge."

Harriet had no need of a midwife. The doctor was a different story. With Harriet's three brothers possessing an uncanny ability to break limbs, Fortune's doctor had earned a good living treating them. Trying to make light of it, she said, "Did you hear that, boys? We'll just have to ensure we don't need the doctor during a rainstorm."

When they'd crossed the river, Lawrence gestured toward the first road on the right. "That's the Lazy B ranch." Though partially blocked by oak and pecan trees, the outline of a two-story farmhouse was visible. "A family named Bramble used to live there. Now Zach and Priscilla Webster call it home."

Though his voice had been matter-of-fact, it caught ever so slightly as he pronounced the woman's name. Harriet turned to look at Lawrence, but there was nothing to see. He was as calm as ever. She, on the other hand, must have been suffering from an overactive imagination if she thought that Priscilla Webster meant something special to him.

"The next ranch is where we're going, the Bar C," Lawrence continued. "After that comes the Friedrichs' farm. That's it for this side of the river. You'll get to meet all those neighbors tonight."

Only minutes later they were on Bar C land, approaching the ranch house. It could have been any Texas ranch with one exception. Harriet's quick glance told her that the Bar C contained the normal complement of outbuildings and a

33

corral where two curious horses watched their arrival. There was even a small burial plot shaded by half a dozen trees. What surprised her and what distinguished the Bar C from the countless other ranches she had seen was that, although the barn and other outbuildings were constructed of timber, the house itself was adobe.

"Welcome!" A pretty brunette whose thickening midsection left no doubt that she was great with child emerged from the house to greet them as they spilled from the wagon. This, Harriet knew without being told, was Sarah Canfield, Ladreville's former schoolteacher whose delicate condition, to use Grandma's term, was the reason Harriet and her family were now in Ladreville. The fond glance he gave Sarah left no doubt that the man at her side was her husband, Clay. Though almost as tall as Lawrence and undeniably handsome, somehow Clay Canfield looked like a pale imitation of Lawrence Wood.

Harriet shook herself mentally. It was absurd. She didn't care about the town's mayor. She had learned her lesson with Thomas. A handsome face and sweet words were of no value unless there was substance underneath them. Fixing a smile on her face, Harriet took another step forward. "I'm pleased to meet you, Mr. and Mrs. Canfield."

Sarah shook her head. "Please call us by our given names. I don't know what it was like in Fortune, but you'll discover we don't put much stock in formality here." She turned toward the town's mayor. "Lawrence, I appreciate your escorting the Kirks."

"My pleasure, ma'am."

"You can't fool me." Sarah accompanied her words with a raised eyebrow. "I know you Rangers prefer being active to sitting around and making polite conversation, but I do appreciate your coming."

Harriet gave Lawrence Wood an appraising glance. A Texas Ranger. That explained his commanding presence. The lawmen were famous throughout the state and, Harriet suspected, well beyond its borders. Renowned for their fighting skills and their mastery of outdoor living, their names were frequently spoken in the hushed tones reserved for heroes. Though Ladreville was a charming town, Harriet couldn't help but wonder what had induced Lawrence Wood to leave the Rangers and come here. Today was not the day to ask him.

As Harriet introduced her siblings to Sarah and Clay, a little girl raced out of the ranch house. "Ooh, a girl!" The dark-haired child who bore a strong resemblance to Sarah grabbed Mary's hand and started back toward the house, dragging Mary with her. "Come see my dolly."

Sarah gave Harriet a wry smile. "That's my sister, Thea. As you can see, she's so excited by the thought of female companionship that she's forgotten all the manners I've tried to drum into her. I hope your sister doesn't mind."

"She won't," Harriet assured her. "I suspect Mary will be thrilled to play big sister." Her brothers, on the other hand, were looking anything but thrilled. Jake's prediction of boredom was coming true.

As if he had read her thoughts, Clay Canfield approached Jake. "You boys ever play horseshoes?" When Jake shrugged, Daniel poked him in the side. "C'mon," Clay continued. "We've got time for a game before the others arrive." He gave Lawrence an appraising look. "You too, big boy."

Jake's snicker met with a grin. "I reckon a boy"—Lawrence emphasized the word—"is never too old to play horseshoes."

35

"And we ladies are never too young to enjoy a glass of cool tea." Sarah led the way, ushering Harriet and Ruth into her home.

Harriet's first impression was one of welcome coolness. Even though it was late afternoon, the August sun was still brutally hot. But though the closest trees were too far away to shade the house, its interior was cool, thanks to the thick adobe walls.

"Your home is beautiful." As her eyes adjusted to the lower light, Harriet admired the large central room with its comfortable furniture and colorful braided rugs. "I was surprised by the adobe, though."

Sarah sank into a chair, placing both hands on her abdomen to cradle the child within. "The original house was timber like our neighbors', but Clay and I decided to rebuild with adobe after the fire."

Her words were matter-of-fact, as if a burned house was a normal event. Harriet shuddered as images of another house and another fire raced through her, scorching her with the memory. Though it had been almost seven years, she could not forget what had happened that November day. She cleared her throat, trying to dislodge the lump that had taken residence. "Was anyone hurt?" The words came out as little more than a croak. Ruth said nothing but moved closer and slid her arm around Harriet's waist.

"No, thank God." Sarah emphasized her words with a shake of her head. "We were blessed, but we didn't want to take any chances."

"I understand." Though she directed her response at Sarah, Harriet gave her sister a meaningful look. She hadn't been overreacting when she'd balked at the idea of allowing the family to sleep upstairs. Ladreville was no stranger to fire.

The sound of a multitude of voices interrupted Harriet's thoughts. Her hostess wrinkled her nose and pretended to frown. "Just what I feared. Everyone is arriving at once. I hope you'll be able to remember all the names. We have five more guests, and it looks like the boys—both big and small—are coming with them."

Harriet shrugged as she and Ruth rose to greet the newcomers. Compared to the challenge she was likely to meet her first day of school when she faced a room of strangers, five was nothing. "Since there are six of us, including three boys who delight in answering to each other's names, I suspect you should save your concern for your other guests."

Sarah laughed and began the introductions, leading Harriet and Ruth toward a blond man and an older couple whose resemblance announced that they were his parents. "I'd like you to meet our neighbors to the south, Frau and Herr Friedrich and their son Karl."

It appeared Karl had inherited his father's medium height and stocky build, while his almost painfully thin mother had given him her blue eyes. Though his parents' hair was now liberally streaked with gray, Harriet could see that it had once been the same sandy blond as their son's. With his square face and undistinguished features, Karl Friedrich was not a handsome man. Moreover, he lacked Lawrence Wood's distinguished air. Harriet bit the inside of her cheek to stop her errant thoughts. A man's appearance wasn't important. Hadn't she learned that lesson with Thomas? What counted was what was inside him. She managed a quick smile for the Friedrich family.

"*Willkommen*." Frau Friedrich accompanied her greeting with a broad smile.

"Welcome to Ladreville." Her husband seconded her wishes. "We're glad to have a teacher for our new school."

Karl stroked his beard. "I'm glad to have pretty girls in Ladreville." He was, Harriet was certain, referring to Ruth. She was the pretty Kirk sister. Harriet was the bossy one, or so the residents of Fortune claimed. But, instead of smiling at Ruth, Karl directed his next words to Harriet. "I see you have good strong brothers too. Your parents must be proud. Will they be joining you here?"

"Our parents are no longer alive." She had mentioned that in her correspondence with Michel Ladre, though she had felt no compunction to describe the circumstances of their deaths. "*There are things which others need not learn.*" Grandma had been speaking of Harriet's parents' lives. If she had been alive, Grandma would have declared that the manner of their deaths benefited from similar circumspection.

"I'm sorry. If there's anything Otto or I can do, you need only ask." To Harriet's surprise, Frau Friedrich hugged her. Harriet could not remember the last time anyone other than Ruth or Mary had hugged her. Perhaps it should have seemed awkward, being embraced by a stranger, but there was no denying the warmth that spread through her at the simple gesture of comfort.

A soft cough reminded Frau Friedrich there were others waiting to greet the Kirks. As the motherly woman stepped aside, Harriet looked up at one of the most beautiful women she had ever seen. Tall and slender, with strawberry blonde hair and brilliant green eyes, she was Harriet's vision of the perfect woman. Not only was she gorgeous, but she was accompanied by an even taller dark-haired man whose smile said he adored her. This was, Harriet knew instinctively, genuine love, the kind she had read about in books, the kind that had eluded her.

"Sarah went back to the kitchen to check on something," the woman said with a kind smile, "so we'll introduce ourselves. I'm Priscilla Webster, and this is my husband, Zach."

"You live on the Lazy B, don't you?"

Priscilla nodded. "It sounds as if you've been given the grand tour of Ladreville, such as it is."

"The tour of this side of the river, at any rate. Mr. Wood pointed out your ranch as we rode by." Harriet looked at the man who had accompanied her to the Bar C. Though Lawrence Wood kept his eyes fixed on Zach, Harriet suspected the heightened color in his cheeks was caused by Priscilla's beauty. Harriet couldn't blame him for being entranced.

"Lawrence," he said, correcting Harriet's formality.

"I don't care what they call you," Zach Webster announced as he clapped Lawrence on the back. "I'm glad you're here tonight. We need to talk about the rustlers."

The former Ranger's expression sobered. "Did you lose more cattle?" The answer was muffled as Lawrence and Zach headed to the far corner of the room.

"Men!" The moue Priscilla made only emphasized her beauty. "All they want to talk about is business."

"Whereas we women have more important things to discuss—like fashion." Sarah rejoined them. "Our mercantile has some lovely yard goods and the latest designs," Sarah added.

"Does the mercantile also carry school supplies?" Fashion was not Harriet's topic of choice. Her clothing and her siblings' were serviceable. If they weren't dressed in the current style, well . . . it wasn't as if she were trying to attract a husband. She wasn't like Mr. Thackeray's Becky Sharp.

Almost as if she'd read Harriet's thoughts about *Vanity Fair*, Sarah shook her head, but her words revealed that she was responding to Harriet's question, not her musings. "You don't need to worry about supplies. The school is well provisioned." Sarah looked down at the evidence of the baby she carried beneath her heart. "If this one doesn't keep me awake all night, I'll meet you at the school tomorrow morning. Now, it's time to eat."

The meal was an enjoyable one, with tasty food and pleasant conversation. Harriet found herself seated between Karl and Lawrence, both of whom kept her engaged in conversation. It was only during the lulls that Harriet noticed how studiously Lawrence avoided looking at Priscilla, who was seated on his other side, and how stilted his responses to her questions were. Unaffected by whatever was causing the constraint between Lawrence and Priscilla, Mary and little Thea chattered at their corner of the table, apparently speaking to Clay's father, who was confined to a wheeled chair and said even less than Ruth.

"So, tell me what brought you to Ladreville." Priscilla leaned forward ever so slightly to address Harriet.

"I thought everyone knew. I answered Michel Ladre's advertisement."

Priscilla wrinkled her nose. "I knew that. I was simply curious why you wanted to move so far from your home."

Harriet took a sip of water as she tried to phrase her reply. "I wanted a better future for my family." A future where Ruth could overcome her shyness, where Mary had friends, where

Daniel and Sam could grow into men, and where Jake would not be tempted to break the law. "There was nothing tying us to Fortune, and Michel Ladre made Ladreville sound very appealing."

That was enough about her family. Harriet looked around the table. "I can guess when the Friedrichs arrived, but what about the rest of you? Have you lived here all your lives?"

Laughter greeted her words. Clay gave his wife a fond glance as he said, "I'm the only one who was born here, but I left, never intending to return. It took Pa's illness to bring me back and the love of a good woman to keep me here."

"I was a mail-order bride," Sarah admitted.

Ruth sighed and spoke for the first time in a long while. "How romantic."

Sarah's smile faded. "Clay wasn't my intended groom. It's a long story."

"Fortunately," her husband said, "there's a happy ending."

"I came to help Clay's father run the ranch," Zach announced, "and wound up with a ranch of my own, not to mention the most beautiful bride in the state of Texas."

"I was looking for adventure, never dreaming marriage would be the greatest adventure of all." The smile Priscilla gave Zach was luminous.

Harriet smiled too, pleased at how she had diverted attention from herself and her family. Only one person had not joined the discussion. "What about you, Lawrence? What brought you to Ladreville?"

His eyes darkened, and for a moment Harriet thought he would refuse to answer. When he did, though his lips quirked in a smile, it did not reach his eyes. "I came to build a bridge."

As the conversation turned to the merits of spanning the

Medina, Harriet felt Lawrence relax. This man, she suspected, had as many secrets as she did. This was not the time to uncover them. Instead, she shot a warning glance at her brothers, who had started to fidget.

As if he realized how boring bridge construction might be to young boys, Karl asked what they planned to do for the three weeks until school started.

"Harriet says we need to work," Daniel announced. "We all have to earn money."

"And what would you do to earn money?" Karl asked, stroking his beard again. It was, Harriet had come to believe, an unconscious gesture he made when he was pondering something.

"Play with the goats."

The snicker had come from Lawrence. Harriet glared at him, then turned back to Karl, who was regarding Daniel with apparent seriousness. He, at least, understood children. "Well, son," Karl said, "I'm afraid I don't have any goats, but I could use a few strong boys to help with the crops." He looked at Harriet. "I can't pay them a lot, but they'd be welcome to have dinner with us. That would save you having to cook for them."

"That would be fine." The truth was, even though she'd told the others it was important to earn money, Harriet's pay would cover their expenses. What she wanted was to ensure that her siblings' time was gainfully occupied and that they learned the lessons of hard work. This was the start of a new life for all of them, and she intended that life to have a firm foundation. "How soon would you like them to start? Tomorrow?"

Jake groaned.

"He's in love with her."

Harriet continued to draw the brush through her sister's hair in the nightly ritual they'd begun so many years ago. First Harriet would brush and braid Ruth's hair; then her sister would return the favor. "Which story are you reading now?" In the last year, Ruth had begun to share Harriet's fascination with books, and the sisters frequently spent a few minutes each evening discussing whatever Ruth had read.

Ruth started to shake her head, then appeared to think the better of it, since Harriet still wielded the brush. "It's not a story. Mr. Wood is in love with Priscilla. Didn't you see the way he wouldn't look at her? He's love struck, just like in the books."

"Nonsense." While it was true Harriet had noticed Lawrence's apparent discomfort, she didn't want to admit she had considered her sister's explanation. "It's more likely they had some kind of disagreement. Besides, Priscilla is married."

"That never stopped true love. Think about Lancelot and Guinevere."

Harriet began to braid her sister's hair. "You think about them," she said more tartly than she had intended. "I've got lessons to plan." The last thing she needed was to think about Lawrence Wood and unrequited love.

She was still telling herself that an hour later as she slid between the sheets. Why then did she keep picturing a tall blond man with deep blue eyes? It was nonsense. Pure and utter nonsense.

3

It was totally absurd. Lawrence ran his shaving brush through the lather. There was no reason he should have dreamt of her and absolutely no reason his waking thoughts should drift to her so often. He picked up his razor, frowning when he recalled the way his Bible had fallen open to the second chapter of Genesis. It never opened at the beginning, and yet the first verse his eyes had seen this morning was Genesis 2:24: "Therefore shall a man leave his father and mother, and shall cleave unto his wife." Absurd. Oh, not the idea of marriage. At one time he'd thought Priscilla was the woman God had chosen for him, but he'd soon realized that what he'd felt was mere infatuation coupled with the desire to protect her. Knowing how foolish he'd once been made being near Priscilla downright awkward. That was why he'd avoided her since he'd returned to Ladreville after resigning from the Rangers. Unfortunately, there'd been no way to refuse Sarah's invitation. Why on earth had the woman placed them next to each other? Though he knew she hadn't intended it, Sarah's seating arrangement had turned last night into one of the most uncomfortable evenings Lawrence could remember, almost as uncomfortable as some of the times he'd spent with his sister.

"You see yourself as one of those knights in shining armor," Lottie had announced when he'd told her he was leaving the Rangers. He couldn't recall what his sister had asked, but somehow he'd found himself speaking of Priscilla. "You want to help everyone. That's all right, Lawrence, but don't confuse concern with love. They're not the same." Lottie, who'd been happily married for fifteen years, considered herself an expert on the subject of love.

Lawrence knew he was not. He was an expert at apprehending criminals. That's why he was here. It was true he'd wanted to leave the Rangers and settle down, but he had not wanted the settling down to be in Ladreville. What man would willingly return to the place where he'd made a fool of himself? But the prodding had been clear. He'd felt it deep inside himself, and though he'd prayed and prayed, God's answer remained constant: go to Ladreville.

Lawrence had listened to his Lord. He'd signed a six-month contract to serve as Ladreville's mayor and sheriff, and he'd do his best to bring honor to those offices. But marriage? That was not part of his plan. So why had he been drawn to Genesis this morning and why did images of Ladreville's new schoolmarm keep flitting through his mind? There had to be a logical reason.

Perhaps it was because Miss Harriet Kirk was unlike any woman he'd met. It started with the fact that Lawrence had never seen a woman care so little about her appearance. She wasn't as beautiful as Priscilla—no one could be—but she

45

would be downright pretty if she took a few more pains. You didn't have to be a fashion expert to notice that Harriet's dress was even dowdier than Frau Friedrich's. As for color, his sister Lottie could spend hours expounding on the proper colors a blonde should wear, and yellow was not one of them.

Lawrence stared into the mirror as he wielded the razor. The last thing he needed was to nick his throat.

He could almost understand why Harriet had been wearing that mousy brown suit for traveling. Though undeniably ugly, it was probably practical. But why had she exchanged the ugly suit for a dress of a particularly putrid shade of yellow? Didn't she know that the color made her look sallow? Lottie had refused to wear anything yellow, and she'd appeared appalled when she'd seen Lawrence in buckskins, announcing that they did not flatter him. As if he cared! The problem with buckskin was that when wet, it stretched and could only be described as slimy. Then, when it dried, it shrank, becoming even more uncomfortable. That was the reason—the only reason—he no longer wore buckskin. It had nothing to do with flattering colors or anything related to vanity.

Unlike other women, Miss Kirk did not appear to possess a bit of vanity. But she possessed many other things, not the least of which was a tart tongue that she made no attempt to tame.

Lawrence frowned as he considered his reflection. He'd missed a spot. He picked up the razor again and removed the offending whiskers before he rinsed his face. He reckoned it was difficult having the care of five children, but it seemed no one had taught Miss Kirk that honey caught flies. She hadn't minced her words about anything, from her disapproval of her brothers' behavior to her admiration for Mrs. Stowe's *Uncle Tom's Cabin*.

He couldn't disagree with her opinion of the boys. They were unruly. But there was no reason to have been so passionate about the book. She claimed to have been born in Texas. If so, surely she knew this was a slave-owning state and that espousing abolitionist ideas was not the best way to gain the townspeople's confidence. While it was true that no one in Ladreville owned slaves and that there had been no slaves in the Old Country, the residents were Texans now, and Texans did not appreciate the government telling them what they could or could not do. Someone ought to explain that to her, but it wouldn't be him. No, sirree.

Harriet Kirk was like a gnat, small, constantly buzzing around, annoying as could be. That must be why he kept thinking about her. It couldn't be anything else.

Harriet walked around the school, considering it from every angle. It appeared well built and generously proportioned. The location was convenient, at least for her, for it had taken less than five minutes to walk here. She drew in a deep breath, enjoying the fresh air as she gazed at the grounds. The town had chosen an excellent site. Not only did the schoolyard possess a large open field that would be ideal for playing tag, but it boasted several huge live oak trees. It wouldn't be difficult to hang a couple swings from those spreading branches. Best of all, the grounds fronted the river. When spring came, the children could search for minnows and tadpoles. They would consider it an adventure, not realizing that the tiny creatures would be part of a science lesson.

Harriet returned to the front and looked at the building again. It would be perfect, if only it were stone. *There will be no cheroots here. No one will be sleeping. There's no danger.* Though her brain formed the thoughts, her heart did not accept them, and she shivered. When she heard the sound of an approaching horse and buggy, she turned, grateful for the distraction.

"I'm sorry I'm late," Sarah said as she dismounted and tied the horse to the hitching post. She looked down at her abdomen. "The little one kept me awake most of the night. I wish I could teach him . . ." She smiled as she explained, "Clay's convinced we're having a boy. Anyway, I wish I could convince the baby to sleep when I do, but Priscilla says that's unlikely."

Harriet raised an eyebrow, wondering how Priscilla Webster had become an expert on pregnancy. "Does Priscilla have children? I thought she and Zach were recently wed."

"That's true. She has no children yet, but she's Ladreville's midwife." Sarah shook her head in mock dismay. "I don't suppose Lawrence mentioned that. Men get embarrassed by things like childbirth."

Harriet doubted that anything would embarrass Lawrence Wood. The man was confidence incarnate. "He said that the town's doctor and midwife lived on your side of the river, but he didn't name them."

"What a terrible hostess I was! I didn't think to tell you that Clay's a doctor and Priscilla serves as our midwife. Now, let's go inside and see what you think of the school." Sarah climbed the steps and started to open the door.

"Wait for me!"

Harriet turned to see a brunette who was almost as short

as she rushing toward the school. Young and pretty with warm brown eyes, she had an engaging smile and a dress that Harriet guessed was the latest fashion. It must be new, for Harriet had never before seen three-quarter-length bell-shaped sleeves over lace-trimmed undersleeves.

Sarah's smile of familiarity told Harriet that the newcomer was her friend. "This is Isabelle Rousseau. Sorry," Sarah corrected herself quickly. "This is Isabelle Lehman. She married the town's miller two weeks ago, and I keep forgetting her new name." She turned to her friend, continuing the introductions.

Isabelle directed her smile at Harriet. "As you might imagine, the grapevine has been buzzing with the news of your arrival. Everyone wants to meet you, and Eva—she's my stepdaughter—could hardly sleep for excitement when she heard you had a young sister. She's hoping for a playmate." Isabelle took a shallow breath before adding, "Eva's seven."

The woman's enthusiasm was contagious. "That sounds perfect. Mary's eight and always complaining about being the youngest in the family, so I'm sure she'll be thrilled that Eva's a bit younger." And if it worked out, one of Harriet's hopes in coming to Ladreville would be realized: Mary would have friends.

"What do you think?" Sarah opened the door and ushered Harriet into the schoolhouse.

Though musty from having been closed, the school was even more appealing than its exterior promised. With room for thirty students, a large chalkboard, and a good-sized desk for the teacher, it was well appointed. The side walls each boasted a window, but Harriet noted with approval that the windows were positioned high enough to discourage excessive daydreaming, and the cloakroom wall blocked the view of the door. Apparently the school's designer understood how easily children were distracted. There was only one flaw, but there was no point in mentioning it. Instead, Harriet forced her lips into a smile and said, "This is the nicest school I've seen."

"You look as if something's wrong." Furrows formed between Isabelle's eyes.

Harriet frowned at the realization that she had not hidden her concern. There was no point in lying. "I wish the building were stone or brick."

Sarah's eyes widened. "Why? Are you worried about fire?"

Harriet nodded. The story would come out at some point. She might as well tell these women. "My parents died when our house burned. I've worried about fire ever since."

Sarah slid an arm around Harriet's waist and hugged her. "I'm so sorry. It wasn't fire, but I lost my parents as well."

"It's been seven years." Harriet wouldn't tell either Sarah or Isabelle about the years before the fire, her parents' erratic behavior and the nights she had prayed they would leave and never return. She doubted either woman would understand, and she had no need of pity.

"I feel so fortunate, because my parents are still alive," Isabelle said. "I don't know whether you've had a chance to explore Ladreville, but they own the mercantile. We've got most anything you might need there."

Taking in a deep breath of air that still smelled of chalk, Harriet seized the change of subject gratefully. "I do need some new clothing for my family. Ruth's stopped growing, but the boys and Mary shoot up faster than thistles."

"We can help with that." Isabelle started to list the types of ready-made clothing that the mercantile carried.

As if she realized that her friend could continue indefinitely,

Sarah interrupted. "You might want something new for yourself."

Though Isabelle nodded, Harriet did not. What she had was perfectly serviceable. Besides, it wasn't as if she wanted to waste money on frippery. Even when her grandparents had been alive and the Kirks were the wealthiest family in Fortune, Grandma had insisted on sensible clothing, claiming it was important that people liked them for their character, not their money. "I have plenty of dresses," Harriet said firmly. "It's the children I worry about."

Isabelle was not dissuaded. "We have lovely yard goods. There's a light blue muslin that would highlight your eyes."

Though she wanted to insist that she didn't need to highlight her eyes, Harriet remained silent. The women meant well. They simply didn't understand.

"Isabelle's the town's expert on fashion," Sarah said. "She won't steer you wrong."

She wouldn't, indeed, because there would be no steering, not toward light blue muslin, not toward anything. "Thank you, both," Harriet said as politely as she could manage, "but I'm content with the dresses I have. They're suitable for teaching."

"Certainly." The look Sarah gave Isabelle said the discussion was closed. "Is there anything else I can show you here?" She gestured around the room. When Harriet shook her head, Sarah announced that she would head home. "I seem to tire more easily these days."

As they waved good-bye to Sarah, Isabelle touched Harriet's arm. "Do you mind if I walk home with you? I want to invite your sister to meet Eva."

"No, I don't mind; I'd enjoy the company." At home in

Fortune, she had been careful to keep her relationships purely businesslike. Grandma had insisted that, as the founding family, the Kirks were Fortune's upper class and should not associate with what Grandma called the "common folks." It was only when she'd become an adult that Harriet had realized that while Grandma's attitude might have been appropriate in her native England, it was the antithesis of the American dream and it had led to the Kirks' isolation. Her resolution that they would not make the same mistakes here in Ladreville was part of the reason Harriet insisted that everyone work. It was also the reason she sought friends for her siblings. And herself. Mary wasn't the only one who needed friends.

"I wonder if Sarah will miss teaching," Harriet said as she and Isabelle crossed Hochstrasse. It was a busy intersection with the post office, the school, and the German church occupying three of the corners, while the space directly across from the school was nothing more than a large field. That, Isabelle explained, was where town gatherings were held, including the sunrise service on Easter, the Independence Day celebration, and the harvest festival.

"I imagine the baby will keep Sarah busy, and then there's always her matchmaking." Isabelle gave Harriet a conspiratorial smile. "Priscilla and Zach did most of it, but I know Sarah was the one who started it. Without her, Gunther and I might not be married."

"I guess every town has its matchmakers." Though several women had stopped to greet Isabelle and make Harriet's acquaintance, this part of Rhinestrasse was devoid of other pedestrians. Isabelle and Harriet were opposite the livery now, at the end of rue du Marché with Harriet's house only a few yards away. "Fortune was smaller than Ladreville, but we had two women whose primary function appeared to be matchmaking." Neither of them had wasted time on Harriet once she had refused a widower who had viewed her siblings as a burden. "She's not just bossy; she's fussy," the matchmakers had declared, but Thomas paid them no heed. He was different, or so she'd believed.

"I suspect Lawrence will be Sarah's next candidate. He's twenty-eight, you know. Old enough that Sarah's getting worried he'll remain a bachelor." Isabelle's voice brought Harriet back to the present. "Lawrence's contract is for only six months, but I know Clay wants him to stay permanently. I think that's another reason Sarah would like him to find a wife." As they approached Harriet's home, Isabelle stopped and raised both eyebrows. "Be careful, Harriet. Sarah might decide you're the right wife for Lawrence."

It was outrage that made her pulse accelerate. Of course it was, not the prospect of life with the tall, handsome man whose eyes spoke of secrets and sorrow. "I'm sorry to disappoint you and Sarah, but there are several reasons why that will never happen. Don't forget that my contract with the town says I cannot marry for at least a year. Besides, no one is interested in a woman raising five children. By the time they're grown, I'll be a confirmed spinster."

Isabelle frowned. "That sounds lonely to me."

The Kirk residence was anything but lonely when everyone gathered for supper that evening. The boys were all slightly sunburned, as if they'd forgotten to wear their hats during the day, but the color in Mary's cheeks was a blush.

"I churned the butter," she announced proudly as she laid a plate of the golden spread on the table. Though it wasn't as smooth as when Ruth made it, it was an admirable first attempt. Harriet praised her youngest sister and watched her blush grow. It took so little to make the child happy.

"I did better than that," Daniel crowed. "I mucked out the stable."

Harriet smiled. Her two youngest siblings were best of friends, but that didn't prevent them from engaging in a gentle rivalry.

"Yeah," Sam said, "me and Daniel—"

"Daniel and I," Harriet said firmly as she took a serving of green beans.

Her brother frowned at her. "Aw, sis, school ain't started yet."

"Good grammar is important year-round, and you know better than to say 'ain't.'"

Sam's lips twisted in annoyance before he nodded. "Okay. Daniel and I"—he emphasized the words—"we got to use pitchforks."

When Harriet had finished congratulating Daniel and Sam on their manly activities, she turned to her other brother. "What about you, Jake? Did you clean out the stable?"

"Nah. The old slave driver—"

"That is no way to refer to Mr. Friedrich." It appeared that Jake's mood had not improved.

"Do you want the story or not?"

"Only if you keep a civil tongue in your mouth."

"Fine." Jake reached for a slice of bread and slathered butter on it, making it clear that he had no intention of speaking again.

Daniel had no such compunction. "Jake got to harness the horses. He's so lucky."

Rolled eyes and an exasperated look were Jake's only response. Harriet turned toward Ruth, who had been unusually silent ever since she had announced that she hated going to the market. "Supper is delicious, Ruth. Thank you for making it."

Ruth gave a dramatic sigh and looked at Jake, as if searching for an ally.

Mary tugged on Harriet's hand. "I helped too."

"Yes, you did. Thank you, Mary." As her sister smiled, Harriet took a deep breath. At least the three youngest children were happy. Ruth and Jake would adjust. They'd have to.

"I'm going to do it, Mutter." Karl Friedrich entered the kitchen, sniffing appreciatively. If he wasn't mistaken, his mother had made chicken and dumplings, one of his favorite dishes. Had she somehow guessed they would have a reason to celebrate tonight?

She brushed the flour from her hands and turned to face him. "Do what?"

"Take me a wife." He'd been thinking about it ever since last night, and the answer was clear. This was what he was meant to do. "You've been saying it was time I married, and you were right. She's the one for me."

A small frown crossed his mother's face. "Who is this woman?"

Karl supposed it was only normal that Mutter would be concerned. After all, she would have to share her kitchen with his wife. But when she heard the woman's name, he knew she would be relieved. "Miss Kirk. Harriet."

His mother's frown did not ease. If anything, it deepened. "But, son, you've only just met her. She seems like a fine woman, but . . ."

"She'll be perfect. Didn't you see how she kept those children in line? There's no nonsense about her. She'll be a good helpmeet, and those boys can work on the farm. I tell you, Mutter, she's perfect."

His mother folded her hands and was silent for a long moment. This was not what he had expected. He had thought she would be pleased. When she spoke, her voice was solemn. "It is true your father and I would like to see you married. If this were the Old Country, we would already have chosen a bride for you, but it's not as easy here. We can't simply go to a woman's parents and arrange a marriage. Women here expect to be courted."

Karl shrugged. Was that all that was bothering Mutter? "So, I'll court her." How difficult could it be?

4

"We need to catch those rustlers," Lawrence said as he looked at the western end of the Bar C and Lazy B ranches. He could feel the blood rushing through his veins. This was why he'd come to Ladreville, to uphold the law, not to think about marriage, a gray-eyed schoolmarm, and a child who reminded him of the worst day of his life. "The courts may not believe taking a dozen head of cattle is as serious as stealing one horse, but the way I figure it, stealing is stealing, and it's wrong."

"You won't get an argument from me." The dark-haired man whose eyes were as blue as the Texas sky tugged on the brim of his hat in a futile attempt to block the sun.

"Here's where it happened." Zach extended his arm to the left.

Lawrence squinted, then nodded. The rustlers had chosen well. The rolling hills that characterized this part of the state were a bit higher here, and the underbrush showed less evidence of grazing. Combined, the two provided adequate hiding spots for men and horses. The cattle wouldn't be spooked, and if other humans ventured into the area, the rustlers had cover. Most importantly, two of the hills joined to create a narrow divide, not quite a canyon, but close enough for rustlers' needs.

"It makes sense," Lawrence said. As much as he hated to admire criminals' brains, he had to admit that these had shown more sense than others he had chased. He gestured toward the divide. "It would be easy to herd the cattle this way, and once they're in the narrows, there's no chance to turn around. After that, it's simple enough to drive them somewhere else and change the brand." The rustlers had taken advantage of the open grassland on the other side of the defile and had herded the cattle in different directions, making it impossible to track them.

Lawrence hobbled Snip, then studied the ground. Though the cattle had trampled most of the grass, a few horse prints were visible. "I'd say three men were involved." He pointed to the different horseshoe patterns.

Zach scuffed the ground, as if looking for clues. "I thought the rustlers might have been Comanche. I heard they were in the area, but it doesn't seem likely, since these horses were shod."

Lawrence heard the disappointment in Zach's voice. Better than most, he knew how strong the desire to find wrongdoers could be. That was why he had joined the Rangers, because he'd wanted to see justice done. "The horses might have been stolen. At this point, there's no way to tell." Lawrence strode back to Snip and mounted the palomino. "I'm afraid there's nothing more I can do other than promise to keep an eye out in this direction." The problem, and he was certain Zach knew it, was that rustlers were wily. There was no telling when—or if—they'd return.

Zach's nod said he'd heard Lawrence's unspoken words. "Thanks. I hope you'll come back to the Lazy B and have supper with us. The least I can do is offer you a home-cooked meal."

"Another time, maybe."

"What's wrong with today?"

Nothing, other than the fact that it would be downright embarrassing. Sitting next to Priscilla at the Bar C had been bad enough. It would be worse with fewer people around to carry the discussion. As he started to invent an excuse, the image of Harriet's face broke Lawrence's concentration. Though he knew she was miles away, in his mind she was glaring at him, those gray eyes fierce behind the spectacles, her lips pursed with disapproval. "Coward," he could almost hear her say. As much as he wanted to, Lawrence couldn't deny that his reluctance to have supper with Zach and Priscilla might not be prudence but cowardice.

"All right," he said, forcing enthusiasm into his voice. "I'll come."

As they rode up the lane toward the Lazy B's main house, a woman hurried onto the porch. Tall and slender, almost unbelievably beautiful with that sunset-colored hair and those grass-green eyes, she gave her husband a smile so filled with love that it made Lawrence's stomach do a summersault. So this was what being married was like, coming home to a woman who acted as if the sun rose and set in you. A lump rose to Lawrence's throat as he wondered whether he'd ever find a woman who looked at him that way.

Priscilla descended the steps and smiled again when her husband wrapped his arm around her waist. "I see you convinced Lawrence to come." She wrinkled her nose as she pretended to frown at Lawrence. "Did Zach warn you about my charcoal biscuits?"

"Now, Priscilla, that was only once." Zach gave his wife a fond smile as he said, "She's a good cook."

"And he's a tolerant husband."

Lawrence laughed at the couple who were so obviously infatuated with each other. "You two remind me of Sarah and Clay." Though he had expected that seeing Priscilla again would be embarrassing, it wasn't. Perhaps he was fully recovered. Lottie had said that would happen, that one day he would regard Priscilla as just a woman, not the one he'd once thought he fancied.

"That's what marriage does to you." Zach opened the door for his wife, then followed her into the house. "You ought to try it."

Priscilla turned, her eyes wide with feigned shock. "Zachary Webster, I never thought I'd hear you say that. After all the trouble we had with Isabelle and Gunther, I was sure you'd sworn off matchmaking."

"Matchmaking? Who's matchmaking? All I did was make the observation that marriage is good."

"My sister says the same thing," Lawrence admitted. "I'll tell you what I told Lottie: all the good women are taken." He looked around the house that Zach had bought soon after he married Priscilla. Although Lawrence had visited the Lazy B a number of times, this was the first time he'd been inside. To his surprise, as he studied the building, his thoughts were focused not on its owners but on the woman who had stared at a half-stone house with horror. Would Harriet like this one? A formal parlor stood on the right side of the center hall, with the dining room on the left. Stairs led to the second story sleeping quarters, and there appeared to be two more bedrooms at the rear of the first floor. It was a pleasant house, probably large enough for Harriet and her siblings, but it lacked the primary attribute she appeared to seek: a stone exterior.

"You never know when you'll meet the right woman." Zach's words brought Lawrence back to the present. "Who knows? She may ride into your life when you least expect it. That's what happened to me."

Priscilla nodded toward the door. "If you two wash up, I'll have supper on the table in five minutes."

Lawrence wasn't certain whether he should be flattered that Priscilla served him in the kitchen. The other invitations he'd received had included a meal in the dining room using what were obviously his hostess's best dishes. Priscilla appeared to be treating him like part of the family. Perhaps she realized that his years with the Rangers made him more comfortable with tin plates than fancy china.

"I'm amazed at all the changes in Ladreville." Zach buttered a perfectly browned biscuit, holding it up as if toasting his wife. "I've been here only a bit more than a year, but it's starting to seem like a different town."

"Do you suppose that's because there's no one named Ladre here any longer?" Lawrence had had qualms about taking the position of mayor and sheriff, knowing that he was expected to fill the shoes of the man who'd founded the town and given it his name.

"That's part of it." Zach nodded as he cut a piece of sausage. "Michel Ladre kept a pretty tight rein on folks."

"And you don't think I will?"

It was Priscilla who answered. "I suspect you'll be fairer.

Even though he claimed not to be biased, it seemed to me that Mayor Ladre sided with the French settlers more often than not."

"I haven't seen much evidence of hostility since I've been here." When he'd first brought Priscilla to Ladreville after the stagecoach she'd been traveling in had been attacked and her parents killed, Lawrence had been aware of the tension between the French and German immigrants. Although they were now Texans and Americans, the centuries of war they'd endured in their native Alsace had led to deep-seated mistrust that occasionally erupted into fights. That had been one of the reasons Clay had insisted the town needed a mayor with experience enforcing the law.

Priscilla smiled as she refilled Lawrence's glass. "Isabelle and Gunther's marriage helped. The townspeople are taking credit for their happiness now, but it wasn't always that way. We even had talk of tar and feathers."

"I'd like to believe their wedding ushered in a new era," Zach said. "We've got a new mayor and a new teacher."

"Don't forget that we'll soon have a new minister." When Lawrence raised an eyebrow, Priscilla continued. "Didn't you hear? Pastor Sempert asked the church headquarters to send a replacement. He claims he's too old."

"He is elderly," Lawrence agreed. "But too old? I'm not sure about that." Though Lawrence had met the German church's pastor and guessed him to be close to seventy, in his experience men of God worked until the day they died. "How do you decide when you're too old to work?"

Zach grinned. "For me it's simple. The day I can't rope a calf is the day I hang up my spurs."

"What about you, Lawrence?" Furrows had formed between

Priscilla's eyes. "You left the Rangers, and I'm certain it wasn't because you're too old."

Lawrence chewed slowly, buying time as he considered how much of the story to tell them. "I was tired of being a nomad," he said. That was true and was all that he'd shared with Clay when he'd agreed to come to Ladreville, but Priscilla's expression led him to continue. "You're right. It was more than that. I didn't like some of the things I saw Rangers doing. There were times when they took the law into their own hands." It was odd. A few months ago, he would have said "we," but now he thought of his former companions as "they." "I was part of Callahan's company. I tell you, there was no reason to sack and burn Piedras Negras. The Mexicans hadn't done anything wrong."

Lawrence frowned as he thought of the group of Rangers who'd headed south, purportedly to recapture Indians, but who had let anger and their hatred of the Mexicans prevail. As a result, a town of innocent people had been destroyed.

"Wasn't Callahan mustered out?" Zach asked.

"Yeah, but I still can't forget what happened." Though he hadn't lit any of the torches, Lawrence hadn't stopped the rampage, either, and that weighed on his conscience. "I almost left the Rangers then."

Priscilla shook her head. "I'm glad you didn't. Who knows what would have happened to me if you hadn't come by that stagecoach when you did." Her eyes darkened with remembered pain. "You were my knight in shining armor."

Odd. That's what Lottie had called him. Lawrence stared at the far wall as thoughts raced through his mind. The fact that Priscilla needed him explained his former fascination with her. It made sense that he saw himself as some sort of hero, but that didn't explain Harriet. She was not a damsel in distress seeking a knight in shining armor. If there was ever a woman who did not need rescuing, it was Harriet Kirk.

She didn't need him, and yet still he thought of her. At the most inconvenient times, Lawrence would picture that delicate nose whose tip turned up ever so slightly, giving her an air of impudence, and he would smile. When he looked at the river and saw the sun glinting on its surface, he would remember how her eyes sparkled behind her spectacles, even when she was trying to look serious. And when he heard the soft sound of leaves rustling in the breeze, he'd be reminded of how the asperity in her voice vanished when she spoke to little Mary.

No matter where he went, no matter what he did, Harriet Kirk was there. It was annoying. It was absurd. It had to stop. Harriet was not a damsel in distress. She was an enigma, and Lawrence did not like enigmas.

❧

"Time to settle up." Though the man's voice was pleasant, Thomas didn't like the way he looked at him, almost as if he thought that he, Thomas Bruckner, would not be able to pay. Just because he'd had to borrow a bit last week didn't mean he wasn't flush today. He was, for he had helped himself to Uncle Abe's collection box. The sanctimonious old prig called it an offering, but Thomas knew it for what it really was: a tax on the citizens of Fortune and a mighty hefty one too, expecting them to pay a tenth of all they earned for the privilege of hearing Uncle Abe preach.

Thomas bit back a smile. They might not have known it, but this week Fortune's churchgoers had staked him in a night of poker. And what a night it had been, all except for the last hour. He'd been on a roll, winning more money than ever. But then the cards had changed, and now this beady-eyed man with the greasy black hair was holding out his hand.

"Sure thing." Thomas reached for his moneybag. There'd be enough in there. Of course there would. He counted out the coins, frowning when the bag was empty and the man still held out his hand. "Well, what do you know? I reckon I'm a bit short." Thomas gave the man his innocent look, the one that made most folks believe his stories of hard luck.

Beady-eyes appeared unimpressed. "Mr. Allen ain't gonna be pleased, seein' as how you owe him close to a hundred dollars."

The amount of his debt might have made him choke, but Thomas barely heard it. His brain had stopped, paralyzed by the name Beady-eyes had pronounced. "Mr. Allen? Mr. Herb Allen?" The words came out as little more than a squeak. Everyone in this part of Texas knew better than to mess with Herb Allen. He was as mean as they came, and, if the stories were true, thought nothing of flaying a man alive if he didn't repay his debts. Thomas blanched at the prospect. How on earth had he wound up in one of Herb Allen's establishments?

"I'll get the money," he promised.

Beady-eyes's laugh sent chills down Thomas's spine. "You do that, and if you know what's good for you, you'll do it fast. Mighty fast." Beady-eyes pointed at the door. "Now, git out, and don't you come back till you got Mr. Allen's money."

Though the evening air felt cool compared to the saloon, it did nothing to dry the sweat that poured down Thomas's face. How had he gotten himself into this predicament? Luck had always been with him, and even when it hadn't started out that way, he'd managed to turn things around. A smile and some glib words worked magic. When had he lost his touch?

Thomas frowned as the image of a slip of a gal flitted before him. Harriet. It was her fault. If she'd married him, he wouldn't be in this pickle. But snooty Miss Harriet Kirk had refused him. Thomas frowned again as he recalled the day she'd announced that she wouldn't marry him if he were the last man on Earth, all because he didn't want to be saddled with her bratty sisters and brothers. Of course, he hadn't let the town know what she'd said. Instead, he'd told everyone that Harriet wasn't the woman for him, and they'd believed him. Everyone believed him. Everyone except for Harriet.

He swung his leg over the saddle and spurred his horse. Harriet might have read more books than anyone in Fortune, but book learning didn't mean a thing. No, sirree. What mattered were the things you couldn't learn from a book, like how to sweet-talk folks.

A smile crossed Thomas's face. That was the answer. She'd been riled. That's all that had happened. She didn't mean it. He'd get her back, and when he did, his problems would be over. All it would take was a bit of sweet-talking, and the richest gal in Fortune's money would be his.

"I don't understand what's wrong with you." Harriet looked at the brother who was refusing to climb into the wagon. Jake had been sulking for two days. Now sulking had turned into a mutiny. "I thought you liked Frau Friedrich's cooking."

"It's better than Ruth's." Though he muttered the words, he shot a glance at Ruth. Harriet bit back a sigh. Something was definitely wrong if Jake was antagonizing Ruth. Since they'd moved to Ladreville, the two had been allies. Why, then, was Jake goading her?

"You ungrateful beast!" Ruth reached down from the wagon and thumped Jake's head. "Just for that, I ought to put ipecacuanha in your milk."

Jake's lips twisted. "Go ahead, sis. Maybe I'd be too sick to work."

Harriet had had enough. "Stop squabbling, both of you. Jake, get into this wagon, or you won't eat anything—not even ipecacuanha—for a week. It was kind of Frau Friedrich to invite us to Sunday dinner, and I expect you to behave." Though she addressed her last words to all five siblings, she had few worries about Sam, Daniel, and Mary. It was only the older two who had been out of sorts, with Jake surlier than she'd ever seen him and Ruth moping constantly. Whenever she'd asked, they'd both claimed that nothing was wrong. They were lying.

"Oh, how pretty." Harriet smiled as she guided the wagon toward the Friedrich homestead. Though the boys had spent six days a week here for the past two weeks, this was her first visit. Why hadn't they told her how extensive the gardens were? Harriet smiled again. Being boys, they probably hadn't noticed the flowers. The house was an ordinary farmhouse, a two-story timber building that resembled the one on the Lazy B ranch. What made it special was the riot of blossoms that tumbled from window boxes and the immaculately groomed flowerbeds that surrounded the house. Someone—probably Frau Friedrich—spent many hours with those plants.

"I've never seen such beautiful flowers," Harriet told her

67

hostess as soon as she was on the ground. She smiled at the older woman, who was dressed in her Sunday best, a deep blue dress with a white lace collar. Her husband stood at her side, his arm around her shoulders, while Karl beamed from the other side of the wagon. He had greeted Harriet, then insisted on helping her dismount from the wagon. Now he was aiding Ruth. Though the family was accustomed to climbing in and out of the wagon without assistance, Harriet had to admit that Karl's gallantry and the broad smile that accompanied it were a pleasant change from Jake's and Ruth's sour faces.

"Are those petunias?" she asked, pointing at the brilliant red and white blossoms.

Frau Friedrich nodded. "I brought seeds from the Old Country. Not many survived, but I'm enjoying the ones that did."

Her husband gave her a fond smile. "Greta had the best garden in the Old Country. Everyone wanted to learn how she did it."

"But I wouldn't tell, any more than Otto would share the secret of his wheat and corn crops."

Harriet stared at the two older Friedrichs, amazed by the visible love flowing between them. Though she'd read about it, she had never seen people her parents' age behaving this way. Love, she had thought, ended as soon as the marriage was official. At least that's what she imagined had happened to her parents.

Harriet blinked and forced her thoughts back to the present. Flowers and crops. That's what they were discussing, not marriage. "What is the secret?" she asked.

"Do you think they'll tell you?" Karl had appeared at

Harriet's side. Though he was standing a proper distance away, her nostrils twitched at the scent of hay, horse, and bay rum, and she found herself remembering Lawrence's clean scent the day he'd escorted them to the Bar C and how it seemed tantalizing, not cloying. Harriet shook herself mentally. It was absurd to be thinking of Lawrence. He was the mayor, the sheriff, nothing more.

"Manure."

For the second time in less than a minute, Harriet stared at Frau Friedrich, embarrassed that her thoughts had wandered. That wasn't like her. "I beg your pardon?"

The older woman smiled. "Manure's the secret. Otto and I used more fertilizer than our neighbors. That's why our crops grew better."

Of course.

Frau Friedrich led them into the house. The interior was far different from the homes Harriet had lived in in Fortune. Even her grandparents' house, small as it was, boasted separate rooms for each major function. Here, the kitchen was small and dominated by a large stove, and there was no separate dining room, simply a table sitting in a corner of the large front room. Though functional, the furniture was devoid of the intricate carvings that had characterized her parents' and grandparents' homes. But, though simple, this house was spotless. The windows gleamed, and not a speck of dust was visible. Frau Friedrich spent her days cleaning, not . . .

Harriet forced those thoughts aside as she and her sisters carried platters and bowls of food to the table. At the other side of the front room, Sam and Daniel were engrossed in a game of checkers, while Otto and Karl appeared to be coaching them. If it hadn't been for Jake staring out the window and obviously choosing not to be involved in his brothers' pastime, it would have been a scene of familial peace. Harriet took a deep breath and let the warmth flow through her. This was what she had sought for so long, a normal family.

When she returned to the kitchen, Frau Friedrich handed her a pitcher of buttermilk. "Would you fill the children's glasses?"

"Certainly. What about the rest of us?"

"We'll have beer."

As the blood drained from Harriet's face, she managed to say, "No!" before memories blotted out the present.

"Pour me another one." Father glared at Mother as he plunked the empty glass onto the table.

"No, Jacob, I won't. You've got to stop this. It's bad enough that you spend your days at the saloon. I don't want you drinking here where the children can see you." Somehow, she managed to ignore baby Mary, who squalled in the corner. Mother had insisted that Mary could sleep in a basket, claiming that was what the other children had done. But Mary was larger and more active than Sam and Daniel had been, and she cried when she was left alone.

"It's my house, and I'll do what I want." Father picked up the bottle and stared at it. "Don't need a glass. Whiskey tastes fine straight from the bottle." To prove his point, he took a long swig.

As her husband emptied the bottle and reached for another, Mother picked up her skirts and ran to her room, oblivious to Mary's frantic cries.

All pretense of a normal family life had fled. What mattered was the whiskey. Father couldn't live without it, and Mother, unable to stop him, spent most of the day staring into the distance, lost in her own private world. Each morning, Father would be remorseful, promising that today would be different, but it never was. By the time Harriet brought her siblings home from school, Father was on his way to oblivion, and Mother lay sleeping in their room.

Harriet had hidden it as long as she could. First, she swore the younger children to secrecy. That had been easy, for none of them wanted to admit that they no longer had functioning parents, that Harriet was the one who cooked their meals and mended their clothing once Mother began spending her days in her room, unable to cope with Father and the fact that the money was running out. Somehow Father had managed to squander most of his inheritance. Though no one in Fortune would admit it, Harriet suspected that more than drinking took place in the saloon and that Father had been gambling.

Once Grandma and Grandpa died, it had become harder to pretend that they were still the wealthy Kirks, the pride of Fortune. Harriet had learned to make do with little, but it had been difficult to care for baby Mary. Eventually, though she'd protested, Harriet had managed to coax her into drinking cow's milk. Then, knowing that neither parent would care for her during the day but unwilling to remain at home and forfeit her own education, fifteen-year-old Harriet had started taking her youngest sister to school with her, claiming her mother was suffering from female ailments. As she had expected, the schoolmaster did not question her explanation.

But one day she could hide the problem no longer. Father must have been smoking, and something—perhaps a match, perhaps his cheroot—had set the house on fire. By the time Harriet arrived home, the house was a smoldering mass and her parents were dead.

"Are you all right?" Frau Friedrich's voice brought her back to the present. "You look so pale."

Harriet stared at the tall German woman. She looked so normal, but Father had looked normal too, before he reached for the whiskey bottle. Her hands shaking with dread, Harriet forced herself to take a deep breath. She knew what would happen. There would be one drink, then another, then still another. And then . . .

As if she sensed her fear, Ruth put her arm around Harriet's waist and hugged her. "We don't drink spirits," Ruth said calmly.

Frau Friedrich laughed. "Nor do we. This is root beer."

5

Harriet tried not to smile as the children filed into the room, grousing about the fact that they had to come to school. It had been the same in Fortune. No one seemed to welcome the first day of classes. Today, Ladreville's students had even more cause to complain. Though Harriet found the weather perfect, their grumbles announced that they did not appreciate the steady rain. Harriet did, for even though the rain had spattered her spectacles as she'd walked to school, it meant there would be less temptation to go outside, and that would make her job easier. Almost as good, the day was cooler than normal for September. That would translate into less drowsiness. Fortunately, though it was downright chilly outside, the warmth the children radiated meant they would not need the stove. That was truly a blessing, for the thought of having to one day light a fire in this wooden structure made Harriet shudder.

She glanced at her watch. Five more minutes. Then she would call the class to order. In the meantime, she studied the children as they entered the schoolhouse, knowing they were eyeing her with curiosity and, in some cases, concern. A new teacher, she knew from experience, was cause for anxiety.

She recognized a few of the pupils, including Eva Lehman, Isabelle's stepdaughter. In the three weeks since they'd moved to Ladreville, the little girl had become Mary's closest friend and was undoubtedly one of the reasons Mary was happy here. The boys were a different story. Her brothers stood in the back of the schoolhouse, as far away from Harriet as they could manage. She bit back another smile, realizing that some things would never change.

Jake, Daniel, and Sam had hated the fact that she was their teacher in Fortune and couldn't understand why she had to work outside their home. Perhaps it had been a mistake, but she hadn't wanted them to know that most of the family fortune was gone, and so she had pretended that she had accepted the position as schoolmarm simply to ensure that they received a good education. Desperate for a new teacher when Mr. Harrod ran off with the mayor's daughter, the town council had agreed to hire Harriet, and—as far as she knew—no one suspected that her salary was the Kirk family's primary source of income. Fortunately, the small stash of gold coins she'd found when they'd moved into her grandparents' house had helped maintain the illusion of wealth.

When she had decided that they would move to another town, the younger children had thought it an adventure until they'd learned she would once again be their teacher. Then they'd begun to complain. Harriet wouldn't dwell on that. Living in Ladreville had brought good things. Though Ruth remained reclusive, both Mary and Harriet had a new friend. Furthermore, Chet wasn't here. Though Harriet had never been certain whether he or Jake was the instigator, one thing was clear: those two were trouble when they were together.

"Good morning, children." It was time for school to begin. As a few titters greeted her, two of the older boys stalked to the front.

"You the teacher?" the first demanded. He stood at least eight inches taller than Harriet and seemed to take pride in his height, for he made a point of looking down at her, ignoring the fact that his dark hair tumbled onto his face when he did. His companion, whose resemblance announced that they were brothers, stood next to him, forming a human wall between Harriet and the rest of the class. The two were big and brawny, and judging from the vacant expression in their eyes, blessed with fewer than normal brains.

"Indeed, I am." Harriet kept her voice firm, knowing there was only one way to deal with bullies like these. Though the challenge had come sooner than she had expected, she had known there would be one and that how she handled it would set the tenor for the school year. "Kindly take seats in the back row."

"What if we don't?" The second boy sneered at her, his brown eyes filled with scorn.

"You will do as Miss Kirk says."

Harriet blinked in surprise. She had been so intent on staring down the bullies that she had not heard him approach, but her surprise paled compared to the boys'. They wheeled around, their expressions almost comical when they saw Ladreville's sheriff standing next to them, his hand on his six-shooter. Their earlier bravado vanished, and they seemed to shrink several inches. Harriet would have been amused if she hadn't been so angry. The man had no cause to interfere.

Didn't he realize that his actions had undermined her authority?

"Mr. Wood, what are you doing here?"

He glared at the boys and pointed to the back of the room, then waited until the two bullies had meekly taken seats there. "As Ladreville's mayor, it's my responsibility to begin the school year by welcoming the students."

Harriet doubted that. She had seen the way he had assessed her each time they had met and knew that he was like Thomas, underestimating her simply because she was short and thin. She might be unable to match Lawrence's physical strength, but that did not mean she was unable to maintain discipline. She'd show him. Taking a deep breath and willing her voice to remain level, Harriet faced her pupils.

"Boys and girls, please take seats—any seats. I'll assign your permanent spots later." The clatter of footsteps was followed by the whisper of clothing as thirty children slid onto the benches. When the room was silent, Harriet gestured toward Lawrence. "We have a special guest today. Please greet Mr. Wood, our mayor. I expect you to listen quietly as he speaks and to afford him the same courtesy you would me."

Turning toward Lawrence, Harriet saw his lips twitch as if he were amused. Surely she was mistaken. There was nothing even remotely amusing about her words. She must have been mistaken, for when he spoke, his voice betrayed not a hint of a smile.

"Ladreville is fortunate to have a teacher of Miss Kirk's caliber." He paused and looked around the room, fixing his gaze on each student in turn. "I expect you to obey her. I do not want to hear of any problems." He touched his six-shooter, as if reminding the class of its presence and his role

76

as the town's sheriff. "Just because the jail cell is empty now doesn't mean it has to remain that way."

A collective gasp and the sound of bodies shifting nervously on the benches greeted his pronouncement. Harriet steeled her face to remain impassive, though inside she fumed. The threat was as unnecessary as his visit. Now she'd have to deal with its aftermath, but he, of course, had not considered that. Though she had once felt a connection to him, sensing that he had painful secrets, today Lawrence Wood had proven to be like Thomas, needing to establish dominion over everyone he met. The sooner he departed, the better. She waited until the room was again quiet before she turned to Lawrence. "Thank you, Mr. Wood. I am certain that my pupils are looking forward to a year of learning as much as I am."

Fortunately he recognized the dismissal and strode from the schoolhouse, pausing only to look down at the two boys who had been harassing her. When the door closed behind him, Harriet picked up a slate and prepared to write. "Now, class, I want you to tell me your names and the grade you were in last spring." The school year had begun.

The day passed quickly. The older boys—Henri and Jean Fayette—tested her authority several times more, then admitted defeat and sat quietly. As she had expected, the humiliation of having to stand in front of the class and demonstrate their ignorance proved to be an effective incentive to good behavior. There had been no need for Lawrence to threaten them.

With the bullies silent, the class settled down to their lessons, and—to Harriet's delight—several of the students appeared to be more advanced than she'd expected. The only problem was that the youngest children, especially the little girls, shied from her when she walked through the school-room, checking their work. Perhaps they were naturally bash-ful and feared she would call on them. It was the only reason Harriet could imagine, unless they were still remembering Lawrence's tale of jail cells.

She looked out the window and nodded when she saw that the rain had stopped. Once again the weather favored her plans. "We have one more lesson before dismissal." A round of groans greeted her announcement. "We are going to practice leaving the school as quickly as possible but in an orderly fashion." Groans turned to puzzled expressions. "When I give the command, I want Henri to open the door and hold it open until the last person has left. The rest of you will stand up and leave, one row at a time, starting with the back of the room. Walk; do not run. You are to cross Hochstrasse and meet me in the open field."

Eva's hand shot into the air. "Why do we have to do this? Mrs. Canfield never made us do that."

Harriet nodded. "That's a good question, Eva. We're prac-ticing what we would do if there were an emergency. I want to be sure everyone knows how to get out safely."

Though the youngest students still appeared frightened, they all followed the instructions, and within two minutes were assembled in the field. "You did very well." Harriet favored them with a smile. "All right, boys and girls; school is dismissed."

Class might be over, but her work was not. It was time to set a few things straight. Harriet waited until her pupils had dispersed before heading for the mayor's office, pausing only briefly to admire the three-story stone construction. What a pity this house hadn't been available for her family.

"Miss Kirk." Lawrence rose as she opened the door to what appeared to be the main room on the first floor. Furnished with a large desk, two chairs, and several huge maps of Europe, as well as portraits of a number of dour-faced men whom Harriet assumed were the former rulers of Alsace, this was clearly the mayor's office. "To what do I owe this honor?"

She accepted the chair he offered, knowing that was the only way he would sit. If there was one thing Harriet did not need, it was to have this man looming over her. She was far too aware of him as it was. Throughout the day, though she knew it impossible, she had caught the scent of his soap when she inhaled. And when she'd looked at her German students with their blond hair and blue eyes, she had found herself comparing them to this man. Surely, she had told herself, his hair wasn't a brighter shade of gold. Surely his eyes were not a deeper blue. But they were. She had not imagined it. Just as she wasn't imagining the curiosity that now colored those sapphire-hued eyes.

Harriet cleared her throat as she reminded herself of the reason she'd come. It was not to stare at this man, no matter how attractive he might be. Deliberately, she looked around the room, her eyes registering the large window on one wall and the partially open door that revealed Ladreville's sole jail cell. "That wasn't necessary, you know."

His brows rose. "What wasn't necessary?"

As if he didn't know. Once again, anger began to simmer, and when she spoke, her voice was laced with asperity. "It wasn't necessary to visit the school this morning. I'm perfectly capable of handling my pupils. I don't need you to threaten them. The little ones were frightened for the rest of the day, probably imagining themselves in your jail cell."

Lawrence's brows lowered as suddenly as they'd risen. "Let's get a few things straight."

Harriet nodded. That was precisely the reason she was here. But her momentary agreement with the town's mayor ended as he continued. "First of all, I came because it was my duty. The townspeople expect me to keep everything running smoothly, including the school. I needed to be certain that was happening." He paused, and his face softened ever so slightly. "Although you didn't appreciate it, I also came as a courtesy to you. I thought you might like both adult companionship and a show of support. Obviously, I was wrong." Before Harriet could reply, he said, "Thirdly, if your pupils are afraid, have you considered they might be afraid of you?"

That was preposterous. Harriet stiffened her spine and glared at the man who had made such an absurd allegation. "Me? Why?"

Though the corners of his mouth twitched as if he wanted to laugh, Lawrence's voice was serious as he said, "You can be rather forbidding, especially when you frown. Unfortunately, that seems to be most of the time."

Just like a man. He was in the wrong, but rather than admit it, he was trying to shift the blame to her. "That's not true."

"Isn't it? You haven't smiled once since you came in here."

"If I haven't smiled"—and she wasn't certain that was the case—"it's because this is not a frivolous conversation."

"Perhaps not, but there are always reasons to smile."

"Like the fact that, no matter what I do or say, Jake is belligerent and Ruth mopes around the house?" Harriet clapped her hand over her mouth. Had those words really come from her? What on earth was the matter with her that she was confiding personal affairs to a man who was practically a stranger? "I'm sorry. I never should have said that. My family is not your concern."

As he nodded slowly, his eyes met hers and she saw sincerity reflected in their blue depths. "Perhaps not directly," he agreed, "but I was serious when I said I came to the school to offer adult companionship. I won't claim that I know anything about raising or teaching children. I don't."

Though his tone remained even, Harriet saw the flash of pain in Lawrence's eyes. It was gone almost as quickly as it appeared, replaced by something that looked like sympathy. Not pity, but sympathy. Harriet relaxed as she recognized the difference.

"Sometimes it helps to talk about problems," Lawrence continued. "You don't have to solve them all yourself."

"Thank you, but . . ."

"I know." He nodded again, and this time there was no doubt about it. He was forcing himself not to smile. "I know you're used to being self-sufficient. I'm not trying to change that. All I'm saying is that I'm here if you need a friendly ear."

Harriet could feel her eyes widen in astonishment as she considered the day from a new perspective. Had she been wrong in thinking Lawrence wanted to interfere? What if he really was offering friendship? No one had ever made such an offer; certainly not a man. Even Thomas, who had professed undying love, had not been a friend. "I don't know what to say."

"There's no need to say anything." Lawrence smiled, and before she knew what was happening, Harriet felt herself smiling in response. "I just want you to know that I'm not the enemy."

She looked at him, seeing the earnest expression on his face. "No," she said slowly, "you're not."

"If we agree on that, can we dispense with some of the formality? My friends call me Lawrence."

"And mine call me Harriet."

"Thank you, Harriet." The smile on Lawrence's face set her pulse to racing in ways that even Thomas's most fervent declarations of love had not.

6

The new minister had arrived. Lawrence grinned. Even though he disliked its proximity to the river, his house possessed the advantage of a central location. Not only was it sandwiched between the post office and the lawyer's office, but it was also directly across from the block of Hochstrasse he privately called "Church Row" because it held the town's two churches and their respective parsonages. If the stories that he had wanted to control the town were accurate, Michel Ladre had chosen wisely when he built his house here, for it afforded a clear view of most of Ladreville's activity. Without straining, Lawrence could see who was headed for the mercantile and who entered the other establishments on Hochstrasse. The only problem was that the post office jutted out a bit, preventing him from viewing the school and its prickly teacher.

Lawrence reached for his hat and headed toward the door. He didn't understand Harriet. For someone so young, she seemed to carry a huge chip on her shoulder. It seemed that she expected the worst of everyone. Look at how she'd misinterpreted his visit to the schoolhouse. While it was true that he'd been concerned about her ability to control the class and wanted to establish some rules for the students, he hadn't been lying when he'd told her that he'd come for her benefit. But she'd been convinced that he'd sought to undermine her authority. Why? He could understand her wariness if she'd been a Ranger. Because their job put them in contact with some mighty undesirable creatures, Rangers quickly learned to trust no one. But Harriet was a teacher. Surely that experience had not engendered such suspicion. And, though he didn't doubt that it had been difficult, it was hard to believe that the strain of raising five siblings had caused her prickliness. Lawrence settled his hat on his head and touched his holster, assuring himself that the six-shooter was in place. There was no point in speculating. If ever there was a woman who defied understanding, it was Harriet Kirk. Her behavior was even more baffling than Lottie's. Though they'd parted amicably, Lawrence would eat his hat if the prim, proper, and prickly Miss Kirk ever accepted his offer of a friendly ear. But Harriet was not his problem. He had duties, and they did not include trying to fathom the mind of Ladreville's schoolmarm.

"You must be our new minister." Lawrence studied the man who had climbed out of the wagon and was hitching the horses to the post. Though the town had been buzzing with the news that Pastor Sempert's replacement was due any day, no one seemed to know anything about him. He was not what Lawrence had expected. Though he couldn't explain why, Lawrence had pictured a short, dark-haired man. Like Pastor Sempert, the stranger was tall, probably an even six feet, but his shoulders were not bowed, and while Pastor Sempert was sturdily built, this man was almost painfully thin. Lawrence had seen scarecrows with more substance.

He extended his hand for a shake. "I'm Lawrence Wood, Ladreville's mayor and sheriff for the next four and a half months."

The man's grip was firm, and when he smiled, his ordinary features lit with enthusiasm. "You're right. I'm Pastor Russell, but please call me Sterling." To Lawrence's surprise, the new minister's voice bore no hint of a German accent. "I certainly hope I'll be serving Ladreville for longer than four months." He gave his dust-covered wagon a rueful glance. "It seems like it took me almost that long to get here from Pennsylvania."

Lawrence had heard something about the new minister being fresh from a seminary somewhere back East. Though the townspeople had hoped for someone to be sent from the Old Country, that hadn't happened. "How was the journey?"

"Long." Sterling Russell's lips quirked in another smile, and he ran his hand over his brow, laughing as he shook off drops of perspiration. "Someone should have warned me about the heat."

"Heat?" The man's expression told Lawrence that, unlike Harriet Kirk, he wouldn't mind a little joking. "This is a cool spell." It wasn't, of course. The sun had emerged from the rain, seemingly determined to compensate for the two days of cool weather. "You should have been here last month. August is a real scorcher." That was no lie. Even the Hill Country's trees couldn't block the sun's intense rays.

Glancing down the street, Lawrence saw a gaggle of women leave the mercantile and head in this direction. Nodding shortly, he gestured toward the parsonage and started walking. The new minister did not need a welcoming committee before he had a chance to get settled.

As Lawrence and Sterling approached the small stone edifice, Pastor Sempert emerged from the parsonage, looking older and more tired than Lawrence had ever seen him. His gait slightly unsteady, he greeted the young minister with a warm smile. "I regret that these old bones don't move as fast as they used to. Now, come inside, and I'll show you around. You're welcome too, Lawrence."

Lawrence shook his head. "I'd be in the way, but I'm just across the street." He addressed his words to Sterling Russell and gestured toward his new home. "Come anytime you're free."

The younger man grinned. "I hope you don't regret the invitation."

"I won't." Though the minister was not what he had expected, instincts honed by years of having to judge a man within seconds told Lawrence that Sterling Russell would be a friend. That was a welcome thought, even if Lawrence would be leaving Ladreville in a few months. A man might as well enjoy those months as much as he could.

"Mayor Wood, we need to speak to you." The first group of women had dispersed, but two more women had come from the opposite direction. Lawrence tried not to frown, though judging from the sour expression on the short, dark-haired woman's face, he suspected he would not enjoy the next few minutes, especially since her companion wore an equally forbidding expression. The two women had obviously dressed for the occasion, for they both sported what Lawrence guessed were their Sunday bonnets. Made of straw, the dark-haired woman's had bright pink ribbons and dried flowers on one side, while her companion's hat boasted blue ribbons and several long bird feathers. The hats were festive; the women's faces were not. Whatever Flowers and Feathers wanted to discuss, the likelihood was that it would not be pleasant.

"Shall we go inside my office?" Lawrence gestured toward the building across the street.

Feathers shook her head. "What we have to say can be said here. We don't mind if others overhear us."

"Certainly." The only good Lawrence could see from that statement was that it was unlikely the conversation would be lengthy. The two women wouldn't want to stand on the sidewalk indefinitely, particularly if Pastors Sempert and Russell returned to unload Pastor Russell's wagon. While they might not care about the rest of its citizens, Lawrence doubted that the women would be willing for Ladreville's religious leaders to overhear them. "What can I do for you ladies?"

Flowers pursed her lips before she announced, "You've got to stop her."

Though he couldn't explain why, Harriet Kirk's face flashed through Lawrence's mind. He dismissed the thought. Surely the schoolteacher wasn't the object of these women's anger. But as Feathers continued the explanation, Lawrence knew his first instinct had been correct. "She's frightening our children," Feathers said.

"Who?" It was a formality, but he had to ask. And then he had to learn why these women had made such allegations.

"Miss Kirk, the schoolmarm." Flowers identified the cause of her concern.

For what seemed like the hundredth time since he'd arrived, Lawrence wondered why he'd ever thought himself suited to be Ladreville's mayor. Though he hadn't agreed with everything the Rangers had done, there was no doubt that he knew how to catch bandits. Dealing with irate women was another story.

He kept his face impassive as he looked at Flowers. "What exactly is she doing that frightens them?" Though Harriet's expression could be formidable, Lawrence doubted that children would report that to their parents. He could imagine his own mother's reaction if he'd come home from school, complaining that the teacher frowned at him. Ma would have told him he was lucky that's all she had done.

"She keeps talking about emergencies," Feathers said.

"She makes them practice leaving the schoolhouse quickly."

Clearly annoyed that Flowers had interrupted, Feathers seized the moment to announce, "My Hortense is scared. She worries that something horrible will happen to us."

"André has nightmares. He says he's afraid he won't be able to get out of our house in time."

Lawrence suspected that if he didn't interject a question, the two women would continue their litany of complaints indefinitely. Besides, he needed to clarify the problem. "Are your children afraid to go to school?" That was how the conversation had begun, with the women claiming that Harriet frightened their children. Now it sounded as if the fear was centered on their homes.

As Flowers shook her head, her pink bonnet ribbons bounced. "André isn't. He says she's an even better teacher than Mrs. Canfield." The compliment was delivered grudgingly.

"What about your daughter?" Lawrence turned to Feathers.

The woman shrugged. "Hortense never said she didn't want to go. Most mornings she leaves earlier than she needs to."

Though the women would not agree, it was clear that while the problem may have originated with Harriet Kirk, it was now the mothers' responsibility. Still, Lawrence was enough of a politician not to say that. "I'll convey your concerns to Miss Kirk." He grimaced as he listened to himself. Look at what had happened. He'd been in Ladreville less than two months, and he was starting to sound as pompous as Michel Ladre. What would he be like after another four and a half months? Worse, what if his time here didn't end in January? The women had their problems. His was, despite the announcements he'd placed in newspapers all across Texas, no one appeared interested in replacing him.

"Will you do it soon?" Feathers asked.

"Yes, ma'am." Lawrence tried not to frown as he imagined Harriet's reaction.

"We're going to the German church tomorrow." Harriet delivered what she knew would be an unwelcome announcement as the family gathered for breakfast. As she'd expected, the boys groaned in protest. Though the family had alternated between the two churches, the children had expressed a preference for the French services, a fact Harriet suspected was due to the presence of stained glass. With neither service being conducted in English, the younger Kirks complained about boredom. At least the French sanctuary offered more visual stimulation. "I know it's our week to go to the other one, but the German congregation has a new pastor," Harriet said. "Common courtesy says we should be present for his first service."

Mary gave Harriet a pleading smile. "Can I sit with Eva? She's my friend."

It was a good idea. The church would probably be more crowded than normal, meaning the Kirks would not have a pew to themselves. Perhaps they could share with Isabelle, Gunther, and Eva. "I'll talk to Isabelle today."

∽

"We'd love to have you sit with us." Isabelle's brown eyes sparkled, and her face glowed as she smiled. As she did each Saturday, she was working at the mercantile, helping her parents on what was normally the busiest day of the week. To Harriet's surprise, when she'd entered the store, she'd discovered only three customers waiting in line. Though a few others wandered through the aisles, the women fingering lace-trimmed handkerchiefs and studying the rows of spices while the men discussed the relative merits of nails and screws, there was less of a crowd than she'd expected. It was, Isabelle claimed, the morning lull.

The pretty brunette leaned across the counter, her smile turning conspiratorial. "I'm glad you'll be with us." Isabelle laid a hand on top of Harriet's and squeezed it. "I can't begin to tell you what a difference Mary has made. Eva's so excited about having a friend that sometimes she goes a whole day without asking me when I'll give her a baby brother or sister."

It wasn't only Eva who was excited about having a friend. Harriet reveled in the pleasure of being able to confide in Isabelle. She raised an eyebrow as she looked at the woman who'd become her friend. "Are you . . . ?"

"Increasing?" Isabelle completed the sentence. "Not yet." She lowered her voice, as if to keep her mother from overhearing. "I want a baby, but Gunther is afraid. You see, his first wife died in childbirth. I keep telling him that I'm perfectly healthy, but Frieda was too." As the door opened and two more customers entered, Isabelle's voice assumed a business-like tone. "I'm sorry. I shouldn't be boring you with those stories. Now, would you like a new ribbon for your hat?"

Harriet shook her head. Madame Rousseau, Isabelle's mother, had tried to sell her a lace jabot the last time she'd visited the store. The trouble was, they didn't seem to understand that Harriet had no need of frivolous clothing. It wasn't as if she were a young girl trying to attract a husband. "My old ribbon is serviceable."

"We have some lovely colors. The dark blue would be particularly fetching."

Isabelle pulled out a spool of ribbon. There was no doubt that the shade was pretty. Still, Harriet did not need it. Her hat ribbons were all brown, a color she had chosen because it did not show soil and would not clash with any of her clothes. "No, thank you."

Good-naturedly, Isabelle shrugged her shoulders. "You can't blame me for trying."

❧

Lawrence frowned as he glanced out the window and saw Harriet leaving the mercantile. As much as he wasn't looking forward to it, this would be as good a time as any to talk to her. He grabbed his hat and hurried outside. Though the calendar showed that autumn was only a few weeks away, the day was hot and oppressively humid, as if a storm were brewing. That storm, he feared, would pale compared to Harriet's fury when she heard of Feathers and Flowers's complaints.

"Harriet," he said when he reached her side, "may I walk

you home?" Where did she get such unbecoming clothing? The dress she wore made her look as pale as an onion.

Oblivious to his unspoken sartorial criticism, Harriet raised an eyebrow. "Aren't you afraid of setting tongues wagging?" The almost playful tone in her voice surprised Lawrence and made him regret that he would probably puncture her lightheartedness.

"Perhaps I should wear a sign saying 'official business.'"

Feigning alarm, she placed one hand over her heart. "Does that mean you're going to arrest me?" This was a new Harriet, a woman who could laugh.

Lawrence waited until they had crossed rue de la Seine before he answered. Now that they were on the block he had christened Church Row, there would be fewer ears listening, for many of the shoppers who frequented the mercantile turned on rue de la Seine as they headed for the open-air market. "If you were looking forward to a diet of bread and water in the jail, I'm afraid I'll have to disappoint you, but I do need to advise you that several mothers expressed their concern over the emphasis you're placing on exiting the school quickly." Lawrence almost groaned at his stilted phrases. Sitting in Michel Ladre's chair was definitely affecting his brain. "From what I've heard, you practice the same thing at home." After Feathers and Flowers's conversation, Lawrence had spoken to several other parents and had learned that, although a few of the children were concerned, most simply found it an odd practice.

"That is true." They were in front of the French church now, but Harriet spared no glances for the graceful building with its stained glass windows. All traces of mirth were gone as she pushed her glasses back on her nose and regarded Lawrence. "I don't believe there is anything in my contract that precludes such activities." This was the old Harriet, no-nonsense Miss Kirk. "To the contrary, my contract clearly states that I am responsible for the welfare of the pupils while they're in my care."

She was correct. Lawrence had reread the contract to be certain Harriet wasn't violating any of its terms. Though he had thought it highly unlikely that anyone as meticulous as she would even consider bending a rule, he'd had to check. She was within her rights, and yet there had to be a way to placate the women. "Perhaps you could assign a little less importance to egress," he suggested.

Those gray eyes that had sparkled only a few minutes ago turned steely. "I could, but I will not." Harriet looked into the distance, and he had the impression she was debating what to tell him. When she spoke, her voice was flat, as if she were reciting multiplication tables, not a personal tragedy. "My parents died when our house burned. If the fire had happened during the night, my whole family might have perished."

Though the sun beat on his shoulders, making him wish they had paused under a tree, Lawrence shivered. So much made sense now. No wonder Harriet had been distressed by a partially wooden house. No wonder she seemed overly protective of her siblings. No wonder she worried about her pupils. She had good reasons. "I'm sorry." The words were inadequate, but Lawrence had nothing else to offer. "I didn't know. You're right, Harriet. What you're doing is wise. I'll support you every way I can."

❦

As he dressed for church the next morning, Lawrence was still thinking about her, marveling at what he had learned.

93

Harriet Kirk was stronger than he'd realized. He had known she had had responsibility for her siblings for seven years, but he had thought their parents had died of smallpox or ague, not something that could have been prevented. How had that affected her? Had she blamed herself for the fire? Did she believe she bore the responsibility, as he did for Lizbeth? Lawrence's heart reached out to Harriet, for he knew just how heavy the burden could be. Perhaps that was why Harriet was so prickly.

She remained in his thoughts as he entered the German church half an hour later and saw her seated in the second pew with her siblings and Gunther Lehman's family. Today, in honor of Sterling Russell's first service, the German church held more people than normal, for many of the townspeople, both French and German, had come to hear him.

Lawrence slid into a pew near the back of the church and bowed his head in silent prayer, waiting for the service to begin. Though simpler than the French church, with plain instead of stained glass windows and a rough-hewn cross that the parishioners had fashioned from a local oak tree their first year in Ladreville, it was a holy place, and Lawrence found the peace he craved whenever he entered the sanctuary. A few minutes later he rose with the rest of the congregation as the two ministers emerged from the sacristy.

"He's so young." The man seated directly in front of Lawrence whispered the words to his wife.

She nodded solemnly. "He doesn't look German."

Lawrence felt a sinking in the pit of his stomach as the service began and the parishioners' discomfort seemed to grow. Not only did Sterling not look like a German, he also did not speak like one. The two men shared responsibility, but while

Pastor Sempert recited the liturgy in German, Pastor Russell's portion was delivered in English, a fact that appeared to bother many of the parishioners. Though Lawrence heard few comments, he observed pursed lips and frowns whenever Sterling spoke. *Lord, open their hearts*, he prayed. *Let them see that Sterling is your servant. Let them hear the words he is speaking, not the language he uses.* But the rustles and fidgets that accompanied the young minister told Lawrence his prayer had not been answered.

When it was time for the sermon, Pastor Sempert approached the pulpit. Straightening his shoulders, he stood for a moment, silently looking at his congregation, his eyes glistening with emotion. How difficult it must be, Lawrence thought, to say farewell so publicly.

A smile crossed the elderly minister's face. "Today is special," he said, his voice slow and deliberate, "for it marks my final day as your pastor. Pastor Russell's arrival brings change for all of us, but it is time. That is why I have chosen Ecclesiastes 3, verses 1–8, as the text for my sermon." Though normally he left it on the lectern, today the minister picked up the large Bible. "To every thing there is a season, and a time . . ." The Bible fell with a thump as Pastor Sempert clutched his head. A second later, he lay crumpled on the floor.

A collective gasp rose from the congregation as they stared at their stricken shepherd. Sterling gathered the older man in his arms, cradling him as he might have a child, while Clay rushed forward. Instinct propelled Lawrence out of the pew. Though he knew little about doctoring, he might be able to assist Ladreville's only physician.

Clay's face was inscrutable as he looked at Pastor Sempert, but Lawrence didn't need a degree from the Massachusetts

Medical College to know the minister's condition was serious. The ashen cheeks, the pain-filled eyes, and the lips twisted into a horrible caricature of a smile told the tale. Clay looked up at Lawrence. "Let's get him into his office." He turned toward Sterling. "Pastor, you'd better comfort your parishioners." Though no one had left the church, the townspeople were whispering, and Lawrence saw many dart anxious glances at the chancel.

Only minutes later, Clay had completed his examination. "Apoplexy." His diagnosis confirmed Lawrence's fears. "It will take a miracle for him to recover."

Behind them, loud voices filled the sanctuary. Lawrence nodded briskly. Though Clay no longer needed him, it appeared Sterling might require assistance in keeping the peace. When he entered the church, Lawrence frowned. The congregation was standing, and many had left their pews to approach the front. Though Sterling appeared calm, Lawrence was reminded of a picture he had seen of Christians in the Roman arena, awaiting certain death.

"It's your fault." The burly man who was glowering at Sterling was practically shouting. "If you hadn't come, Pastor Sempert would be alive."

"You killed him!" A woman pointed her finger at Sterling. This was worse than Lawrence had feared. The parishioners' resentment of Sterling was so strong that it had become irrational. Without even knowing Pastor Sempert's true condition, they were blaming Sterling for it. Instinctively, Lawrence's hand moved to his hip. He had never fired a weapon in a church. God willing, he would not have to today.

Before Lawrence could say anything, Harriet pushed her way between the accusers and the young minister. Though she was half the size of the bully, the man retreated under the force of her glare.

"You should all be ashamed of yourselves," she said. Unlike the others, she was not shouting, yet her voice carried clearly through the church. "Is this any way to conduct yourselves in the house of the Lord?" Without waiting for a response, she continued. "You call yourselves good Christians. If you were, it seems to me you should be praying for Pastor Sempert's recovery and thanking God that he sent us a new minister at the exact time we needed one."

A few people hung their heads; others murmured something that sounded like an apology. Lawrence stared in amazement at the way Harriet had controlled what had become an angry crowd. Somehow she had chosen the exact words that had quieted them and changed their anger into chagrin.

Lawrence faced the congregation. "Pastor Sempert is still alive," he announced. "Dr. Canfield is doing everything he can. In the meantime, I suggest we follow Miss Kirk's advice." He nodded at Sterling.

The young pastor straightened his shoulders and gazed out at his flock. "Let us pray."

7

"I could never have done that." Ruth's eyes filled with tears, and she blinked to keep them from falling.

Harriet wasn't certain which surprised her more: her sister's words or the tears. If Ruth had been chopping onions, Harriet would have blamed watery eyes on the aromatic vegetable, but she was peeling carrots. "Done what?" she asked.

"What you and Pastor Russell did—stand up in front of everyone when they were angry."

Though Harriet was still appalled at the congregation's reaction to Pastor Sempert's apoplexy, her heartbeat had returned to normal well before she had arrived home. What remained was dismay that the citizens of Ladreville could have been so cruel, blaming the new minister for something that was clearly not his fault. She had hoped that Ladreville would be different from Fortune, but it appeared it was not. Harriet pushed her spectacles back on her nose as she said, "For me it wasn't much different than standing in front of a classroom."

Her hand clutching the paring knife as if it were a lifeline,

Ruth shook her head. "There were more people in the church, and they were bigger than your pupils."

"That's true." Some of the parishioners were almost as tall as Lawrence and burlier, their arms and shoulders bearing witness to years of hard work. "But bullies are the same regardless of their size." Harriet had learned that the day Thomas had berated her for refusing his proposal of marriage. "You can't let them see that you're afraid. That's what they want." She looked down at the potato she was peeling and began to dig out its eyes. "I felt sorry for Pastor Russell. This wasn't a very pleasant welcome." Her frown faded as she recalled her own welcome. Though businesslike, Lawrence had been cordial that first day.

"I wonder if he'll leave now." Ruth cut the carrot into chunks and arranged them around the pot roast.

"I doubt it. His contract is until January."

The furrows that appeared between Ruth's eyes spoke of her puzzlement. "I didn't realize ministers had contracts." She reached for another carrot.

"Oh!" Harriet felt blood rush to her face as she recognized her mistake. "You're right; they don't." Why, oh why, had her mind been wandering? Why had she been thinking of Lawrence? It must be because she'd been recalling the way he had greeted her when they'd arrived. That must be the reason she had made such a silly response. What a ninny she was!

Two hours later when they gathered around the long table in the dining room, the boys were still talking about what had occurred in the German church. Though the younger ones had heard of apoplexy, it was the first time they had seen someone stricken, and they were both curious and a bit alarmed.

"Chet was right," Jake declared.

Harriet doubted that. "In what way was he right?"

Jake shoveled food onto his plate. It was only when he'd taken more than his share that he looked up. "He said there was no God. What happened this morning is proof. If there really was a God, he wouldn't have let the minister suffer like that." Grabbing a biscuit and slathering it with butter, he said, "The way I see it, either there is no God, or he's a mean one."

Before Harriet could respond, Mary's face contorted with anger. "You're wrong, Jake. Eva told me that God is good. She prayed for a new mother, and God gave her one." Refusing to look at her oldest brother, Mary turned to Daniel and Sam. "We need a father, so I'm gonna pray for one. You oughta do that too."

Jake dropped his fork, not caring that it clattered against the plate. "You're just a silly little girl. You don't know nothing. We don't need a father, and even if we did, God wouldn't give us one."

"I am not silly." Mary burst into tears. "You're just mean." She hiccupped, then glared at her brother. "I hate you."

Harriet laid down her utensils and gave Jake a stern look. The morning's events had taken their toll on everyone, but that didn't mean she could allow Jake to disparage his sister. "There was no call for your comments. I expect you to apologize to Mary."

"I will not. We don't need a father."

"Jake!" Though Harriet did not raise her voice, the children all knew that tone. It meant she had reached the end of her rope, and they faced serious consequences if they disobeyed her.

"That's another thing we don't need—you pretending to be our mother." Jake's voice seethed with resentment. "Ruth and I are grown up. We don't need you." He pushed back his chair and stormed out of the room, leaving his heavily laden plate as evidence of his anger. Jake never missed a meal.

In the silence that followed his exit, Harriet took a deep breath. Jake was wrong. They did need her, all of them. She knew that. Still, his lack of gratitude stung. Didn't he realize that everything she had done was necessary? If she hadn't taken care of them when their parents died, the good citizens of Fortune would have separated the family, placing them on different farms. Some of them might even have wound up in an orphanage. But Harriet had ensured that they remained together, that they had a home and food and clothing. And this was what she got in return?

She took another deep breath, trying to calm her thoughts. Everyone was overwrought, distressed by what had happened at church. Pastor Sempert and Pastor Russell—indeed, the entire German community—had more important problems than she.

"Ruth," she said with a faint smile for her sister. "I think we should take some food to the parsonage. Pastor Sempert might be able to eat some of your blancmange."

Ruth nodded. "Anything for the poor man."

"I've never seen a woman act like that." Karl took another potato from the bowl and laid it on his plate. Though normally Sunday dinners were spent discussing the pastor's sermon, there had been no sermon today, only those appalling moments when Pastor Sempert had been stricken and when

Harriet had quieted the congregation. If he hadn't been there, Karl would not have believed it possible.

"That's because she's an American," his father said. "She wasn't raised the way women in the Old Country were."

"But she was strong, Vater." Surely his father would appreciate that.

"Ja, she is." Mutter's expression was solemn. "I wonder, though, if she is the right woman for you. Marriage is for a lifetime. You need to be sure."

"I am sure."

Vater nodded slowly. "This is America. Things are different here. Why don't you take some time to get to know her and her family before you begin to court her?"

"Vater is right. We all need to get to know her."

Karl knew all he needed to. Harriet was strong; she would give him sons to work on the farm; and in the meantime, she had three brothers who would be good field hands. But he could not disobey his parents, and so he nodded. They'd soon see that she was the perfect wife for him.

❧

"Good afternoon, Harriet."

She turned and smiled. There was no mistaking either the man or the horse. Lawrence owned the only palomino in Ladreville, and though there were other blond men, no one else had the same broad shoulders and muscular legs.

"Where are you headed?" he asked as he drew Snip next to Harriet's wagon.

"I'm paying a call on Sarah and her baby." Isabelle had delivered the news that Clay's prediction had been right. He and Sarah had a baby boy whom they'd named Robert in honor of Clay's father, although they planned to call him Rob. That was why Harriet was on the west side of the Medina.

"Clay is one proud papa," Lawrence told her. "He said his family is complete now that he has a son and a daughter."

"A daughter?"

Though Lawrence nodded, Harriet saw the puzzlement in his eyes. "Clay adopted Sarah's sister. Thea's his daughter now."

Harriet took a deep breath, composing herself before she said, "Sarah's lucky. Most men don't want a ready-made family." No one in Fortune had.

The look Lawrence gave her was long and piercing, and Harriet suspected he knew the answer to his question before he posed it. "Is that why you're not married?"

"One of the reasons." She decided to make light of the question. "I can't abandon my sisters and brothers even though they might wish it. Jake, in particular, thinks I'm too strict."

"And you're not?"

"Of course not."

Lawrence grinned. "You sound like my sister Lottie. She made it her mission in life to boss me, but if you asked her, she'd claim otherwise."

Though she detected no resentment in his voice, instinct told Harriet that Lawrence was not close to his sister. "Do you see her often?"

He shook his head, confirming her supposition. "Lottie has a family of her own now—three boys—and my time with the Rangers didn't often take me in her direction."

"Not even for Christmas?"

"'Fraid not." Lawrence's tone announced that the subject was closed.

103

Though they chatted of inconsequential things until they reached the Bar C, Harriet's mind continued to whirl. Christmas was meant for families, but it seemed that Lawrence had none—not a real one, anyway. Perhaps that was the reason for the sadness she had seen in his eyes the day she'd met him.

There was no sign of sadness when he touched his hat brim in farewell and said, "When you get back to Ladreville, you might want to pay a call at the post office. Steven Dunn—he's the postmaster—has a letter for you."

"A letter for me?" Harriet could not imagine who would have written. Though her destination was not a secret, she had not expected to hear from anyone in Fortune.

This time Lawrence's lips curved into a smile. "As far as I know, you're the only Harriet Kirk in Ladreville. Steven's mighty anxious to meet you. Seems he's heard a lot about the new schoolmarm. All good, of course."

Lawrence's faintly teasing tone made Harriet reply in kind. "Then don't you dare tell him the truth. He might withhold my oh-so-important missive if he knew that I was a stern taskmaster who frightened small children."

Harriet was still smiling when she entered the ranch house. She had no sooner admired the baby and given Sarah the gift she'd brought when the door opened again.

"Ach, Sarah, let me look at that son of yours." Frau Friedrich bustled into the room, Thea trailing behind her. Seeming to move with more energy than three other women, the tall German woman planted herself directly in front of Sarah and bent down for a better view of the baby. "Isn't he precious?" Her smile was warm as she looked at the mother and child. "You and Clay make beautiful babies. You need to have many more, at least one girl."

She straightened and gave Harriet a long look. "As dearly as I love Karl, I've always wanted a daughter."

And I've always wanted a real mother.

Harriet stared at the letter, reading it for the third time. When he'd handed it to her, Steven Dunn had asked if it was from a gentleman admirer. Hardly! Thomas Bruckner was not a gentleman, not in any sense of the word, and he had never admired her—only the fortune he believed she possessed. But according to the single sheet of thick paper she held, he regretted the way they'd parted and wanted her to return to Fortune as his wife. There was, Harriet noted, no mention of her siblings. Either he'd forgotten they existed or he assumed they would stay in Ladreville when she raced back to Fortune to accept his offer of matrimony. In either case, Thomas was wrong, as wrong as he'd been the day he'd first proposed marriage.

Crumpling the paper and tossing it into the stove, Harriet smiled. Fortunately, she didn't need Thomas to make her life complete. It might not be perfect, but life in Ladreville was good. Surprisingly good.

"I told you you'd regret that open invitation you issued the day I arrived." Sterling Russell settled himself in one of the chairs in front of Lawrence's desk. It had happened so often that it had become almost a routine. More days than not, the young minister would arrive soon after breakfast and share a second cup of coffee with Lawrence before he returned to the parsonage to spend the rest of the morning reading to Pastor Sempert. It was, Sterling claimed, the only thing he could do for the man who'd once been the heart of the community but who was now an invalid, unable to walk or speak.

Though he couldn't vouch for Sterling, Lawrence enjoyed their time together. Sterling didn't feel the need to fill every moment with talk. Instead, he'd sit quietly for minutes on end. That made what he did say feel more important, even if it was nothing more than an amusing anecdote.

"You must be joshing. I don't regret it for a minute. Who else would help drink my terrible coffee?" Making coffee wasn't supposed to require extraordinary talents, but judging from the flavor of the dark liquid he brewed each day, it required more than Lawrence possessed.

Sterling took a sip before giving Lawrence a mischievous grin. "You need a wife."

The room was cool. There was no reason his face should feel hot or why indignation should rise faster than smoke from a bonfire. Lawrence clenched his fists, trying to control his temper. It was bad enough that his Bible kept opening to passages about marriage—today it had been the wedding at Cana—but now Sterling thought he needed a wife. Was this some sort of conspiracy?

"Why would I need a wife?"

The young minister pointed toward his mug. "For one thing, she might be able to make decent coffee."

"I could hire a housekeeper to do that." Lawrence would have to do that soon, because the house needed cleaning, and his prowess with a broom was even less than his skill as a cook.

"Ah, but there are other reasons for a wife—like companionship."

106

"Snip's a pretty good companion."

Sterling raised an eyebrow. "God didn't intend man to live with a horse." As Lawrence frowned, he added, "End of today's sermon. But, if you do decide to take a wife, I'd advise you not to delay. I hear that Ladreville's short supply of eligible young women is dwindling. According to three different sources, Miss Kirk received a letter from a gentleman admirer. The town's already speculating that it'll need a new teacher next year."

"At least hiring one won't be my problem." His contract would be over, he'd be gone, and Harriet Kirk would be nothing more than a memory. Still, Lawrence couldn't help wondering about her gentleman admirer. When they'd spoken on the way to the Bar C, she had acted as if marriage was a far distant event for her. The Ladreville grapevine must be wrong.

"Women!" Sterling said with a grin. "We'll never understand them."

Lawrence was smiling as his friend left the office. He was not smiling a few minutes later when Karl Friedrich stormed through the door, his face set in a scowl.

"You've got to help me, Sheriff. Someone cut my fences again. If I hadn't noticed it, those blasted cattle would have eaten all my wheat." Though the stocky blond farmer usually spoke good English, this morning his accent was so thick that Lawrence could hardly understand him. What he did understand was that he needed to visit the Friedrich farm and search for the culprit.

Lawrence could not recall a less pleasant ride. Normally, once he'd steeled himself for the crossing, he enjoyed being on the other side of the river. With only three ranches, it was quieter than the town itself, and he could let Snip gallop. Normally that left both him and his horse in a good mood. Normally. Today Lawrence was forced to listen to a litany of complaints.

"Farming was supposed to be easier with the Kirk boys helping," Karl announced when they'd forded the Medina. "It sure hasn't worked out that way. There's problem after problem."

"Do you think one of the Kirks is responsible for the fence?" That was the only reason Lawrence could imagine for Karl mentioning his helpers.

"Ja." He spat the word. "That Jake is nothing but trouble. I knew it from the first day."

"Then why did you hire him?" Lawrence knew that the Friedrichs had bought the Preble ranch soon after the town was founded and had converted it to a farm in 1845. If Karl and his father had managed the farm on their own for more than ten years, surely there was no reason to hire someone Karl didn't trust.

"I need help. Vater," he said, using the German term for father, "is too old to be working the way he has these past years. The boys seemed like an answer to prayer, but I tell you, Sheriff, they're not."

Lawrence and Karl had reached the Friedrich farm and were following the fence line, riding slowly enough to inspect it. "Here it is." Karl pointed to a stretch of fence that bore signs of recent repairs. "You can see where it was cut."

Though Karl remained mounted, Lawrence slid off Snip and walked along the fence, searching for clues. It was unlikely, he knew, that there would be any, but he wouldn't be doing his job as sheriff if he didn't look. He had almost given up when he spotted a scrap of fabric caught on the fence. Plucking it off the wire, Lawrence stuffed it into his pocket.

As far as he knew, there was only one person in Ladreville who had a shirt of that particular shade of green.

"Are the Kirk boys on your farm today?" he asked as he mounted Snip.

"Ja. They spend every Saturday here."

Lawrence nodded. That made his job easier. "I want to talk to them, starting with Jake."

"Then you think one of them did it?"

Lawrence shrugged. "It's possible." He would say no more until he'd spoken with Jake, for it was also possible—although unlikely—that there was an innocent reason for a piece of Jake's shirt to be on the fence.

"I see your shirt is ripped." There was no point in pre-ambles, particularly when dealing with a boy who swaggered toward him, a chip as big as the state of Texas sitting on his shoulder. As a matter of courtesy, Lawrence had taken Jake aside, not wanting his younger brothers to overhear the conversation. The consideration, it appeared, was lost on Jake.

Lawrence took a deep breath. Though he remembered the awkwardness of being Jake's age, the body that had sprouted so quickly it felt like a stranger's, the yearning to be treated as an adult, he could not condone what Jake had done. There was a distinct line between right and wrong, and Jake had crossed it.

"Yeah?" Jake practically snarled the word. "So what? I must have caught it on something in the stable. Old Man Karl has lots of nails."

Lawrence gave Jake a look that would have had grown men quailing. It had no effect on Harriet's brother. Evidently, the boy was too young to recognize danger. Though he did not raise his voice, Lawrence laced it with contempt. Jake deserved no less. "There are a couple problems with your story, but let's start with the fact that you owe Mr. Friedrich some courtesy. I don't imagine your sister would like you referring to him that way."

Jake's lip curled. "Look, mister, I don't need another sermon. I get them every Sunday."

"You're going to get more than a sermon from me, Jake. I don't like liars, and that's one whopping lie you told about your shirt. You didn't catch it on a nail in the stable. I found the piece on the fence, just a couple feet from where it was cut."

"So?" The boy was the picture of belligerence, practically begging Lawrence to smash his face. Lawrence fisted his hands, then forced himself to relax them. Punishment would come later. First he needed a confession.

"So," he said, turning Jake's question into an answer, "I think you're the one who's responsible for Mr. Friedrich's cut fence."

"What are you gonna do about it?"

"I'm going to start by taking you home. We'll see what Harriet says."

❧

"Why did you do it?" Harriet stared at her brother, wondering if a stranger had taken over the familiar body. This person looked like Jake, but he wasn't acting like him. Of course, if she were being truthful, Jake hadn't acted like himself in a long time, and it had only worsened since they'd come to Ladreville. The signs of rebellion had been there; today was simply the most visible manifestation and proof that leaving Fortune had not solved Jake's problem.

"Why, Jake?" Harriet demanded, glaring at him. Though he hadn't liked it, she had forced him to sit while she remained standing. At least this way she towered over him, rather than having to look up at him.

"Why does it matter? All you care about is what happened." Anger and resentment weighted his words, giving them the force of darts, and like darts, they penetrated her skin.

Harriet bit back her own anger, forcing herself to remain calm. "That's not true. I care about you." Why else did Jake think she had spent so many years working to keep the family together? Or did he even think about that? Probably not. He was so caught up in his own sense of misery that he didn't consider anyone else. She was the one who had to think of others, and right now she was stymied. What punishment could she invoke that would show Jake the error of his ways?

"If you cared, you wouldn't have made us leave Fortune, and you sure as shootin' wouldn't have made me work on that miserable farm," he snarled, his tone reminding her of an angry dog. "I hate farming."

Harriet nodded slowly. That was the answer, a punishment befitting the crime. "It's a shame you don't like it, because you're going to be doing a lot of farming. We're going back to the Friedrichs, and you're going to apologize to Mr. Friedrich. You're also going to work for free until you've paid for the damage." The insolent expression on Jake's face made Harriet add, "Because you won't be earning any money, you're going to help Ruth with her chores. You can stay home from school on Mondays and do the laundry."

Jake jumped to his feet, his hands balled, his eyes dark with anger. "That's not fair! You're as bad as he is." Though Harriet hadn't thought it possible, Jake's fury increased. He

111

took a step toward her, and for a second she feared he would strike her. Instead, he snarled again. "I'll bet he told you to make me do girls' work."

"Who?" Jake must realize that she hadn't spoken to Karl since she'd learned of the cut fences. As soon as Lawrence had left, Harriet had confronted her brother. There had been no consultation with Karl. Furthermore, if Jake were thinking straight, he would realize that Karl would not suggest laundry as a punishment. He would be more likely to propose a lengthy visit to the woodshed.

Jake's lips twisted, turning his normally handsome face into a grotesque mockery of her brother. "The sheriff." He spat the words. "I hate him, and I hate you, and most of all I hate Old Man Karl."

And I hate the boy you've become. Harriet took a deep breath, trying to control her own anger. "Be that as it may, you are going to apologize to Mr. Friedrich, and you are never again going to refer to him as Old Man Karl."

"But he is old." Jake clenched his fists. "He acts like he's a hundred years old."

"Jake!" Harriet glared at her brother. "That's enough. Now, come with me. You have an apology to deliver."

The apology was mumbled and so obviously insincere that Harriet wanted to strangle Jake. Still, he had said the words. Now he would begin to work off his debt.

His face still flushed with anger, Karl shook his head. "The boy needs more than that. If he were my son, I'd give him a thrashing he wouldn't forget."

Jake leaped forward, his fists clenched. "You're not my father and you won't ever be. Do you hear me? Never!"

8

"What's wrong?" Isabelle was more than a little out of breath as she grabbed Harriet's arm and tugged her to a stop, and though she was dressed as fashionably as ever, a lock of hair had escaped from her intricate coiffure and hung down her back.

Though Isabelle had posed the question, Harriet could have echoed it, for it was unlike her friend to be anything but perfectly groomed. Instead, she asked, "What makes you think something's wrong?"

Laying her hand over her heart as if to slow its beat, Isabelle shook her head. "Isn't it obvious? You were practically running down Rhinestrasse."

"That was a brisk walk," Harriet countered.

"Maybe for a horse. You looked as if you were trying to escape someone. I tell you, Harriet, when I looked down the street and saw you, I was so frightened that I thought about calling the sheriff."

Harriet blanched. She didn't need Lawrence seeing her

when she was in this state. It was bad enough that Isabelle had found her. "I'm sorry you were alarmed. I'm perfectly safe." She gestured toward the empty street. "As you can see, there's no one else here." That was part of Rhinestrasse's appeal. At this time of day, there were few pedestrians and even fewer carriages. Harriet could walk to her heart's content without having others join her or comment on her pace. A brisk walk, she had discovered years before, did more than almost anything to clear her mind. And today she needed that. That's why she had been pacing up and down the street since school had ended. Unfortunately, that had not resolved her problem.

"So, what's wrong?" Isabelle could be like a terrier, unwilling to let a subject go once she'd dug her teeth into it.

"Now, child, no one needs to know what happened." Her grandmother's words emerged from the recesses of Harriet's mind. *"If you don't admit it, it's nothing more than a rumor."* But Grandma was wrong. Denying something didn't make it disappear, and lying to a friend was just plain wrong. Harriet turned to Isabelle. "It's Jake. I don't know what to do about him."

Isabelle released her grip on Harriet's arm and slid her arm around her waist, giving her a quick squeeze. "I heard there was some problem at the Friedrichs' farm."

This was what she had feared: public knowledge of Jake's misdeeds. "Are there any secrets in Ladreville?"

"Not many. It was the same way in the Old Country. Maman says it's human nature to gossip."

Gossip or not, the problem remained. Though Harriet could have continued walking for another hour, she stopped at a fallen log and suggested they sit. When Isabelle gave a

114

grateful sigh, Harriet knew she had been right in thinking her friend wasn't accustomed to exercise. "I don't understand," she admitted. "My brother has always been a good boy. There were the normal childhood pranks, of course, but nothing malicious until a year ago. Jake found a new friend then, and he was a bad influence."

"Is that the reason you left Fortune?"

One of them. "How did you guess?"

Though Isabelle had been staring into the distance, she turned to face Harriet, her expression solemn. "My family had a similar experience in the Old Country. Léon got into trouble and would have been jailed if we hadn't left. That's why we came to Ladreville."

"Léon a troublemaker? I would never have thought that." Harriet had met Isabelle's brother on several occasions and had found him to be a serious, hardworking young man.

"Maman said it was a stage of growing up. She must have been right, because once we arrived here, there were no further problems. He still plagues me with his teasing, but I don't think that will ever end."

Harriet nodded. "I don't mind the squabbling, because I know it's normal, but I worry about Jake. He's like a stranger, filled with hatred."

"Perhaps it's only anger." Isabelle gave Harriet's hand a quick squeeze. "Sometimes they're hard to separate."

Isabelle's touch warmed her, and the concern she heard in her voice told Harriet she had not been wrong in confiding in her. Isabelle understood; she wanted to help. "You could be right," Harriet admitted. "Jake does seem angry most of the time. I've asked, but he won't tell me why, and recently he's gotten this notion that I'm going to marry Karl Friedrich.

Even when I told him I wasn't planning to marry anyone, I could see he didn't believe me."

Isabelle shrugged, as if to say she'd expected that. "Boys his age aren't logical, and they don't trust anyone older them. Besides, there've been some big changes in Jake's life. You brought him to a new town, so he has to make new friends." Isabelle watched as a mockingbird spotted a squirrel and chased it out of the tree. "That's hard enough, but now he's working on the farm too. Did you know that Léon used to work there?" When Harriet shook her head, Isabelle continued. "It didn't last very long. Though Léon didn't say much, I imagine Karl is a stern taskmaster. Is Jake used to that?"

Harriet hadn't considered that possibility. "I don't suppose he is. I've tried my best, but I'm not as strict as I ought to be, either at home or at school."

As the corners of Isabelle's lips turned up, she said, "Eva's happy about that. She says you make it fun to learn."

That was the first good news Harriet had heard all day. "I wish I could believe that, but no matter what I do, other than Eva, the young children seem afraid. I don't understand it."

Once again Isabelle's expression sobered. "They are afraid. They're afraid of you."

"Of me? Why?" Lawrence had claimed that was the case, but Harriet hadn't wanted to believe it. "What am I doing wrong?"

Her friend shook her head. "It's not what you're doing. It's the way you look."

Harriet tried not to sigh. Once again Lawrence had been right. He had said she looked forbidding. That must be what Isabelle meant. "I've been trying to smile more often."

116

"It's not that." Isabelle studied her gloves as if the buttons contained the mysteries of the universe. At length, she looked up and met Harriet's gaze. "There's no easy way to say this, but your clothing and the way you wear your hair can seem . . ." She paused, then said rapidly, "You appear *un peu* intimidating to small children."

A little. If Harriet had had any doubts that Isabelle was uncomfortable with the subject, her use of a French phrase would have quenched them. Though she knew Isabelle spoke French with her family, she was normally scrupulous about not lacing her English conversations with French words.

"What you really mean is more than a little, isn't it?"

"I'm afraid so. Eva said the others think you look like a scarecrow." When Harriet's back stiffened, Isabelle laid a cautioning hand on her arm. "Now, don't be offended. It's not hard to fix. If you come to the mercantile tonight, we can get started."

"I'm not sure." Harriet had more important things to worry about than her hair and clothing, things like her brother's anger.

Isabelle raised an eyebrow. "Do you want to win over your pupils or not? The choice is yours."

When phrased that way, there was only one answer. As Harriet nodded, Isabelle gave her a triumphant smile. "I'll see you at 7:00."

There was no reason to feel as if she were facing a firing squad. Isabelle was her friend. She wanted to help. But no matter how often she tried to reassure herself, Harriet could not dismiss her apprehension. It felt as if a hundred butterflies had taken residence in her stomach, all beating their wings furiously as they tried to escape.

"Come in." Lighting the way with a lamp, Isabelle led Harriet through the mercantile to a back room. Filled with cartons and crates, this was obviously the stockroom. It was also more private than either the main part of the mercantile or the Rousseaus' home on the second story. Someone—perhaps Isabelle—had cleared a space for a wooden chair and a small table. The latter held a second lamp along with a comb, brush, and assorted hairpins.

"We'll start with your hair," Isabelle said as she gestured toward the chair. A moment later, Harriet's spectacles carefully placed on the table, Isabelle had removed the pins and was brushing Harriet's hair. "This is beautiful," she said softly. "You shouldn't hide it."

Harriet didn't hide her hair; she merely arranged it in the simplest style possible. "I don't have time to fuss with it."

"Nonsense. That might have been true a few years ago, but even Mary is old enough to dress herself." Isabelle continued drawing the brush through Harriet's hair, straightening the long locks. "Once you heat the curling iron, it will take less than ten minutes."

"Curling iron? We don't own one."

A low chuckle greeted her words. "Isn't it fortunate that we just happen to sell curling irons?"

In far less than ten minutes, Isabelle had coiled Harriet's hair at the base of her neck, leaving a few strands free. Those strands were soon curled. "How does that feel?"

"Strange. I'm not used to hair touching my face." When Harriet turned her head, the curls bounced against her cheeks. It was a distinctly odd sensation, almost as if she were a

118

different person. Harriet patted the back of her head. Normally she pulled her hair into a tight bun at the middle of her head. This one seemed looser, and it was positioned far lower. "Are you sure the bun is secure?"

Isabelle's eyes sparkled with mirth. Though butterflies were still rampaging through Harriet's stomach, filling her with a combination of dread and anticipation, her friend was clearly enjoying herself. "It's called a chignon, and yes, it's secure." Isabelle took a step backward, tipping her head to one side as she studied Harriet. "*Magnifique*," she announced.

When Harriet reached for her spectacles, wanting to see if she looked as different as she felt, Isabelle shook her head. "Not yet. Let's get you out of that dress."

Harriet looked down at the medium brown calico that had been new five years ago. "There's nothing wrong with it."

"Indeed not . . ." Isabelle pursed her lips in feigned indignation. "If you want to look like a mouse. A dead mouse, that is." Without waiting for a reply, Isabelle crossed the room and opened a tall cabinet. "Your hair is so pale that you ought to wear bright colors, like this." She pulled out a garnet red gown. "Let's see if it fits."

Even without her spectacles, Harriet could see that this was finer than anything she had owned. Not only was it made of broadcloth, which Ruth had told her the fashion books referred to as "lady's cloth," rather than the sturdy calico of her weekday clothing, but the skirt was fuller, requiring extra yardage. The extravagance did not end there. It had slightly puffed sleeves, and the bodice boasted tiny tucks and delicate ivory buttons. "Where did you get this?" Harriet asked as Isabelle slid it over her head, carefully protecting her new coiffure. Though the mercantile carried a few ready-made bodices, she had not noticed any frocks.

"I made it."

Isabelle acted as if that were nothing, though Harriet knew how many hours of work must have gone into the tucking alone. "When did you do this?" She had only agreed to consider new clothing this afternoon.

"I started the first day I met you." Isabelle's laughter filled the room. "Gunther tells me I meddle too much, but I was determined to see you in a pretty gown."

"This isn't just pretty. It's beautiful." Harriet's hands caressed the fabric, delighting in its soft texture. Calico might be more practical, but there was no denying the pleasure of the almost silky weave. "I've never had anything this fine." Grandma had claimed there was no reason to waste money on furbelows, and all too soon, there had been no money to waste. Harriet began fastening the buttons.

"It's about time you thought about yourself." Isabelle's voice held a slight hint of asperity. "Ruth and Mary are more stylishly dressed than you."

"Not anymore." Harriet pivoted on her heel, enjoying the sensation of the soft fabric swirling around her. "I don't know how to thank you, Isabelle. This fits perfectly."

Her friend's smile broadened. "Wait until you see how you look." As Harriet replaced her spectacles, Isabelle dragged a full-length looking glass from behind the cupboard. "What do you think?"

Harriet stared at the mirror, astonished by the sight. Those were her spectacles and her eyes. That was her nose, and yes, that was her mouth, but everything else looked different. The hairdo, which felt so strange, made her look younger, more approachable. Perhaps it was the ringlets, perhaps the color of the dress. Harriet wasn't certain. All she knew was that her face seemed softer, her cheeks rosier. "Is this really me?" As she asked the question, she pictured Lawrence. What would he think? Would he still call her forbidding? Harriet shook her head slightly, trying to chase away her errant thoughts. There was no reason to care about Lawrence's opinion. She was doing this for the children.

Isabelle gave her a quick hug, then took a step back to admire her handiwork. "This is the way you were meant to look."

Harriet's gaze returned to the mirror, for she was almost mesmerized by the transformation. "I can't believe the difference. I feel like Cinderella getting ready for the ball."

"Does that make me the Fairy Godmother?" Isabelle wrinkled her nose. "Gunther will split his sides laughing at that thought."

"How can I possibly thank you?"

"That's simple. Throw out those old clothes you've been wearing and make yourself some new dresses." Isabelle pulled two bolts of fabric off one of the crates. "This deep green would look nice on you. So would the pink."

When Harriet left the mercantile half an hour later, though her arms were laden with packages, her heart felt lighter than it had in years.

Lawrence was bored. He hadn't expected that. The first months had been busy, dealing with the townspeople's complaints. Most of those complaints had been petty, and he'd chafed at the realization that being mayor and sheriff of a small town was far different from the freedom and excitement he'd found as a Ranger, that the justice he wielded was on a smaller, less dramatic scale. Today he would have welcomed a dispute over payment for one of William Goetz's tables. Instead, he was sitting in his office, staring at those gloomy maps and even gloomier portraits from the Old Country, wondering what to do.

He ought to be glad there were no more problems on the Friedrich farm and that the rustlers had left Zach's cattle alone. He ought to be happy that his days had been free of complaints about Harriet and her insistence on efficient exits from the schoolhouse. Instead, he was bored.

He couldn't even visit Sterling, for he knew the minister was writing a sermon for his ever-dwindling congregation. Each Sunday fewer people entered the German church. Though Lawrence knew Sterling was concerned, he claimed there was nothing anyone could do. "You can't threaten to arrest them if they don't come to church," Sterling had said. "All you can do is pray that God will soften their hearts." And so Lawrence prayed, but that did not bring the parishioners back.

He stared at the wall again, frowning at the maps. Michel Ladre had been proud of them, declaring they were evidence of the turmoil his emigrants had escaped. That might have been true ten years ago, but today Lawrence found them annoying. The townspeople were Texans now. If maps and pictures were going to hang on the wall, they ought to be maps of Texas or even of the United States of America. The portraits should be of the governor and president. Alsace, Lorraine, France, and Germany no longer had any relevance.

Knowing that someone would undoubtedly complain but not caring, Lawrence pulled everything from the wall. The spots where the pictures had been were brighter than the surrounding surface, leaving no doubt that something had once hung there. He could buy some whitewash at the mercantile and fix that. At least while he was painting, he would not be bored.

But as he left his office, Lawrence found himself turning left. Though the mercantile was to the right, it seemed that his feet had other ideas, for they headed toward the school. He wasn't planning to visit Harriet. Of course he wasn't. But, as long as he was almost there, he might as well check on the students. The students. Not Harriet.

The children were outside, the younger ones running in circles, playing tag and appearing to be having a good time, the older boys engaged in building a human pyramid while the girls watched, probably hoping to see the pyramid collapse in a tangle of arms and legs. Everyone appeared to be healthy and happy. His mission was complete. And yet Lawrence climbed the steps and entered the schoolhouse.

"Harriet?" He stared at the petite blonde-haired woman who stood at the chalkboard, her back toward him, writing lessons. This woman wore a fashionable red dress, and her hair was softer than Harriet's. She was the right height, the hair was the right shade, and this was obviously where Harriet should be, but Lawrence wasn't certain he wasn't seeing a stranger. No-nonsense Harriet Kirk did not own a fashionable dress, much less one in a color other than putrid yellow or dirty brown, and she most certainly did not wear her hair in a style that even Lottie would envy.

As the woman turned, Lawrence felt his jaw drop. This woman was beautiful. No, that was too mild a word. She was stunning. She was spectacular. She was . . . "What . . . ?

How . . . ? Why . . . ?" Though the questions whirled through his mind, Lawrence's tongue refused to form complete sentences. It was embarrassing. Here he was, sounding as tongue-tied as a schoolboy, all because he found himself in the presence of a beautiful woman.

Harriet—for it most definitely was Harriet who stood by the chalkboard—smiled. "You forgot who, where, and when." She was amused by his discomfiture, and there was nothing he could do about it.

Lawrence tried to look away, but his eyes were as disobedient as his feet had been when he'd told them to go to the mercantile. "I came to see how your brother was faring." Though it wasn't the truth, it was the first coherent thought to emerge from his mouth.

The sparkle behind those spectacles told Lawrence that Harriet had seen through him, though she pretended to believe his explanation. "He's not happy working for Karl," she said, the warmth in her voice betraying her inner smile, "but I don't think anything would please Jake these days. As for the other . . ." She held her skirts and made a mocking half-curtsey. "Isabelle is responsible. She told me I looked like a dead mouse."

"You don't look like a mouse anymore, dead or alive." What an inane thing to say! Lottie would cringe and tell him he knew nothing about speaking to a woman. That was self-evident.

The corners of Harriet's mouth turned up again as she pretended to fan herself. "Why, thank you, Mr. Wood. Your flattery would turn a girl's head."

"Harriet, you know I was a Ranger. We believe in plain speaking." That was true, but it didn't explain why he was

124

having so much difficulty with this conversation, why he felt so flummoxed. He couldn't deny it, though; just the sight of Harriet turned his thoughts to quicksand. Who would have guessed that she would emerge as a beautiful butterfly?

～ى

"I'm surprised your mother never taught you to make pickles." Though Frau Friedrich's voice was even, Harriet sensed the disapproval.

"Mother was busy with all the children." She wouldn't tell her that Mother had no time to make pickles because her days were spent locked in her room. "Besides, I don't think she liked the flavor." Harriet enjoyed the sweet and sour flavor of what Frau Friedrich called bread and butter pickles and had asked for the recipe. The German woman had insisted that, rather than simply write out the instructions, she would show Harriet how she made them.

"The important thing is to not overcook the cucumbers." Frau Friedrich had let Harriet mix the pickling solution and pour it over the sliced cucumbers and onions. "Once it comes to a boil, it's time to put everything into the jars." Deftly, she ladled the aromatic mixture into the first of the canning jars, tightening the lid. "Now, you try."

To Harriet's dismay, she spilled fully a quarter of the pickles on her first attempt. "I'm afraid I need more practice."

"Don't worry. You'll get it right before you know it." The older woman's voice was warm and encouraging, so different from the strident tone Harriet associated with her mother. "Now, try again."

By the time the twelfth jar was filled, Harriet had managed to drip only a little over the edge of the jar.

125

"*Sehr gut*. Very good," Frau Friedrich translated. "Now, let's sit a spell. I made a kuchen I thought you might like." She brought out the fragrant coffee cake and cut two generous slices. "Enjoy it."

Harriet enjoyed far more than the coffee and cake. She enjoyed every moment of her visits to the Friedrich farm. They had started one Saturday when Daniel had forgotten his jacket. Afraid that he would be cold, Harriet had taken the garment to the farm. When she'd arrived, Frau Friedrich had insisted she remain for a bite to eat and a bit of conversation. The bit of conversation had stretched into an hour, and when Harriet had taken her leave, it had been with the invitation to return each week.

"I miss the companionship of another woman," Frau Friedrich had said when Harriet protested that she might be imposing. "You'd be doing me a favor by coming."

But the favors, Harriet was certain, were being conferred on her. Though Jake might resent working for Karl, Harriet looked forward to her time at the farm. Karl was invariably friendly to her, never failing to say something complimentary about either Daniel or Sam. If there was nothing memorable about their conversations, no sparring, not even the joking banter that had begun to characterize her conversations with Lawrence, Harriet didn't mind. The true appeal of her visits to the farm was the time she spent with Karl's mother. When she was in the older woman's company, she felt as if she were doing more than visiting a neighbor. Instead, she had the sensation of being enfolded in warm arms, of being surrounded by love.

The door opened, and Karl strode into the kitchen. "Mutter, I saw Harriet's wagon and . . ." He stopped, his mouth agape when he spotted Harriet. Blood rushed to his face, then quickly receded.

His mother chuckled. "What's the matter, Karl? Haven't you ever seen a woman in a new dress?"

It was more than the dress, Harriet knew. This was the first time she'd visited the Friedrichs since Isabelle had taught her how to style her hair. Frau Friedrich had commented on the change, saying she liked the new Harriet. Karl's reaction was different. He stared at her, his gaze moving from the top of her head down to her waist, which was all that the table revealed, and back to her crown.

It wasn't the first time someone had stared at her. Lawrence had, as had the schoolchildren. Harriet's youngest pupils had grinned when they'd realized the stranger in front of the classroom was only Miss Kirk, confirming their approval with smiles instead of cringes when she called on them. This was different. While the children's gazes had warmed her and Lawrence's had made her feel beautiful, Karl's seemed almost disapproving. But that was silly. Why would he disapprove of a new hairstyle and dress?

"I almost didn't recognize you." His voice sounded strained, and Harriet wondered if that was the reason for his disapproval. Karl disliked surprises. He stroked his beard as he said, "I came inside to see if you would like to attend the harvest festival with us. Mutter makes the best chocolate cake for it."

According to Isabelle, the harvest dance was the primary social event of the autumn, an evening that everyone in Ladreville looked forward to. With activities for all age groups, families came as a unit, bringing baskets of food. And while each family was responsible for its supper, the evening culminated in a feast of shared desserts. Karl had not been exaggerating when he'd described his mother's cake. Even Isabelle, who favored French pastries, admitted that everyone tried to have a slice of Frau Friedrich's chocolate cake. "Thank you, Karl," Harriet said with a small smile, "but I can't leave my siblings alone." Though they would be tired the next day, Harriet wanted them all to attend the social.

Karl slapped his forehead. "What a *Dummkopf* I am! The invitation is not just for you. Your whole family is invited." He turned to his mother. "Isn't that right, Mutter? We want you to share our supper."

When Frau Friedrich nodded, Harriet smiled. Jake would not be pleased, but the rest of the family would enjoy being with the Friedrichs. "In that case, thank you. I accept." For one night, they'd be part of a true family.

"This deep blue calico is beautiful." Harriet touched the bolt of fabric that Isabelle had set aside for her. "Thank you for ordering it."

"It's my pleasure." Isabelle gave Harriet a wry smile. "The town's buzzing with the news that you spend a lot of time on the Friedrichs' farm. Everyone figures it's because you're planning to marry Karl when your contract expires."

While Isabelle spoke, blood drained from Harriet's face. How foolish she had been, not realizing that a town as fond of gossip as Ladreville would misconstrue her afternoons with Frau Friedrich. It was true that Karl always spoke to her while she was there and that he had been the one who had invited the family to the festival, but that wasn't courting. Harriet had been courted by Thomas, and she knew the difference. Karl was simply being friendly.

"The whole idea is preposterous," she said, her voice harsher than normal. "I'm not planning to marry anyone. It's true I go to the farm, but it's to visit Karl's mother. She's teaching me German cooking." Harriet gritted her teeth, trying to dismiss the unsettling images that Isabelle's words had provoked. "The grapevine is wrong. Completely wrong." But she had agreed to attend the fall festival with the Friedrichs. What would the town make of that? And what would Lawrence think?

9

"I'll race you to the tree."

Lawrence tried not to let his surprise show. He hadn't been surprised when Sterling had suggested they spend the afternoon together. Being cooped up in the parsonage with an invalid had to be difficult. That was one of the reasons Lawrence had recommended they do something more strenuous than simply talking. Unfortunately, the times he and Sterling had walked along the streets of Ladreville, they'd been met with blatant shunning by the people who should have been Sterling's parishioners. Being on horseback meant they could escape the town and its disapproval. But it was one thing to ride slowly on the roads as they'd done before, quite another to race across the field. An Easterner didn't realize how rough the fields could be and how one misstep could result in a horse breaking its leg. Still, there was no denying the enthusiasm in Sterling's eyes.

"You're on." When they'd left the livery, they'd headed south on Hochstrasse and were now standing at the intersection of Potomac Street. The American-named street marked not only the end of Hochstrasse but also the end of the town. From here for the next half mile there was nothing but open fields and the massive oak tree that Sterling had chosen as their destination. It was an ideal spot for a race.

Lawrence leaned forward, urging Snip to a gallop. An instant later they were flying across the field. Though he had thought he would keep his horse reined in to give Sterling half a chance, Lawrence was startled when the minister's mount passed him. Somewhere, this man had learned to ride. Not only ride, but ride well.

"C'mon, Snip. Let's show them what you can do." The horse needed no encouragement. Always competitive, Lawrence's palomino hated nothing more than losing. Though he won, the victory was a matter of inches. "It looks like you studied more than preaching at that seminary," Lawrence said when he and Sterling were once more riding abreast.

A grin split the minister's face. "Surprised you, didn't I? Folks seem to think a parson can't do anything other than preach. The truth is, I learned to ride as a youngster. I wish I could do it more often, because it's a great way to clear my head."

Lawrence had never ridden for pure pleasure. For him, a horse was part of his job. Always had been, and probably always would. But he understood the need to sort out one's thoughts and relax. Though few might admit it, everyone had the same basic need. Even Harriet, as self-reliant and confident a person as he'd ever met, took long, brisk walks that Lawrence was willing to bet were designed to clear her head.

He'd seen her striding as if pursued by an angry javelina and wondered what troubled her so deeply. Perhaps it was her family. Jake was undeniably a handful. It could also be her pupils, although Lawrence doubted that. If there were any problems at the school, he'd have heard of them. He hoped Karl Friedrich wasn't the cause. Though he couldn't picture them as a couple, for a few days the town had buzzed with speculation of a June wedding. But gossip was fickle, and it was a long time until June, and so the matrimonial rumors had been eclipsed by discussion of what many considered to be preposterous: Lawrence's proposition that they construct a bridge across the Medina.

He turned to his companion. "Is your head clear, or do you want to try that again?"

"And risk being beaten twice? No, thanks. I'll let you savor your victory for a while before we have a rematch."

"Can you get away tomorrow?" Lawrence asked as his eyes scanned the horizon, looking for intruders. Though there was no reason to expect rustlers or hostile Indians, old habits were slow to die. Nothing appeared amiss. A hawk soared overhead, searching for its next meal. On the opposite bank, Clay's cattle grazed peacefully. It was a typical autumn day in Ladreville. Only a Ranger would have imagined anything else.

Lawrence turned back to Sterling and continued his invitation. "It would be a slower ride, but I'd appreciate your company. I'm going to the other side of the river to look for evidence of rustling."

His friend's eyes lit with pleasure. "Even though I ought to be writing my sermon, I'd rather do that." He looked around. "I guess you haven't found any clues."

"Whoever they are, these rustlers are wily. They cover their tracks well. And, surprisingly, they're not greedy. They could have taken more cattle last time, but they didn't."

"Yet you think they'll be back."

Lawrence nodded at the man who rode slowly by his side. For an Easterner, Sterling understood a lot about the West. Or perhaps it was that he understood people. "The Bar C and the Lazy B have the best cattle in the Hill Country. It's almost irresistible."

The smile Sterling gave Lawrence was wry. "I wish my sermons were irresistible. It's mighty discouraging seeing only a handful of people in the church."

Each week fewer people attended, but Sterling didn't need him to voice those words. "You know you can count on me and the Kirks." Lawrence had been surprised to see Harriet at services each Sunday, for she had previously alternated with the French church.

Sterling nodded. "I appreciate your support and that of the Kirks. Did you know that Harriet brings something soft for Pastor Sempert to eat three times a week? She's as regular as clockwork, coming every Monday, Wednesday, and Friday on her way to school. This week she let her little sister carry the pudding. The child was beside herself with pleasure when Pastor Sempert managed to smile at her."

Lawrence could picture the scene, for he recalled how excited Lizbeth had been when he'd let her carry a basket of eggs one day. He hadn't told his sister that the eggs were hard-cooked and that she couldn't break them. There was no point, Ma had said, in spoiling Lizbeth's fun. Even as a youngster, Harriet probably hadn't needed the admonition to be careful with Mary's feelings. For her, it would have been instinctive, for if ever there was a woman born to be a mother, it was Harriet.

"I'm worried about the other parishioners—the ones who

came from the Old Country," Sterling continued. "It seems they won't accept me as God's messenger. It makes me wonder why he sent me here."

They had turned around and were making their way back to Ladreville, neither one in any apparent hurry. Lawrence reined in Snip and looked at his friend. "Did you come willingly? I didn't. I kept fighting the idea of living in Ladreville, but I couldn't shake the conviction that God wanted me here. I wish I knew why."

Though Sterling's eyes were serious, Lawrence saw no condemnation in them. "I believe God has a reason for your being in Ladreville, and I don't believe it's simply to protect Ladreville's citizens or to serve horrible coffee." Sterling's expression sobered. "I don't think God is finished with you. I believe he had other reasons for leading you here."

Memories of the Bible passages he'd read flashed through Lawrence's mind. Today the book had opened to the story of Jacob's love for Rachel and what he'd had to do to gain her father's approval. Almost every day it seemed as if Lawrence was drawn to verses about marriage. Why? Was God mocking him, or was there another reason? He wouldn't ask Sterling and risk a second discussion of Lawrence's need for a wife. Instead, he raised an eyebrow. "Why do you think God sent you to Ladreville and not some other place?"

To Lawrence's surprise, Sterling hesitated. "I'm not certain any longer. Back in Pennsylvania when I received the call, I thought God's plan was for me to help make Ladreville more American. I believed that was the reason the people at church headquarters chose me instead of someone from the Old Country. Now I don't know. How can I bring about change if no one listens to me?"

Lawrence had no answers, but half an hour later as he removed Snip's saddle and began to curry him, he nodded slowly. Perhaps Sterling was right. Perhaps God had brought him to Ladreville for more than one reason. Perhaps his next mission was to help his friend.

᳃

Nothing! Thomas kicked the door so hard that the flimsy wood splintered. He had kept a smile on his face when the postmaster shook his head and informed him there was no mail, but now that he was back in his uncle's miserable excuse for a stable, there was no need for pretense. Thomas was angry, and he didn't care if the horses knew it.

Why hadn't she written? More importantly, why hadn't she come? What was wrong with her? Thomas kicked the door again. It made no sense. Women would do anything for him. Even Uncle Abe, who claimed that Thomas was headed for fire and brimstone, admitted that his nephew had been given more than his share of charm. So why hadn't Harriet responded? What was wrong with the woman? Didn't she understand that Thomas needed her? Now he'd have to invent another excuse and hope that Herb Allen's business kept him in Houston for another month.

Sweat trickled down Thomas's neck. He had to find the money. He had to! His stomach churned at the prospect of being the object of Herb Allen's anger. This was all Harriet's fault.

᳃

Her hands were clammy and shook more than an oak leaf in a windstorm. Her legs were even worse. They threatened to buckle at the mere thought of taking a step. Ruth sank onto the bed, thankful no one was home to witness her cowardice. "It's time you took credit for all those delicious puddings," Harriet had said this morning at breakfast. "You can deliver it today." And then she'd waltzed off to school as if she hadn't just asked Ruth to do something as impossible as swimming to Africa.

Ruth took a deep breath, trying to calm her nerves. It did no good, for when she exhaled, her breath came out in tiny spurts, not the long, steady stream of air that she had heard was so beneficial. What was wrong with her? She couldn't even breathe properly.

She clenched her hands, trying to steady them. Just the thought of meeting others, of having to talk to them, filled her with fear. Harriet didn't understand. She had no problem being with strangers. Ruth did. The only places she felt comfortable were home and church. There were no strangers at home, and once the worship service began, she was not required to talk to anyone. All she had to do was listen . . . and watch.

Her breathing started to slow as she thought of him. He was the strongest person she had ever met, stronger even than Harriet. Week after week he climbed into the pulpit and faced a congregation that seemed to barely tolerate him. She heard the nasty comments, the people who said they would never accept him as their minister. Though whispered, the accusations were so loud that she knew he must be aware of them, and yet he gave no sign. Instead, he acted as if he had been welcomed by his parishioners, as if they were not open in their conviction that he could never replace Pastor Sempert.

Forcing herself to her feet, Ruth took another deep breath,

and this time she managed a slow exhalation as she thought of Sterling Russell. Though her hands trembled, she pinned on her everyday hat and slid her hands into her gloves. At least they hid the clamminess that still had not vanished.

Minutes later, she was outside, willing her feet to take yet another step. As a light breeze rustled the trees, a bird trilled its contentment. Ruth was not content. She was scared. If only there were a back entrance, she wouldn't have to venture onto Hochstrasse with its curious passersby. But there was no back entrance, and so she braved the stares of women heading to the mercantile, keeping her head down, pretending to be concentrating on the sight of her neatly buttoned shoes. Left, right. Left, right. It felt like hours before she arrived at the parsonage, but at last she raised the knocker.

"Good morning, Miss Kirk." Though he did his best to hide it, Pastor Russell's voice could not disguise his surprise at finding her outside his front door. Why would he expect her, when she had done nothing more than nod greetings each Sunday? He had never even heard her voice. His was as friendly as ever as he said, "Come inside and tell me how I can help you."

No! She wouldn't go inside. Instead she held out the basket. "Pudding. I brought pudding for Pastor Sempert. And for you, if you want it." As the words tumbled out of her mouth, Ruth kept her eyes fixed on the front step. She didn't want to see his pity. She didn't want to know that he regarded her the way the townspeople did, as an object of ridicule. Quiet Ruth. Mousy Ruth. The silent sister. She had heard it all, first in Fortune, now here in Ladreville.

"Thank you, Ruth." To her surprise, he did not take the basket from her. Instead he touched her chin, tilting her head

137

up so that she was forced to look at him. "Thank you," he said again, and this time he smiled at her. "Are you certain you won't come in?"

She shook her head. "Maybe next time."

Where had that come from? All Ruth knew was that somehow this man's smile had chased away her fear.

Harriet liked this time of the day. Classes were dismissed; the school was empty; she could enjoy a few minutes of peace as she planned the next day's lessons. Once she returned home, the bedlam would resume, with Ruth and Jake grumbling, the younger boys squabbling, Mary feeling put upon. It was here in the silent classroom that Harriet found respite and a sense of renewal. Occasionally Isabelle would visit her, but most days she was able to savor the solitude.

As the creak of the floorboards announced someone's arrival, Harriet looked up. Blood drained from her face and her heart began to race at the sight of Lawrence's somber expression. What had Jake done this time?

"Come in." Somehow her voice sounded normal. Though she wanted to blurt out her questions, Grandma had instilled in her the need to observe social niceties. She rose and offered the sheriff her chair. "I'm afraid you won't fit in the pupils' desks." Even her oldest student was inches shorter than this man who towered over the majority of Ladreville's citizens.

He shook his head. "There's no need. I can stand, or . . ." Lawrence pulled the dunce's stool from the corner, placing it near her desk.

Despite herself, Harriet smiled. "You're the first person who volunteered to sit there."

"Is it frequently occupied?"

"Other than by my brothers, no."

Though pupils inevitably squirmed when they were seated in front of the class on the high stool that made everyone, from the youngest to the oldest, look a bit ridiculous, Lawrence seemed at ease there. "I'm surprised they'd misbehave in school."

Harriet noticed that he wasn't surprised by the mischief, only the location. Her heart sank another notch as she tried to imagine what Jake had done. "It's difficult for them, having me as their teacher. The other boys egg them on, but . . ." She gave Lawrence a long, appraising look. "I don't imagine you came here to discuss the dunce stool. What has Jake done?"

The sheriff's blue eyes widened slightly, as if he were surprised by her question. "Nothing." Lawrence shook his head to emphasize his answer. "Is that why you thought I was here?" When she nodded, he leaned forward, his expression earnest. "I'm sorry if I alarmed you."

As relief flowed through her, Harriet managed a small smile. "It's simply that you looked so serious. I thought there was a problem."

"There is. I'd like your opinion about something, but I assure you that it doesn't concern your family."

Relief mingled with surprise that this man, who was the cynosure of the town, sought her opinion. That had never happened in Fortune. "I'll help if I can. What's wrong?"

"It's Sterling. Pastor Russell," he clarified. "The man's become my friend, but even if he weren't, I'd want to help him." The tightening of Lawrence's lips made Harriet think he was trying not to frown. "It can't have escaped your notice that fewer people attend church each week. That's not good

139

for Sterling, and it's not good for the parishioners, either."
A mirthless laugh escaped those expressive lips. "I can't very
well order everyone to go to church, can I? The truth is, Harriet, I don't know what to do."

And that admission cost him. Harriet saw the pain in his
eyes and recognized its source. She hated it when she could
not resolve a problem. How much more difficult must it be
for a Ranger to admit to being powerless?

Before she could say anything, Lawrence leaned forward
again. "The reason I'm here is I wondered whether you had
any ideas."

Harriet pursed her lips, trying to find an answer. When
her pupils were absent too often, she visited the parents to
learn why they were truant. Pastor Russell could do that, but
what if his parishioners refused to let him enter their homes?
Though she had never faced that problem, it was possible the
minister might. How distressing that would be! And even if
he did speak to them, how could he persuade them to return?
When dealing with truants, Harriet would point out that the
parents weren't getting value for the money they paid for a
teacher. There were no such arguments for churchgoers.

Reluctantly she shook her head. "I doubt there's anything
you or I could say that would help. We're native Texans, and
that puts us in the same category as Sterling. The congregation wants someone from the Old Country, someone who
speaks German and understands their customs." Sterling
Russell did not meet any of those criteria. "I'll keep thinking
about it, but right now I have no suggestions."

Lawrence's eyes darkened with disappointment. "I was
afraid of that. I've been wracking my brain, but I haven't
come up with anything either." He slid off the stool and

walked to the bookshelves that lined one of the side walls. "Are you sure there are no answers here?"

Harriet shook her head. "Not in those particular books. They're adventure stories and fairy tales for the younger children. I use them as a reward for finishing their lessons." Though it had surprised her, even the older students seemed to enjoy the stories. Oh, they pretended not to listen, but she caught them looking interested, and once she had heard two of the senior boys discussing *David Copperfield*.

"You enjoy books, don't you?"

"I couldn't live without them." Harriet rose and stood by Lawrence's side, fingering the spines of her favorite stories. "I can hardly recall the time when I didn't read. Books have always been my refuge."

It was a mistake. She knew that the instant the words left her mouth. She had revealed a part of herself that no one needed to know. Perhaps he wouldn't notice. But Lawrence turned, his expression thoughtful. "I've never heard them described that way."

The only possible course was to attempt to deflect his curiosity. "Haven't you ever wanted to escape a rainy day?" Harriet would not mention that reading had helped her escape far more than inclement weather and that she had chosen books as her companions to block out the sight of her father with his constant companion: whiskey.

"Books can transport you to another time and place." She pulled *David Copperfield* from the shelf. "I've never been to England, but Mr. Dickens makes it so real that I feel as if I've wandered along the lanes of Suffolk." As she had hoped, Lawrence's expression changed. Now he looked at the book, not her. "Don't you believe me?"

He shrugged. "Let's say that I'm a bit dubious." He sounded downright unconvinced. "Other than the Bible, I haven't read anything since I left school, unless you count Wanted posters."

"I don't." Impulsively, Harriet handed him the book. "Let's change that. Why don't you give Mr. Dickens a chance?"

Lawrence gave her a speculative glance. "What do I get if I enjoy him?"

"Another book."

"And if I don't?"

"I'll clean your office for a month." Though Lawrence had said nothing to her, the grapevine had reported that he was having difficulty finding someone to clean his office and the jail cell.

"You'd do that?"

Harriet nodded. While cleaning was not among her favorite pastimes, she was willing to wager that Mr. Dickens's prose would keep her from having to wield a mop and bucket.

Lawrence stuck out his hand. "You've got yourself a deal."

10

"Harriet." Though her smile did not falter, Frau Friedrich's eyes widened with surprise and the faintest hint of alarm as she looked up from her ironing. "I didn't expect you today." Like many of the town's residents, Frau Friedrich was highly organized, with specific activities planned for each day. Tuesday was the day for ironing, not Harriet's visits.

"I didn't mean to worry you," Harriet said, wishing she had thought to send a message ahead. Though she wasn't normally impulsive, riding to the farm after school had been a spur of the moment decision, one she hoped she would not regret. "I won't stay long," she promised, "but I wanted to talk to you."

Ever since Lawrence had told her of his concern for Sterling, Harriet had sought a way to help him. This morning when Pierre Berthoud had been absent for the fourth day and she'd resolved to pay a visit to his home, she had felt as if the fog had lifted. While Pastor Russell might not choose to

143

question his parishioners, there was no reason Harriet should not talk to someone who had become a friend.

"Anytime, my dear." Frau Friedrich's smile broadened, and her voice softened. "You're always welcome here." She placed the flat iron back on the stove and motioned toward the kitchen table. "Sit down and tell me why you've come, other than to brighten an old woman's day."

"You're not old." It was true that her hair was gray and her face creased with years of smiling, but Harriet never thought of Karl's mother as old. "I didn't know where to turn, other than to you." Though the older woman's eyes sparkled at the thought, Harriet doubted they would continue to sparkle when she heard the reason for her visit. "My grandmother told me it was rude to ask personal questions, and this is definitely personal, but I can't think of any other way to learn what's happening."

Frau Friedrich nodded slowly. "Go on, my dear. I'll help you as best I can."

That was what Harriet had been counting on. Being French, Isabelle was still an outsider to the rest of the German community, but the Friedrichs were held in high esteem. If Harriet could convince them to return to church, others would follow. She took a deep breath. "I noticed you no longer attend church services, and I wondered why."

As she had feared, Frau Friedrich's lips thinned, and she remained silent for a long moment. When the German woman spoke, her voice was harsher than normal. "Ach, Harriet, you do ask hard questions, don't you? I think you already know the answer to this one. It's the new minister. He's too young, and he doesn't speak German. How can we respect him?"

Her words confirmed Harriet's suspicions. Though most

of the townspeople spoke English, at least haltingly, thanks to Sarah Canfield's efforts, they still preferred church services conducted in their native language.

Harriet looked around the room as she searched for an argument that might sway the older woman. There had to be something. Her eyes lit when she spotted the new curtains. To Frau Friedrich's dismay, the ones she had brought from Alsace had disintegrated in the strong Texas sun and she'd been forced to sew a new pair. "It will take awhile to become used to these," she had told Harriet when she commented on the change. "They're too bright now, but they'll fade." Perhaps that was the answer.

"I imagine Pastor Sempert was young once." Harriet kept her voice neutral, as if the thought had just occurred to her.

To her surprise, Frau Friedrich chuckled. "Indeed, he was. I can remember his first weeks in our church back in Alsace. My mother kept complaining that he couldn't possibly know anything because he was still wet behind the ears." The chuckle died as color rushed to Frau Friedrich's cheeks. "It appears I'm following in my mother's footsteps, doesn't it? That's not very Christian, is it?"

Harriet knew better than to agree. Instead, she said, "I believe Pastor Russell is doing the best he can. Perhaps he's like your curtains and needs to fade a bit to fit in, but he seems earnest, and his sermons manage to keep my brothers from fidgeting. I consider that little less than a miracle."

As Harriet had hoped, the older woman smiled. "What you've said is true. The least Otto and I can do is make an effort to get to know him." Frau Friedrich's voice was once again thoughtful. "Church is not the best place for that. I think I'll invite Pastor Russell for dinner next Sunday."

"I imagine he'd like that. It must be lonely eating alone most of the time." Lawrence had said that the minister's housekeeper prepared meals but that the ones he had tasted would win no blue ribbons. That was one of the reasons Harriet sent food to the parsonage, that and the desire to let both ministers know she supported them.

The sparkle returned to Frau Friedrich's eyes. "I'll make my chocolate cake," she said. Her eyes narrowed slightly. "There's one string attached to my invitation. You and your family need to come too."

"Thank you. We'll all enjoy that." All except Jake.

⁊

"Do you think they'll come tonight?" Zach whispered the words.

"I don't know." As he peered through the branches that disguised the mouth of the cave, searching for signs of intruders, Lawrence's pulse returned to normal. He had thought he'd heard a horse, but careful watching had proven that to be a false alarm. "The arrow Sterling and I found was definitely Comanche, so it's clear they've been in the area." He had been elated by the discovery, telling Sterling it was the first lead he'd had. That elation had begun to fade.

Lawrence looked at Zach, who was pulling their next meal from his saddlebag. "Your cattle are the most likely reason they were here. As I told Sterling, they're irresistible." A single steer would provide the tribe with meals, not to mention hides for clothing and shelter. "I can't promise the Comanche will return this month, but it's common knowledge that they prefer to hunt by the light of the full moon."

That was the reason Lawrence and Zach were camped in a

small cave near the defile where the rustlers had herded cattle the last time. Those cattle—what Clay Canfield's father used to refer to as "gold on the hoof"—were milling around the pasture only a few hundred yards away. The branches Lawrence and Zach had dragged in front of the cave hid its opening, while the smell of the cattle masked any aromas from their meals. Though their horses were clearly unhappy with being confined in such a small place, they had retired to the far end of the cave, momentarily content to munch their oats.

Tonight was the last of the three nights Lawrence had planned to be here. In addition to the night of the full moon, he had chosen the ones immediately before and after, not knowing when—or if—the Comanche would hunt.

"I'm beginning to think they're not going to come," Zach said as he handed Lawrence a jar of beans, grimacing at the prospect of another cold meal. They both knew they could not light a fire for fear of alerting the Indians. Fortunately, the nights had been warmer than normal for October, but there was no denying the fact that unheated food was not particularly appealing.

Lawrence opened the jar. "I hate to admit it, but I think you're right. We'll wait until daybreak, just in case, but I doubt we're going to see anyone tonight."

As he chewed a piece of beef jerky, Lawrence thought of the many nights he'd subsisted on nothing more than dried meat and water. Tonight's beans should have made it a veritable feast, and yet he found himself wishing he were back in Ladreville. He could have had a hot meal at the saloon before he returned home to discover what happened to David Copperfield in the next chapter. Instead, he was here on what appeared to be a fruitless vigil.

"I'm sorry I wasted your time," Lawrence said. "Next time I'll come alone."

"You will not." Zach's vehemence surprised Lawrence. "They're my cattle. I can't expect you to protect them single-handedly."

"That's the Ranger way." Oh, it was true that they did some things in bands, but most of Lawrence's work had been solitary.

"You're no longer a Ranger," Zach pointed out.

"You're right. Most of the time I don't miss it, although I have to admit I never imagined I'd be the mayor of a town." Nor had he imagined himself enjoying a novel. Nor, for that matter, had he imagined himself looking forward to sparring matches with a schoolmarm.

Zach finished the last of the beans and scoured his bowl with a hunk of dried grass. "Isn't it amazing the plans God has for us?"

"I'm still waiting to learn what he has in store for me."

"So, what did you think of *David Copperfield*?" Harriet smiled at the tall blond man who looked so comfortable in her classroom. Though she wanted to tell him about her conversation with Frau Friedrich and how the German woman had volunteered to invite Pastor Russell to her home, Harriet hesitated. The grapevine had been quick to report that Lawrence had failed to catch the cattle rustlers, and some of the more acerbic tongues had wagged with the speculation that the sheriff had grown soft since he'd left the Rangers. It would be unkind, Harriet decided, to raise Lawrence's hopes when the possibility existed that they would be shattered. It

148

was, after all, possible that the Friedrichs' disapproval of the new minister might persist, even when they knew him better. And so Harriet resolved to keep the conversation focused on less volatile subjects, like books.

Lawrence laid the volume in question on top of her desk and placed a hand on it. It was an almost possessive gesture, a far cry from the reluctance with which he had accepted the book a week ago. "I can't say that I liked Uriah Heep very much."

Harriet took a deep breath, inhaling the faintly musky scent that was Lawrence's alone. Even if she were blind, she'd recognize him by it. A combination of hair oil, soap, fresh air, and the man himself, it lingered in the room and in her memory long after he was gone.

"I'm not surprised," she said with another smile. "No one does. But here's the real question: did Mr. Dickens make you forget you were in Ladreville, Texas?"

Lawrence pulled the dunce stool closer to her desk and settled on it. His lips twitched with amusement as he delayed his answer, knowing she was waiting for it. When he spoke, the amusement turned into a full-fledged smile. "Amazingly, yes. I looked up one day and was surprised that the sun was shining. You see, the scene I was reading had taken place at night, so I expected to look out at dark skies and drizzle. Instead, I saw one of our perfect Texas blue skies. Amazing."

Harriet wasn't certain what was more amazing, Lawrence's enthusiasm or her reaction to it. Though she took pleasure in teaching her students, the satisfaction she felt when one of them mastered a particularly difficult lesson did not compare to seeing Lawrence so animated over a book. She wished she understood the difference. Perhaps it was because he was an

adult and adults were reputed to be less receptive to learning. That didn't seem to be the case with Lawrence. Harriet
didn't know why she was so pleased, but she was.

"Does this mean you'd like another book?"

He nodded, and his lips quirked in a wry smile. "As much
as I was looking forward to having you clean my office, you
won the wager, fair and square."

༝

Lawrence looked at the woman seated behind the desk.
Gone was the prim and proper schoolteacher with the severe
hairdo and unflattering clothing. In her place was a young
lady who would turn heads anywhere she went. Right now
that woman was giving him a smile warmer than the August
sun. "I'm glad," she said. "Books can be friends."

Lawrence tried not to frown. That was all well and good,
but he wanted more than an inanimate object to be his friend.
He wanted Harriet. In the long hours while he'd waited for
the rustlers, he had thought about his time in Ladreville.
There were things he could be proud of: the arguments he'd
settled, the way the town appeared to have accepted him. But
the memories that circled through his head, refusing to be
dismissed, were of the hours he had spent with this woman.

It was true that he had enjoyed *David Copperfield*; however, it wasn't only the story that had intrigued him, but the
knowledge that Harriet had read it. As he turned the pages,
Lawrence found himself wondering what she thought of a
particular scene, whether she had reacted to the characters
the way he had. Wouldn't Lottie laugh? Neither one of them
had ever been called a bookworm, yet here he was, eager to
discuss a long book with a schoolteacher. That was one thing

150

he would not include in his next letter to his sister. She didn't need to know about Harriet . . . yet.

When they finished their review of *David Copperfield*, Lawrence knew two things: he and Harriet had very different views, and yet they agreed on the most important aspects of the book. It was exhilarating, hearing her opinions and knowing that she would listen to his.

He slid off the stool and walked around the schoolroom, envisioning it filled with students, with Harriet standing in front, a small but commanding presence. To think he'd once considered her a gnat, tiny and annoying. Now he viewed Harriet as a hummingbird, beautiful, brightly colored, and bursting with energy. Like the bird, each time she entered his life, she raised his spirits.

"Tell me about your family," he said as he returned to the stool. "Do they love books as much as you do?" He would need to know that and so many other things if he were to court Harriet.

Court Harriet? Lawrence heard his breath escape in a whoosh. Where had that idea come from?

ॐ

"The food is delicious, Frau Friedrich." No one could doubt the sincerity of Sterling's words, for this was the second heaping plate of Wiener schnitzel and spaetzle that he had emptied.

From the opposite end of the table, Herr Friedrich gave his wife a proud smile. "My Greta is the best cook in Ladreville."

Harriet nodded her agreement. The dinner was going even better than she had hoped. Oh, it was true that Jake was fuming, resenting the fact that he had to be at the same table as his nemesis Karl, and Ruth blushed even more than normal when she learned she would be seated between Sterling and Karl, but everyone else appeared to be enjoying both Frau Friedrich's wonderful cooking and the company.

She smiled at Herr Friedrich. "Your wife is a marvelous cook. That's why I've asked her to teach me some of her secrets. It would be good if I could make more than coffee."

"Harriet is an awful cook." Daniel stuffed a biscuit into his mouth and continued speaking. "Everything she makes is lumpy, even the porridge."

"The gravy is the worst," Sam announced. "Lumpy, lumpy, lumpy."

"Now, boys, that's no way to speak of your sister." Karl leaned forward and frowned at them. "You need to show respect. And don't talk with your mouths full." Though his words were directed at the younger boys, Mary cringed under the force of Karl's disapproval. Frau Friedrich had placed the four youngest children on one side of the table, with Sterling, Ruth, Karl, and Harriet on the other. Being under constant adult scrutiny did nothing to improve the youngest Kirks' manners.

"They're only telling the truth," Harriet said, trying to defuse the situation. "The family is fortunate to have Ruth. We'd probably starve if it weren't for her." Predictably, Ruth blushed and lowered her head.

While Sterling murmured something to Ruth, Karl turned toward Harriet, approval shining from his eyes. "It's good that you learn Mutter's recipes. They will serve you well when it's time to feed your husband."

Like her siblings' behavior, this was not a subject Harriet cared to discuss. "There's no husband in my future," she said steadily. Inexplicably, the image of Lawrence danced before her. It must be because she'd been thinking of *Uncle Tom's*

152

Cabin and wondering whether he was enjoying it. That had to be the reason—the only reason—she had pictured him.

At her side, Karl stroked his beard. "Ach, Harriet, a woman like you would make a good wife." According to Isabelle, the rumor mill had lost interest in her and no longer linked her name with Karl's. That was excellent news and could be one of the reasons Jake had seemed almost like his old self. Harriet couldn't let Karl do anything to change that. As she opened her mouth to deliver a retort, Sterling interjected himself. "These pickles are particularly tasty." Harriet suspected he cared less for pickles than for peace, a supposition that was confirmed when he turned to Herr Friedrich. "Now, sir, tell me about your wheat. Gunther says it's the finest in the state." The awkward moment had passed.

Half an hour later, dinner was over and Harriet was helping Frau Friedrich wash dishes.

"You were right, my dear," the older woman said as she swirled soapsuds in the basin. "Pastor Russell is a good man. Otto, Karl, and I will be in church next Sunday."

Harriet's heart filled with warmth. This was why she had come, to solve a problem. "Thank you. I know Pastor Russell will be pleased." And so would Lawrence. Harriet glanced at the cuckoo clock that hung on the kitchen wall, calculating how long it would be before she could tell him the good news.

"I'm not done," Frau Friedrich said as she handed Harriet a plate to dry. "I plan to pay a few calls this week. It's time our congregation started acting like Christians again."

Harriet nodded. If only every problem were that easy to resolve.

11

Each day was easier. Her knees no longer knocked when she left the house, and yesterday she'd actually spoken to a woman at the mercantile. Ruth had been so excited about that feat that she had wanted to rush to the parsonage and tell Sterling, but that would not have been seemly, and so she had waited until this morning. It was unseemly enough that in her thoughts she called him Sterling rather than Pastor Russell. No one other than God knew her thoughts, but if she had visited the parsonage twice in one day, others might have noticed, and she couldn't let that happen.

"You look happy," he said when he opened the door and ushered her inside. That was another difference. Ruth had overcome her fear enough to enter the parsonage. Last week she had even ventured as far as Pastor Sempert's room and had delivered the vanilla custard to him. His smile, crooked and distorted as it was, had made her feel as if she'd slain a dragon. Perhaps she had—the dragon of dread.

"I am happy," she told Sterling, quickly recounting

yesterday's trip to the mercantile. "I know it doesn't sound like much but . . ."

"Nonsense. Each step is important. Now, tell me what you're planning to do about the harvest festival."

The harvest festival was only a fortnight away, and though Ruth had cajoled, pled, and outright refused to attend it, Harriet still expected her to go with the rest of the family. How was Ruth to endure a whole evening at the festival? It wasn't like church, where all she had to do was listen. People would expect her to join in conversation. And then there would be another meal with the Friedrichs. She closed her eyes, trying to blot out the memory of Sunday dinner with them.

The older Friedrichs were nice enough, or they would be if they didn't expect her to converse. Unfortunately, both Herr and Frau Friedrich were outspoken in their opinions and seemed to think that everyone else should be too. But at least they were pleasant, unlike Karl. He was so gruff that Ruth wasn't surprised Jake didn't like him. She didn't care for him overly much herself, especially when he looked at Harriet as if she were a horse he was considering buying. Harriet had her faults—perhaps more than her fair share—but she was not an object. If she had had more courage, Ruth would have told him that.

"I don't know what I'm going to do," she admitted. "Unless I'm ill, I suppose I'll have to attend it."

Sterling was silent for a moment. "I think you should do more than simply attend. I think you should participate." As Ruth felt the blood drain from her face at the very prospect, he continued. "I heard the committee needs a woman to serve punch. Why don't you do that? A pretty girl like you shouldn't remain on the sidelines."

Ruth gulped. He thought she was pretty? "You think so?"

"I know so. You can do it, Ruth. I know you can."

And so, although it had not been her intent, Ruth found herself agreeing to stand behind a table and ladle punch at the town's harvest festival, all because Sterling Russell thought she was pretty.

❦

"Sit down, Jean-Claude. If you tease Hilda once more, you'll spend the rest of the day on the dunce stool." And it would not, Harriet knew, be anywhere nearly as pleasant an experience as having Lawrence there. Jean-Claude would fidget; the other children would snigger; she would be forced to assume her most forbidding expression. Though the boy took his seat and only glowered at Hilda, Eva Lehman began to cry. "What's wrong?" To her dismay, Harriet's voice held more than a little annoyance. It seemed everyone was out of sorts today, including her.

Eva looked up, her face mottled by tears. "I forgot how much three times three is. Mama Isabelle and Vati will think I'm a dummkopf." Something was definitely amiss today, for the child was more distressed than Harriet had seen her. Normally Eva was careful to speak only English, but here she was referring to her father as Vati and letting another German word slip in, all because of a multiplication table.

"Your parents and I don't expect you to have memorized them yet," Harriet said gently. "It takes time." And that was the problem. Her pupils were eager to learn, but they were also easily discouraged, expecting everything to happen immediately and becoming disappointed when it didn't. Though this was not a problem she had encountered in Fortune, Sarah confirmed that she'd noticed the same phenomenon last fall. What the students needed was patience. Unfortunately, that was not part of Harriet's lesson plan.

It ought to be. The thought refused to be dismissed. While the children recited today's Bible verse and chanted the times-three multiplication table, part of Harriet's mind continued to worry, chasing the thought the way a dog might his tail and with the same predictably frustrating results. She was accomplishing nothing, absolutely nothing.

It was late afternoon when Harriet glanced out the window. The schoolyard looked the way it always did, the grass thin in the areas where the children played tag, totally missing under the two swings. And yet at one corner of the yard a small patch of goldenrod flourished, as if in defiance of the children's activity.

That's it. Harriet felt a bubble of excitement rise to her throat as she considered the possibilities. The more she thought about it, the better the idea seemed. While there were no guarantees that it would work, it was certainly worth trying. "Wear your oldest clothes tomorrow," she told the children as she dismissed class. "We have a new project."

"What are we going to do tomorrow?" Daniel demanded at supper that night. It was the same question she had heard from half a dozen students as they'd filed out of the schoolhouse. Her brother was going to get the same answer she gave them.

"You know I can't tell you. It wouldn't be fair to the other pupils."

"They're not fair to us." Though normally possessed of a sunny disposition, tonight Sam was frowning. "They all think we're your favorites."

157

"Of course you are, but only at home." To Harriet's surprise, Ruth spoke before she had a chance to reply. "You know Harriet can't play favorites at school. But she could tell me."

Harriet intercepted the mischievous glance her sister gave the boys. Something was different about her tonight. Ruth seemed calmer, almost serene, and it wasn't like her to become involved in the family's squabbles. Though Harriet was curious about the reason, right now she needed to deal with her brothers.

"I could tell Ruth," she admitted, "but I won't."

Mary scrunched her face into a grimace. "You're mean. Ruth would have told us."

Which was precisely the reason Harriet would not confide in her. "You'll find out tomorrow, along with everyone else."

≈

Thomas tried not to groan as he dragged himself to his feet. The man Herb Allen had sent to deliver his message had made sure there was no misunderstanding.

"Mr. Allen don't like cheaters," the man had announced as he landed a punch to Thomas's ribs. "No, sirree, he sure don't like folks who don't pay." Another blow. "You got one more week. Seven days." Seven kicks accompanied the statement. "If you ain't got his money then, you'll be sorry. Real sorry."

Thomas was sorry now. Sorry he'd had the misfortune to lose money in one of Herb Allen's establishments. Sorry he'd let this miscreant catch him unaware. And sorry—oh, so sorry—that his letter to Harriet had been lost. That had to be what had happened. It was the only explanation. If she'd received his letter, she would have returned to Fortune. He knew it.

His gait unsteady, Thomas made his way back to the parsonage. There was no other choice. He'd have to ask Uncle Abe for the money. The old man had started locking up the offering, but surely once he understood the urgency, he would agree.

He did not.

"The Bible warns us that we will reap what we sow." Leave it to Uncle Abe, Fortune's esteemed parson, to quote the Bible. Thomas almost spat in disgust. "It's unfortunate you've gotten yourself into this predicament, but . . ."

"It wasn't my fault. The other guy cheated."

Uncle Abe seemed unimpressed. "Be that as it may, you brought it on yourself. Gambling is wrong, and you know it."

There had to be a way to convince him. Repentance. That was the trick. Uncle Abe was always talking about people needing to repent.

"You're right," Thomas said, though the words threatened to choke him. "I was wrong. I've learned my lesson. I'll never gamble again." At least not in a saloon Herb Allen owned. "All I ask is that you help me this one time."

"No." His uncle looked at Thomas as if he were a piece of dirt. "The only way you'll learn the lesson is to face the consequences. The full consequences."

But Thomas couldn't, not when the consequence might be death. "Please!" Oh, how it hurt to grovel.

"No. And don't ask again. I won't change my mind."

He had to get the money. He had to. Thomas grimaced as he hoisted himself out of the chair. There had to be a way to get that money, but he could think of only one. Harriet. He grimaced again. There was no time to waste. As painful as it

159

would be to mount a horse, he had no choice. He would go to Ladreville, and when he returned, he would have Harriet . . . and her money.

⊷

"But it's October, Miss Kirk." Jean-Claude stared at her as if she'd lost her mind when she announced their project. "No one starts a garden in October."

"We do," Harriet countered, struggling to contain her grin. Children were so predictable. Though most of them approached anything new with enthusiasm, Jean-Claude could be depended on to complain.

Harriet looked around the classroom, nodding slowly at the pleasure she saw on most faces. "Now, let's practice our orderly exit as we go outside." Despite Jean-Claude's skepticism, the pupils were soon squealing with delight at the prospect of playing in the dirt rather than being quizzed on spelling. At the end of the morning, Harriet smiled as she surveyed what they'd accomplished. It had been dirty work, digging the bed, pulling out grass, raking rocks, but no one had complained, not even Jean-Claude.

"Excellent progress, children. We'll have the finest flower garden in Ladreville."

Eva's knit brows telegraphed her confusion. "How can we? We didn't plant anything."

"We'll do that tomorrow." There was plenty of time to sow the seeds today, but Harriet wanted them to wait. This was, after all, a lesson in patience.

As the afternoon progressed and she found herself glancing at the clock dozens of times, she realized it was a lesson she also needed. Today was the day Lawrence would return

Uncle Tom's Cabin, and she—silly Harriet—was counting the minutes until he arrived. She never felt this way when she and Isabelle planned to meet. As much as she enjoyed conversing with her friend, anticipation never sent frissons down her spine. Seeing Lawrence was different.

It was only because she wanted to hear his reaction to the book. There was no other reason why Harriet found an hour with him more exciting than her visits with Isabelle. And it was only because she enjoyed discussing literature that she wished she and Lawrence could meet more than once a week. She wouldn't suggest that, of course. It would be highly improper to impose on him, for Lawrence was a busy man. Besides, Harriet would do nothing to give the rumor mill any more grist. Once a week was seemly. Anything more frequent would provoke comments.

She smiled when she heard the heavy footsteps that could only be his. Rising to greet Lawrence, she blurted out the first words that came to mind. "No book?" His hands were empty. "Haven't you finished it?"

He nodded, his blue eyes sparkling with what appeared to be amusement. Was she that transparent? Did he know how much she enjoyed his company?

"Yes." Harriet gulped at the swift response. How embarrassing! She lowered her eyes, then raised them again when she realized Lawrence had not read her thoughts but was simply answering her question about the book. "I didn't think you'd mind if I lent it to Zach and Priscilla. I wanted them to see what all the fuss is about."

"Does that mean you liked *Uncle Tom's Cabin*?"

Rather than reply, he strode to the corner and brought the dunce stool close to her desk. It was only when Harriet was seated that he answered. "I wouldn't say I liked it, but I will admit that it made me think."

"And what did you think?"

His smile took years off his face, giving Harriet a glimpse at what he must have looked like a decade ago. "I think," he said slowly, drawing out each word, "that the reason you recommended that particular book is that the author is named Harriet."

She pretended to be annoyed. "The next thing I know, you'll accuse me of having written it."

"Did you?" He acted as if that would not surprise him.

"No. I read books, but writing's not the life for me."

"I wouldn't dismiss the idea. Your life may be too full right now, between teaching and raising your siblings, but that won't always be the case."

It was flattering, having someone believe she was capable of writing a book as powerful as Mrs. Stowe's masterpiece, but Harriet couldn't let Lawrence continue to think she was that talented. "Perhaps I won't always be so busy, but I'm a reader, not a writer."

He gave her another playful grin. "Thanks to you, I've joined the former group." Leaning forward, his hands on his knees, his expression turned serious. "Tell me, Harriet. Don't you think Mrs. Stowe—the other Harriet—exaggerated the evils of slavery?"

It was a valid question. "I don't know. Despite Jake's claims to the contrary, I've never met a slave." When Lawrence raised an eyebrow, she explained that her brother believed working for Karl Friedrich was tantamount to being sold into slavery. "As much as he hates farming and having to do what he considers women's chores, I think the punishment is working. Jake seems to have realized the consequences of his behavior."

"I'm glad. I have to admit that your brother worried me. I've seen others his age continue on the wrong road."

Unbidden, the image of Thomas Bruckner's almost cherubic smile flashed through Harriet's mind. She didn't want to think about Thomas, not today or any day. Even slavery was a more pleasant topic than the man whose angelic face and sweet words had almost convinced her that he loved her. She thanked God every day that she'd overheard Thomas boasting that he'd find homes for her siblings before the wedding. "I won't be saddled with the brats," he'd announced. And, as it turned out, he hadn't been saddled with her either.

Harriet forced thoughts of Thomas away and fixed her gaze on Lawrence. "The reason I've never met a slave is that Fortune is a farming community," she explained. "Like Ladreville, the farms were small enough that there was no need for slaves. I know it's different in other places, particularly on the cotton plantations, but I do think Mrs. Stowe makes a good case for abolition."

"Even if it would destroy the economy of the slave-owning states, including Texas?"

"I don't know." That was beginning to sound like a refrain, and yet Harriet could not regret initiating the discussion. This was what she sought, the exhilaration of talking about more than lesson plans and the latest fashions. "What do you think about the news of so many bank failures?"

Lawrence sighed. "Unfortunately, it isn't only banks that are failing. I read that several railroads have gone bankrupt and that other businesses are teetering on the brink. People are calling it the Panic of 1857 and saying it might be worse than the one we had in 1837." Lawrence's eyes were solemn as he said, "When I read Mrs. Stowe's book, I couldn't help but wonder what would happen if slavery were abolished and planters suddenly had no workers. The cotton wouldn't be planted or picked; the planters would have no money; they couldn't buy goods. Everything might collapse. That's one of the reasons I haven't called a town meeting to vote on the bridge. I don't want to do that while there's so much uncertainty."

Harriet blanched at the thought. Though she had no recollection of the earlier panic, the problems this one was causing were ominous. Still, she wasn't certain Lawrence and the slave owners were right in believing that abolition would destroy the country.

"You make a compelling argument," she admitted, turning so she could watch Lawrence's expression. "And yet is there any way to justify cruelty to another human being? Is there any possible reason to excuse a man like Simon Legree?"

Lawrence shook his head. "The answer is no, even though slave owners claim that slaves are their possessions, not human beings." Rising, Lawrence walked to the window and stared outside for a long moment. When he turned, she saw concern etched on his face. "I tell you, Harriet, I don't know how this will end. There's so much emotion on both sides."

The way he looked, as if he'd taken the weight of the slavery debate on his shoulders, made Harriet wonder if she'd made a mistake in urging that he read *Uncle Tom's Cabin*. "Your next book needs to be something happier," she said with a bright if forced smile. "I would offer you one of Jane Austen's stories, but I don't imagine you'd enjoy them." As she described the world of Regency England, Lawrence shook his head, agreeing that it held no interest for him, but she saw that the diversion had accomplished her goal. His mood was lighter. When he left, it was with a copy of Washington Irving's *Sketchbook* in his hand.

Harriet remained in the schoolhouse, looking around the room that once again felt empty. She and Lawrence would probably never agree on slavery or Mrs. Stowe's book, but that didn't matter. What mattered was the time they spent together. For the hour that he was there, Harriet felt alive—truly alive. It was the way she felt when she was with Isabelle, but so much better.

Harriet gathered her books and slid them into the satchel as she prepared to return home. Isabelle was a dear friend, but Lawrence was . . . She paused, searching for the correct word. Special. That was it. Lawrence wasn't simply a friend; he was a special friend, and oh, how wonderful it was to have a special friend, if only for a few months. For when January ended, so too would Lawrence's time in Ladreville.

Harriet bit her lip, trying not to think about that. There was no benefit in dwelling on things she could not change. She shouldn't spend time worrying about the future. Hadn't she taught her siblings that? Instead, she would enjoy each and every minute of the present. It was all she had.

12

"I'm glad you decided on a new dress for the festival." Ruth moved back to study the frock she had pinned onto Harriet for a preliminary fitting. Deep green with gold braid trim, it was both simple and elegant at the same time. "As Ladreville's new teacher, you're sure to be the center of attention."

Harriet smiled, as much at the beauty of her new gown, which was reflected in the long mirror Ruth had brought into the parlor, as her sister's words. Even though Grandma would have disapproved, calling it self-indulgent, Harriet could not deny the pleasure she found in wearing attractive clothing. Still, she doubted Ladreville's citizens would notice. "I imagine the townspeople will be more interested in Sarah and Clay's son than me. Babies always take the limelight." And that was good. Harriet wanted her family to blend into the community, not stand out.

"You or Rob." Ruth unpinned a seam to adjust the fullness of one sleeve. "It doesn't matter. I'm simply thankful that it won't be me. No one pays any attention to the ladies who pour punch."

Harriet felt her jaw drop as her sister's words registered. "You're going to pour punch?" A month ago, Ruth had offered up vehement protests against attending the festival. Now she was planning to participate? What had happened? Harriet stared at her sister, trying to understand. "You know there's more involved than just pouring punch. You'll have to talk to some people." Admittedly, if Ladreville was like Fortune, most guests would say little more than "please" and "thank you" with an occasional "good evening" thrown in for good measure, but still . . . for someone as shy as Ruth, even such minimal social contact would be painful.

"I can do it." Ruth poked another pin into the sleeve, then stepped away so that Harriet could see her reflection in the mirror. "I know I can."

Ignoring her gown, Harriet kept her eyes on her sister. "You look like my sister, but you don't sound like her."

Ruth smiled. "I feel different. It's hard to explain, but I feel lighter now, as if I've cast away a heavy yoke, and it's all because of him."

"Him?" Ruth had spoken with a man? Harriet studied the face that she knew as well as her own. Ruth looked older, and yet at the same time, her expression reflected almost childlike wonder.

"Sterling." Ruth blushed. "Pastor Russell. I know you probably didn't expect it, but I started talking to him when I took the blancmange to the parsonage. I can't explain it, but he made me realize I had no reason to be afraid of other people. And, Harriet, he . . ." Though Harriet hadn't thought it possible, Ruth's blush deepened. "He said I was pretty."

167

Harriet's heart began to sing with joy. "Oh, Ruthie." The childhood nickname slipped out. "Of course you're pretty." And Sterling Russell was a miracle worker. It didn't matter how he'd done it, he'd made one of Harriet's dreams come true. He'd helped Ruth emerge from her chrysalis.

༄

"You're planting a garden?" Though there was no dirt under her fingernails, Lawrence had heard the story from half a dozen citizens, and when he'd walked to the schoolhouse this afternoon, he'd seen the evidence.

Harriet fisted both hands on her hips in what Lawrence hoped was feigned indignation. When she adopted this pose, Harriet reminded him not of a gnat or a humming-bird but an angry hornet. She pursed her lips, but despite the stern expression, Lawrence sensed that she was trying not to laugh.

"The schoolmarm in me wants to inform you that you have an incorrect subject and verb tense. It's the children who did the work—not me—and it's done—past tense." The lesson delivered, Harriet laughed, and the smile she gave him warmed Lawrence's heart more than a fire in January. "The truth is, essentially you're right. The children and I have planted a garden."

"In late October?" That was part of what had surprised him, that and the thought of Harriet digging in the dirt.

"It's a winter garden," she announced, as if that should be evident. "Frau Friedrich told me which seeds to plant. Most of them won't sprout until spring, but a few will come up soon. The rest will give us something to look forward to."

Her enthusiasm made Lawrence want to continue the

discussion. "I didn't realize agronomy was part of the curriculum."

As Harriet moved to her chair behind the desk, a sweet perfume filled the air. It was probably nothing more than soap. Lawrence knew that his mother and Lottie had scented their bath soap with flowers. Harriet probably did the same. But whatever it was, the scent teased his nostrils and made him want to pull that silly dunce stool closer to her.

Seemingly undisturbed by his nearness, Harriet shook her head. "It isn't, but I needed something to teach the children patience."

Patience. That was something he could use. Lawrence had to admit that he'd never considered gardening as a way to gain it, but didn't Ecclesiastes say there was a time to sow? Perhaps Harriet was right.

She smiled at him again. "I won't claim it's as difficult as chasing bandits, but being cooped up in a classroom with two dozen fidgeting pupils is not my idea of a good day. Besides, I've always loved flowers. Even though we didn't have many at our home in Fortune, I enjoyed the ones we did."

"I gather that your mother was not a gardener."

Harriet's face darkened. "No," she said shortly. "She was occupied with other things. Now, tell me what you thought of *Oliver Twist*."

The lighthearted moment had ended. Harriet couldn't have made it clearer that she wanted to change the subject than if she'd announced it in those words. Though Lawrence complied, all the while they discussed Oliver and Fagan, a part of his mind pondered her change of mood. What had bothered her? Was it the thought of her former home, or was her discomfort somehow connected to her mother? He wouldn't pry, but he couldn't help wondering. And so, as he made his way back to the stone building that was his home, he continued to think about Harriet and the flowers she loved. He'd told her about the spread of bluebonnets that Clay and Zach claimed was the finest in Texas, promising that he would return to Ladreville to take her there next spring, but he wanted to do more.

That was it! Lawrence grinned as he climbed the front steps. He turned around, considering, then shook his head. Not now. Though he shared the children's lack of patience, it would be unwise to enter the mercantile now. Harriet might stop by, and then the surprise would be spoiled. He couldn't let that happen. Having it be a surprise was almost as important as the item he planned to order, for somehow, though she had never said it, Lawrence knew surprises—at least pleasant ones—had been all too rare in Harriet Kirk's life. That was going to change.

⌁

"You look very fetching today." The smile that accompanied Karl's compliment softened the lines of his face, making him almost handsome. Not as handsome as Lawrence, but . . . Harriet pushed that thought firmly aside. There was no reason to be comparing Karl and Lawrence, no reason even to be thinking of the town's mayor. Karl was the man who had invited her and her family to the harvest festival.

"Thank you." Harriet laid her hand in his and let him help her into the buggy. Though it was only a short distance from her home to the field where the dance would be held, he had insisted that he would escort her and her family there. The reason was now evident, for instead of the sturdy wagon the

170

Friedrichs normally used when they came to town, Karl was driving a new buggy.

"I've never seen such a fine carriage." Harriet admired the highly polished brass and wood and let her fingers trail over the soft leather seats. Her family had owned a similar carriage until Father had sold it to pay for his whiskey. Forcing back the unwanted thoughts, she called to her siblings.

The boys, undoubtedly at Jake's instigation, refused to ride with Karl, and when Ruth volunteered to ensure that they reached the party together, Harriet agreed that they could walk alongside the buggy rather than ride. She and Mary would accept Karl's offer. Surely with the rest of the family so close, no one would misconstrue her reason for being in the wagon.

"Where are your parents?" Harriet asked as she settled onto the front seat while Mary scrambled into the one behind her and Karl.

"They're setting up our spot." Karl flicked the reins, setting the buggy into motion. "Mutter wanted to get there early so everything would be perfect."

"Knowing her, it will be." Harriet glanced to the left as they crossed rue du Marché and waved at the approaching family. The children who scampered in front of their parents were her pupils, dressed in their Sunday best. Turning back to Karl, Harriet smiled. "Your mother is a wonderful woman. You're fortunate to have such loving parents." Though she knew the past could not be changed, she could not help wondering what her life would have been like if her parents had been different, if Father's love of strong drink and Mother's inability to cope with it had not exceeded their love for their children.

"Ja." Karl nodded solemnly. "But a man longs for more than parents. He wants a family of his own—a wife and children." He reached across and laid his hand on Harriet's, giving it a little squeeze. "God did not make man to live alone."

The gleam in his eyes, not to mention the touch of his hand on hers, made Harriet uneasy, for it reminded her of Thomas. She did not want to encourage Karl, nor did she want to provide grist for the rumor mill. Most of all, she did not want to be courted, especially not by this man. Deliberately, Harriet turned to look at Mary, her movement dislodging Karl's hand.

"Mary!" Harriet frowned at the sight of her sister hanging over the side of the buggy, apparently trying to touch the ground. "Get back inside. You could hurt yourself that way."

Karl scowled as he glanced at the rear seat. "She needs a father. I know you do your best, but sometimes a child needs a father's hand. I—"

Unwilling to hear the conclusion of his sentence, Harriet stretched her arms toward her sister. "Come here, Mary." As the child scrambled over the seat, Harriet settled her between herself and Karl. "Mary made butter today, didn't you, sweetie?"

Her sister nodded and turned toward Karl, enthusiasm lighting her face. "I showed Eva how. Her mama never let her use the churn." Though Frau Friedrich had insisted there was no need for the Kirks to bring anything, Mary, bursting with pride over her newly acquired culinary skills, had pleaded that she be allowed to make a dish of butter for the evening. The slightly lumpy spread now rested in a cut glass bowl that had belonged to Harriet's grandmother.

Though Karl nodded, his pursed lips told Harriet he was

not pleased by the interruption. A minute later, he hitched the horses to one of the posts that had been provided for the day's festivities and helped both Harriet and Mary out of the buggy, frowning ever so slightly when Mary cradled the butter dish in her hands.

Placing a hand on her sister's shoulder to keep her from running and possibly dropping the butter, Harriet walked slowly. The large field across the street from the school was no longer empty. Instead tables carried from the two churches were arranged around the perimeter, leaving an open space in the center where families would eat and where the dancing would later take place. The air was redolent with the aromas of roasted meat and chicken and the tangy smells of cabbage and pickles, while the sound of children's shrieks punctuated the low murmur of the adults' conversation. All of Ladreville, it appeared, had come to the festival.

"This way," Karl said as he led them to his parents.

"We got here just as fast walking," Jake muttered as he strode next to Harriet. "We didn't need him." The last sentence was punctuated with a glare at Karl. Before Harriet could admonish her brother, Karl's father stepped forward. If Herr Friedrich was aware of Jake's animosity toward his son, he ignored it, instead clapping Jake on the shoulder the same way Harriet had seen him greet his own son.

"The womenfolk can take care of the food," Herr Friedrich said with a grin. "Let's us men play some horseshoes."

Over the din of hundreds of individual conversations, Harriet heard the clank of metal on metal. She smiled, knowing that Jake would enjoy the game as much as he appreciated being referred to as a man. Herr Friedrich understood boys.

Harriet looked around, wondering how she could help

Frau Friedrich. Since one end of the quilt already boasted a tablecloth, and delicious aromas emerged from the large pots of food placed on it, it appeared little remained to be done.

After she'd given Mary silverware and asked her and Ruth to roll it in napkins, Frau Friedrich smiled at Harriet. "You help simply by being here," she said as she patted Harriet's arm. "For many years I prayed for a daughter, but God did not bless me with one. I think he was waiting, knowing he was going to bring you into my life. I thank him every day."

Tears pricked Harriet's eyes, and she dashed them away. "I'm honored," she said as she hugged the older woman. "Now, let me do something. I need to set an example for the others."

Half an hour later, Karl and Herr Friedrich returned, trailed by the Kirk boys. "Has anyone seen the mayor?" Karl asked. "It's time to get started."

Harriet didn't know why she was surprised at the thought that Lawrence would be here tonight. Admittedly, he had said nothing about attending the dance, but he was the mayor. It made sense that he would have to make an appearance. She looked around, searching the crowd for the tall blond-haired man who inexplicably figured in so many of her thoughts. "There he is."

He was making his way to the center of the field. Clad like the others in his Sunday finery, Lawrence was an imposing figure with his broad shoulders and confident stance. The way the crowd parted before him reminded Harriet of Moses and the Red Sea. If Moses had been half as imposing as Lawrence, it was no wonder his people had followed him.

When Lawrence reached the center of the field, he raised his voice. "Ladies and gentlemen, your attention please." Though he was not shouting, the crowd grew silent, and everyone turned to watch him. "I have been told that it is customary for the mayor to open the festival with a speech." He paused, his expression droll as he added, "A lengthy speech." When a few people tittered, Lawrence smiled. "I thought it was time to start a new tradition, one of brevity. And, so, with no further ado, let me welcome you to Ladreville's fall festival." He looked around the field, his eyes pausing occasionally as they rested on a familiar face. "I'm here as your mayor." He laid his hand on his six-shooter. "I trust the town will have no need to seek me in my capacity as sheriff." The titters became laughter. When Ladreville's citizens were once more silent, Lawrence turned to Sterling, who now stood next to him. "Pastor Russell will lead us all in giving thanks for our food." As the prayer concluded with a resounding amen, Lawrence raised his head. "Let's eat!"

"I doubt anyone will complain that that was too long," Harriet said. The speed with which the crowd had dispersed, everyone hurrying toward their quilts, told her they were either hungry or anxious for the dancing to begin.

"Mayor Wood's a good man," Karl agreed. "I wonder where he went."

Harriet looked at where Sarah and Clay sat with the rest of their family as well as Priscilla and Zach, thinking they might have invited Lawrence to join them, but he was not there. Where had he gone? It seemed a shame that the town's mayor had to eat alone.

"Would you pass me the pickles?" Karl touched Harriet's arm and gave her a broad smile when she handed him the plate. Jake scowled. Sam and Daniel appeared to be in the midst of a contest to see who could eat the most chicken, while

175

Mary chattered, telling Herr Friedrich more than he could possibly want to know about the garden she had helped plant and how she and Eva had churned butter. Though Ruth could hardly be called garrulous, she held her own in a discussion with Frau Friedrich.

A lump lodged in Harriet's throat. It all looked so normal. A bystander would not realize that they were not a family but simply six orphans being befriended by neighbors. The lump grew, and tears pricked Harriet's eyes. This was what she wanted. This was what she had tried to create for her siblings: a warm, caring family.

"Sehr gut," Herr Friedrich said as Sam took the last piece of chicken. "Do you see this, Greta? The boys enjoyed your food."

"We all did." Ruth smiled as she rose. With the main courses finished, it was time for her to take her place at the punch table. Other women were already making their way to the long table where desserts awaited the revelers.

Harriet stood. "I'll walk over with you." Though Ruth seemed unusually poised this evening, Harriet was afraid that her courage might desert her when she was faced with a line of strangers.

But Ruth shook her head. "There's no need. Besides, I hear the musicians tuning their instruments. The dancing will start soon."

"If you're sure . . ." As Ruth nodded, Harriet gave her sister a quick hug. "You'll be fine, and you're right—I did promise the first set to Karl."

"I'll be the envy of every man here." Karl tucked Harriet's hand into the crook of his arm and led her toward the center of the field. "I'll have the prettiest gal in Ladreville for my partner."

"The second prettiest." Gunther Lehman fell into step next to Karl. "My wife holds top honors."

Though Isabelle blushed at the compliment, Harriet noticed that she looked paler than normal, almost as if she were ill. "I don't want to listen to Gunther and Karl talk about crops." Isabelle linked her arm with Harriet's, drawing her away from the two men. "We've got more important things to talk about, like your dress. It turned out well."

"I can't take any credit. Ruth's the one who chose the design and did all the sewing. All I did was stand still for fittings."

"You've got a talented sister. I have to admit, though, that I was surprised to see her at the punch table." Isabelle glanced in that direction.

"Surprised doesn't describe the way I felt." Harriet chuckled as she recalled her initial reaction. "Shocked or dumbfounded would be closer." She turned to watch her sister. Though Ruth appeared as confident as the other woman behind the table, dispensing punch and smiles to the townspeople, when a tall brown-haired man approached, she blushed. How sweet! Harriet smiled at the realization that Sterling Russell had brought the becoming color to Ruth's face, turning her from pretty to downright beautiful. Little Ruthie was growing up. Soon she'd be thinking about marriage. Harriet swallowed, trying to dissolve the knot that formed in her throat every time she considered life with her siblings gone. It was foolish to worry about that now, for it would be many years before she was alone.

While Karl and Gunther discussed crops and flour and the musicians continued to assemble, Isabelle entertained Harriet with stories of her stepdaughter's antics. "Eva said all the little girls think you're pretty now. And, judging from the way Karl keeps staring at you, he agrees."

Karl was a far less pleasant topic than Ruth. He'd been different tonight, and Harriet did not like the difference. Karl was a friend, but no matter what he said or did, that was all he would ever be. Though a day ago she would have thought it unlikely, she had to admit that his behavior tonight continued to remind her of Thomas, making her wish she had not agreed to dance the first set with him. It was too late to undo that, but instead of dwelling on the German farmer's unwelcome touches, Harriet turned to Isabelle. "Are you all right?" she asked. "You look a bit pale."

The young Frenchwoman laid a hand on her midriff. "My stomach's been queasy. It must be something I ate."

Harriet's eyes narrowed as she considered the possibilities. It could be bad food, or it could be something else, something far more pleasant. This, however, was not the place to air her suspicions.

"It's time to line up for the first set," Karl announced. The musicians had finished their tuning and sat next to their instruments, their fingers ready to turn wood and strings into music.

Harriet took her place next to Karl. This was why they had come. For the adults, the dance was the culmination of the day. As she moved across the grass, dipping, twirling, clapping her hands in time to the music, Harriet's thoughts whirled faster than her feet. Who would have thought that Karl, sturdy Karl with his heavy tread, would be such a good dance partner? There were no more unwelcome touches, nothing more than the dance required. For the moment, Karl was a friend. He seemed to sense Harriet's lack of experience and compensated for it, softly coaching her as they made their way through the intricate steps, smiling with approval when she mastered them. He was clearly enjoying himself, and—thanks to him—she was discovering that dancing was fun.

And yet . . . Harriet shivered as she tried to understand her sudden uneasiness. She looked around, searching the crowd for her siblings. Ruth appeared relaxed as she stood behind the punch bowl; Mary and Eva played at one side of the field; the boys were part of an impromptu ball game on the other side. They were fine. So, why did she feel so strange? Isabelle was smiling up at Gunther, her color restored. Frau and Herr Friedrich were dancing with gusto. Even the weather was cooperating, providing an evening that was cool but not cold with stars twinkling above. Everything seemed perfect, and yet something was missing. What could it be?

෴

He was probably the only person in Ladreville who wasn't happy to be here. Lawrence leaned against one of the tall oak trees as he watched the crowd of revelers. He never had liked dances. Oh, it wasn't the dancing itself that bothered him but the resemblance to Independence Day celebrations. There were too many people in one place and not enough attention being paid to individuals.

He took a deep breath, exhaling slowly as he reminded himself that it was not his job to keep children out of the river. With some luck, the cool weather would take care of that. It *was* his job to ensure drunks did not hurt others. As much as he would have liked to be anywhere else, he had been warned that some men invariably overindulged, not in the punch the town provided but in the jugs of whiskey they smuggled onto the grounds, two of which he'd already confiscated. That was why he was here—to keep the peace, not to count the number of times Harriet had danced with Karl. Eight, but he wasn't counting. Of course he wasn't. Just as he wasn't watching where she went when Karl began to dance with another woman.

Lawrence had no intention of following Harriet, and yet, if he didn't, why were his feet taking him to the punch table when that was clearly her destination? It certainly wasn't because he wanted any of the sticky sweet beverage Ruth and that other lady were purveying. Yet here he was.

"Would you like a glass of punch, Mr. Wood?" To Lawrence's amazement, Ruth did not duck her head when she addressed him.

"Thank you." Lawrence nodded and held out his hand for the glass she proffered. "I'll take one for your sister too." It was surely his imagination that Ruth found something amusing in that. What possible amusement could anyone find in a simple act of courtesy?

"I thought you might like this." Lawrence held out the cup to Harriet as she approached the table, still unencumbered by Karl.

"Thanks. Dancing made me thirstier than I expected." She swallowed the pink liquid, then wrinkled her nose, as if she found the sweet concoction as unpleasant as he had.

Lawrence took the cup from her and placed it with his on the table reserved for dirty dishes. "Other than the punch, are you enjoying the dance?"

As Harriet nodded, a tendril of hair bounced against her cheek. Did she have any idea that a man might want to tuck the lock behind her ear? Of course not. Harriet was not a woman to flirt. Her words proved that. "At first I didn't want to come, but being here made me realize that Isabelle was right. This is part of the community." That was the Harriet he knew. Sensible Harriet.

From the corner of his eye, Lawrence saw Karl approaching. If he didn't act quickly, the man would monopolize her again. "Would you like to walk a bit?" Lawrence could leave the gathering for a few minutes. After he'd parted the farmers from their whiskey jugs, there had been no more disturbances.

Harriet raised an eyebrow. "You're not dancing?"

"Despite Lottie's efforts, I never became more than a passable dancer. I'm afraid I'd crush your toes." As a puzzled expression crossed Harriet's face, Lawrence realized she might not remember who Lottie was. "Lottie's my sister."

"That's right. Your older sister."

His only sister since that summer day two decades ago, but that was not a topic he chose to introduce. "Yes. Shall we walk, or have you promised all the dances?"

"They're not all promised, and yes, I would enjoy a walk." Harriet looked around, as if assuring herself that her siblings were accounted for. "I imagine the river is pretty with the moon shining on it."

She was probably correct. By tradition, Lawrence had been told, the harvest festival was held on the October Saturday closest to the full moon. Tonight was cloudless and, if a person wanted to gaze at the river—which Lawrence most definitely did not—the moon would undoubtedly be reflected in its surface. Most people would find it pretty, but Lawrence was not most people. He started to suggest another destination, then realized that would involve an explanation he didn't want to make. There was no reason to tell Harriet about Lizbeth. Her own family created enough worries; Lawrence

181

wouldn't add to them by discussing his. It was easier to put his discomfort aside and simply walk to the river.

He tucked Harriet's hand into the crook of his elbow and headed toward the water. Nothing would happen. Harriet was an adult, not a child. As for himself, he would focus on the warmth of her hand on his arm, not the deadly depths of the river.

"It's cooler than I realized," Harriet said when they'd crossed Hochstrasse.

Lawrence nodded. Perhaps this was the excuse he sought. "Crowds always generate a lot of warmth. We can turn around if you like."

She shook her head, setting the tendrils to bouncing again. "No. It feels good."

He should have realized that nothing deflected Harriet from a goal. She wanted to see the river, and nothing would stop her. They were parallel to the school now. Lawrence tried again. "Are you sure you don't want to check on your garden's progress? Some of the plants might be night-blooming."

A peal of laughter greeted his words. "You won't let me forget that, will you? I know you don't believe it, but you'll be sorry next spring when that garden is the showcase of Ladreville."

"I'm not doubting you. It's simply fun to see you get riled up." Besides, watching Harriet pretend to bristle helped him not think about rivers and Lizbeth.

She raised an eyebrow. "Is that so? My siblings might beg to differ with you. They don't like to see me riled."

"That's because you're their boss. Lottie still tries to tell me what to do, even though we're both grown."

"I hope I won't do that, but I have to confess that I can't imagine what it will be like when they're gone."

They had reached the riverbank and had turned, walking slowly to the south. This was the part of the river Lawrence would see if he used the back rooms of his house. Though Gunther claimed the mayor's home had one of the nicest views of the Medina, Lawrence had given it no more than a cursory glance. A river was a river. Some saw it as a source of life-giving water. Gunther regarded it as the energy that drove his mill. Lawrence knew it for what it truly was: a potentially deadly force. But he wouldn't speak about that. It was safer to confine the discussion to siblings—Harriet's siblings.

"They'll be grown before you know it. Ruth's already a woman, and Mary's what?—seven?"

"Eight," Harriet corrected. Lawrence smiled as he thought of the little girl who was turning out to be as feisty as her oldest sister. He had encountered her outside the schoolhouse several times when he'd visited Harriet, and—though he could not explain when it had happened—the sight of her no longer evoked memories of Lizbeth. Instead, he simply saw her as Mary, an appealing child in her own right. Tonight he was fortunate enough to be strolling with her sister, who was far more appealing.

"A few minutes ago I felt as if something was missing from the evening. Now I know what it was: being here, seeing this." Harriet gestured toward the river. "It's so beautiful." Her voice was soft, almost reverent. Though Lawrence would never agree with her about the river, he had to admit that the moment was close to perfect. He was alone with the most fascinating woman he'd ever met.

Removing her hand from his arm, Harriet took another

step toward the water. "Oh, look," she said, leaning forward and gesturing to something floating lazily downstream. "Isn't that—"

Perhaps the grass was damp. Perhaps her shoes were worn and slippery. Perhaps she simply lost her balance. Lawrence didn't know. All he knew was that Harriet was tumbling headfirst toward the river. *Oh no!* The image of Lizbeth's lifeless body flashed before him. *Not again!* For the space of a heartbeat Lawrence stood frozen with horror before he leapt forward. "Harriet," he shouted as he wrapped his arms around her waist and tugged her against him, catching her before she landed in the water. "Harriet!" Her body was warm; her arms clutched his; he could hear her breathing. She was safe!

Though he could feel her heart pounding with alarm, Harriet's eyes sparkled as she looked up at him. "Thank you. I hadn't planned to take another bath today."

A bath? Lawrence frowned. She acted as if falling into the river would have been a trivial occurrence. Didn't she realize what could have happened? He tightened his grip on the woman who had managed to irritate him, the same woman who haunted his thoughts and dreams. He had to make her understand.

"A bath is the least that could have happened. You could have drowned like Lizbeth."

13

At last! There was no one waiting in line for another cup of that all too sweet punch. He didn't understand why so many people went back for second and third helpings. One had been more than enough for him. He'd rather drink water from the river than that swill. But that wasn't important. What was important was taking care of that man.

Jake hurried to the table, determined to talk to the sister who for years had been his only ally. "We've got to stop him," he announced without preamble. "That man is turning into a shadow. Every time I look, he's there."

Though the night was cool, a flush rose to Ruth's cheeks as she shook her head. "You're wrong," she insisted, sounding more like Harriet than herself. "Sterling came only three times, and he never stayed any longer than was seemly."

Jake stared at his sister, trying to understand. Had Ruth been drinking the other punch, the one that had some sort of spirits in it? That was the only reason he could imagine for her blush and that nonsensical response.

"Sterling?" he demanded. "Who's Sterling?"

Ruth's face turned an even deeper pink the way it had the time Harriet caught her reading a book when she should have been cooking dinner. "Pastor Russell. That's what I meant. Pastor Russell. He just wanted to make sure I was all right." Ruth was more flustered than Jake had ever seen her. That must be why she wasn't making much sense. She glared at him as she added, "I don't know why I'm explaining all this. You're not my keeper."

"No, but he plans to be."

Furrows formed between her eyes. "Who are you talking about?"

Who did she think? The man in the moon? Girls could be so dumb. "Karl, of course. Haven't you noticed the way he won't leave Harriet alone?" Surely ladling glasses of punch wasn't so engrossing that Ruth hadn't been able to see what was going on practically in front of her. She wasn't blind without her spectacles like Harriet. "I tell you, Ruth, Karl wants to marry her. We can't let him do that. He's a mean man. He'll turn Harriet and us into his slaves. Don't you see? We'd have to move out to the farm and work there every day."

Blanching, Ruth shook her head, but Jake saw the doubt in her eyes. Maybe she wasn't so dumb. After all, she'd been the first to say she didn't like Thomas, that his smiles held something sinister. But Ruth's expression reminded Jake of Harriet and the way she didn't have to say anything to make him feel like a little boy.

"I'm sure you're wrong." Though Ruth's voice was low, she enunciated each syllable, just like Harriet. What had happened to the old Ruth, the one he could count on in a pinch?

"Karl may be courting Harriet, but he doesn't want us all on the farm."

Dumb. Dumb. Dumb. She didn't understand. "You're the one who's wrong, Ruth. I tell you that man is looking for free help. A wife and slaves." When Ruth shook her head again, Jake clenched his fists. He should have known better than to think she would help him. "Someone's gotta stop him, and I guess it's gonna be me."

❧

"Lizbeth?"

"She was my sister." Though the moonlight glinted off her spectacles, Lawrence saw tears welling in Harriet's eyes as the past tense registered. He clenched his fists, wishing he had clenched his teeth. He should never have mentioned Lizbeth. He certainly hadn't planned to, but fear had propelled his words. In the years that he'd been a Ranger, he had learned to hide his feelings, to act based on reason, not emotion. And yet in the space of a second, his training was forgotten, replaced by raw fear. There was no way to retract Lizbeth's name.

Harriet looked up at him, confusion clouding her eyes. "I thought Lottie was your only sibling."

"She is now." Lawrence slipped off his coat and wrapped it around Harriet's shoulders. He wasn't certain whether it was the cold or the belated realization that she could have been hurt, but something was causing her to tremble. Perhaps the additional warmth would help. One thing was certain: they needed to leave the riverside.

Lawrence kept his arm around Harriet's waist, gently leading her back toward the gathering as he started his explanation. "Lizbeth was four years younger than me—three at the time—and it seemed she was always following me. Sometimes I was happy about that. I remember calling her my little puppy, because she trailed after me the way one of the dogs did. But most of the time she seemed like a pest. That's why I used to hide so she couldn't find me."

Harriet laid her hand on his arm and squeezed it. He noticed that the trembling had stopped, and her voice held a hint of amusement. "I remember doing that with Ruth, and the boys still try their best to shake off Mary."

"You make it sound innocent," he said. "No one died because you were hiding."

She stopped and looked up at him, those big gray eyes solemn. "Whatever occurred, it couldn't have been your fault. You were only seven."

Lawrence urged her to keep walking. Somehow it was easier to talk while he was moving. "I know that now, but for years I was haunted by the belief that I should have saved her."

"What happened?"

They had reached Hochstrasse and were moving steadily toward the site of the festivities. Lawrence slowed his pace, not wanting anyone to overhear. "It was the annual Independence Day celebration. There was a parade, speeches, a picnic, and then lots of games." He stared into the distance as memories of a hot sunny day flooded through him. "I don't remember where my parents and Lottie were. All I remember is that Lizbeth wanted to be my partner for the sack race, and I refused. I called her a silly little girl. The last time I saw my sister alive, she was crying and telling me I was mean."

Lawrence swallowed deeply, trying to chase away images that were more than two decades old. "I won the race.

Afterward, I was celebrating with my friends when I heard a splash. Somehow Lizbeth had fallen into the river." His voice was calm, but inside his heart ached with the realization that if he had let Lizbeth race with him, she might still be alive. "There had been a recent rain, so the water was deeper than normal, but it wouldn't have mattered if it had been only four feet deep. Neither of us could swim."

Though she said nothing, Harriet tightened the grip on his arm. "I jumped in to save her, and I almost drowned myself." Oddly, Lawrence had few memories of that. Perhaps they had been obliterated by the horror of Lizbeth's death.

"Oh, Lawrence." Harriet's voice was choked with tears. "I can't imagine how awful that must have been. It was terrible when my parents died, but a child's death is worse—much worse."

He wouldn't tell her that even now he sometimes dreamt of a small coffin being lowered into the ground, and that each time he would waken shaking. Harriet didn't need to know that. Instead Lawrence forced a light note into his voice. "I learned to swim, but . . ." He paused for dramatic effect. "I have to admit that I've never been comfortable around rivers."

"And I made it worse by insisting on walking by the river and then slipping." Harriet stretched her hand up and stroked his cheek. It was nothing more than a simple gesture of comfort, and yet its effect was far from simple. Her hand was soft, her touch as gentle as an autumn breeze, and like the breeze that carried scents across the evening air, her fingers sent warmth flowing through him. Somehow, some way this woman's touch chased away the darkness and the pain, leaving in their place the realization that while he had been unable to save Lizbeth, what had happened that summer day had

189

shaped his life, leading him first to the Rangers and now to Ladreville. It was all part of God's plan.

᳝

It was farther than he'd thought. Thomas winced as he turned over. This sleeping on the ground was mighty rough on the body, but what was a man to do? He couldn't spend his last coins on a bed, not that there were any in sight. This part of Texas was more desolate than anything he'd seen, and it was all that farmer's fault.

Thomas had reckoned it would take no more than three days to reach Ladreville, but here he was on the fifth day, and he still hadn't gotten there. That cursed farmer had told him to turn right at the crossroads, when he should have turned left. Left. Left. Left. That's what the old codger should have said. But he hadn't, and now Thomas was lost somewhere in a land that was fit for nothing more than scorpions and javelinas.

First things first. He had to get to Ladreville and convince Harriet to marry him. Once that was done, he'd find the farmer, and the man would pay. Yes, sirree, he'd pay.

᳝

"Where were you?" Karl's light blue eyes reflected worry and something else, perhaps a bit of anger. "You should have told me you were going away."

Harriet shivered. Ever since she'd returned Lawrence's coat, she had felt cold. More than that, she'd had an odd sensation of bereavement, as if she had lost something important. That was absurd. She had looked around the celebration, assuring herself that her siblings were all there. Though she hadn't

190

seen Jake, the others were safe. Jake was probably sitting on the ground, playing jacks with the other boys. She was fine. It was Lawrence who had suffered the loss. Even though it had been more than twenty years ago, the loss was still shaping his life. No wonder he felt so strongly about constructing a bridge over the Medina. Harriet shivered again. She couldn't restore Lawrence's sister, but she could help him convince the townspeople they needed a bridge.

"Where were you?" Karl repeated his question.

"I went for a walk along the river," Harriet said as calmly as she could. What should have been an ordinary walk had been anything but that. First there was that awkward slip when she'd found herself heading face first into the water, only to be yanked back at the last second. Next came those seconds of unexpected warmth being held by Lawrence. How wonderful it had felt to be in his arms, to be so close that she could hear his heart beat and savor the fragrance that was his alone. Though he had meant nothing more than comfort, Lawrence had chased away the chill and, more than that, he had restored her sense of equilibrium.

Then came his revelation, uncovering the deep facets that made Lawrence so special. Harriet had seen the handsome man, the strong man, the former Ranger, the current mayor and sheriff. Tonight she had discovered the vulnerable boy.

When Harriet was seven, days had been spent with Grandma and Grandpa. Grandma had claimed it was because Mother was busy. At the time Harriet hadn't understood, for when she and Ruth returned home for supper, Mother was almost always asleep. But Harriet didn't mind. Days in the stone cottage were exciting as Grandpa introduced her to the magic that could be found between the covers of a book. Those had been happy days when death was only a word. Lawrence had not been so fortunate, and Harriet's heart ached for the loss he had endured and the guilt that had plagued him for so long. Young as he was, Lawrence had felt responsible for his sister's death, and though he tried to make light of it, Harriet knew all too well the burden responsibility could place on a child. This, she suspected, was the reason he continued to distance himself from Lottie; he feared losing her.

"You should have told me." Karl's words brought Harriet back to the present. She looked around, searching for Lawrence, but he was not in sight. When they'd reached the gathering, he had told her he needed to walk around to ensure that no one was imbibing too heavily.

"I would have gone with you." Karl placed his hand on the small of Harriet's back and led her toward the center of the field where the dancers were gathering once more. It appeared that while she had been gone, the musicians had rested and the townspeople had enjoyed a second helping of dessert.

"Thank you." Harriet tried not to flinch at the warmth of Karl's hand on her spine. He was merely being courteous, she reminded herself; it wasn't fair to compare him to Lawrence. The fault was hers, for she had been rude in leaving the dance without telling Karl. He was, after all, her escort for the evening. As such, Harriet owed him basic kindness. There was no need to tell him she had not been alone, just as there was no need to tell him she had lost her desire to dance. Even though all she wanted was to be alone to reflect on what she had learned, she couldn't do that without hurting Karl's feelings. Still, there might be a way to postpone their return to the dancing. "Is there any of your mother's cake left?"

Karl nodded. "She saved you a piece."

"Excellent."

They were walking toward the Friedrichs' quilt when Harriet saw Lawrence approaching, his hand firmly gripping Jake's shoulder. Her heart sank as she realized that neither one looked happy.

"What's wrong?" she asked, though the coward inside her did not want to know. Lawrence's expression told Harriet that, whatever it was, it was serious.

He nodded toward her and Karl. "I need you both to come with me." His voice seethed with barely controlled anger, causing the lump that had formed in Harriet's throat when she'd seen Jake and Lawrence together to grow.

Karl fisted his hands as he glared at Jake. "What did that young whippersnapper do?" he demanded at the same time that Harriet cried, "Oh, Jake, what have you done?"

Jake remained silent, his expression so belligerent that Harriet wanted to slap his face. When he refused to answer, Lawrence said, "He slashed the seats in Karl's buggy. I'm afraid they're beyond repair."

So quickly that Harriet did not anticipate it, Karl lunged forward and grabbed Jake, wrapping his hands around his throat. "You fiend!" Karl shouted as he began to throttle him. "That was the finest buggy in Ladreville."

An instant later, Lawrence yanked Karl away. "I'm the sheriff here," he said firmly. "I'll administer justice."

"I'll tell you what justice he needs." Karl's voice was filled with venom, and he kept his hands fisted, as if looking for an opportunity to pummel Jake. "It'll start with a trip to the woodshed."

Though Karl had been angry the day Jake had cut the fence, today his fury seemed boundless. Harriet moved so that she stood between him and her brother. Karl was right; Jake needed to be punished, but a beating would not restore Karl's buggy. She looked around, wondering who had overheard the exchange. Would the Kirks be the subject of gossip tomorrow? *"The Kirk name must not be besmirched."* As her grandmother's words echoed through her head, Harriet wondered how she could have prevented Jake's vandalism. Perhaps if she hadn't left the gathering, she would have seen Jake near the buggy and been able to stop him. Oh, why had she agreed to walk with Lawrence? But even as the question formed, Harriet knew two things: she couldn't have stopped her brother and she wouldn't have missed the walk with Lawrence for anything.

"The crime is a serious one." Lawrence was speaking to Karl. "I'll treat it as such." He took a step toward the irate farmer. "It appears you're mighty riled. I suggest you go back to the dance. Harriet and I will handle this."

Karl shook his head. "I told you I could handle it."

"Not as long as I'm the sheriff." Lawrence laid a hand on Karl's shoulder. Whether he meant to comfort or restrain him, the firm grip kept Karl from attacking Jake, and that was a blessing. "I'll come out to the farm on Monday to discuss retribution," Lawrence continued as he walked a short distance, escorting Karl toward the dancers.

"What's retribution?" It was the first time Jake had spoken.

Trying to keep her own anger under control, Harriet forced herself to make a civil reply. What she really wanted was to shake some sense into her brother. How could he have done this? Didn't he know that he was jeopardizing his future? "It means the repair of Karl's buggy."

Jake scuffed his foot, then kicked an acorn. When it sailed

into the air, landing a few yards away, he grinned with apparent satisfaction. "I'm not gonna do it. He had it coming."

Harriet's anger grew. It was bad enough that he'd damaged the buggy. It was even worse that he felt no remorse. "There is no excuse for destruction of property," she said in her most severe schoolmarm voice.

"Indeed there is not." Lawrence stood on Jake's other side, the seemingly casual way his hand rested on his six-shooter announcing that he would tolerate no argument. Though he directed his words at Harriet, she saw that he was keeping his eyes fixed on her brother. "It appears that this is a lesson Jake needs to learn. This, however, is no place for a discussion. Let's go to my office."

They walked in silence, Jake shuffling and making exasperated huffing sounds, Lawrence keeping his hand firmly on Jake's shoulder, Harriet trying to bite back the fear that welled inside her. What if the citizens of Ladreville were like Fortune's townspeople? Would Jake ever live this down? Harriet preceded the men up the steps and waited until Lawrence opened the door, ushering them into his office. When he'd lit two lamps, chasing the shadows from the room, she saw that he had made a few changes since the last time she'd been here. The desk was angled so that he could look out one of the windows. The large maps of Europe and the gloomy portraits that had decorated two walls were gone, leaving brighter patches of paint in their place.

"Do you have any idea how to stop this behavior?" Though Lawrence stood over Jake, the words were addressed to Harriet. The anger was gone, replaced by a firm but almost kind tone that reminded Harriet of how safe she had felt when he'd gathered her close to him.

"I wish I did. I've never seen Jake like this." Her brother snorted, as if denying her defense of him. "Oh, he had his mischievous moments, but he was never malicious."

"I hate being here." Jake spat the words as he directed his anger at her. "You should never have made us leave Fortune. I had friends there."

"The wrong kind of friends."

Lawrence perched on the corner of the desk. "Whether or not you like it, Jake, you live in Ladreville now, and that means you will abide by its laws. The citizens of Ladreville expect me to protect them and their property."

Jake snarled. It was the wrong response. Lawrence narrowed his eyes, and his voice was cold as he said, "Since you obviously do not respect property, it's time for you to learn just how much a buggy is worth and how long it takes to earn that amount of money."

"I only wrecked the seats."

Oh, Jake, Harriet wanted to cry, *stop being so insolent. You're only making this worse.* Instead, she said firmly, "Be quiet, Jake. The sheriff is in charge here."

"I know school is important to you." Lawrence nodded at Harriet as he spoke. "But I'm afraid Jake will not be attending until he's paid off his debt."

"Good. I hate school."

"That's enough, Jake." Harriet grabbed his arm and shook it. "You've done enough damage today." She turned toward Lawrence. "How will he pay for the repairs? His wages from Karl aren't very high, and after what happened tonight, I wouldn't blame Karl if he refused to allow Jake to work for him."

Though Harriet kept her eyes focused on Lawrence, she

196

heard Jake's exaggerated sigh. Even if Karl continued to hire her brother, nothing good would come of it.

As Jake shuffled his feet and sighed again, Lawrence shook his head. "Jake won't be working for Karl. He'll be working for me." Lawrence gestured toward the walls with their obvious signs of missing pictures. "He'll start by painting this room. After that, the whole house needs a thorough cleaning."

"That's woman's work!" Jake emphasized his frustration by beating his fists on the desk.

"Hush! You'll do what Lawrence orders." If the situation hadn't been so serious, Harriet might have smiled at the fact that Lawrence was finally achieving what he'd sought since he arrived: finding a housekeeper.

Lawrence was not smiling as he looked down at her brother. "Make no mistake, Jake; you're going to work, and you're going to work hard." It was no wonder Lawrence had been such a successful Ranger. Simply the tone of his voice was enough to make Jake cower. If he'd drawn his gun, Harriet doubted even the most hardened of criminals would have resisted.

"It will be two or three months before you're able to pay Karl for the damage you've done," Lawrence continued. "In the meantime, you will be here every day at 7:00, and you'll work until 6:00. Your only day off will be Sunday, but I expect you to spend the morning in church."

"That's not fair!" Jake scowled at the lawman.

"That's the way it's going to be."

Jake fisted his hands again as he glared at Lawrence. "I hate you just like I hate Karl."

"Jake!"

Harriet's brother paid her no heed. His eyes dark with emotion, he stared at the sheriff. "I hate you."

If he thought he'd rile Lawrence, Jake was mistaken. "Hate, love—it doesn't matter to me. All I care about is that you do the work I set out for you."

That was fair enough, but Jake didn't see it that way. He jumped to his feet, his face suffused with anger. "Don't think you can be my father," he shouted. "I don't need one."

Harriet blinked in astonishment. Lawrence had done nothing even remotely paternal. Why did Jake think he regarded him as a son?

But Lawrence appeared unfazed by her brother's outburst. "No, you don't," he agreed. "What you need is to be the man of the family. You should be the one who's setting the example." The look he gave Jake was almost pitying. "I've got to tell you, Jake, the example you've been setting is mighty poor. You need to change that if you expect Sam and Daniel and little Mary to respect you."

Harriet watched, astonished by the change in Jake's expression. From sullen and resentful, it had been transformed. Somehow, Lawrence had reached him, touching a cord deep inside him that, no matter how many times she had tried, she had never reached. Was this what Jake sought—the recognition that he was almost an adult? It was true that she had never told him she expected him to be the man of the family, but she didn't treat Jake like a child. Did she?

14

"Miss Kirk! Miss Kirk!" Eva's cry of excitement preceded her as she rushed into the schoolhouse, her blonde braids flying behind her. "Come look!"

"What is it?" Though she guessed there was only one thing that would bring a child in from the midday recess early, Harriet wanted Eva to have the thrill of announcing the news.

"They sprouted. Six of them." She reached for Harriet's hand and tugged. "Come look."

Harriet shook her head as she looked down at Isabelle's stepdaughter. She had been the only one of the schoolchildren who had commented on Jake's absence. The others, Harriet surmised, had heard the tale from their parents. Fortunately, though gossip had been rife for several days, the story of Jake's vandalism had been eclipsed by the rumor that Michel Ladre and his wife had been seen boarding a ship in Galveston, apparently bound for Europe. The idea that the town's founder was returning to the Old Country was so shocking that nothing else seemed important.

"We'll wait until everyone returns," she told Eva. "Then we'll go out again. We can practice our orderly exit." The past few days had been cool and rainy, and Harriet had forgone the egress lessons, even though she knew that soon she would have to light the stove. Despite the increased possibility of a fire, the children could not continue to shiver in the classroom. "It's your surprise," she said to Eva, "so you can lead us outside."

The smiles on the children's faces when they saw the sprouts and the barrage of questions they fired at her told Harriet they would accomplish little this afternoon when they returned to the schoolhouse. Bowing to the inevitable, she spent the time that would have been devoted to geography discussing the role of warmth, moisture, and sunshine in a plant's life. Though she stressed how much time was required, Harriet suspected that was one lesson her pupils were not absorbing.

"I'll check the sprouts tomorrow," Pierre Berthoud announced when class was dismissed.

"And I'll come on Sunday," Anna Singer volunteered.

"There'll be lots more on Monday" was little Heidi Gottlieb's prediction. But when the students returned on Monday, there were still only six plants. Though those six had grown over the weekend, the children were not satisfied.

"When will the others sprout?" Heidi demanded.

Harriet would not lie. After all, the garden was meant to teach them patience. "Maybe not until spring."

Anna's scowl left no doubt of her opinion. "That's too long."

Pierre nodded. "I don't want to wait."

But they had to.

❦

The boy had mastered the art of sullenness. The first day he had complained constantly, harping on the unfairness of the world in general and Lawrence in particular, until in desperation Lawrence had announced that he would half Jake's wages if he continued. That had done the trick. The complaints had stopped, though they'd been replaced with silence punctuated by groans and hisses. Now Jake stood near the door, his posture openly defiant. It would be a long three months until he'd worked off his debt.

"We're going to the livery today," Lawrence said, watching for a reaction. "Klaus needs some help."

The reaction wasn't long in coming. Jake clenched his fists and abandoned his insolent slouch. "I thought I worked for you."

"You do. I'm hiring out your services." Jake had finished painting not just the office but also the town's one jail cell. He had, Lawrence had to admit, done a fine job. Though Lawrence suspected Jake had wanted nothing more than to fling the paintbrush—fully loaded with paint, of course—at him, he'd controlled his temper and had demonstrated a real flair for smooth brushstrokes. He had even done a passably good job cleaning the house, if you didn't count the deliberately overturned pail of water that had ruined a carpet and the windowpane that just happened to break when he polished it. Knowing that Jake's goal was to rouse his anger, Lawrence had done nothing more than point out that the cost of a rug and replacement glass would be added to Jake's tally. "At least another month, possibly two," he'd said, trying not to cringe at the thought of having Harriet's rebellious brother underfoot for so long. Lawrence wasn't certain who was bearing the brunt of the punishment.

"I didn't agree to work at the livery." Jake took a step forward before he reconsidered. A scowl might mar his otherwise handsome face, but he appeared to have learned a lesson or two, starting with the fact that violence was not permitted in this room.

"I hate to point this out to you, Jake, but your agreement isn't necessary. The night you decided to vent your anger on Karl Friedrich, you gave up a lot of rights. In the eyes of this town, you're a criminal now." One of the reasons Lawrence was taking Jake to the livery was that he wanted to mitigate that perception. Perhaps if the town's law-abiding citizens saw Jake working diligently to repay the damage he'd caused, they'd consider him less of a threat to their property.

Though he had not told Harriet, lest he deepen the fear he'd seen on her face when she'd learned what Jake had done, a delegation of citizens had cornered him outside his office the next afternoon, demanding to know how he proposed to deal with such blatant vandalism. They'd left, only partially mollified, when he'd explained the nature of Jake's punishment.

The boy glared at him. "So now I'm gonna have someone else telling me what to do."

Lawrence understood Jake's complaint. He'd joined the Rangers in part because he liked the idea of being on his own, of making decisions and not having a boss watching over him. "I'm afraid that's pretty much the way it's going to be until you've settled your debt."

Jake shook his head, his expression mutinous. "I hate people ordering me around. That's what Karl did, and Harriet's no better." He shook his head again, as if reconsidering. "She's worse. She doesn't just order me to do things; she treats me like a child."

202

Lawrence tried not to smile. If there was one thing Jake would not appreciate, it was amusement. "Older sisters do that," he said as solemnly as he could. "At least mine always did. Lottie made sure I knew she was the one in charge."

"I hate that." Jake kicked the chair. "I hate the way Harriet thinks she's my mother and my father."

Lawrence nodded. There had been times when he had thought he had three parents, and he'd resented Lottie's attempts at domination. Harriet, however, had no choice. "It seems to me your sister was thrust into that role when your parents died."

Jake shook his head again. "That didn't change anything. They weren't real parents."

Lawrence tried to mask his surprise. "What do you mean?" he asked casually, knowing that the key to getting Jake to talk was to appear not to care. Meanwhile Lawrence's brain whirled. Was it possible that the Kirk children had been adopted? Harriet's correspondence with Michel Ladre had said nothing of that, but why would it? Ladreville's mayor had no reason to know her family history other than the fact that she was now responsible for five siblings. "What do you mean, not real?" Lawrence asked again.

His eyes firmly fixed on the floor, Jake muttered, "Nothin'." Silence had returned.

❧

"Harriet." What perfect timing. There she was, emerging from the mercantile at the same time he returned from taking Jake to the livery. "If you have time, would you like to see the work Jake's done?"

She checked her watch before nodding. "I have a few

minutes until I'm due back in school. Sarah's visiting, and she'll watch the children until I return. I don't want to take advantage of her, though, so I shouldn't be too late."

That was Harriet, conscientious to a fault. Lawrence opened the door and escorted her into his office.

"It looks much better," she said as she surveyed the now uniformly colored walls. "I don't miss those gloomy pictures."

"Or the maps of Europe. We're all Texans now."

Behind the spectacles, her gray eyes sparkled with amusement. "You and I were born Texans."

"That's true, but it doesn't hurt to remind the others. Sterling thinks that's the reason he was sent here, to make the town more American."

"It hasn't happened yet, has it?" Harriet settled into one of the chairs in front of his desk. Perhaps it had been a mistake, offering her some of his terrible coffee. He had hoped she would relax enough that he could ask about her parents, but instead they were speaking of Sterling and his still diminished congregation.

"No," Lawrence admitted, "and I can't think of a way to change that. Sterling is my friend. I'd do anything in my power to help him, but this is well beyond my power. It's going to take an act of God to turn the citizens of Ladreville into Texans."

"I'm beginning to think that's what Jake needs too, one of God's miracles. Moving here didn't work." As Harriet took a sip of coffee, he could tell she was trying not to grimace.

Rather than apologize, he asked, "What happened in Fortune?"

"Jake was associating with at least one boy who was a pernicious influence."

How like Harriet to use a word with three syllables when one would have sufficed. "Have you noted any deleterious effects from the move?" Lawrence knew big words too . . . at least one.

She placed the cup on the desk without taking another sip. "The fact that Jake is working for you is proof that leaving Fortune didn't solve the problem. I wish I knew what would."

Lawrence had no answer, and he sensed this was not the time to introduce the subject of her parents. "How is the school garden?"

Judging from the way Harriet wrinkled her nose, he had chosen the wrong subject. "I'm afraid I have some disgruntled pupils. I think they expected flowers in November."

"You have shoots."

"True, but they want more. I'm having second thoughts about the whole idea. No one believes me when I tell them things are happening underground. I guess the concept of dormancy is too much for them."

Lawrence wanted nothing more than to wrap his arms around her and tell her not to worry about her brother or her pupils, but he couldn't. Not only would that be unseemly, but he couldn't guarantee that there would be no further reason for worry. Instead he gave an exaggerated shrug. "It's a good thing I'm not the teacher. I'd pull out my six-shooter and order everyone to believe me." When Harriet smiled at the prospect, he added, "Mark my words. They'll believe you in the spring. A garden is not a dumb idea."

"It's not a dumb idea," Isabelle announced as she placed a piece of gingerbread next to Harriet's glass of milk. When

205

school had ended, Harriet had suggested Eva return home with Mary, and she'd headed to the Lehman house, knowing she would find both a welcome and answers inside the cozy kitchen. No matter what Lawrence said, he wasn't a parent. Harriet suspected he was simply trying to soothe her feelings and told Isabelle that.

Her friend disagreed. "Nonsense. I can't imagine Lawrence Wood sparing anyone's feelings. He's as honest as they come—sometimes painfully honest. When Gunther asked him if the town would pay for repairs on the dam, he pointed out that the dam served only one purpose and that was to turn Gunther's millstone, so it was Gunther's responsibility to keep it in good shape, and recently Lawrence has been outspoken in saying the town needs a bridge. Gunther and I agree with him on that, but most people think it's an unnecessary expense." Isabelle gave a Gallic shrug. "What I'm trying to say is, you can trust Lawrence to tell the truth."

Isabelle took a bite of the gingerbread, frowning ever so slightly. "It needs more cloves," she said. When Harriet demurred, Isabelle simply smiled. "You can be honest. I'm being honest with you when I tell you that Eva was so excited the day she found those sprouts that she would hardly eat supper, and it was her favorite chicken stew. She kept telling Gunther and me how wonderful it was to have a garden and how special you made her feel when she was the first to spot the seedlings."

"They were all excited the first day. It was afterward that they became discouraged. Now I have to listen to Henri Fayette grousing that a garden is stupid."

"Oh, Henri." Isabelle shrugged again. "He was born complaining. Eva doesn't think it's stupid. She listened when you told the class about seeds getting ready to sprout." Isabelle laughed as she poured herself another glass of milk. "I have to admit that it was a bit awkward. Eva asked me if the seeds were like a baby growing in its mother's stomach."

It wasn't a bad analogy, even though it was not one Harriet would have used. She gave her friend an appraising look. "Is there any special reason why that thought might have come to Eva's mind?" Isabelle's pallor at the fall festival was gone, replaced by a glow that reminded Harriet of Sarah holding her newborn son.

Isabelle shrugged again. "She might have heard Gunther and me talking about a new baby," she admitted.

The pieces all fit. First the pallor, now the glow. Harriet remembered the changes when her mother had been increasing. "Is that why you've been queasy?"

"I'm not sure yet, but it might be. I'm praying it is."

"Oh, Isabelle." Harriet rose and hugged her. "I'm happy for you."

The lovely Frenchwoman frowned. "It would be wonderful, if only Gunther were happier. The whole idea of childbirth scares him."

"Isn't that true of most men? My father fled the house at the first sign and didn't return for days."

Blood drained from Isabelle's face. "Your mother's confinements lasted that long?"

"No, but Father wanted to be sure." The truth was, he'd felt the need to celebrate the impending birth with strong drink and had been too drunk to walk home. Harriet had insisted her mother deserved a bouquet, and she and her grandmother had been picking flowers when they found him sleeping underneath a tree after Ruth's birth. That had been the first time Grandma had admonished Harriet not to tell anyone what she'd seen. When the boys and Mary were born, Harriet hadn't bothered looking for her father. Mother hadn't asked for him, and Harriet had learned that disturbing her father meant a cuff on the head.

"Gunther had better not do that."

He won't hit Eva. Harriet almost blurted out the words before she realized that Isabelle was worried about her husband's deserting her. "I'll have Lawrence arrest Gunther if he tries to escape," Harriet said lightly.

Isabelle grinned. "It's a good idea, if Lawrence is here. No one knows whether he'll stay past January. Gunther's tried to convince him to remain, but he said he wasn't sure he would."

"Oh. I'd forgotten." While she and Lawrence talked about everything from the financial panic to books to wallpaper for his house, they had not discussed his plans for the future. Harriet took a sip of milk, trying to mask her confusion. Though Isabelle's gingerbread was delicious and had assuaged her hunger pangs, an emptiness settled deep inside as she thought of Lawrence's leaving and what it would mean to her. Ladreville wouldn't be the same without him. It would be as empty and colorless as she felt right now.

She took another sip of milk. She couldn't stop him; she wouldn't even try, for he deserved to follow his dreams, wherever they led him. And yet, the prospect of life in Ladreville without Lawrence seemed bleak. He was her friend, and she would miss him. More than she had dreamt possible.

❦

The church was fuller than Harriet had ever seen it, the pews packed with French citizens as well as Germans. It appeared the whole town had come to pay its last respects to Pastor Sempert, who had died the previous morning. It was now Saturday afternoon, and the church was crowded beyond capacity. Twelve people sat in pews designed for ten, while still others stood in the narthex. A few late-blooming flowers graced the altar, but the predominant odors were hair oil and ladies' toilet water. In honor of the town's elderly minister, it appeared that Ladreville's citizens had bathed earlier than normal this week. Harriet, squashed between Ruth and Daniel, was thankful for that.

More than the scents and the sounds of soft murmurs, Harriet felt as if she was surrounded by sorrow. The people she had met as she'd entered the sanctuary grieved, and Ruth sobbed audibly. No one, it seemed, was unaffected. The elderly minister had been loved by his congregation and respected by the entire community.

Without a doubt, his death was a milestone in the town's history, the end of an era. What would the future bring? Would his death unify or further divide the German-speaking population? Though church attendance had grown a bit since Frau Friedrich had instituted her campaign to bring others back, it was still only half what it had been when Pastor Sempert had conducted services. Yesterday when Harriet had ridden to the Friedrich farm to deliver the sad news, Frau Friedrich had admitted she feared there would be backsliding and that Pastor Russell would be left with only a shell of a congregation. Her eyes red-rimmed from tears, Ruth had expressed the same concern. Harriet wondered whether her sister's tears were for the town's former pastor or its new one, for Ruth's conversations were peppered with Sterling's name, and though she would not admit it, Harriet suspected that her visits to the two ministers had become the highlight of her sister's life.

The music ended and a hush filled the church as Pastor Russell took his place in front of the altar. "We are gathered together to lay to rest the man who guided this congregation for many years. Though I knew him for a far shorter time than most of you, I know that, as much as he loved this life, Pastor Sempert longed for the moment when he would be taken home to his heavenly Father. That moment has come. He is now at rest, and it is for us who remain to continue the work he began."

The only sounds were a few soft sobs and the shuffling of pages as several children searched for the next hymn.

Though Harriet expected Sterling to continue with the funeral service, to her surprise, Père Tellier, the minister of the French church, rose from his seat in the first pew and joined Sterling. Short of stature and slender, he was not an imposing figure, and yet when he spoke, all eyes were on him.

"Pastor Russell has graciously granted my wish to speak of my friend. This will not be a eulogy. What I want to share with you today is the last conversation I had with Pastor Sempert. It was the day Pastor Russell was expected to arrive."

As Ruth wiped her eyes, Harriet squeezed her hand, wishing there were some way to comfort her. Perhaps Père Tellier's words would accomplish that.

The French minister leaned forward, as if seeking a physical contact with the congregation. "My friend spoke of the man who was coming to replace him. I must admit that I was surprised when he confessed to being disappointed when he learned that the church was sending a man from Pennsylvania. You see, he had expected someone from the Old Country, a man who spoke German far better than any Pennsylvanian could, a man who understood your customs."

Harriet heard feet shuffling and a few embarrassed coughs as at least some members of the congregation realized that they shared the same sentiments.

"You all know that when Pastor Sempert was displeased, everyone knew it. The day he learned the new minister's identity he was convinced that our Lord had made a mistake, and he wasted no time telling him exactly that. I'll leave you to imagine that conversation. Fortunately, there was no fire and brimstone." The coughs turned to chuckles.

"Unfortunately, there was also no response, and that made Pastor Sempert angry. He told me he spent a week being angry with our Lord for refusing to understand that he, Pastor Sempert, knew what was best for his congregation. That week, he confessed, was the loneliest of his life, for he had distanced himself from God. Finally, in desperation, he prayed. And this time, instead of praying that God would do what he wanted, he prayed for understanding. It was only then when Pastor Sempert truly meant the words 'thy will be done' that he learned what God had in store for him . . . and for us. It was then that he realized God wanted Ladreville to become an American town, one that looks forward to the future and not only back to old ties. That was why Pastor Russell was sent here. It was God's will."

Père Tellier looked out at the congregation, his eyes moving slowly from pew to pew. "Our friend and pastor found his peace that day, just as he is at peace now. I know that he would want you to share that peace. The question is, can you? Are you ready to take the step that he did? For I caution you that the only real peace is found when we accept God's will."

The French minister paused, his head bowed in silent prayer. When he raised it, he looked directly at the parishioners. "You have come here today to honor Pastor Sempert with your presence. That is as it should be, but I ask you to honor his memory in another way, one that may be more difficult. Will you honor him and, more importantly, our God, by welcoming the new shepherd our Lord has sent us?"

The murmurs turned into a single sound, the sound of hundreds of voices saying amen. Harriet smiled, and when she looked to her side, she saw that Ruth's tears had dried, and she too was smiling. It had taken a man's death and another's eloquence to convince them, but the congregation finally had a new pastor.

15

Harriet took a deep breath as she walked around the class-room, straightening desks and checking that the ink bottles were closed. She did not need an encore of yesterday, when Marie Seurat had bumped into Pierre Berthoud's desk, over-turning a full bottle of ink and destroying the pages he'd so carefully copied. Though it had been an accident, Pierre had refused to accept Marie's apology and had sulked all afternoon while Marie had shed copious tears, convinced that she had ruined her life, not simply Pierre's composition.

A quick glance outside confirmed Harriet's suspicions. Yesterday the two children had been sworn enemies. Today, with the mercurial emotions so characteristic of youngsters, they were playing peacefully in the schoolyard, the contre-temps apparently forgotten.

Harriet's smile faded as she looked at the garden, now ignored by her students. Perhaps Lawrence and Isabelle were correct, and the garden wasn't a bad idea. When spring came, everyone would enjoy it. The problem was, it wasn't accomplishing Harriet's goal of teaching the children patience. They had deplorably small quantities of that particular virtue at any time, and it was worse now. With the cooler weather, they were less anxious to go outdoors, especially to check on a plot of ground where nothing appeared to be happening. Soon she would have to find new activities to amuse them during their recesses. Soon she would have to light the stove. Harriet shuddered. She'd postpone that as long as she could. In the meantime, there had to be something to keep her pupils occupied.

Her eyes lit on the calendar that hung next to the chalkboard. November was more than half over. In less than a fortnight, it would be December, and then . . . Harriet's pensive expression turned to a grin as she pictured the last page of the calendar. That was it. Clutching the prospect of a new activity to her the way a sassy squirrel does acorns, Harriet returned to her desk and started making lists of questions. She glanced at the clock again, counting the hours until she could dismiss school and talk to Isabelle. Her friend would have the answers.

Two hours later, class was over and Harriet was gathering her papers when she heard the door open. "Isabelle!" Harriet rose and hurried toward the pretty brunette. Dressed in a forest green frock with pale gold trim, Isabelle could have graced the pages of *Godey's Lady's Book* or Frank Leslie's *Gazette of Fashion*. "Did you read my mind? I was planning to visit you this afternoon."

Isabelle shook her head. "No mind reading. I was just so excited that I couldn't wait to tell you the news." Her brown eyes sparkled, and a becoming flush colored her cheeks. "Do you want to guess?"

There was only one thing Harriet could imagine that would cause so much happiness, but she didn't want to be the one to pronounce the words. It was far better to let Isabelle make her joyful announcement. "I'm not good at guessing," Harriet prevaricated. "Why don't you tell me?"

Isabelle clasped her hands, then flung them wide and pirouetted. "I'm expecting!" she cried. "Priscilla confirmed it."

Though not unexpected, this was joyous news indeed. "Oh, Isabelle, I'm so happy for you."

"There's more." Isabelle's lips twitched, as if she were trying to control her smile. "She thinks I may be carrying twins."

"Oh, my!"

Isabelle's laugh filled the schoolhouse. "That's what I said. At least," she admitted with a sheepish grin, "that's what I said when I could talk. At first all I could do was stare at Priscilla. I was sure she was wrong." Isabelle's eyes sparkled again. "Just think, Harriet. These will be the first twins in Ladreville. Even Gunther is excited about that. But how will I ever take care of two babies? I've never even cared for one. I don't know anything about babies." Isabelle's words came out faster than the water over her husband's waterwheel.

Harriet smiled at her friend. "You'll have lots of help—maybe more than you want. If I know Eva, she'll try to adopt one of the babies as her own, and your mother's close by." When Isabelle's expression remained dubious, Harriet added, "So am I. I may not be a mother, but I've had lots of experience with children, and I'd be glad to help you."

Her face once more wreathed in a smile, Isabelle threw her arms around Harriet. "I knew I could count on you. Oh, I'm so glad you came to Ladreville!"

215

For the next few minutes, Isabelle chattered about her quea-siness, the need for two of everything, and possible names for the babies. Then she clapped a hand over her mouth and frowned. "How selfish of me! You said you had planned to visit me today. Was there a special reason?"

"Nothing as special as your announcement, but I did want your advice." When Isabelle settled into one of the front desks, Harriet pulled out her own chair. "I was considering having the children perform a Christmas pageant. What do you think?"

Isabelle nodded so vigorously that a curl escaped from her chignon. "It's a wonderful idea. We've never had a pageant, but the parents loved it when their children marched in the Independence Day parade, so I'm sure they'd be even more excited about this." Furrows formed between her eyes, as if she had considered all aspects of the plan and found some-thing missing. "Where will you hold it?"

Harriet didn't need to consult her list. Finding a suitable location was the first item on it. "That's one of the things I wanted to discuss with you." She gestured around her. "The school is obviously too small, and it's too cold to expect people to sit outside. That only leaves the churches, and they're uncomfortable when everyone attends one."

Isabelle nodded. After Pastor Sempert's funeral, she had lamented the crowded conditions. "So what are you going to do?"

"The only solution I could find was to have two perfor-mances, one in each church."

Isabelle was silent for a moment, as if considering. "That's a good idea, but don't be surprised if a lot of parents come to both performances. I know Gunther and I would if Eva were in the pageant. You may wind up with crowded churches, anyway."

Harriet frowned. "I hadn't considered that possibility." She'd have to speak to the ministers about setting up extra chairs. "I've also been worrying about costumes. Would you—"

"Of course," Isabelle interrupted. "I'd be insulted if you didn't ask me to help. Maman and I will choose some fabric, and as soon as you've decided who will play Mary and Joseph and the wise men, we'll start sewing."

That was the reaction Harriet had hoped for. Still, she couldn't let Isabelle underestimate the effort. "It may be more work than you're expecting. I want all the children to be involved." That was an important element of Harriet's plan. She gave Isabelle a wry smile. "We'll have a lot of shepherds. A lot."

Isabelle appeared unfazed by the idea. "Then we'll enlist the mothers. Most of them are accomplished seamstresses."

"Unlike me."

Laughing, Isabelle nodded. "I wasn't going to say that. God gives us all different talents. Yours is teaching, raising children, and planning the pageant." She flashed an arch smile. "But you're right. I won't trust you with a needle and thread."

Harriet pretended to be annoyed. "I can always count on you to keep me humble. Now, is there anyone whose permission I need?"

"The ministers, of course." Isabelle tipped her head again, as she was wont to do when she was considering a particularly weighty subject. "You should also ask Lawrence." Harriet raised an eyebrow, surprised by the suggestion. "When Michel Ladre was here, he insisted on approving everything that affected the town. I don't think Lawrence is that strict, but it couldn't hurt to ask him. I can't imagine that he'll disapprove."

✑

He did not.

"It's a good idea." Lawrence settled into the chair next to Harriet. "Do you need any props?"

Harriet looked around his office, impressed with the difference the fresh coat of paint Jake had given it made. Even with the pale sunlight of late autumn, the walls seemed to glow. "We have all the shepherds' crooks we need, so all that's left is a manger. I thought I could borrow one."

Lawrence wrinkled his nose. "Not a good idea. The farmers are always using theirs, and—more importantly—you won't like the smell." To emphasize his words, he held his nose in mock horror.

"I don't need a stable, but I can't imagine the pageant without a manger."

"I wasn't suggesting you try to do without one. I think you should have both a manger and a stable, and I have just the person to build them for you."

Harriet didn't try to hide her surprise. "I was afraid William Goetz would be too busy." When they had discussed the pageant, Isabelle had told her he was the only carpenter in Ladreville and that his services were in great demand as Christmas approached.

"William won't be too busy if someone else does the work and all he has to do is supervise."

"That sounds logical, but who would that someone else be?"

"Your brother."

218

Her boot heels made little sound as she strode down rue du Marché. That was one of the advantages of strolling on this street rather than on Hochstrasse's wooden boardwalks. Though the latter kept her skirts from becoming splattered with mud after a rain, Harriet found it more satisfying to walk briskly on the packed earth. That was why she chose this street for her almost-nightly peregrinations. That and the privacy. There were few houses on this stretch of the road, and none of the commercial establishments remained open past dark.

She smiled as she increased her pace, enjoying the acceleration of her heartbeat. Everything was going well with the pageant. The children were excited; the parents were pleased; even Jake was in a better mood. Harriet knew that the credit for the last went to Lawrence. Though she would not have dreamt it possible, Jake had become a different person since he started working off his debt. He certainly complained less frequently. That might be because he was tired—Lawrence hadn't exaggerated when he'd warned Jake that he would work hard—but Harriet suspected her brother's newfound serenity came at least in part from the fact that he was learning new skills.

Jake seemed to enjoy that. While he'd grumbled about being sold into slavery when he'd started working at the livery, the complaints had ceased after the first day. Instead, Jake had begun regaling the younger children with tales of the horses. In the past, Harriet might have cautioned him about the blatant hyperbole, but she was so pleased by his improved mood that she'd bit her tongue. What harm could there be in letting him pretend to be a hero? Perhaps that was

219

what Jake needed. Perhaps his fascination with horses would lead to a vocation. Now she hoped he would find carpentry equally rewarding.

Harriet smiled again. One thing was certain: Lawrence kept her brother too busy to get into trouble. Jake might be missing school, but it appeared that he was learning more valuable lessons than her books could offer him. Working for Lawrence was giving him an education in life.

Lawrence. Harriet's smile softened as she realized how he dominated her thoughts. This wasn't like those first few weeks when Thomas had come to live with his uncle and Harriet had been overwhelmed by the fact that an almost unbelievably handsome young man was paying attention to her. She had soon discovered that Thomas's sweet words were false, that he didn't love her, and that he felt nothing but contempt for her family. Lawrence wasn't like that. He'd never indulged in sweet words, had never claimed to love her. Instead, his actions had demonstrated that he cared about her and her siblings. Lawrence had been a true friend, honest and reliable, a fine example for Jake. It was no wonder she thought of him so often.

When she reached the end of rue du Marché, Harriet paused, debating whether to follow her normal pattern and turn around or proceed onto Potomac and return home via Hochstrasse. Though the latter route provided more variety, it forced her to pass the saloon. Unlike the stores on rue du Marché, the saloon would be open, welcoming men who indulged in strong spirits, men who might spill out the door, their unsteady gait and slurred words testament to the whiskey they'd consumed. While that had happened only once, it had been enough to convince Harriet to take an alternate course.

She started to turn around, then stopped. Isabelle had mentioned a new display in the mercantile's front window, insisting that Harriet would enjoy seeing it, but she'd been too busy to stop by the store after school. If she continued on Potomac to Hochstrasse, she would be able to peer into the plate glass window and see what had excited Isabelle. It was the least she could do for her friend after all the work she was expending on the pageant. Resolutely, Harriet turned onto Potomac.

She walked briskly, enjoying the cool night air. Though still two blocks from the river, she was aware of the water here, for its moisture scented the air. Harriet breathed in deeply, enjoying the heaviness of the humidity. Lawrence might fear the river, and he had good cause, but she reveled in the sound of life-giving water flowing gently downstream. She couldn't hear it yet, but she knew it was there, and it comforted her.

When she reached Hochstrasse, the sensation of nearing the river increased. Her smile broadening, Harriet considered detouring to walk by the river. It was there, at the end of Potomac, that the town had agreed to build a bridge. The campaign had been easier than she had expected. Despite the predictable complaints about higher taxes, when Lawrence had volunteered to contribute half his wages, Ladreville's citizens had agreed to raise the remaining funds. With construction scheduled to begin in February before the spring rains swelled the Medina, it was the town's unspoken expectation that, even though his contract was set to expire in January, Lawrence would remain long enough to see his project completed. And that was good, at least for Harriet.

She looked down the street. There was time to stroll by the river, for Ruth wouldn't expect her home for another half hour. Her decision made, Harriet quickened her pace, then stopped abruptly as a man emerged from the saloon.

It couldn't be. Harriet felt the blood drain from her face, and her hands grew clammy. Why was Lawrence coming from that den of iniquity? Surely he was not one of the men who spent each night there. Surely he knew better. But what if he didn't? What if he was like her father? Harriet stood frozen, her teeth chattering with fear, until a thought warmed her. Of course. Lawrence was the town's sheriff. That was why he was in the saloon. Undoubtedly he'd been called to break up a dispute.

"Good evening, Harriet." The man in question touched his hat brim in greeting and crossed the street to join her. "I didn't expect to see you outside."

Her foolish fears dissolved faster than sugar in hot coffee, and Harriet smiled as Lawrence approached. Why had she doubted him, if only for an instant? She knew Lawrence, and he was not a drunkard. "Walking helps me relax," she explained. "I go out most nights, but I don't usually come this way."

"I'm glad you did." He stepped onto the boardwalk and bent his arm, silently urging her to place her hand in the crook of his elbow.

Harriet took a step closer. A second later she gasped as her nose registered the odor of whiskey. She sniffed again, not wanting to believe her senses, but there was no doubt. Lawrence had liquor on his breath.

"*Just one more.*" Images flashed before her eyes. Father was holding the bottle, filling the glass again. "*Just one more.*" Was that how it had been tonight? She stared at Lawrence, the man she had thought she knew. What a fool she was!

She'd been duped by Thomas, and though she had thought she'd learned her lesson, she had not. She'd trusted this man. "You've been drinking."

"I had a whiskey," Lawrence admitted, as if it were of no consequence.

Harriet recoiled in horror. That was how it started—with one drink, then a second, and then another until the bottle was empty. "How could you? Don't you know how harmful whiskey is?" Her voice was shrill and filled with anger. Though Lawrence appeared startled, he said nothing. Harriet clenched her fists, trying to control her disappointment. "I thought I knew you. I thought you were different." Before he could respond, she picked up her skirts and began to run.

"Harriet, come back." She heard the sound of Lawrence's voice and his boot steps behind her. "We need to talk." Though she knew his longer stride would easily catch her, he did not appear to be hurrying. Perhaps he thought she would turn around. Perhaps he thought her anger would dissipate. He was wrong.

"Never!"

෪

"I don't know why I have to eat with him." Jake accompanied his words with a snarl. It was no less than Harriet had expected, which was why she'd made the announcement to him separately, rather than waiting until they were all seated for supper. Overall, Jake's mood might have improved, but one thing had not changed: his dislike for Karl Friedrich.

"It's a matter of common courtesy," Harriet said calmly. Experience had taught her that the best way to deal with Jake was to refuse his bait. No matter what he said or did, she could not display anger. "We've been the Friedrichs' guests many times, and we need to reciprocate."

"You do." Jake pointed a finger at her, his voice rising with audible fury. "I don't. I don't ever want to see Karl Friedrich again. Not ever. Do you hear me?"

Harriet heard him. In all likelihood, everyone in the house did. Jake's words echoed through her brain. Never again. That's what she had said about Lawrence, but it wasn't true. She wanted to see him again. She wanted to resume their friendly bantering. But she also wanted to be assured that the whiskey she had smelled had been an aberration, that it was the last drink he would ever take. And that assurance, she knew, would not be forthcoming, for she had heard that Lawrence patronized the saloon almost every night. He was, it appeared, if not a slave to Demon Alcohol, at least a close acquaintance. But Lawrence wasn't the subject of today's discussion. Karl was.

Harriet nodded slowly, acknowledging her brother's words. "I don't know how many times I have to tell you, but you're wrong about Karl. He is not courting me, and he does not want to be your father." Since the night of the fall festival, there had been nothing remotely familiar about Karl's behavior. He had treated her with courtesy but nothing more. If he had had any romantic thoughts about her, it appeared they had been destroyed along with his buggy seats. "You may not want to see him again, but I wouldn't be surprised if Karl felt the same way." When she and Ruth had discussed inviting the Friedrichs, Harriet had wondered if they would accept or if they would hold Jake's behavior against the whole Kirk family.

"I hope he does. Maybe then he won't come." A satisfied

smile crossed Jake's face. "If he does, I'll stay at the livery. I'd rather eat oats with the horses than anything with him." Jake laced the last word with contempt.

The open defiance was vintage Jake. Though she bit back her anger, Harriet responded with her firmest tone, the one that brooked no dissention. "You'll eat here and you'll be civil to all our guests. Even Karl. Now, I don't want to hear another word about it."

She did not. From the moment Karl and his parents arrived, Jake said not a word. Instead, he feigned laryngitis. Harriet might have been amused by her brother's ingenuity had it not been for the fact that, though he remained silent, his expressions were eloquent. Scowls and frowns were interspersed with patently disdainful glances, leaving no one to doubt his displeasure with the family's guests. Tonight even Frau and Herr Friedrich were included in Jake's disapproval, apparently being punished for the sin of giving birth to Karl. It was intolerably rude, and yet Harriet had little recourse. Had he been younger, she would have sent Jake to his room and insisted that he remain there until he was ready to apologize. She would not do that today, for that was exactly what her brother wanted.

"Permit me," Karl said when the table was laden with food and everyone had gathered around it. As he pulled out Harriet's chair and seated her, Jake glared.

"It was very kind of you to invite us." Frau Friedrich smiled her approval of the canned beans. Inspired by the pickling lessons, Harriet had decided that she and Ruth could can some beans, and although they'd had their share of problems, at least the results were edible.

"I'm thankful you could come. I know how busy you are."

"Dairy cattle are the problem," Herr Friedrich explained. "They need to be milked twice a day."

When Daniel and Sam poked each other, apparently finding amusement in the farmer's schedule, Ruth gave them a stern look. "They're trouble," she said. For a moment, Harriet wondered whether she was referring to her brothers. "But the milk and cheese are delicious." It appeared Ruth wasn't commenting on her siblings. "I used to enjoy milking our cow in Fortune."

Harriet stared at her sister, startled by both the revelation that she had taken pleasure in their cow and by the number of words she had strung together. The old Ruth would have spent the evening studying her plate as if it contained answers to the world's mysteries and would have exchanged no more than two or three words with their guests. The new Ruth was surprisingly social. If this was the result of the time she had spent with Pastor Russell when she delivered food to the parsonage, Harriet could not complain. At least one of her siblings was being polite.

Karl leaned toward Ruth and grinned. "You're welcome to milk our cows anytime you want."

Though Ruth smiled, Jake glowered and snorted, sounding more like a pig than a cow as he shoveled food into his mouth and chewed with it half open. Once again, he was testing Harriet, daring her to banish him. Perhaps she should for the Friedrichs' sakes, but she hated the idea of letting Jake win. Instead, she tried to deflect attention from her brother's poor manners by channeling the conversation toward innocuous subjects. But, whether she spoke of the weather, the upcoming pageant, or Frau Friedrich's plans for their Christmas tree, Jake's response was always the same: a sullen expression and more barnyard noises.

"Have you thought about what you'll do next year?" Studiously ignoring Jake, Karl directed his question to Harriet.

She nodded. Surely this topic would not provoke Jake's anger. "I expect to be teaching again, if the town renews my contract." Though Lawrence had not reported any further complaints about her, there was always the possibility that something—perhaps Jake's behavior—would convince the townspeople that she was unfit to be their schoolmarm.

Karl's lips turned up in an enigmatic smile. "Perhaps you will be the one not to renew the contract," he suggested.

Harriet blinked. "Why would I do that? I enjoy teaching." Especially now that her pupils' enthusiasm was rekindled by the pageant.

Daniel made a well in his mashed potatoes and began to fill it with the serving of beans Harriet had insisted he take, dousing the mixture with a generous helping of gravy. Harriet tried not to smile at her youngest brother's attempt to mask the flavor of a vegetable he detested. She should be thankful he wasn't glowering at their guests.

Oblivious to the fact that Mary, who normally enjoyed green beans, had emulated her brother, somehow managing to splatter gravy on the tablecloth, Karl gave his mother a knowing smile before he turned back to Harriet. "You wouldn't renew your contract if you were planning to marry."

There was a moment of silence as his words registered. Then, before Harriet could respond, Jake jumped to his feet. "Not you! She won't marry you! My sister deserves better than you, you old goat!" Without waiting to be excused, Jake stormed from the room.

An hour later, Harriet stood next to Ruth, drying the dishes her sister was washing. Though the elder Friedrichs had insisted they were returning to the farm to complete their daily chores and that was the reason they could not stay for dessert, Harriet knew otherwise. Nothing she could say could mitigate the damage Jake's outburst had caused. When her temper cooled, she planned to deal with him. She would have to reprimand him for his behavior, though she suspected that would accomplish nothing. No matter how often she spoke to him, where Karl was concerned, Jake remained irrational.

"Karl was right, you know." Ruth handed her a plate. "You should consider marriage." As Harriet started to sputter, Ruth continued, "Not Karl, but what about Lawrence?"

Marry Lawrence! That was even more absurd than the thought of becoming Karl's wife. "What a preposterous idea."

"Why?" Ruth swirled another plate in the rinse water before she handed it to Harriet. "He's a good man, well respected. Even Jake tolerates him. You could do worse."

What a night. First Jake's rudeness, now Ruth's silly suggestion. Though she was tempted to ignore the latter, Harriet knew Ruth would persist until she received an answer. "You know I don't plan to marry until Mary is raised," she said as calmly as she could, "but if I did, there are many reasons why Lawrence would not be the man I chose." She stretched onto her tiptoes to slide the stack of plates onto their designated shelf. "I know you're not going to rest until I tell you what they are, so here are three." Harriet held up her right hand, the fingers curled into her palm. Raising one, she said, "He drinks." A second joined the first as she added, "He doesn't want a ready-made family. And, most importantly," she said as she raised her ring finger, "he doesn't love me."

Ruth's snort reminded Harriet of Jake. What was happening to this family that everyone was becoming contentious and resorting to crude noises?

"So you say." Ruth shook her head slowly. "I think you're wrong about his feelings. I think you're afraid of love."

16

It was the oddest town he'd ever seen. Thomas looked around, his lip curling at the sight of half-timbered buildings. Didn't these folks know that Texans didn't build houses like this? A house was made of stone or wood. Only foreigners would think you should use both. But that's what this town was, a bunch of foreigners. He heard them talking, and even the ones who spoke English were almost impossible to understand.

Why on earth had Harriet decided to come here when she could have remained in Fortune as his wife? Surely by now she would have seen the error of her ways. Every other woman would have, but Harriet was stubborn. There was no telling what she was thinking.

Thomas walked slowly, choosing the quietest streets. If Ladreville was like Fortune, there'd be nosy people just waiting to report that a stranger had entered their precious town. He couldn't let that happen. If he was going to convince Harriet to marry him, he needed surprise on his side. That and his charm would do the trick.

He looked around. It wouldn't be hard to find the school. And then . . . Thomas grinned in anticipation.

※

"Women! I'll never understand them." Lawrence frowned at his companion, then shrugged as he leaned back in the saddle. He was a churl to even introduce the subject. It wasn't Sterling's fault that he was in a rotten mood. It wasn't even the fault of the cloudy day. The problem was, Lawrence had lain awake most of the night as he had for the past week, reliving his encounter with Harriet. Predictably, by morning his head hurt almost as much as it had the one time he'd had too many whiskeys.

He probably should have declined the minister's invitation, but he had thought—wrongly, it turned out—that a brisk ride might improve his disposition. Besides, Snip needed the exercise. And so he and Sterling were on the opposite side of the Medina, letting their horses cool down after a gallop.

The air was thick and damp, presaging a storm, but that didn't appear to faze Sterling. He grinned as he swatted a fly that buzzed around his nose. "Women are definitely one of God's mysteries. I'm not sure he meant us to understand them, but he did send them to us for a reason."

"To make our lives miserable?" Lawrence was only half joking. His life had certainly been miserable since that night outside the saloon. At first he'd thought Harriet would calm down in a day or two, but when he'd approached her after church, she'd pretended she didn't see him, and when he'd addressed her on the street, she had given him a look that would have chilled an August day. How was a man supposed to patch up a quarrel—if that's what it was—when the other

231

party wouldn't speak? "I swear, women are creatures from another world."

Sterling chuckled. "You sound like my father when he and Ma had a row. He'd threaten to leave the farm and never return. The next thing we knew, they were kissing." As Snip whinnied, almost as if he understood the conversation, Sterling laughed again. "Believe me, when my brothers and I were growing up, we almost preferred the arguments to the kissing. That was mighty embarrassing to young boys."

For the first time this morning, Lawrence smiled, recalling portions of his childhood. "I know what you mean. When it happened, my sister used to claim that our parents were mushy. I have to confess that for the longest time, I didn't understand why she thought they resembled cornmeal mush. All I knew was that I didn't want to watch any show of affection. I would have headed for the hills if there'd been any near us. As it was, I'd hide in the barn until I thought the mushiness was over."

As a breeze rustled the oak leaves, Sterling stared into the distance. "Still, a man reaches a time when he looks at women differently, especially if a special one catches his eye."

Lawrence shot his friend an appraising look. It seemed that he wasn't the only one who was in an odd mood this morning. The tone of Sterling's voice had changed, humor replaced with something else, something almost wistful. "It sounds as if someone has caught your eye."

Sterling nodded but kept his eyes fixed on the grove of trees, as if hoping to spot the mockingbird whose cry filled the air. "I didn't expect it, but I can't get her out of my thoughts."

Though Lawrence steeled his face to remain expressionless, he understood what Sterling was saying. Thoughts of a certain schoolmarm cropped up when he least expected them, and they refused to be banished, even though the schoolmarm banished him.

"I didn't think so at first." Sterling was still speaking, oblivious to the direction Lawrence's thoughts had taken. "But now I believe she'd be the perfect helpmeet for me."

Lawrence glanced down at Snip to hide his confusion. It appeared this was not a passing fancy or a simple case of infatuation. Sterling sounded serious. "Are you going to tell me who the special lady is?"

The minister turned back to Lawrence, a broad smile crossing his face. "You might as well know. It's Miss Kirk."

"Harriet?" Lawrence felt the way he had when a bandit had shoved the end of a rifle into his stomach: shocked, sick, and more than slightly foolish. Sterling and Harriet? Lawrence couldn't picture them together, and yet there was no denying the fatuous look on his friend's face.

That look turned to mild horror. "Never! It's the other Miss Kirk I fancy. Ruth."

Lawrence's heartbeat returned to normal. "The shy one," he said softly. It was easier—far easier—to imagine Sterling with Ruth. Still, he wondered how such a timid woman would fare as a parson's wife.

"She's only shy until you get to know her." It seemed that Sterling had read his mind. "Last week she took exception to something in my sermon and didn't hesitate to tell me."

"That sounds like Harriet. She's pretty plainspoken, at least with me."

Though Sterling had once again been staring into the distance, he turned and looked at Lawrence, his expression appraising. "Harriet's a fine woman, but she's not the one for me."

Perhaps it was Sterling's expression; perhaps it was the tone of his voice, which had altered ever so slightly. Whatever the reason, Lawrence's hackles rose. "Don't look at me like that. Harriet's not the one for me, either. She practically took my head off because I'd had a glass of whiskey, and she hasn't spoken to me since. For the life of me, I can't figure out why."

Though Snip tossed his head, as if he shared Lawrence's frustration, Sterling nodded solemnly. "There's an easy way to learn what's bothering her."

Surely that wasn't amusement tingeing Sterling's words. There was nothing amusing about being ignored by Harriet. Though his first instinct was to demand the information from Sterling, Lawrence forced an amiable tone to his voice. "If you know the secret, I'd be much obliged if you'd share it with me."

Sterling shook his head. "It's more entertaining to watch you squirm."

"And I thought you were a man of God."

"That doesn't stop me from enjoying a moment of satisfaction watching a big, tough Ranger felled by a slip of a woman."

"Be careful." Lawrence tightened his grip on the reins. "This big, tough Ranger is thinking about planting his fist on your face."

"You'll have to catch me first."

Before Lawrence knew what he intended, Sterling leaned over his horse's neck, and the two were off, racing toward the pecan tree whose blackened trunk was evidence of a long-ago lightning strike. Sterling had only a second's advantage, but that was enough to make Lawrence unable to catch him.

"Congratulations. It appears that you've been practicing," Lawrence said when they were once more riding side by side.

"I have," Sterling admitted, "and since you were kind enough not to rearrange my face with your fist, I'll tell you the secret." He took a deep breath, exhaling slowly in a deliberate attempt to heighten the suspense. "The secret is . . ." Another pause. "Ask her."

"Ask her?"

Sterling grinned. "It's simple enough. You open your mouth and words come out. Of course, considering what you've told me about Harriet's mood, you might want to take a peace offering."

"What on earth is that?"

"Some little thing to sweeten her disposition. The mercantile's bound to have something." Sterling's lips twisted into a rueful smile. "Here's another bit of advice for you. You might want to claim that whatever you buy is for your sister. Otherwise, Ladreville's grapevine will have you married before you even set foot inside the schoolhouse."

"Well, well, well. If it isn't the little schoolmarm."

Harriet spun around so quickly that the chalk fell out of her hand. She'd been writing the next day's lessons on the board, but the sound of a voice she had never thought to hear again had driven every other thought from her brain.

"Thomas! What are you doing here?" There was no mistaking either the voice or the deceptively handsome face. Though he was of only medium height, Thomas Bruckner's dark brown hair and eyes combined with flawlessly formed features made him a man few women could refuse. Why had he sought out the one who *had* refused him?

He smiled, his lips curving into an expression most people would have described as cherubic. "I came to see you." He smiled again and took another step toward her. "What I see is that you've changed. You're more beautiful than ever."

Harriet dismissed the compliment, knowing it to be as false as everything Thomas said. "You're wrong. I haven't changed, and I can't imagine why you wasted your time coming here."

"Now, Harriet, don't be hasty. I know we had a misunderstanding when we parted, but . . ."

"There was no misunderstanding. You asked me to marry you. As I recall, you practically ordered me to marry you. I refused. How could there possibly be a misunderstanding about that?"

Though his lips stayed curved in a smile, Thomas's eyes were cold. "Surely you can't mean to remain here, teaching foreigners' children when you could be home in Fortune, living a life of ease as my wife."

How dare he be so condescending? Harriet straightened her spine and glared at Thomas. "As odd as it may seem to you, remaining here is exactly what I intend to do. This is my home now, and those people you call foreigners are my friends."

"But I want to marry you."

"I can't imagine why. You told me I was stubborn and waspish. Why would you want to marry a woman like that?"

"Because I need . . ." He stopped abruptly, his voice changing subtly as he said, "Because I care about you."

She shook her head. "You care about only one thing, and that's yourself." As she remembered the rumors of

Thomas's gambling debts, she added, "If this is about money, once again you're wrong. There is no money, and even if there were, I would never give it to you. Go back to Fortune and find yourself someone else. I will never, ever marry you."

"But you have to."

"No, Thomas, I do not." Harriet pointed at the door. "You're the one who needs to do something. Leave."

"You haven't seen the last of me."

Seconds later, Harriet sank into her chair, her legs weak with relief. It was typical Thomas, insisting on the final word, but at least he was gone.

⌒◦

He felt silly, carrying a bag of candy in his pocket. It didn't seem like the kind of thing Harriet would appreciate, but Madame Rousseau had assured him that all women—including his purportedly fussy sister—would enjoy a sweet. So, here he was, feeling distinctly awkward as he opened the door to the schoolhouse.

"Good afternoon, Harriet," Lawrence said as he walked through the cloakroom. The best approach, he had decided, was to pretend this was a normal visit, that their last encounter had not occurred.

She rose. Though her lips pursed in disapproval, it was her eyes that caught his attention. Even the glint of light on her spectacles could not disguise the fear. Was this why she had shunned him? But why would she be afraid of him?

"I didn't expect to see you. I thought I made myself clear that night."

So much for pretense. It appeared that Harriet had not

changed her mind or even softened her attitude. The only good thing Lawrence could say was that she was talking to him. Gentleness wasn't working; he'd have to take a different approach.

"I beg to differ," Lawrence said, his voice as firm as if he were dealing with a hardened criminal. "You might have thought you were clear, but I'm confused."

She stopped a foot away from him, her gray eyes cold as she said, "How could you misunderstand something as simple as 'never'?"

This was definitely not going the way he had hoped. Perhaps he should have started by offering her the candy. It was too late for that now. Harriet would see the gift for what it was, a ploy to sweeten her disposition.

"I understood the word," he admitted, "but I hoped you didn't mean it."

"I did." Her expression changed, fear once again replacing anger. What was it she feared? But when she spoke, Harriet's words were defiant. "I choose not to associate with drunkards."

Not for the first time, Lawrence wished he'd asked Jake about his sister. He had considered doing exactly that but had hesitated because Jake was his employee, albeit not of his own volition. Somehow, it seemed wrong to presume on that relationship and pump him about Harriet. "That seems reasonable enough," he said, keeping his voice lower than normal. Who would have thought that his years with the Rangers would help him today? One of the things he'd learned was that a calm, almost soft voice could defuse an angry situation. "I would prefer not to associate with drunkards, either. However, I am not a drunkard."

Harriet drew herself up to her full height and glared at him. "How can you deny it? I smelled the whiskey on you."

He nodded. There was no point in disputing something she knew to be the truth. Still, he wanted to be certain she understood the situation. "One drink does not make a man a drunkard."

"But one drink leads to another."

"Not always." He watched her closely. It hadn't been his imagination. Harriet was fearful. Though she tried to hide it, the very subject of whiskey made her tremble. Lawrence felt a sense of kinship, for he was no stranger to fear. The way his heart raced each time he crossed a river was proof of that. He softened his voice again as he asked, "Why are you so angry with me?"

Harriet turned and walked toward the window. The tilt of her head and the slight slump of her shoulders told him she was debating whether or not to answer him. He wouldn't push. With a woman like Harriet, that would accomplish nothing. Nothing positive, that is.

At last, she turned to face him, though she remained at the window. "I didn't want anyone to know."

"I can keep secrets," he said firmly. "Whatever it is, I want to understand. I want to be your friend." The truth was, there were times when he thought he wanted more than that. Friendship was a way to start, and if it led to courtship . . . well, that wasn't bad, was it?

Harriet nodded slowly. "All right, but you must promise never to tell anyone—not even Sterling."

When he agreed, she made her way to her desk and sank onto the chair, gesturing to Lawrence to take a seat. It was only when he was settled on the dunce stool that she spoke again.

239

"My father was a drunkard." Though the words were shocking, she pronounced them as if she were reciting nothing more important than a multiplication table. "I don't know when it started, but I can't ever remember him not drinking, and it got worse once Ruth was born. After that, it seemed to me whiskey was all he cared about. Mother couldn't stop him, so she spent her days either sleeping or staring into the distance." Harriet's eyes darkened, giving Lawrence an idea of the effort it took to reveal her past to anyone. "I learned early on to take care of myself. I remember going to church one Sunday. I was so proud that I had dressed myself that I didn't visit my grandparents that morning, and so I hadn't realized that my shoes didn't match. The other children laughed at me. Even the parents gave me pitying looks." She gazed toward the window, obviously composing herself. "I didn't go back until my grandmother taught me to match shoes and comb my hair."

Lawrence's heart went out to the little girl who'd had such a difficult childhood. He wanted to wrap his arms around her and assure her that no one would ever again hurt her, but he couldn't make that assurance. No one could. Instead, he sat quietly, watching as this brave woman opened the deepest recesses of her heart.

"Things worsened when Ruth was born. If it hadn't been for my grandparents, I don't know what we would have done. They watched over us at first, but Grandma died when I was eleven. After that, there wasn't much Grandpa could do. By the time Sam arrived, I was used to being in charge."

So much was becoming clear. That was what Jake had meant when he'd said Harriet had acted like his mother even before their parents died. Though she had not borne the children, it appeared that she had had almost total responsibility for them. Poor Harriet!

"I'm sorry." The words were inadequate. How could mere words express the feelings that surged through him? This wonderful, prickly woman's story threatened to bring tears to his eyes. But Lawrence did not cry. Not ever. Not since the day Lizbeth had drowned.

"It can't have been easy," he said. Harriet had been a child raising children. When had she had a chance to be a youngster herself? The answer, Lawrence suspected, was never.

"It wasn't easy for anyone," she said quietly, "but it was worse when our parents died. Whiskey killed them." Again, her words were matter-of-fact, giving no hint of the emotions that must have accompanied the events she was describing. Was this how she dealt with the past, by insulating herself from it?

"What happened?"

"You know they died in a fire. What I didn't tell you is that Father caused it. We'll never know how it started, but it seems he was so drunk he didn't notice the house was on fire, and Mother must have been asleep. When I brought the others home from school, there was nothing left but charred ruins and . . ."

The way her voice trailed off told Lawrence she had found not just charred wood but her parents' bodies.

"Oh, Harriet." It was no wonder that she feared both fire and drunkenness. She had a good reason. "I don't know what to say."

"There's nothing to say." She removed her spectacles and began to polish them.

Without the spectacles, Harriet looked younger, more

vulnerable, reminding Lawrence of the child she had once been. It was then that he remembered the candy. Lawrence pulled the bag from his pocket and handed it to her. "I brought this for you."

For a moment the only sound was the loud ticking of the clock on the back wall. Harriet stared at the bag, as if trying to decide whether or not to accept it. When she did, Lawrence exhaled the breath he hadn't realized he was holding. Her lips quirked into a wry smile as she opened the bag and recognized its contents. "Were you hoping to sweeten my disposition?"

Though that was the intent, he wouldn't have phrased it that way. "It was meant to be a peace offering."

"Thank you." Harriet waved the bag under her nose, sniffing deeply. "Lemon drops are my favorite." Holding out the bag, she offered him one. When he refused, she popped one into her mouth. "Delicious," she murmured.

"I'm glad you like them." It had been a lucky choice. Lawrence watched her enjoying the tart candy. "What would happen if you ate them all this afternoon?" he asked as casually as he could.

Harriet gave him a wry smile. "I'd have one very sore stomach."

He nodded. "Would you blame the candy?"

"Of course not!" Her tone left no doubt that she considered the question preposterous. "It would be my fault. I should know better than to eat a whole bag of sweets."

For the first time since he'd arrived, the conversation was going the way Lawrence had hoped. "I agree. You should know not to eat too much candy, and a man should know not to drink a whole bottle of whiskey."

Harriet's face paled and she jumped to her feet, her eyes

once again flashing with anger. "You're wrong, Lawrence. It's different. Eating too much candy would hurt only me, but whiskey harms others. Look what it did to my family. Father's drinking killed him and Mother, and . . ."

Though she didn't complete the sentence, Lawrence knew she was thinking of the terrible toll it had taken on her and her siblings. Because her father had been unable to control himself, Harriet's childhood had been almost unbearably difficult, forcing her to adopt an adult's role when she was still a youngster.

"I learned the lesson very early," she said, her voice cracking with emotion, "and it's one I'll never forget. That's why I cannot trust anyone who drinks."

Lawrence thought of the men who spent each evening in the saloon. Though few left as inebriated as Harriet's father apparently had been, more than one lurched as he made his way out the door. Who knew what happened when the men reached their homes or what effect their time away and the money they spent at the saloon had on their families? Lawrence had enjoyed the taste of whiskey, and he'd only once lost control and drunk too much. Until today he had seen no wrong in what he'd done. But now . . .

"You're right." He stood at Harriet's side, not daring to touch her but wanting her to know he understood. "I cannot promise that I won't go into the saloon again. That's part of my responsibilities as sheriff. But I can promise you that I won't take another drink."

♥

She was lying. Thomas had played poker long enough to know when someone was lying, and Harriet was most

243

definitely a liar. She had money. Of course she did. It had to be stashed somewhere in her house, that funny-looking building only a block or so away from the school. Sure as frost in December, that's where it was. The only problem was, he'd have to wait another day. By the time Miss High and Mighty Harriet threw him out of the school, the other children were back home. Thomas grinned at the thought of the Kirk fortune. Harriet was right. He didn't need her. Once he had the money, he'd be on easy street. No debts, no wife to tie him down, nothing but piles of silver and gold. He'd have the life he had always wanted, compliments of Harriet.

≈

Harriet stared out the window. Though there was only a light breeze at ground level, the clouds were scudding across the sky as if propelled by a fierce wind, playing peekaboo with the stars and the tiny sliver of a moon. It was a night meant for a stroll, but even the brisk walk she'd taken had not corralled her thoughts. They continued to whirl, a maelstrom of images that chased away any hope of sleep. Thomas and Lawrence. Lawrence and Thomas. Anger and hope. Fear and friendship. It had been the most tumultuous afternoon she could recall.

Seeing Thomas had disturbed her more than she wanted to admit, leaving her shaky and fearful. When he'd courted her in Fortune, he'd been charming, the perfect gentleman until the day she'd confronted him with the words she'd overheard. Even then, though angry and belligerent, he hadn't frightened her. Today Thomas's eyes reflected desperation, and desperate men were dangerous. Harriet knew that from the tales Lawrence had told of his life as a Ranger. She could only hope that Thomas finally realized that she was not an heiress and that she had no intention of returning to Fortune and marrying him.

Lawrence was different. Harriet smiled, thinking of the lemon drops he'd given her. They were as sour as her mood had been when he'd arrived. She hadn't wanted to see him, hadn't wanted to talk to him, and she certainly hadn't intended to tell him about Mother and Father. Harriet didn't want anyone in Ladreville to know what had happened. Ruth knew better than to speak of their father's drinking, and Jake had only the faintest memories, while the others had been too young to recall their father's drunken state. Harriet gripped the windowsill, reflecting that, thanks to her, the secret was a secret no more. And yet she could not regret telling Lawrence. There had been something truly cathartic about sharing the worst part of her life with someone who cared. For he did care. She had read that in his eyes. He cared enough about her feelings that he had agreed not to drink again.

No. Harriet shook her head. He hadn't agreed; he had volunteered, and there was a huge difference. Mother had begged Father to stop, but he'd paid no heed to her pleading. Lawrence, once he'd understood how Harriet felt, had chosen to change his life. She had sensed no hesitation on his part, simply a desire to make her happy. And he had. His promise had chased away fear, sowing seeds of hope. Those seeds, Harriet knew, would germinate more quickly than the ones her pupils had planted.

Lawrence was not like her father. He was not like Thomas. He was . . . She paused, seeking the correct word. A friend?

He'd been a friend today, but somehow the word seemed inadequate. She took a deep breath and smiled. The word didn't matter. What mattered was that he had come to the schoolhouse and they'd resolved their problems. Life was better when Lawrence was part of it.

17

Something was wrong. Harriet knew it the moment she entered the house. The kitchen was empty. Not only was Ruth not there, but there were no signs of supper, no pots on the range, no delicious aromas wafting from the oven.

"Ruth!" Was her sister ill? That was the only reason Harriet could imagine for the absence of supper preparations, but Ruth was never ill. "Ruth!" she called again.

"I'm up here." Her sister's voice was faint, as if coming from the front of the house.

Her shoes clattering on the stairs, Harriet raced to the second story. "Where are you?" she cried as she reached the landing.

"In your room."

Seconds later, Harriet's eyes widened as she entered her bedchamber. Every garment she owned lay on the floor. Her trunk had been overturned, its contents strewn across one corner of the room. And her books—her precious books— had been knocked off the shelves with such force that some of the spines had split. Ruth sat in the midst of them, trying to restore order.

"What happened?"

Though Ruth's face was white, her voice remained calm. "I heard someone up here when I returned from the market, but by the time I got here, he was gone. When I looked out the door, I didn't see anyone."

"Oh, Ruth." Harriet knelt next to her sister and wrapped her arms around her. "You shouldn't have come up here. He could have hurt you."

Ruth shook her head. "There wasn't any danger. The intruder left before I got close to him."

"Ruthie, please don't take chances like that again. I couldn't bear it if something happened to you." Unbidden, the memory of Lawrence's young sister invaded Harriet's thoughts. Though decades had passed, he had not fully recovered from her death. "I can't lose you."

Ruth placed her hands on both sides of Harriet's face and waited until her sister met her gaze before she said, "Don't worry. I'll be fine."

Harriet hoped that was true. She rose to her feet and looked around. "Were any of the other rooms disturbed?"

Ruth shook her head as she stood. "Just yours." Tears filled her eyes as she looked down at the damaged books. "Who could have done this?"

"Thomas." Harriet had no doubts about the intruder's identity. This was not a simple burglary; it was an act of revenge.

"Thomas Bruckner? But he's hundreds of miles away."

Harriet shook her head. "He was at the school yesterday."

The remaining touch of color drained from Ruth's face. "You didn't say anything."

"There was nothing to say. I told Thomas to leave because I never wanted to see him again. I thought he was gone." Harriet managed a wry smile. "It appears I was wrong."

Ruth clasped her hands, as if trying to still their trembling. "We'd better tell the sheriff."

"There's no need. Thomas won't be back." Now he knew without a doubt that she had no gold.

⌇

"How does this look?" Harriet turned to her sister, relieved that Ruth appeared calm. For several days after Thomas's break-in, she had been nervous. Now, she seemed to have regained her normal composure. The two women had been sitting in the parlor for several hours since supper, lengths of fabric in their laps, and not once had Ruth mentioned hearing strange noises. Instead, her fingers had moved quickly, plying a thread and needle. Unfortunately, while Ruth had finished two shepherds' costumes, Harriet had only one item to display. She handed it to her sister.

"This is perfect." Ruth turned it over, admiring it from every side. "It looks like a babe in swaddling clothes. No one will guess that you used Mary's rag doll."

Harriet chuckled. "The real magic is that I didn't have to sew a stitch. Pins did the trick." She doubted she'd ever learn to sew as well as Ruth. Even little Mary demonstrated more skill than she did. But somehow, she had managed to create what looked passably like the baby Jesus.

Ruth returned to the seam she was finishing. "Have the children learned their lines?"

As was the case each evening, conversation revolved around the pageant. Harriet smiled when she realized that most of her conversations, whether at home or at school, concerned it. Though she had envisioned the pageant as a way to occupy her students, it had grown into a project involving the entire town. Parents stopped her on her way to or from school, asking questions about their children's roles. Even adults whose children were either too old or too young for school were curious about Ladreville's first school play.

"Some of them have memorized their lines," Harriet said, answering Ruth's question. "But I suspect that at least a few will forget them at the performance. They'll all be excited about their costumes and the audience." She smiled at her sister. "I'm glad you're willing to be a prompter."

Ruth's needle glinted in the lamplight as she sewed another seam. "Being behind the scenes is no problem," she said firmly. "I think I could even manage to deliver a brief announcement if needed."

"I wouldn't ask you to do that." While it was true that Ruth had changed over the past couple months, becoming more confident and seeming to have overcome her fear of strangers, Harriet wasn't certain how she would handle the strain of having all eyes focused on her. That was far more difficult than pouring punch at the fall festival.

"I know, and I'm grateful." Ruth laid down her needle and thread and flexed her fingers. "This is going to be the best pageant ever."

Harriet couldn't help it. She laughed. "Since it's the first one, that's a certainty. I simply hope there are no major problems." Just as she hoped there would be no problem with the angel's wings she was cutting out for Mary's costume. It would be embarrassing if her own sister's wings were uneven.

"No one will notice, even if there are snags." The way

Ruth was looking at the wings made Harriet suspect she was referring to them as well as forgotten lines and missing props. "The parents are almost as excited as the children. I heard them talking in the mercantile."

"You went to the mercantile?"

Ruth nodded as if it had not been a major undertaking. "I needed a few things for Christmas."

So did Harriet. She had been so engrossed in the pageant that she had not given much thought to gifts for her family. "Did you see anything the boys would like?" Fortunately, she had already ordered several books for Ruth and a doll with a porcelain face for Mary, realizing that her youngest sister was now old enough to put aside her rag doll.

A hint of embarrassment crossed Ruth's face, but her voice was steady as she said, "I knew you'd be busy with the pageant, so I chose their gifts."

Harriet steeled herself not to react. The last time Ruth had been involved in selecting gifts, she had suggested toys that were too old for the others, and she'd burst into tears when Harriet had explained their unsuitability. What had she done this time? But when Ruth listed the items she had chosen, Harriet nodded. It wasn't only Mary who was growing up. Harriet couldn't have done better if she'd tried.

"Perfect," she said, repeating Ruth's term of approbation. As Ruth basked in the compliment, Harriet decided to introduce the subject that had been hovering in the back of her mind ever since she had refused Frau Friedrich's invitation for the Kirks to spend Christmas with them. As much as she enjoyed Frau Friedrich's company, she wouldn't risk ruining Jake's holiday. It would be difficult enough, spending this first Christmas in a new place. At least in Fortune they had been familiar with the town and its customs. "It seems to me that Christmas will be lonely for people without a family."

When she had asked Lawrence how he spent holidays when he was a Ranger, he'd seemed surprised. "They were like every other day," he'd said. "I worked." Harriet doubted this year would be any different, but surely Lawrence deserved more than a solitary meal at the saloon. Though he might not be close to his own family, she was willing to share hers with him.

Ruth nodded. "I imagine it would be. Fortunately, there are few without families in Ladreville." The town hadn't been established long enough for there to be many people without parents, children, or spouses. Even single men like Karl had parents close by, and Granny Menger, who had been the town's sole childless widow, had died the month before the Kirks arrived.

"There are at least two. What do you think about asking Lawrence and Sterling to have dinner with us?" Harriet had feared it might be awkward if Lawrence felt he was being singled out, so she had decided to invite the only other person in Ladreville with whom Ruth was comfortable. "What do you think, Ruth? I know it would mean extra work."

Though Harriet had expected a protest, Ruth shook her head. "Not much extra. I'd still cook the same things, just a bit more. I think it's a good idea. Let's do it."

Lawrence grinned as he strode toward the schoolhouse. There might be a chill in the air, but his heart was warm with anticipation of the time he would spend with Harriet. How glad he was that they were friends again! Despite her sharp tongue—or perhaps because of it—being with her was invigorating. Harriet challenged him as no one else did and made him look at the world from a different view. Today, though, there would be no time to discuss books, for today he planned to show her the newly constructed stable and manger. As the person in charge of the pageant, she needed to approve it. More importantly, he wanted her to see what her brother had accomplished.

For his part, Lawrence had been impressed with Jake's work, and though he hadn't expected to, the truth was, he'd come to care for the boy. Though he could not condone what Jake had done, he understood the young man's frustration. Life had seemed difficult enough when Lawrence was Jake's age. How much worse would it have been if his pa hadn't been there to guide him?

As it was, Jake learned quickly, and once he set aside his unhappiness at being forced into what he used to call slave labor, he had proved to be a reliable worker. It was true that he had not evidenced much contrition, and Lawrence still wasn't certain what had provoked the destruction of Karl's buggy, but one thing he did know was that the boy needed attention and a man to influence him. For the time being, he was that man. As for the future . . . Lawrence wasn't certain what it would hold or even what he wanted it to be. What mattered was the present. This was his time with Harriet, and Lawrence planned to savor every minute.

She was waiting when he entered the schoolhouse, her coat buttoned, her hat firmly placed on her head. As she greeted him, Harriet tugged on her gloves.

"I'm glad to see you're wearing those." Lawrence nodded toward the mittens. "You'll need them today. It feels cold enough to snow."

She raised an eyebrow. "Does it do that here?"

"From what I've heard, not often, but it's also not impossible." As she preceded him down the steps, he apologized for his lack of a carriage. Since the Ladres had taken both their wagon and buggy when they left town, Lawrence had only his horse. It was, he had assured Clay when he'd been hired, sufficient for his needs, and that was true. Normally. But today it would have been nice to have been able to offer Harriet a ride.

She smiled and took a deep breath of the cool air. "I enjoy walking. Don't you?"

"Not very much," Lawrence admitted. Walking had been for those who couldn't afford a horse. But now, with Harriet's hand on his arm, he was beginning to reconsider his opinion. "We lived far enough from town that I rode to school." He continued his explanation as they turned left onto Rhinestrasse. Their destination was halfway between Hochstrasse and rue du Marché on Potomac Street. While it was slightly shorter to take Hochstrasse, Lawrence preferred the less traveled rue du Marché, reasoning that there would be fewer interruptions there than on the main street.

"I guess you could say that I lived on a horse." Was it his imagination, or did Harriet tighten her grip ever so slightly? Whether or not she had, it was definitely pleasant, feeling her fingers on his arm. A man could get used to this.

"My brothers are very impressed with your horse." Harriet's tone was as casual ever. The additional pressure must have been his imagination. "He's the first palomino they've seen."

"Snip's a good mount. He's gotten me through some tight spots." Though many of the Rangers had lamented the government's failure to provide horses, Lawrence had been glad that he'd been able to select Snip. A horse was a bit like a wife. Not just any one would do. "Snip saved my life once."

This time there was no doubt about it. Harriet tightened her grip and slowed her pace so she could look up at him. When she did, her eyes sparkled with mirth. "Be careful not to say something like that around Daniel and Sam. They'll insist that you tell them the whole story."

"They're good boys." But they were also easily impressed. Lawrence suspected that was the reason Harriet was warning him: she didn't want their heads filled with tales of life as a Ranger. He couldn't blame her. Perhaps if he hadn't heard so many stories of brave and daring deeds, he would not have joined the Rangers. But if he hadn't, he might never have met Harriet. That was not a pleasant thought.

"They are good boys," she agreed as they turned onto rue du Marché. "I haven't had problems with them. Of course, they're still young. Jake's wild streak didn't start until he was twelve." Harriet frowned. "That's Sam's age."

"I think Jake is learning his lesson. If I'm right, the younger boys will learn from his experiences, and you won't have the same problems with them."

"I hope so. Jake seems happier lately." Harriet paused to greet Frau Bauer as she left the market. When the older woman was out of earshot, Harriet continued. "I know that's thanks to you. I suspect Jake would be angry if he knew I was saying this, but it's obvious to me that he looks up to you. Thank you, Lawrence. You've helped my brother in ways I could not."

Pleasure rushed through Lawrence. Was this how knights of yore felt when they'd slain a dragon? "I was only doing my job."

Harriet wrinkled her nose. "Perhaps. Or perhaps you were giving a fatherless boy a bit of parental guidance."

"Jake doesn't want a father." And Lawrence didn't want a nearly grown son. "I'd like to think I was serving as an older brother."

"Whatever you call it, you've set a good example and taught him some valuable lessons. I don't know what we'll do when you leave. I know your contract ends in January."

"That's true." Oddly, Lawrence hadn't thought about the end of his term recently. At one point, he had been counting the weeks until his contract was over. Now he found himself thinking about the construction of the bridge and the speech he knew he'd have to deliver at the Independence Day celebration. He'd even wondered whether Harriet would change the format of the Christmas pageant next year.

He gave her a reassuring smile. "I won't leave until Jake has paid for Karl's buggy and I've caught Zach Webster's rustlers. I owe you both that much."

"Thank you." Harriet's lips quirked in a wry smile. "My grandmother taught me not to pry, but one question's been bothering me ever since my family and I arrived here, and only you can answer it."

Lawrence slowed their pace, not wanting to arrive at the carpentry shop until they'd finished this discussion. He wasn't certain what surprised him most, the fact that something had perplexed Harriet or that she had waited so long to ask. "What is it?"

"Your contract." Color rose to her cheeks, as if the question embarrassed her. "Why is it so short? I thought most contracts were like mine, for at least a year."

He should have known that she'd recognize the discrepancy.

Lawrence was silent for a moment, debating what to tell her. "I insisted on the short time frame," he told her. Deciding that she deserved the whole truth, he added, "I didn't want to come to Ladreville, because it reminded me of a down-right embarrassing time in my life." When she said nothing, simply looked up at him with those big gray eyes, he said, "I had been infatuated with a woman, and I didn't want to have to face her again."

"Priscilla." It was a statement, not a question.

"How did you know?"

"Things were awkward between you two the night we all had supper at the Canfields' ranch. Ruth thought you were in love with her."

Lawrence shook his head, determined that Harriet under-stand. "Never. I confused sympathy with love, but I was never in love with Priscilla. It was like a schoolboy's infatuation, nothing more serious. For a while, though, the very thought of how I'd acted made me cringe."

He'd expected her to murmur something sympathetic. What he didn't expect was Harriet's saying, "I know. I made the same mistake myself. At first I believed I was in love, but then I realized how mistaken I'd been, and I felt like a fool."

"You could never be a fool."

She chuckled. "I hope to never repeat the experience, but, yes, Lawrence, I was a fool. I thought he loved me."

Though she laughed again, this time it was a brittle laugh, and Lawrence heard the undercurrent of pain. They had reached the end of rue du Marché and turned right onto Potomac, leaving only a hundred yards to William Goetz's shop. Though Lawrence wanted to say something, anything, so that Harriet knew she was loveable, the timing was all

257

wrong. This was neither the time nor the place for a declaration of his feelings.

As his eyes adjusted to the comparative darkness, Lawrence heard Jake's voice. "Harriet, what are you doing here?" Surprise mingled with what sounded like annoyance. Did Jake find his sister's visit an intrusion? Though the carpenter's shop was open to the public, and members of the community would wander in to view William's projects, Lawrence hadn't considered the possibility that Jake might not want Harriet to see him at work.

"I thought she should see what you've done." Lawrence emphasized the first word, trying to ensure that Jake knew Harriet was not to blame. Though she was smiling again, he did not want to be responsible for causing her any more pain.

"All right." Though Jake's voice sounded grudging, Lawrence heard the undercurrent of fear and realized that he was nervous. He wanted Harriet's approval but wasn't certain he would receive it.

"Back here." Jake led the way to the rear of the shop. As they passed him, the town's carpenter looked up and nodded briefly, then returned his attention to the chest he was constructing. "Here it is." Casually, as if Harriet's opinion mattered not a whit, Jake gestured toward the stable he'd built.

His sister's response was instantaneous. "Oh, Jake!" Harriet ran her hand over one side of the small building. "This is so much more than I expected." Though the shape was unmistakable, instead of the crudely hewn planks that might have formed a working stable, this one boasted finely finished wood. Ducking her head as she entered the child-sized building, Harriet crouched down to touch the manger. "It's beautiful."

William Goetz laid down his plane and joined the others. Of medium height with light brown hair and eyes, the carpenter had no distinctive features, and yet when he smiled, a man knew he could trust him. That was one of the reasons Lawrence had asked him to employ Jake.

"This young man shows promise," William told Harriet, placing a proprietary hand on her brother's shoulder. "If he wants to become a carpenter, I would be willing to have him apprentice with me."

Jake's intake of breath told Lawrence this was the first he'd heard of the offer. It was a generous one, for William had been one of the citizens who hadn't wanted Jake inside his shop for fear the boy would destroy it. It had taken Lawrence's personal pledge of restitution before William agreed to train Jake.

Harriet gave the carpenter a warm smile before flashing another at Lawrence. "Thank you both," she said, her expression lighter than Lawrence had seen it in weeks.

"What about me? Don't I deserve some thanks?" The boy in question put his hands on his hips and glared at his sister. "I did the work."

"Yes, you did. Thank you, Jake." She gave the manger another soft pat before she left the stable. "This will make the pageant extra special. What a talented brother I have."

A flush colored Jake's face, and he dipped his head in embarrassment. "So, Mr. Wood," he said in an obvious attempt to deflect the attention from himself, "are you looking forward to Christmas at our house? Ruth's mincemeat pie is the best."

Christmas at the Kirk house? What was Jake talking about? Lawrence turned toward Harriet, his raised eyebrows telegraphing his questions.

She shrugged. "I had planned to invite you, but Jake has beaten me to it." Harriet gave her brother a fond look before her gaze settled back on Lawrence. "My family and I request the pleasure of your company on Christmas Day." She delivered the invitation with admirable formality, her diction reminding Lawrence of the descriptions of town criers in several of the books she'd lent him. Before he could reply, she added, "As Jake said, Ruth's pies are delicious, and so is the rest of her meal."

Lawrence swallowed deeply as he considered the generosity of Harriet's offer. Other than the day when he'd ordered the surprise for Harriet, deciding it would be an ideal Christmas gift, he hadn't thought much about the holiday. It was true it would be his first in Ladreville, his first as the town's mayor and sheriff, but he had assumed he would spend it as he had the past three or four Christmases: alone. Thanks to Harriet, he would not. Perhaps she was only being neighborly. Perhaps this was her way of thanking him for helping Jake. Then again, perhaps the invitation meant that she enjoyed his company as much as he did hers. Lawrence could only hope that was the case.

"Are you certain?"

Harriet nodded. "Yes. We all want you to come. Isn't that right, Jake?"

The boy scuffed the floor with his toe, releasing the pungent smell of freshly cut wood as his boot crushed some shavings. "Yeah. I mean, yes, ma'am." Confused, Jake added, "Yes, sir." When no one spoke, he blurted out, "Yes, somebody." Laughter met his words.

"Thank you. I'd be honored." Lawrence felt his spirits rise. The Ladreville grapevine, which prided itself on its accuracy,

260

must be wrong. It appeared that Karl was not courting Harriet, for if he were, surely they would spend Christmas Day together.

Lawrence grinned.

～

"Oh, Miss Kirk, the pageant was wonderful," Madame Seurat gushed. The first performance had ended, and the parents gathered in the back of the French church to congratulate the players.

Though she knew they would be tempted to rush toward their parents, Harriet had insisted that the children leave single file, starting with the youngest members of the cast.

"But this isn't school," Eva had wailed, obviously anxious for Isabelle and Gunther's praise.

"It's important to have an orderly exit, no matter where you are," Harriet had explained. As more groans ensued, she relented and allowed them to leave in pairs. She waited until the children had had some time for felicitations before she walked toward the narthex, where she was soon surrounded by adults.

"I don't know how to thank you," Madame Seurat continued. "Marie was thrilled to be one of the angels. Her papa and I call her our little angel, but seeing her in that costume . . ." Her voice broke. "Why, it brought tears to my eyes. I can't thank you enough."

Half an hour later, when the Frenchwoman's praise had been repeated dozens of times and the church was beginning to empty, Lawrence made his way to Harriet's side. "Everyone seems to think this was the best idea since Ladreville was founded," he said softly.

Though she felt as limp as a wet rag, Harriet managed a smile. The performance had gone well. The French church had been packed with proud parents and curious townspeople, none of whom seemed to notice the mistakes. It had been good that Ruth was seated behind the pulpit to prompt the children, because, as Harriet had predicted, a number forgot their lines. One shepherd dropped his crook, and a wise man carried his gift upside down. But those were minor imperfections, and no one minded. What mattered was that Ladreville's children had taken part in a story of timeless beauty.

Harriet looked up at Lawrence and smiled. Dressed in his Sunday finery, he was by far the most handsome man in town. Of course, it didn't matter what he wore. Even in workday clothes, he was the most handsome man in town. "I couldn't have done it without you."

"Jake did the work."

Harriet disagreed. "I wasn't simply referring to the stable and the manger." Although they had been widely admired after the performance. She had watched her brother preen when several of the men had clapped him on the shoulder in approbation. "I heard how you convinced the townspeople to create a pageant fund so that Isabelle's parents were repaid for their goods and William didn't have to donate the wood. That was very kind of you, Lawrence."

"The pageant is for everyone in Ladreville. I thought everyone should have a chance to be part of it." He shrugged as if the task of convincing the town to loosen their purse strings had been insignificant. Harriet was certain it had not been easy, particularly this year when they'd already agreed to an extra assessment to construct the bridge and when stories of the Panic made people more cautious than normal.

The country's widespread financial worries were part of the reason Harriet was grateful that the Rousseaus and William Goetz would be reimbursed for their costs.

"Once again, I don't know how to thank you."

"I'm your friend," Lawrence said, looking down at the petite woman who figured in so many of his dreams. "Friends help friends."

"Then thank you, friend."

Harriet extended her hand. Though he knew she meant for him to shake it, Lawrence raised it to his lips and pressed a kiss on the back. It wasn't what he wanted to do. What he wanted was to draw her into his arms and hold her close; what he wanted was to kiss her lips and caress her soft skin, but this was not the time or place.

18

Thomas frowned at the sound of church bells. It was all her fault. Here it was, Christmas Eve. He should have been home, sleeping in a warm bed. Instead he was halfway between Ladreville and Fortune in a town so small he didn't bother to learn its name, watching people stream into the church. He knew what the minister would say, for he'd heard Uncle Abe recite the story so often he had it memorized. They'd all smile at the story of a babe in Bethlehem, and then they'd sing hymns, praising the infant Jesus. And when it was over, they'd go home to succulent feasts, while he was stuck out here, facing another night of sleeping on the cold ground.

Thomas slowed his horse as he considered his actions. What he needed was money, but it didn't look like anyone in this miserable town had much. Oh, he could search a few houses, looking for a hidden stash, but there was no point in risking being caught, not when it seemed there wasn't enough silver here to matter. Still, there was no reason to sleep outdoors tonight. If he played his cards right, he could get a hot meal and a soft bed. Christmas made folks generous. When they learned his plight, the tale of a man with no place to sleep would remind them of the story they'd just heard, the one about a family forced to stay in a stable because there was no room at the inn. He nodded. That's what he'd do. Hitching his horse, he made his way into the crowded church.

An hour later, Thomas grinned. The ploy had worked exactly as he'd expected. In truth, it had worked far better than he'd expected. He'd chosen a seat next to a couple with graying hair and no children nearby. Experience told him they'd be the easiest marks. When they'd introduced themselves after the service, he'd let slip the fact that he was passing through, embellishing the story with the tale of his horse's injury keeping him from spending this holy night with his invalid uncle. They'd believed it, lock, stock, and barrel. Before he could say "Merry Christmas," they'd invited him to follow them home. That was what he'd hoped for. But they had given him something else—something far more important than a night's rest. As they'd left the church, the woman had murmured to her husband.

"We need to stop at the school," the old man, who turned out to be the schoolmaster, explained. "My wife wants to be sure we have enough candles." The words were innocent. The schoolmaster and his wife had no way of knowing that they'd triggered new thoughts in Thomas's mind. The school. Things stored there. Of course. That was where Harriet had hid her money. He'd been looking in the wrong place. Exultation raced through his veins. Tomorrow morning he'd head back to Ladreville, and this time he wouldn't be leaving empty-handed. No, sirree.

Thomas grinned. You couldn't ask for a better Christmas gift than that.

～❦

"I'll get it." The excitement in Ruth's voice when she heard the knock on the door made Harriet turn from the table she was arranging and study her sister. Today Ruth looked prettier than ever, but that, Harriet suspected, was not because of her new dress, nor did the flush that colored her face owe much to the heat of the oven. Ever since they'd decided to invite Lawrence and Sterling to spend Christmas Day with them, Ruth had seemed more animated than Harriet could remember. Today, she was practically sparkling as she tossed her pinafore aside and rushed to the front door.

She was too slow.

"Merry Christmas!" Mary tugged the door open and greeted the family's guests. The gust of cool air mingled with the heady scents of pine and candle wax. Though Harriet would not allow the candles on the tree to burn all night, as Isabelle had said was the custom in Ladreville, she had agreed that they could be lighted during the day, so long as someone was nearby.

"Merry Christmas." Sterling and Lawrence formed a duet as Ruth ushered them into the parlor.

Harriet laid the last plate on the table and joined the rest of the family in time to hear Mary shriek. "Presents! You brought presents!" She pointed toward the bulging sack that Lawrence carried.

Harriet stared at the tall, handsome man who was grinning like a schoolboy. When she'd seen him earlier today at the Christmas morning service, he had said nothing about presents. "Oh, Lawrence, you shouldn't have." While it was true that she had wrapped a gift for him, suspecting it might be the only one he would receive, she had not expected him to bring anything.

Unexpected tears pricked her eyelids, and her heart warmed at the thought that Lawrence had taken the time to choose items for her family. His gifts would help make the day special.

Lawrence shrugged, the action emphasizing the breadth of his shoulders. Though his frock coat was not the latest style, a point Isabelle had made the first time she had seen him in church, Harriet thought it suited him. Lawrence did not need fashion to enhance his rugged good looks.

He gave Harriet a quick smile. "Sterling and I wanted to express our gratitude for being included in your holiday." When the expression on the minister's face said he knew nothing about the packages Lawrence had deposited near the tree, the warmth that had gathered in Harriet's heart spread throughout her body. How kind it was for Lawrence to pretend that Sterling had been part of the gift-buying process. Though others might consider him brusque and intimidating, this was the true Lawrence: thoughtful and generous. This was the same man who'd sent tingles all the way to her shoulder when he'd pressed his lips to the back of her hand. Harriet had lain awake most of that night reliving not the pageant but Lawrence's kiss. Now he was here in her home, sharing this special day. Truly, it was good that she'd brought her family to Ladreville, for how else would she have met this wonderful man?

"Can we open them now?" Daniel stared at the packages beneath the tree as if he didn't trust Mary, who had plunked herself next to them, not to open his. Sam's grin told Harriet he had urged his brother to ask the question, while the gleam in Jake's eye gave lie to his feigned nonchalance. Only Ruth paid no heed to the gifts. Her gaze was fixed on the young minister.

Harriet nodded. Though the food was ready to be served, it would not spoil if they waited half an hour. Besides, it was obvious that the younger Kirks were too excited to enjoy even the best of meals. As she settled into one of the wingbacked chairs on one side of the rug, smiling when Lawrence took its companion, Harriet watched her siblings arrange themselves. Ruth perched on the edge of a wooden chair, perhaps because it was the closest to the horsehair sofa where she'd suggested Sterling sit. The other children positioned themselves on the floor only inches from the tree and the packages that so intrigued them.

Contentment rose within Harriet as she thought about the day she had once dreaded. So far, it had been amazingly pleasant. Sterling's sermon had stirred the congregation as he'd asked them to reflect on what Mary and Joseph had felt that Christmas Day almost two thousand years ago. "What do you suppose it was like," he asked, "once the angels and the shepherds left? New parents are always nervous, worrying that they won't know how to care for their child. What must it have been like, knowing this was no ordinary baby?" Harriet had smiled as Isabelle gripped Gunther's hand, no doubt thinking of her impending motherhood.

"Do you suppose Jesus spilled milk?" Mary asked when they returned home. Fortunately, there had been no spilled milk or squabbling as the family ate breakfast, despite the fact that the youngest three were visibly anxious for their presents. Even opening the gifts had been more pleasant than normal, for Ruth's choices had been excellent, filling each of the children with delight. Though Harriet had feared otherwise, it appeared that no one regretted not being in Fortune today. She certainly did not.

As Sterling distributed the packages Lawrence had brought, consulting the tag on each to deliver it to the correct member of the Kirk family, Ruth's smile broadened, and in that moment, she was beautiful.

"Look, Harriet!" Mary held out the bonnet that was a perfect match for the dress her new doll wore. When Harriet gave Lawrence a questioning look, he mouthed the words "Madame Rousseau." It appeared that Isabelle's mother had told him of the doll Harriet had ordered for her youngest sister. But the boys' gifts—jacks for Daniel, a cribbage board for Sam, and a chisel for Jake—were not Madame Rousseau's selections. Harriet knew that as surely as she knew the boys would treasure their presents. She smiled, hoping Lawrence would read her approval of his choices.

"We can't forget our hostesses," he said. In response, Sterling handed Ruth a small bag, while Lawrence held out a flat package to Harriet.

Though Ruth quickly opened the bag and exclaimed over the sweets it contained, Harriet was loath to unwrap her gift. Whatever it was, she wanted to savor the moment. She turned toward her youngest sister. "Mary, I think you'll find two packages on the other side of the tree." Harriet had placed them there when the family had finished opening their gifts. "Would you bring them to me?" She handed Ruth the one for Sterling and watched, bemused, as both her sister and the minister blushed when their hands touched.

Sterling studied the package, turning it over in his hands as if he were considering what the contents might be, though the size and shape indicated it could only be a book. "The gift of your company is more than enough. I don't need a present."

Leaning forward, Ruth shook her head. "Please open it. I chose it for you."

His flush deepened as he unwrapped the book. "St. Thomas of Aquinas." Sterling's tone was reverent as he admired the leather binding. "What a fine edition!"

"It was our grandfather's," Ruth explained. "I thought you might enjoy it."

"Oh, I will." He leaned forward so that his head was practically touching Ruth's, and the two began to converse quietly. With the other children engrossed with their new toys and Ruth and Sterling occupied, Harriet could almost imagine that she was alone with Lawrence.

"This is for you." She handed him the remaining gift.

Though he accepted it, he made no move to unwrap it. "Please open yours first. I hope I wasn't mistaken when I chose it."

Unlike his gift and Sterling's, which were clearly books, the contents of Harriet's package were not obvious. Slowly, so she could extend the moment, she untied the ribbon and slid the paper away, then carefully opened the box. "Oh, Lawrence!" Harriet gasped at the contents. It was a book, but what a book! "I've never had anything like this." She stroked the cover, admiring the embossed leaves and vines, then smiled at the pictures of flowers that graced its pages. The artist's skill was undeniable. "They look so real that I can almost smell them."

Lawrence's eyes sparkled, and she saw that her words had pleased him. "You said you liked flowers, so I thought you might enjoy looking at this, especially during the winter when nothing is blooming."

"It's perfect." She spoke softly, not wanting the others to intrude into her conversation with Lawrence. "I couldn't have wished for anything better." When his smile broadened, she gestured toward the package he still held. "It's your turn now. I'm sure you've already figured out that it's a book."

"I did have a slight suspicion," he admitted with a mischievous grin. "The title will be the surprise." He grinned again at the words embossed on the cover. "*The Aeneid*." Lawrence opened to the first page and began to read, "'Arms and the man I sing.' I've heard of Virgil's epic poem," he admitted, "but I've never read it."

"Like Sterling's gift, it's another one of my grandfather's books. I hope you don't mind that it's not new." Though she tried not to let her nervousness show, Harriet could not disguise the slight trembling of her voice. She had hoped Lawrence would like his gift, but now, faced with the beautiful new items he'd given her family, she wondered whether she had made a mistake.

He waited until she met his gaze before he spoke, and when he did, Lawrence's eyes shone with sincerity. "To the contrary, the book is more valuable because of its age and history." He fingered the leather binding and smiled. "I feel as if you've given me a part of yourself."

Harriet drew in a deep breath, then returned his smile. Thank goodness, she had not made a mistake. She had chosen *The Aeneid* for a number of reasons. First, it had one of the most beautiful bindings in her grandfather's collection. Secondly, as a story of heroic deeds and great adventure, she thought it would appeal to Lawrence. It might even remind him of his days as a Ranger. But most of all, Harriet had selected it because it was one of her favorite tales and she wanted to share it with Lawrence.

Grandpa had had a copy in the original Latin, but this one, which he had acquired soon after they moved to Texas, was English. Since Harriet doubted that Lawrence read Latin, the choice of edition had been simple. What she had questioned was whether he would enjoy the story. Now, seeing his reaction to the gift, she was hopeful that he would.

The afternoon passed more quickly than Harriet had thought possible. Though they lingered at the dinner table for over an hour, savoring the meal Ruth had worked so hard to prepare, and then spent several more hours in the parlor, watching the boys play with their new toys while the adults conversed quietly, it seemed as if only a few minutes had gone by when Sterling rose and declared it time to leave.

"I'd better go too." Lawrence stood, extending his hand to help Harriet rise. Surely it was her imagination that he held it a bit longer than necessary, that he pressed it tighter than convention demanded. Oh, her traitorous imagination! Ever since the night when he'd kissed her hand, she had been filled with memories of how sweet that had felt and wishes that he would repeat it. Harriet's face flushed as she admitted her dreams had been for more than a simple repetition. She had dreamt of Lawrence kissing not her hand but her lips. Foolish, foolish Harriet! Lawrence was her friend. A good friend, it was true, but merely a friend.

"What a wonderful day." Ruth sighed with pleasure after she closed the door behind the two men.

It had been wonderful. The day that had begun so well had continued to improve. Everyone seemed happy, and Ruth . . .

well, the change in Ruth could only be called miraculous. Harriet's formerly reclusive sister had been almost vivacious this afternoon, laughing and actually initiating conversation. The difference was so dramatic that it brought to mind a butterfly emerging from its chrysalis. What could have caused the change? Harriet thought back over the day's events, recalling the flush that had colored her sister's cheeks when Lawrence and Sterling had arrived and the way she had smiled when she and Sterling had conversed. Was he the cause? She knew they were friends, but perhaps there was more than friendship. Could it be that her sister harbored tender feelings for the minister?

Harriet frowned. Though many girls were married by the time they reached Ruth's age, her sister's life had been so sheltered that Harriet did not believe she was ready for such a change. And, if she were being truthful, she wasn't ready, either. Ruth was an integral part of the family. What would they do without her? Suddenly, the bright and shiny, almost perfect day lost its sheen.

Despite efforts to regain her earlier pleasure, when night fell, Harriet was still feeling disgruntled. Realizing there was no point in inflicting her malaise on the rest of the family, she grabbed her cloak and headed outside. Perhaps a brisk walk would restore her spirits. Instead of turning down rue du Marché, as she normally did, tonight she wanted to walk beside the river, and so she continued along Rhinestrasse, not even slowing when she passed the school.

"May I join you?"

Harriet spun around, her spirits rising as fast as Independence Day fireworks at the sound of Lawrence's voice. "Please do." The gloomy thoughts that had plagued her fled, replaced by a swift rush of pleasure.

Harriet smiled as he crooked his arm, inviting her to tuck her hand into it. "We can turn around," she offered. "I was going to walk by the river, but there's no need to do that." Though gently flowing water soothed her, she knew it had the opposite effect on Lawrence.

"I don't mind as long as you stay close to me. You'll be safe if you're holding on to me."

She would indeed, for his arm was strong and comforting, giving her the sensation of being next to a bulwark. There was no danger of falling into the water while she was clasping Lawrence's arm.

When they reached the river, they turned left, heading in the same direction they had taken the night of the fall festival. Tonight, though, there were no sounds of revelers in the distance, nothing but the normal squeaks and slithers of nocturnal creatures.

"I want to thank you again for your invitation," Lawrence said as they strolled slowly along the Medina's bank. "This was the best Christmas I can recall."

Now that she was with him, that was true for her once again. Being with Lawrence restored her equilibrium and revived memories of the happy day. "I feel that way too," Harriet said, tightening her grip on his arm ever so slightly. Though she did not need the physical support, the warmth that emanated from his sleeve reassured her. "I was a little worried about my family, wondering if they'd miss Fortune. They don't have a lot of happy memories of it, but it was the only home they've known." Harriet laughed softly as she said, "My grandmother used to claim that Christmas is the season of miracles. Perhaps it is, because my family was more content than I've ever seen them."

"Perhaps that's because Ladreville has become their home."

"Perhaps." Harriet smiled at the thought. The events of the last month, even Thomas's unwelcome visit, had made her realize that this was her home. She had no desire to leave, especially when she had friends like Isabelle and Lawrence. "I hope that's true. It would be good if they were all happy, but right now that doesn't matter. What matters is that today was a perfect day."

Lawrence stopped and looked down at her, his eyes sparkling with an emotion she could not identify. Though the night was cool and the breeze off the river penetrated Harriet's cloak, Lawrence's expression was as warm as the summer sun. "Not perfect, but close. There is one thing that would make it better."

The look on his face made Harriet's heart skip a beat. "What is that?" Her words emerged as little more than a croak.

Lawrence smiled, and then, as slowly as if he had all the time in the world, he slid his arms around Harriet. Drawing her closer, he smiled again. "This," he murmured as he pressed his lips to hers.

19

"I can't believe it's already 1858." Isabelle shook her head as she poured a cup of coffee for Harriet. The two women were seated in Isabelle's kitchen, where Harriet had come after school.

"The holiday passed quickly." Though the memory of how Christmas Day had ended lingered, Harriet would not tell Isabelle about that. Lawrence's kiss was something she hugged to herself, not wanting to spoil it by sharing it with anyone. Even now, when she knew no one could see her, she would press her fingers to her lips, recalling how firm his lips had been, how their touch had sent sensations flooding through her. Though the kiss had lasted only seconds, the memory was indelibly etched on her brain.

"I was surprised that the students were glad to come back to school after Christmas." She needed to talk about ordinary things, not the extraordinary pleasure she had found in Lawrence's arms.

Isabelle pushed a plate of cookies toward Harriet. "The

novelty of new toys wears off quickly unless they can share them with others."

Harriet nodded. With Christmas being on a Friday, the children had had three days without school. When they had returned, many had brought their favorite gift, wanting to show it to their friends. "The children didn't even complain about nothing growing in the garden. I think they've forgotten it." And Harriet wasn't complaining about that. It was good that her pupils had other things to occupy them.

"Eva hasn't forgotten. She's simply more concerned about her baby brothers."

Harriet couldn't help smiling, for Eva had announced to the entire school that she was going to have two baby brothers. She had even declared that one would be named Harry in honor of Harriet. "I'm practicing so I can take care of a real baby," she had confided when she showed Harriet the baby doll she had received for Christmas.

"What will Eva do if one of the babies is a girl?"

"The same thing we all will. Love her." Her smile fading, Isabelle continued. "I only wish Gunther weren't so worried."

"He's still concerned about your confinement?"

The lovely brunette nodded.

"You're healthy, and Priscilla is an accomplished midwife." Harriet had heard tales of how she'd delivered a breech baby without assistance. Surely twins would be easier than that. "Besides, there's always Clay. The grapevine says he's a first-rate doctor."

Isabelle took another bite of cookie, chewing thoughtfully before she said, "It's probably just my nerves. Maman said ladies in a family way have strange worries and cravings. Still, I can't help wishing the bridge was already finished."

"Why are you so worried?" This was the first time Harriet had heard Isabelle mention the bridge.

"Because both Priscilla and Clay are on the opposite side of the river. What if they can't get to me in time to deliver the babies?"

Harriet reached across the table and squeezed her friend's hand. "Stop worrying, Isabelle. That won't happen."

"Did you hear the news?" Zach asked without preamble as he strode into Lawrence's office. "Rustlers struck Herr Plaut's ranch. Took a dozen head of cattle."

Lawrence rose from behind the desk. Zach's announcement was of far more importance than reading the wanted posters that had arrived in today's mail. Besides, it might help him stop thinking about Christmas night and the way Harriet's lips had felt. Ever since that night, he'd been able to think of little else.

"I don't like the sound of that." Herr Plaut lived near Golden, the closest town, making his ranch less than ten miles from Ladreville. "A dozen isn't enough for most thieves. They could be coming this way." Everyone in this part of Texas knew of Zach's cattle.

Zach scratched his nose and frowned. "That's what I thought. I sure would like to catch them this time."

Lawrence's pulse accelerated at the prospect of stopping the raids once and for all. This was why he'd been hired, to keep the people of Ladreville and their livelihoods safe.

"Looks like it's time for another stakeout. If they want

your cattle, my guess is the bandits will hit within the next three days. The new moon's tonight, and that'll give them the greatest cover of darkness."

Zach nodded. "I'll tell Priscilla I won't be home for a few days."

And I'll tell Harriet.

༺

When was that blasted woman going to leave? Thomas crouched behind one of the large oak trees and glared at the school. The pupils had been gone for half an hour now, all thirty or so of those screaming monsters. What was she waiting for? Was she counting the money? That was the only reason Thomas could imagine for her staying in that little building.

If she didn't go home before the sun set, he'd be stuck here for another day, because there were some things that could not be done after dark, and searching the school was one of them. He couldn't risk lighting a lantern and alerting others to his presence, especially since his legs were still wobbly. Though the old couple claimed it was the grippe, Thomas blamed the Christmas goose they served him for the fever and the ailment that had turned his insides out and left him writhing in pain for more than a week. Even when food no longer turned his stomach, he'd been too weak to walk, and so he'd remained another four days to regain his strength, and all the while, he'd fumed, thinking of the gold and silver waiting for him.

At last the door opened and Harriet descended the steps. Another minute and he could go inside. Another two minutes, and he would be a rich man. Thomas's palms started

279

to tingle at the thought of holding all that money, but as he kept his eyes fixed on Harriet, he frowned. What was she doing? Though she had seemed in a hurry when she'd exited the school, now she stood at the bottom of the steps, almost as if she was waiting for someone.

He looked around, his heart pounding when he saw a man striding briskly toward the school. Though he hadn't met the man, he knew who he was. You didn't have to spend more than five minutes in this miserable town to hear about its most famous resident: mayor, sheriff, former Ranger Lawrence Wood. Why was the sheriff coming here? He couldn't—no, he couldn't possibly—be looking for Thomas. The lump that settled in Thomas's gut gave lie to his brave words, but it began to dissolve when he saw that the sheriff was smiling. Lawmen didn't smile when they were on a man's trail. So why was Sheriff Lawrence Wood looking so happy?

The answer wasn't hard to find. Grouchy old Harriet, the woman who would hardly give Thomas the time of day, took a step toward the sheriff, linking her arm with his, smiling at him as if he were the most wonderful creature on earth. How could she? Thomas clenched his fists and pounded on the tree trunk. Harriet had never smiled at him that way. That lowdown, conniving, cheating woman. She would pay for this.

He waited until they were gone. No point in tempting fate. But once he could no longer see them, Thomas hurried up the steps and entered the school. The money had to be here. He'd find it, and then he'd find a way to punish Miss High and Mighty Harriet Kirk.

An hour later, Thomas could no longer deny the facts. There was no money. There was nothing but books and papers and ink. Nothing. Nothing at all.

He kicked one of the desks, wincing when his toe hurt. She hadn't been lying. The nasty-mouthed woman who had refused to marry him didn't have any money. Thomas kicked the desk again, wishing it was Harriet's face. The last two times he'd seen her she had said she never wanted to see him again. That was fine with him. He didn't want to see her, either, but one thing was certain: he would see to it that Harriet never forgot him. It was time to get even.

He looked around, searching for some way to hurt her. He could destroy those books she thought were so precious. That would rile her. She might even shed a tear for them. But that wasn't enough. Not when he was facing Mr. Allen's demands. Thomas would shed more than tears if Herb Allen's men caught up with him. He'd be shedding blood, and it was all Harriet's fault. She should have married him. She should have given him money. But she hadn't, and now she would pay.

Thomas's eye lit on the stove. The thing Harriet feared most was fire. He grinned. Perfect. He would give that miserable woman the biggest fire of her life.

ॐ

"Did you hear that?" Lawrence whispered the question.

In the darkness he saw Zach nod. "Sounds like horses to me." The two men were camped in the same cave they'd used before, with branches concealing the entrance, their horses hobbled inside with them. Though it was only the first night of their stakeout, it appeared the wait was over. Zach's cattle had proven irresistible.

Lawrence tamped down the rush of energy that always accompanied a fight, reminding himself that patience often paid excellent dividends. Unhobbling Snip, he said, "Let's let 'em

281

all get into the valley. I want to catch them red-handed." If he and Zach did it properly, when these rustlers were brought to justice, there would be no question of their guilt. The culprits might not hang, but they wouldn't see the light of day for a good number of years.

Lawrence positioned himself at the mouth of the cave, watching as the rustlers snuck into the defile. Though he'd expected more, it appeared there were only two of them. Either they were mighty good at rounding up cattle or these two were working alone. That could explain why they'd taken a mere dozen steers from Herr Plaut. A real roundup required more hands.

As the men circled the herd, Lawrence nodded at Zach. "Now!"

Within seconds, they were on horseback, their rifles ready. The rustlers had no chance, for Lawrence and Zach blocked the narrow defile, leaving their quarry no easy escape. "Hold it right there. Drop your guns." Lawrence almost laughed at the intruders' surprised expressions when they saw themselves facing the wrong end of two rifles. Though both of them sported six-shooters on their hips, they had no time to draw. As the six-shooters hit the ground, Lawrence moved Snip between the rustlers and their weapons. "All right, now. Get off." They'd lost their right to ride fine horseflesh.

While Zach kept his rifle pointed at the bandits, Lawrence dismounted and tied their hands behind their backs. "Recognize these varmints?" he asked Zach as he wrapped a rope around each man's waist and tied them to Snip. The would-be rustlers were going to have a mighty long walk tonight.

Zach nodded. "They own the ranch next to Herr Plaut. I heard they'd fallen on hard times."

"Was that it, boys?" Lawrence asked. "Did you figure this would be an easy way to increase your herd?" Though neither one struck Lawrence as being overly bright, they had enough sense to keep their mouths shut. Lawrence looked over at Zach. "I've got a mind to string them from one of these trees, but I reckon the judge should have his say."

The way Zach's mouth twitched told Lawrence he recognized the bluff and was enjoying the rustlers' reaction. Suddenly the prospect of walking ten miles didn't seem so bad, when the alternative was a swift hanging.

By midafternoon, the rustlers were in jail, Herr Plaut was happy to have his cattle recovered, and Golden's sheriff had agreed with Lawrence's suggestion that they and two other neighboring towns band together against future rustlers.

"I guess it's true," Zach said as he and Lawrence headed back to Ladreville. "The Rangers always get their men."

Lawrence raised his face to let the weak January sun warm it. "I'm not a Ranger any longer." If he were, perhaps he would not have this strange feeling deep inside him. Perhaps the wind, which continued to intensify, would not feel as if it were bringing ill fortune along with dried leaves. Perhaps he would not harbor the fear that he was too late for something important.

"You may not be a Ranger," Zach countered, "but you did what you promised. You caught the rustlers. Thanks to you, Priscilla and I will sleep better knowing those two are behind bars."

"It feels good to have that done," Lawrence admitted. But the exhilaration of apprehending the bandits had faded, leaving emptiness in its place, emptiness and the strange sensation that he should not have lingered in Golden. He had fulfilled the terms of his contract; the problems he'd been hired to resolve were gone. Jake was close to working off his debt. Lawrence could pack his bags and go anywhere that caught his fancy, and yet the prospect that had once buoyed him now left him feeling flat. He didn't want to leave Ladreville. It wasn't only the Kirk family that had made it their home. He had too. The quaint little town that had once appealed to him solely because it was where Priscilla lived now had a different, far stronger allure: Harriet.

As his mind pronounced her name, a sense of urgency filled Lawrence. He couldn't explain it. All he knew was that Harriet needed him. Now.

20

"Now, children, class is in session and you need to pay attention." Harriet accompanied her words with a frown, hoping that a slightly forbidding expression would accomplish what admonitions had not. When they'd returned from the noontime break, two of the children had brought new toys for the others to admire, and they were still talking about Eva's baby doll and Pierre Berthoud's dominoes, both of which had been stashed in the cloakroom. "We're going to study geography next. It's a very important subject."

Perhaps it was important to Harriet, but her pupils appeared more interested in the toys. Taking a deep breath, Harriet drew herself up to her full height. "I want utter silence." Though her command was greeted with groans, the children complied, and within seconds the class had returned to normalcy. The wind might be howling outside, but her pupils were quiet.

Harriet smiled as she pulled down one of the two wall maps. This one, a companion to the larger one of the United

States, featured Texas. "Who can show me where the capital is?"

Half the hands went up. When Heidi Gottlieb had successfully located Austin, Harriet asked the class to find Ladreville. As she'd expected, every hand rose.

"Miss Kirk, will you show us where you used to live?" Anna Singer posed the question after Mary returned to her seat, her head held high with pride that she had found Ladreville.

"Certainly." Harriet pointed to the tiny spot that marked her hometown. "Fortune is only half the size of Ladreville, so the print is very small." The mapmakers apparently subscribed to the theory that the type font should indicate each town's population. While there might be some benefit to that approach, it had its drawbacks.

"We can't see it from here," Eva complained, citing the primary drawback.

"Then you may all come closer." Harriet beckoned the class to approach the map. When they were clustered around it and had exclaimed over the distance Harriet and her family had traveled, she asked the students to trace the state's major rivers, starting with the Medina.

"Me! Me! Pick me!"

Harriet tried not to smile at her pupils' enthusiasm. "All right—"

Crack! Whoosh! The sounds came without warning, chasing every thought from her brain. Only fear remained. The shattering glass, the ominous crackle of flames. Was there anything more terrifying? And then there were the smells, the pungent odors of kerosene and smoke. The school was on fire.

Dimly Harriet registered the sight of a broken bottle, shards of window glass, burning liquid and flames. Her heart began to pound, and her head felt oddly light, as if it were disconnected from the rest of her. *Please, Lord, no.* This couldn't be happening. Not another fire.

The deep recesses of her brain shrieked with horror as she realized that someone had hurled a lit bottle of kerosene through the window and that, propelled by the strong winds that had risen this morning, the fire was spreading at an almost incredible rate, fueled by the books and papers and the dry wood of the school itself. *No, no, it couldn't be.* But it was. The floor had begun to burn, creating a band of fire between the class and the door, while flames licked at the edge of the desks. Was this what it was like the day Mother and Father died? Did they see the flames? Did they smell the smoke? Harriet shook herself mentally, tamping down the fear that threatened to paralyze her. What had happened to her parents was unimportant today. All that mattered was getting the children to safety.

"All right, boys and girls." By some miracle, her voice did not tremble. A quick assessment told her there was only one way to save the children. "We've practiced this many times." Harriet moved to the far wall and began to push the desks aside, forming a pathway. Though smoke swirled and fouled the air, the flames had not reached that wall. If the children moved now, they could escape.

"Quickly, quickly." She barked the orders. "No running. Don't fall. Take nothing. We'll meet across the street." Harriet herded her pupils from the schoolhouse, keeping her voice firm and confident, refusing to give in to the terror that even now sent shudders through her. She had never heard of fire spreading so quickly.

Save the children. Please, save the children. There was no point in trying to quench the flames with the cloakroom's single bucket of water. Unless help arrived immediately, the schoolhouse would be destroyed. That mattered not a whit. It could be replaced; the children could not.

Less than a minute later, Harriet stood on the opposite side of Hochstrasse, counting heads. Her prayer had been answered, for they were all here, shivering from the cold wind that even now was blowing the smoke across the river. That was why no one had come to help. The east wind had kept the smoke from spreading through the town and alerting the citizens to the school's plight.

Harriet looked at the children. Though several were coughing from the smoke, no one had been injured. *Thank you.* She wrapped her arms around two girls who seemed the most distressed, trying to comfort them.

"You're safe," she murmured. "The school doesn't matter." As she stroked their backs, their trembling subsided.

"Can we go home?" Jean Fayette asked.

Harriet nodded. There was no reason to remain here. "Tell your parents I'll speak to each of them tonight."

Across the street, smoke billowed from the schoolhouse, and flames licked hungrily at the roof. With the wind fanning the fire, it would take only minutes for the building to be consumed, but the children were safe. Sam and Daniel, resilient as only children could be, were punching each others' arms in some incomprehensible ritual.

As the group dispersed, Mary ran to Harriet's side, tears streaming down her face. "She's gone. Eva's gone."

"It's all right, sweetie. Everyone's going home."

"No!" Mary shook her head violently. "Not home. She wanted her doll."

Horror shot through Harriet, chilling her blood at the same time that her hands began to perspire. Take nothing, she had told the children. That meant Eva's doll was in the school. Surely she hadn't gone back into the inferno. But Mary seemed to believe she had. As the image of her parents' lifeless forms flashed before her, Harriet began to tremble. Not again. She couldn't lose another loved one. She stared at the burning building, her knees so weak with fear that they threatened to collapse. There was no choice. If there was even the slightest chance that Eva was inside, Harriet had to bring her out.

"Wait here." She gripped Mary's arm as she issued the orders. "No matter what happens, do not follow me." One child in that raging fire was too many.

As she ran toward it, Harriet assessed the building that only a few minutes ago had been a simple schoolhouse. The walls were burning, and the roof appeared on the verge of collapsing. How would she get Eva out of there? Was Isabelle's beloved stepdaughter even alive? Harriet had heard that smoke was more dangerous than the flames themselves and that children were more vulnerable than adults.

Though every fiber of her being protested, Harriet raced up the steps, trying to ignore the roaring of the flames and the trembling of her limbs. She could do this. She had to. A little girl's life was at stake.

"Eva!" she shouted as she entered the schoolhouse. The heat was greater than she had expected, fogging her spectacles the way a hot oven did. "Where are you?" There was no answer.

Harriet pushed her spectacles onto her head in a desperate attempt to see. The doll was in the cloakroom. Surely that was where she would find the child. "Eva, where are you?" The smoke was so thick Harriet could barely see outlines of the walls. How could a little girl have survived it? But she had to be alive. Surely God would not be so cruel as to take Gunther's daughter.

Harriet slid her spectacles back onto her nose; it was no use. She could see nothing, nor could she hear. The roar of the fire drowned out all other sounds. Touch was all she had left.

Crouching down, she searched the floor, her hands patting each inch as she looked for Eva. The child was not in the cloakroom, but neither was the doll. The bucket of water lay on its side, its life-giving liquid spilled onto the floor, leaving a faintly damp spot. Was that good or bad? Her head pounding from the smoke, Harriet tried to make sense of what she'd learned. The bucket must have been overturned recently, or the floor would be dry. Surely that meant Eva had been here. Had she found her doll and become confused, going into the schoolroom rather than leaving? It was the only answer.

The flames were closer now, the crackling and creaking louder. In a matter of seconds the roof would collapse. Harriet knew that. She also knew that she could not leave without Gunther and Isabelle's daughter. *Help me*, she prayed. *Dear Lord, help me find Eva.* There was no answer.

He smelled the smoke long before he saw the source. The winter wind carried it for miles, filling his nostrils with the acrid odor, and with each mile, Lawrence's worry grew. This was not normal smoke. There was too much of it for it to be the plumes that rose from Ladreville's houses. That smoke dissipated quickly. This was different. Something was burning, something large, something that was not supposed to be on fire. Deep inside, he knew that, just as he knew that the smoke was the reason Harriet needed him. She feared fire the way he did water. Simply the sight of flames and the smell of smoke worried her. What would happen if she were close to the fire? What would happen if . . . Lawrence refused to complete the thought. Harriet was still alive. She had to be, and he had to reach her. Whatever was happening, he needed to comfort her.

Let me get there in time, Lawrence prayed as he bent low, urging Snip to a gallop. Zach had gone the opposite direction, planning to stop at the Bar C and tell Clay that the rustlers had been apprehended. Lawrence was alone now, racing toward Ladreville. *Let me help her. Please.*

The smoke was thicker here, leaving no doubt that it came from the town itself and not a neighboring ranch. He felt his pulse accelerate and his heart fill with dread. As Snip descended the bank into the Medina, Lawrence shuddered at the sight before him. *Dear God, no. Not the school.*

Trying desperately to block the ominous sounds of flames consuming wood, Harriet crawled as quickly as she could, making her way into the schoolroom, calling for Eva, choking each time she took a breath. Was this how Mother and Father had felt? Had they known this horrible sensation of being unable to breathe, yet needing air so desperately that they opened their mouths again and again?

She stretched out her arms, searching for a small body. Overhead, the beams groaned and shifted. It wouldn't be long. If she didn't find Eva soon, they'd both be trapped.

They'd both be . . . Her mind recoiled, refusing to pronounce the final word. *Help me, Lord. Don't let Eva die.* The rafters creaked; the flames crackled. The end was near. Harriet knew it would soon be over. Dimly, she remembered the prayer Pastor Sempert had offered as he'd sought to understand why Sterling Russell was to be the next shepherd for his flock. *Thy will be done.*

Her mouth too parched to pronounce the words, Harriet prayed silently. Over and over she repeated the words as she crawled through the schoolroom. *Thy will be done.* And then, though the flames roared and the smoke thickened, her fears disappeared, replaced by the greatest calm she had ever known. Was this what death was like? But if she was dead, why would she still smell smoke?

She continued crawling, searching for Eva, until she felt a soft, still form. Unable to see, Harriet traced the body, stopping when her hands touched Eva's face. She had found her. The little girl lay on the floor, her doll clutched in her arms. *Let her be alive*, Harriet prayed.

There was another ominous creak, and with a flash of sparks, one of the roof rafters tumbled to the ground. Flames spiraled ever closer. Another foot. She could make it another foot, she told herself as she dragged Eva into the cloakroom. Just another few feet, and they'd be at the doorway. *Pull. Harder. You can open the door.* And somehow she did.

When she reached the steps, Harriet dragged herself to her feet and hefted Eva into her arms. She had to get her down the stairs. The building was only seconds from total collapse. They had to get away. But Eva's weight was too great, and Harriet's knees buckled. *Help!* she prayed again. *I can't do it alone.* A second later, the burden was lifted.

"I've got her." Somehow, some way, Lawrence was here.

Harriet stumbled down the steps, dragging herself a few yards away from the school before she collapsed on the ground.

"How did you know?" she asked. "How did you know I needed help?"

As Lawrence swept her into his arms, he nodded solemnly. "God told me."

❦

Several hours later, Harriet sat in bed, pillows propped behind her back to keep her upright. Clay had just left, having assured her that Eva would be fine. Though she had minor burns and smoke in her lungs, the little girl would recover. "Children are remarkably resilient," he had announced with a smile. "You, on the other hand . . ." That had been the preface to his declaration that Harriet should not plan to take any long walks for at least a week. "You need to let your lungs heal." Clay had dressed the burns on her hands, leaving instructions for Ruth to change the bandages daily.

"Is it all right for us to come in?" Ruth opened the door a crack and popped her head inside. Judging from the sounds behind her, the other four children were close by.

"Yes." Though she needed time to think, to try to understand everything that had happened today, Harriet knew that her siblings were worried about her. Mary had watched her go into the burning school and had run shrieking to Daniel and Sam, insisting they not leave her alone. All three had been so frightened that no one had thought to go for help.

"I was scared," Daniel said softly when Harriet had assured them that the doctor had pronounced her injuries minor.

"Me too," Sam admitted.

Mary's eyes filled with tears. "Why did Eva go back? I would have given her my doll." Isabelle and Gunther would have bought her another doll—a dozen dolls—if they had known. But no one had realized that Eva was so deeply attached to her new toy that she would risk her life to find it.

"Can I do that?" Mary asked. "Can I give Eva my doll?"

Harriet nodded. "If you want to, you may. That's very generous of you."

"I like Eva. She's my friend."

"It's good to have friends," Harriet agreed. She had Isabelle and Lawrence. Especially Lawrence. A small smile crossed Harriet's face as she thought of how he'd been there at the exact moment she needed him.

"The town's lucky you insisted on practicing egress." Though Jake was still supposed to be working, when he'd heard about the fire, he had asked permission to return home, and William Goetz had agreed that assuring himself of Harriet's health was more important than finishing a bookshelf. "Thanks to you, no one was seriously hurt."

Harriet shook her head. "You're wrong," she said firmly. "I wasn't the one who kept Eva safe. It was God."

Lawrence had waited as long as he could. He'd spoken to Clay and learned that Harriet's injuries were not serious. He'd given her several hours to rest, because Clay had said that was important. But he could wait no longer. He needed to see Harriet, to assure himself that she would be all right.

Lawrence pounded on the door with far more force than necessary. When Ruth opened it, he dispensed with pleasantries. "I have to talk to Harriet."

Her sister ushered him in, her lips curving as though she found something amusing about Lawrence's impatience. "She's in the parlor. I've been turning people away, but I know Harriet would want to see you."

There was no Christmas tree today, no candles decorating the mantel, no reason Lawrence's heart should be filled with joy other than the sight of the woman seated on the settee, wrapped in a quilt. Her face was paler than he'd ever seen it, with a few pieces of sticking plaster marring one cheek, her eyes as gray as the smoke that had drawn him back to Ladreville. Though her hands were bandaged, she held a thick book in them.

How like Harriet! Even after enduring what must have been a frightening experience, she could not be parted from her books. Lawrence knew there was no reason to be surprised. Hadn't Harriet told him she found refuge in books? When she laid it on the seat beside her, Lawrence recognized it as a Bible.

"Harriet!" He crossed the room in four swift strides.

As she rose, Lawrence opened his arms, not sure she'd accept the offer but praying that she would. She did. A second later, she was enfolded in his embrace. Although he longed to hold her so tightly that she could never escape, Lawrence forced his arms to relax. Today Harriet was like a piece of fragile crystal. If he held her too tightly, she might break. It was enough that she was close enough that he could hear her breathing.

"Oh, Lawrence," she murmured, tipping her head up so she could look at him, "it seems as if all I do is thank you, and now I'm going to do it again. Thank you for being there when I needed you." Her voice was hoarse, the result of the smoke, and he could tell by the way she carefully formed each word that it hurt to speak.

"I wish I had arrived sooner." If only he hadn't spent those extra hours convincing the other sheriffs they should band together to prevent future rustling. God had saved Harriet's life, but if Lawrence had been there, perhaps he could have prevented her injuries.

She laid a hand on his, as if to comfort him. "You couldn't have stopped the fire."

Lawrence looked at her bandaged hands. "What happened? Did the stove explode?" It had to be something catastrophic that destroyed the whole building.

Harriet shook her head, and he saw sorrow fill her eyes. "It wasn't an accident. Someone threw a lighted bottle of kerosene through the window. You know how dry everything is. The floor caught fire immediately, and it seemed like only seconds before the desks were in flames." She shuddered at the memory.

Arson. Lawrence hadn't expected that. He frowned, trying to picture the nebulous figure who had deliberately tried to injure—perhaps kill—Harriet and the schoolchildren. "I can't imagine who in Ladreville would have been so cruel. It's one thing to rustle cattle. It's far different to endanger innocent lives." Lawrence laid his hand on top of Harriet's, stroking the bandages that encased her fingers. "Who could be filled with so much hatred?"

Her hands trembled. "The only person I can picture doing something like this is Thomas Bruckner, but he's gone."

"Thomas Bruckner?" There was no one in Ladreville by that name.

"He's someone I knew in Fortune." The darkening of Harriet's eyes told Lawrence the acquaintance had not been a pleasant one. Was this the man she had thought she loved? He forced back the stab of something—surely it wasn't jealousy—and focused on Harriet's next words. "He was here before Christmas. When I didn't give him the answer he wanted, he ransacked my room."

Anger and disappointment surged through Lawrence, anger that someone had violated Harriet's home, disappointment that she had not confided in him. As sheriff, he should have been informed of the crime. But, more than that, as her friend, he should have known she was in danger. "Why didn't you tell me?"

The tightening of Harriet's lips confirmed that she'd read his emotions. When she spoke, her voice was low. "I probably should have, but there wasn't any real damage, and I didn't believe he'd come back."

Lawrence bit back his angry retort. If he'd heard about Bruckner last month, he might have been able to stop him, and then the fire would not have occurred. But nothing would be gained by berating Harriet. Instead he said as calmly as he could, "I wish I'd known. It might have made a difference."

"Perhaps." Harriet sounded skeptical. "The fact is, I don't know that it was Thomas who set the fire. He was angry when he left, but I can't imagine why he would have returned to Ladreville."

Lawrence had seen enough criminals to know there were many possible reasons. "Why did he come here in the first place?"

Color crept into Harriet's cheeks, and she lowered her gaze as she said, "He wanted me to marry him."

"And you refused?"

She nodded. "He didn't love me . . . or my family."

297

21

"Are you certain you feel well enough to go?" Isabelle's brown eyes filled with concern. She had come to the Kirk house with the obvious intention of dissuading Harriet.

"It's only my hands that were hurt, and I won't need to use them tonight." Harriet held up the bandaged appendages. Clay had warned her that she would bear scars, but he believed there would be no other lasting damage.

"It's not just your hands. Your throat was hurt too," Isabelle added the reminder. "Eva still complains about hers."

"I need to attend the town meeting," Harriet said, wincing slightly as the effort of sounding forceful hurt her throat.

Isabelle raised one carefully groomed eyebrow, as if to say that she noticed Harriet's twinge of pain but would not mention it. "All right, but if you turn any paler than you are now, I'll drag you out of there."

"Yes, Mama." When Isabelle looked askance, Harriet laughed. "I figured you were practicing on me so you'd be an expert by the time the babies were born."

"It wasn't that at all." When they both rose to retrieve their cloaks, Isabelle gave Harriet a warm hug. "I simply wanted to keep you safe. It's the least I can do after what you did for us. I don't know what Gunther and I would have done if you hadn't rescued Eva."

"I told you I wasn't the one who saved her. God was responsible."

"But he used you. We won't forget that." Isabelle sighed. "I just wish there were something we could do for you."

Harriet slid her hands into the muff Isabelle had brought, realizing her bandages would make it impossible to wear gloves. "The muff is enough, but if you insist, there is one other thing you can do for me."

"Anything."

"Don't mention Eva's rescue again."

"But . . ." Isabelle stared at Harriet for a moment, her reluctance obvious. At last she nodded. "All right."

By the time they reached the German church, it was crowded, and had Gunther not saved seats for them, Harriet and Isabelle might have had to stand. Even though only Ladreville's adults had been invited to the town meeting, there were enough of them to fill either church. The German one was slightly larger, which was the reason Lawrence had chosen it for tonight's gathering.

Like Isabelle, he had been leery of Harriet's attending before her injuries healed. "You'll never stay quiet," he had said with a smile. Harriet did not dispute his allegation, but it didn't change the fact that she had to be there.

"I called this meeting because as your mayor I have several important things to discuss with you," Lawrence announced when the crowd had quieted. Though he looked as handsome as ever, his eyes were more serious than normal. They held no fear or pain, simply firmness of purpose.

"My reasons are all related to the school. First of all, you know that the fire was no accident. Someone deliberately set it." A low murmur of assent greeted Lawrence's words. The ever-vigilant grapevine had reported the presence of kerosene. "If anyone saw anything suspicious, I ask you to speak to me after the meeting. You'll be talking to me not as your mayor but as Sheriff Wood," he added with a wry grin.

Though several people turned to look at those seated behind them, no one said anything. Harriet wondered if anyone had seen Thomas or whether the fire's instigator was someone seated in the church. As much as she doubted Thomas had returned, the alternative was decidedly less pleasant.

Lawrence paused for only a second before he said, "Next I want to talk about rebuilding the school. Is there anyone here who does not agree that it should be rebuilt? If so, please raise your hand."

There were no raised hands; instead, a dark-haired man Harriet didn't recognize stood up. "We need a school. I ain't disagreeing with that. What I wanna know is how we're gonna pay for it."

"We can't increase taxes any more," a blond man chimed in.

The murmurs intensified as the townspeople voiced their concerns. This was what Harriet had feared when Lawrence had told her he was convening the meeting. Though the citizens of Ladreville supported the concept of education, she worried that it would be difficult to raise the necessary funds.

When she had told Lawrence her concerns, his expression grew pensive. Tonight he merely nodded. "I agree with all of you. We cannot increase taxes, but we need a school, so I have a proposition for you."

Isabelle gripped Harriet's arm. "I knew Lawrence would find a solution," she whispered.

Lawrence's gaze moved throughout the church, resting on one person, then another, as if he sought approval even before he presented the idea. The townspeople, who had been whispering and fidgeting on the pews, became silent as Lawrence opened his mouth once more. "We gathered here just a few months ago to discuss another of Ladreville's needs. That day we agreed to fund a major project. What I suggest to you tonight is that we use the money we allocated for the bridge for the school."

Isabelle gasped and laid her hand protectively on her midsection. "Oh, Gunther," she whispered, "we need the bridge."

At her side, Harriet sat speechless. Perhaps more than anyone in Ladreville, she knew how deeply Lawrence cared about the bridge. Though he'd told her that he viewed it as his legacy to the town, explaining that even after he was gone, it would ensure safe crossings, the bridge was more than that. It was also a way for Lawrence to tame his fears. And now he'd volunteered to abandon the project.

As if he sensed her thoughts, Lawrence said, "You know I was the one who pushed to construct a bridge. I told you it was important. I still believe that, but our need for a school is more urgent."

It was an interesting choice of words—urgency vs. importance. Lawrence wasn't saying that he considered the school more important than the bridge, but he was acknowledging the timeliness of the need for a school. Regardless of the words he used, it was a generous gesture and one that filled Harriet's heart with warmth.

"I like that idea," the dark-haired man said.

"Me too," the other dissenter agreed.

Lawrence nodded shortly, as if he had expected their reaction. "I need a show of hands. All in favor of spending the money on the school instead of the bridge, raise your hands."

As Harriet looked around, she saw there was no need to count the votes. The vast majority of Ladreville's men had their hands in the air.

"Opposed?" Lawrence waited a few seconds before he declared the decision unanimous. "Ladreville will have a new school as soon as we can get it constructed."

Harriet rose. This was one of the reasons she had come tonight. "I'd like to make a suggestion." It was more than a suggestion. She was going to do her best to ensure that the town agreed with her. Sarah had told her how her own pleas had resulted in Ladreville's citizens agreeing to construct a school. Though that first school had met Sarah's needs, it did not meet Harriet's, and, she was willing to bet, it no longer met those of the town.

When Lawrence motioned her to come forward, Harriet walked to the front of the church and stood next to him. "I thank you all for agreeing to rebuild the school." Even though she was speaking as loudly as she could, her voice barely projected to the rear pews, and she saw Clay shake his head in disapproval. He had warned her that overtaxing her vocal cords now might cause permanent damage. That was a risk she had to take.

"There is no doubt in my mind that a school is one of the most important buildings in a town, second only to its churches," Harriet continued. "But I beg you to consider what we learned yesterday. Wood burns very quickly. That's

302

why I ask that the new school be constructed of stone, to make it safer for the children of Ladreville. I even think we need stone floors."

The blond man who'd spoken before shook his head. "That will take longer."

"That is true," Harriet agreed. The stone had to be quarried, which was more time-consuming than felling and splitting trees. "But it will also last longer. If we build with stone, your great-grandchildren will attend school in the same building."

When there was no further discussion, Lawrence asked for a show of hands, then gave Harriet a congratulatory smile after the town agreed that the new school should be constructed of stone.

There was a moment of silence before Gunther murmured something to Isabelle and rose. "What will the children do while the school is being built?"

Lawrence grinned as he looked at the miller. "That was the third subject I wanted to discuss: the interim school. Even if the weather is perfect, it will take some time until the new building is ready. Our children should not go without schooling during that period." A low murmur of assent greeted Lawrence's words. "I understand that before the first school was constructed, classes were conducted in the church halls."

Harriet knew that was true, but she also knew from Sarah's tales that it had been a decidedly unsuccessful experiment, with the French citizens refusing to let their children attend classes in the German church and the Germans denying their children access to the French church.

Lawrence's smile faded and his expression was stern as he said, "I also understand there were problems with that."

When Harriet looked at the audience, several women ducked their heads, as if ashamed, while a number of men shifted uneasily on the pews. Rather than acknowledge their discomfort, Lawrence continued speaking. "My recommendation is that we use only one of the churches this time. That will make it easier for Miss Kirk, since she won't have to move her teaching materials back and forth." The pained expressions faded as the townspeople accepted Lawrence's face-saving suggestion. Thanks to him, though everyone knew otherwise, they could pretend that the only problem with the original school had been Sarah's need to move between two buildings.

"Which one?" the blond man demanded, his voice and posture belligerent.

"That's the question." Lawrence's response was even. He addressed the entire audience. "Which do you think would be better?"

Though Harriet expected the answers to be predictable, with the German citizens recommending their own church, Gunther's reply surprised her. "The French hall is larger," he pointed out.

Monsieur Seurat rose. "But the German hall has more light. That might be better."

The discussion continued with no resolution apparent. "I propose we vote." Lawrence waited until Harriet was once more seated before he called for a show of hands. When the French hall won by a slim margin, he thanked the townspeople and adjourned the meeting.

Within minutes, the church was virtually empty. Though anxious to return to Eva, Isabelle and Gunther agreed to leave only when Harriet assured them that she could walk home alone. "I doubt you'll be unaccompanied," Isabelle said with a mischievous look at Lawrence.

Harriet doubted it too, but whether or not Lawrence walked with her, she needed to talk to him. She couldn't let his wonderfully generous action go unacknowledged. "Thank you," she said, willing her voice to hold out for a few more minutes. "I know the bridge was important to you."

Lawrence took the hand she extended, holding it gently between both of his. "I meant what I said. Right now, the school is more important. If the town is fortunate, we won't have flooding this year, and the bridge won't be that critical. C'mon, let's get you home. I saw Clay frowning and suspect he's not happy that you're here."

"Clay worries too much." He was an excellent physician, but even Sarah admitted that he could be overly protective.

"You might say that about me too. I worry about you, Harriet."

As Lawrence slid his arm around her waist and led her to the door, Harriet forgot the sting of her burns and the rawness of her throat. For the moment there were no worries. There was only the pleasure of being with Lawrence.

༂

"We almost lost her, Mutter." Karl shook his head as his mother offered him a cup of coffee. He needed more than coffee to clear the thoughts that had circled through his head since the day he'd heard of the fire and Harriet's bravery. That was why he was here, sitting in the kitchen on a fine morning when he ought to be outside helping his father. He needed his mother's advice.

"She's the wife I want." Strong and brave, Harriet was the

perfect helpmeet. Though Karl had had doubts since the fall festival when she'd shown herself unable to control Jake, the fire had made him realize that he'd been expecting too much of her. She was only a woman, after all. Disciplining older boys was a man's job. His job.

Mutter laid down her cup and looked at him, a question in her eyes. Though Karl tried not to frown, he didn't understand why she would question him. Hadn't he told her before that he intended to marry Harriet?

"Are you certain, son? Harriet is a fine woman. You know I love her like a daughter, but don't forget that she doesn't come alone. You'd be responsible for the other children too."

This was easy to understand. Mutter was referring to Jake. Karl nodded. "Jake is a problem, but a firm hand will end his mischief. Once the others realize that I won't allow any nonsense, they'll cause no trouble. You'll see, Mutter. Life will be easier when we have them here." His parents were getting too old to do all the farmwork. That was part of Harriet's appeal. She brought workers with her.

Mutter stared at him the way she used to when he was a child and had told a lie, making him as uncomfortable as she had all those years ago. It was silly to feel that way, for he wasn't a boy any longer, and he hadn't lied.

At last she nodded as if she'd heard his thoughts. "Have you spoken to Harriet? Does she know how you feel?"

"Nein. That's why I'm here. I don't know where to start."

The cuckoo clock chimed 10:00, reminding him he should be in the barn repairing tack.

"You need to court her."

Karl tried to bite back his annoyance. "You told me that before, but you didn't tell me how to do it."

306

His mother sighed, and once again he felt as if he were ten years old and had somehow disappointed her. "The first thing you need to do is visit Harriet. That will let her know you care about her."

"But what do I say when I get there?" That was a problem. Karl could talk about crops and farm animals, but those weren't things that interested women.

Mutter sighed again. "All right, son. If you're sure this is what you want, I'll go with you the first couple times."

∼

"Mutter sent this." Karl held out a bowl filled with what appeared to be a soft pudding. "She said it would not hurt your throat."

"Oh, Karl, I feel as if I'm being spoiled." This was the third consecutive night that he'd brought gifts of food from his mother. The first two times, he'd been accompanied by his mother, but tonight he was alone. Harriet accepted the bowl before leading him into the parlor. Though the boys had been playing there when Karl rapped on the front door, the room was now empty, the thumps overhead telling Harriet they'd moved their game to their bedroom.

"Would you like to sit?" She offered Karl a chair and nodded to Ruth to take another. As was true the last two days, he wore clean overalls and a sheepish expression. Ruth claimed he had come courting, but Harriet didn't believe that. If Karl were courting a woman, he'd simply declare his intentions. He wasn't a man for subtleties like flowers, books, or lemon drops. Besides, a man didn't bring his mother if he was courting. Still, Harriet had to admit that it was unusual for Karl to visit three days in a row.

"You deserve to be spoiled," he said. "Mutter and I want to spoil you." Karl's face reddened, as if the subject embarrassed him, and he added abruptly, "I heard Olga Kaltheimer is coming back to Ladreville."

"I don't believe I know her." Harriet wondered why Karl was speaking of someone she had never met. Though she had been introduced to the elder Kaltheimers, there had been no mention of a daughter.

Karl stroked his beard. "Olga was supposed to be the teacher when Sarah left. I heard it was all set; then one day she left town to visit cousins. That's when Michel Ladre advertised for a new teacher. But now Olga's coming back."

That was, Harriet realized, the longest speech she had heard Karl deliver, although why it concerned her was not apparent. "That's good," she said idly. Perhaps Karl was simply searching for a topic of discussion. Or perhaps he thought she needed an assistant, and that was why he mentioned a woman who wanted to teach.

But Harriet was mistaken. Karl shook his head. "Don't you see, Harriet? If Olga returns, you don't have to teach anymore. You could marry and have a family of your own."

Harriet blanched. Was it possible Ruth was right?

A rejected suitor. Lawrence had chased and apprehended more criminals than he could count in his years as a Ranger, but this was the first time he'd sought a rejected suitor. Of course, it was also the first time he'd heard of a man setting a fire because a woman refused to marry him.

"It was Bruckner," he said when he entered Harriet's parlor.

"Thomas?" Blood drained from her face so quickly

308

Lawrence feared she would swoon. Was it possible that she still had feelings for her first suitor?

"I'm afraid so," he said more brusquely than he had intended. "A couple of people reported seeing a stranger in town the morning of the fire. Their description matches the one you gave of him."

Harriet shuddered. "I knew Thomas didn't love me, but I never realized he harbored so much hatred. Even if he was still angry at me, why would he endanger the children?"

Lawrence shrugged. "It's almost impossible to tell what's inside another person's heart." His own for example. What would Harriet say if she knew what he was thinking? Would she be shocked to know that he was remembering how soft her lips had been against his and how good it had felt to hold her in his arms? *Business, Lawrence*, he reminded himself. *You're here on business. There will be time to tell her how you feel once you've caught Bruckner.*

"Don't worry," Lawrence said firmly. "I'll catch him. Rangers always get their men." His lips twitched as he added, "Even ex-Rangers."

༈

"He's courting you, you know," Ruth said as they cleared the table.

Harriet blinked. "He's not even here." Lawrence had been gone for four days now, searching for Thomas. "How could he . . ." She broke off abruptly. "Oh, you meant Karl."

Ruth's lips twitched as if she were trying not to smile. "Who else did you think I meant?" When Harriet refused to answer, she said, "It's not just Jake who's concerned. The town has noticed Karl's frequent visits. They're speculating about whether you'll finish your contract or turn the school over to Olga Kaltheimer this month."

"I have every intention of honoring my contract," Harriet said firmly, "and no intention of marrying Karl Friedrich."

"Does he know that?"

"The subject has never come up."

"It will."

But it did not. Though Karl came every evening, sometimes accompanied by Pastor Russell, sometimes with his mother, sometimes alone, he never stayed long, and while he sat in the Kirks' parlor, he spoke of his farm, of the school, of Olga Kaltheimer's desire to teach. But he never spoke of marriage. And when Harriet spoke of her plans for the coming school year, though he frowned, Karl made no attempt to dissuade her. It appeared that he was simply being neighborly, trying to make her recovery more pleasant. Thank goodness.

Thomas Bruckner wasn't hard to find. Lawrence grinned as he entered the saloon, realizing that it hadn't taken a Ranger's skills to find him. The man hadn't even bothered to hide his tracks. Instead, he'd left a trail a mile wide, making indelible impressions each time he stopped. No one who encountered Bruckner forgot his cherubic face or his devilish temper. It appeared that whatever had angered him enough to set the school on fire hadn't faded, for here he was in a small town a few miles west of New Braunfels, arguing with the barkeeper.

"You cheated me," Bruckner announced as he slammed his fist onto the bar. Harriet hadn't exaggerated. Thomas Bruckner's face might not be handsome in the ordinary sense, but there was something angelic about it. If you could ignore the snarling lips, that is. "I already paid you."

Though it was midday and the saloon was practically empty, the barkeeper wore the faintly harried expression Lawrence associated with men at the end of the night when they'd poured too many drinks and settled too many disputes.

"You paid for the glass you just drank, not this one." The tall, almost emaciated man behind the bar kept a firm grip on the object of Bruckner's anger. "If you want it, you'll pay me. Otherwise, leave."

"I'll leave when I'm good and ready."

As Bruckner reached for his six-shooter, Lawrence put a firm hand on his shoulder. "Let's take a walk."

The man who looked like an angel spun around. "Who . . . ?" He narrowed his eyes, as if searching his brain for Lawrence's identity. "Oh, you . . . the sheriff." Though Lawrence had never met Bruckner, it appeared that some memory had broken through his alcoholic haze. "What are you doing here?"

"I'm looking for answers about a fire."

"I don't know nothing about a fire." The way his eyes shifted gave lie to his words.

Lawrence tightened his grip on Bruckner's shoulder. "I heard you paid a visit to my town."

"So what? You got a law that says I can't do that?" He leaned forward, reaching for the whiskey bottle. Though the barkeeper still held the glass, he'd placed the bottle back on the bar just outside Bruckner's reach.

Shifting his weight so he could nudge the whiskey toward the barkeeper, Lawrence said, "No law against visiting, but we sure do have laws against burning down schoolhouses."

"It's too bad your schoolhouse burned." Though Bruckner

311

attempted to feign innocence, the gleam in his eyes left no doubt of his guilt. "That's a downright shame."

"Yes," Lawrence agreed, "it was a shame. More than that, it was a criminal act, and you're going to pay for it."

"Me?" Bruckner sneered. "You can't pin it on me. I was miles away when the window broke."

"Did I say anything about a broken window?" Lawrence addressed his question to the bartender.

"No, sir." It was clear that the older man's ennui had faded, replaced by amusement at the scene unfolding before him.

"All right, Bruckner. Come with me." Lawrence hauled him to his feet, relieved him of his weapons, and propelled him toward the door. "You've got some explaining to do."

Bruckner's bravado faded in the sunlight. "All I wanted was to scare her." The man was lying. Lawrence hadn't spent a decade as a Ranger without learning to read people. This sniveling excuse for a man was lying. "I figured she'd give me some money if I scared her enough."

Sure. And the sun rose in the west. "Seems to me it's mighty tough to do anything if you're dead."

"Yeah, well . . ." Bruckner's lips curved into a sneer. "She had it coming to her. She should have married me when I asked her. Then the money would have been mine."

Though his fists itched to connect with Bruckner's face, Lawrence forced himself to remain calm. There was nothing to be gained by breaking the man's nose and splitting his lip. He needed to learn what had driven Harriet's suitor to attempt murder.

"What money?" Bruckner kept talking about money, as if Harriet were an heiress.

"The money I needed to repay Mr. Allen."

Now they were making progress. "Herb Allen?"

Though he nodded, there was no mistaking the fear that shadowed Bruckner's eyes. He wasn't as stupid as Lawrence had thought. At least he knew enough to fear someone who killed men as easily as cockroaches.

"You've heard of him?" Bruckner asked.

"I reckon everyone in Texas has heard of him." With the hatred Herb Allen had engendered among the state's criminals, if he didn't travel with a posse of his own, Lawrence doubted he would have lived this long. "How'd you manage to owe him? Gambling?"

"Yeah. The cards weren't with me one night."

Probably a lot more than one night. Herb Allen didn't bother with small debts. He bought up others' notes, then collected on them . . . one way or another. Owing a substantial sum to a man with Herb Allen's reputation explained Bruckner's terror, but it didn't explain his belief that Harriet would be his salvation. "Why did you think Harriet would give you money?"

Bruckner looked as if the answer should be obvious. "Because she was the richest woman in Fortune. Her grandparents practically founded the town. They were rolling in gold."

"Odd. She never struck me as wealthy." If she'd had the fortune Bruckner claimed, Harriet would have had no reason to teach, nor would she have been so concerned about her siblings earning their keep.

"She was rich back in Fortune." Bruckner spat the words as Lawrence tied his hands behind him. "She was rich as can be. I don't know what she did with it, but all that money should have been mine."

"What's going to be yours is a good long time in a jail

313

cell, unless someone in Ladreville decides to string you up." Though he wanted to wipe away Bruckner's dubious expression with the business end of a spur, Lawrence said only, "You could have killed thirty children. The town isn't too happy about that. We've never had a lynching in Ladreville, but there's always a first time." The man blanched.

Lawrence hoisted Bruckner onto his horse, ignoring the man's complaints that he couldn't ride in handcuffs. It would be uncomfortable, but Thomas Bruckner didn't deserve comfort.

Though he had planned to head back toward Ladreville and let Bruckner wait for the judge there, Lawrence reconsidered. It wasn't only this miserable man's existence that was at stake. Lawrence would take his chances with that. But if Thomas Bruckner were incarcerated there, Harriet would be faced with the knowledge that the man she had spurned, the man who had tried to kill her, was close by. There would be gossip—lots of it—mingled with the fear that he might escape. Lawrence shook his head. He couldn't cause Harriet any more pain.

"C'mon, Bruckner. We've got a long ride ahead of us."

22

It felt good to be home. Lawrence untied the bedroll and slung his canteen over his shoulder. After almost a week away, he needed a bath and a shave. A hot meal and a long sleep could wait, but cleanliness was an essential preparation for what he most wanted: a visit to Harriet.

"You look happy." Emerging from the parsonage, Sterling followed him up the steps to the mayor's house. "That must mean you caught your man."

"I did." Lawrence grinned at his friend when he reached the second floor landing. "It felt good to see Bruckner behind bars, but it felt even better to come back here." Lawrence wondered whether Sterling would understand. He wasn't certain he did, at least not completely. All he knew was that while he'd been gone, something had shifted deep inside him. "It may sound strange, but for the first time in my life, I feel as if I'm where I'm supposed to be."

While Lawrence deposited his traveling gear in one corner of his room and searched for a clean shirt, Sterling sank onto the room's sole chair. Though unpadded and straight-backed, it was more comfortable than the floor. "Does this mean you're not going to leave Ladreville?"

"It does. You know, I didn't want to come here, but now I want to stay. I plan to tell Clay and the others that I'll sign as long a contract as they want."

Raising his eyebrow, Sterling asked, "Would a certain schoolteacher be the reason?"

There was little point in dissembling. If matters proceeded the way he hoped they would, it wouldn't be long before the grapevine learned of his interest. "She just might be."

Sterling leaned forward, his grin fading. "You may not want my advice, but if you haven't already done it, you ought to make your intentions known. Ever since the fire, Karl Friedrich has become a daily visitor at the Kirk residence. The grapevine says he's trying to convince Harriet to turn the school over to Olga Kaltheimer so she can marry him now."

"I see." In all likelihood, the fire had jolted Karl, causing him to turn what had appeared to be a desultory courtship into an active one.

"Do you? Ruth won't say much, but I get the impression that Karl's a pretty persistent fellow. He's a nice enough man, but I can't say that I want him as a brother-in-law."

Lawrence, who had been looking for a collar, stopped and stared at Sterling, shocked by the minister's final words. "Brother-in-law? Unless I'm mistaken, there's only one way Karl could become your brother-in-law. When did this happen? I leave the town for less than a week, and you decide you're ready for marriage."

"You know it isn't a new idea. I haven't said anything to Ruth yet, because I'm waiting until after Easter," Sterling

316

explained, "but after that, I plan to ask permission to court her."

Lawrence rose and strode to the window, trying to phrase his words carefully. "Six months ago I never would have pictured quiet Ruth as a parson's wife." He was still having trouble forming the image of Ruth on her own and Harriet without her.

"Ruth has changed, and so have I." Sterling's words brought Lawrence back to the present. "Now I can't imagine my life without her."

"I know what you mean."

"Then take my advice. Don't wait."

Lawrence didn't, though Zach had sent a note, asking him to come to the Lazy B as soon as he could. Even if the rustlers had struck again, Harriet was more important than Zach. Lawrence needed to see her, to relieve her fears about Bruckner and—most importantly—to tell her what was in his heart. Unfortunately, when he reached the Kirk house, Karl was already there.

"Lawrence!" As she opened the door and ushered him into the parlor, Lawrence noticed two things: Harriet's hands were no longer bandaged, and her eyes sparkled. Though there might have been other causes, he wanted to believe the sparkle was due to happiness, just as he wanted to believe she hadn't given Karl that brilliant smile.

"When did you get back?" she asked, her voice still husky from the smoke.

"About an hour ago." His hair was damp, but he no longer smelled like a dusty horse, and his boots would not track mud onto her rug.

"You look tired."

From the corner of his eye, Lawrence saw Karl frown. Though the man had greeted him with a curt nod, he clearly did not appreciate Harriet talking to him. Too bad. Karl had had the week Lawrence was gone to court Harriet or whatever it was he was doing here. Lawrence had no intention of leaving simply because another man was present.

He gave Harriet a broad smile, then favored Ruth with another. Though Ruth was sitting in the corner, obviously serving as Harriet's chaperone, it would be rude to ignore her. "It was a long trip, but it was successful."

"You found Thomas?" Harriet seated herself and gestured Lawrence toward the chair he had occupied each time he'd visited. A stray domino announced that the boys had been playing on the rug at one point, but there was no other sign of the younger Kirks, leaving Lawrence to wonder where they'd gone.

He stretched his legs in front of him, trying to relax. When he'd envisioned this scene, Karl had not been part of it. "Yes," he said. "Bruckner admitted he set the fire." Lawrence wouldn't repeat the other things the man had said. Most of them were unfit for human ears. Harriet's lips tightened, and she pushed her spectacles back on her nose in a gesture Lawrence had come to realize meant she was nervous, but she said nothing.

Karl was not so reticent. "The scoundrel!" He pounded his fist into his palm. "I hope you've got him locked up."

"I do indeed." Lawrence addressed his next words to Harriet. "He's in the Fortune jail."

"Fortune?" Karl's voice rose a decibel. "Why did you take him there? The crime was committed in Ladreville. He should stand trial here. We should decide how he's punished."

Karl's obvious anger confirmed the wisdom of not bringing Thomas Bruckner back to Ladreville. Fanned by fury, the townspeople might not have waited for the circuit judge to arrive but might have taken Bruckner's fate into their own hands. "I'm the sheriff," Lawrence said calmly. "The town pays me to make decisions."

"You're supposed to make good decisions." Karl's expression left no doubt that he did not believe Lawrence had fulfilled that obligation. "We'll see what the others have to say about this." Though his next words were muttered, Lawrence distinguished "contract." Karl, it appeared, was threatening to terminate Lawrence's employment.

Harriet leaned forward, clasping her hands. "I think it was a wise decision," she said firmly. Knowing Harriet as he did, Lawrence was certain it was not by chance that she moved her hands again, as if to remind Karl that she was the one who had been injured. "Thank you, Lawrence." She accompanied her words with a smile. "Sheriff Faulkner will ensure that justice is done."

"Harrumph!" His disapproval evident, Karl rose and took a step toward the front door. "Coming, Sheriff Wood?" Though phrased as a question, it sounded like a command. "Miss Kirk is fatigued."

Rising when Harriet did, Lawrence shook his head. He had no intention of being rushed, simply because Karl Friedrich was ready to leave. "I have some business to discuss with Harriet." Despite his intentions, it was evident that this was not the time to speak of affairs of the heart. Karl had spoiled that, but Lawrence wouldn't let him ruin the whole day.

Harriet closed the front door behind Karl and returned to the parlor. "I worried about you while you were gone," she

319

said when she and Lawrence were once again seated. This time, he noted, she chose the settee, only a foot away from his chair. She had not been this close to Karl. Surely that was a good sign, as were the words she had spoken. If she worried, it must be because she cared.

"I was never in any danger," Lawrence assured her, adding, "unless you count Bruckner's tongue. It packs as much venom as a rattler."

Harriet's eyes clouded. "When I first knew him, Thomas was a sweet talker. He changed."

Sterling had said he and Ruth had changed. That might be, but Lawrence doubted that Thomas Bruckner had ever been anything but a despicable creature. "Perhaps, or perhaps he simply showed his true colors. It seems he got in over his head with gambling debts and owes a pile of money to a man named Herb Allen." Lawrence watched Harriet carefully as he said, "I don't understand it, but he thought you could bail him out."

"Me?" Her surprise wasn't feigned. Lawrence would bet on that.

"He claimed you were an heiress."

She shrugged. "I suppose I was . . . once. The money went pretty quickly after my grandparents died. What my father didn't spend on whiskey, he gambled away. He must have thought there was an endless supply, but of course there wasn't. After he and Mother died, I was fortunate to find some gold hidden in my grandparents' house. That, combined with my teacher's pay, let us continue to live a normal life." Shaking her head slowly, Harriet said, "When he came here, I told Thomas the money was gone. I don't know why he wouldn't believe me."

Lawrence believed her, for everything she said rang true. A once-wealthy family explained the books that had become such an important part of her life and the fact that she had been taught to read at an early age. Harriet's grandparents had had the time and the money to indulge her. It was also logical that her father, more concerned with whiskey than work, would have squandered his fortune, leaving her no recourse but to find a way to support her siblings.

"I hope I never see Thomas again," Harriet said. "I don't think I could trust myself to be civil."

"You won't have to see him unless you return to Fortune."

"I have no reason to do that. Ladreville is my home now."

Lawrence liked the sound of that. "Mine too." Once again, he focused his eyes on Harriet, watching for her reaction as he said, "I've decided to stay."

Her reaction did not disappoint him, for Harriet's eyes brightened, and a smile lit her face. "Oh, Lawrence, I was hoping you would. I'm so glad."

Warmth filling his heart, Lawrence nodded. It was time to leave. Tomorrow would be soon enough to tell her he loved her. Tomorrow they would both be rested, and there would be no Karl to interfere. Yes, tomorrow would be the day.

The man had to be stopped. Jake clenched his fists as he tried to slow his breathing. Tonight Old Man Karl even tried to tell the sheriff how to do his job. Jake knew, because he'd had his ear to the floor. It was bad enough when Karl ordered him and his brothers around. Though Jake hadn't liked that— no, sirree, he hadn't liked it one bit—at least Karl had been paying them. He probably thought that entitled him to treat them like slaves. It didn't, but Karl had only grown worse. Now he thought he owned everyone.

Look at how he treated Harriet. He wanted her to do everything his way, like giving up the school to that woman named Olga. Karl was trying to get Harriet to bend to his will, and she didn't seem to realize it. Though he would have thought she'd learned her lesson with Thomas, that lying sack of scum, it appeared that his normally smart sister was as dumb as dirt where Karl was concerned. If Jake didn't do something, she might even marry the man. Jake shuddered at the thought. That would be a mistake, the biggest mistake of Harriet's life. The biggest mistake in all their lives. As sure as roosters crowed, Jake knew it wouldn't be only Harriet who'd suffer. They all would.

The man was an ogre. Jake wouldn't be surprised if that was the reason Léon Rousseau stopped working for him. Jake had heard that Léon liked farming and wanted his own spread and that he'd once tried to learn from Karl. That had lasted only a couple months. No one else seemed to know why Léon wasn't spending any more time on the Friedrich farm, but Jake knew. Léon Rousseau wasn't dumb. He had figured out the real Karl and hightailed it out of there. The problem was, hightailing wasn't going to accomplish anything for Jake, not with Karl sniffing around Harriet the way he was. Jake clenched his fists again. Someone had to stop that man, and it looked like it was up to him.

He grinned. Old Karl sure had been riled when he'd cut those buggy seats. It had taken months before he'd started sweet-talking Harriet again. Maybe something worse would keep him away forever.

Harriet flung her arms out to the side and twirled around. Had there ever been such a wonderful night? Thomas was in jail; Lawrence had returned; and—best of all—he planned to stay. The bubble of happiness that had formed inside her escaped as a giggle. Sinking onto her bed, Harriet laughed. She couldn't recall the last time she'd giggled. Mary giggled. Sam and Daniel did, although they'd deny it. But Harriet had had little cause for laughter. Until tonight.

The house had come alive the moment Lawrence entered. What had been an ordinary evening listening to Karl speak of crops had become extraordinary, all because Lawrence was there. Though Karl had made no secret of his displeasure, Harriet could only praise Lawrence's decision not to bring Thomas back to Ladreville. The fewer people who knew that the fire had been set out of deliberate malice toward her, the better, for there was no telling how the townspeople might react. But this way, no one would know. Her family could continue to build a life here, a life free from scandal, free from pity. Thanks to Lawrence.

That was good, but what made the evening extra special was the way Lawrence had looked at her when they'd said good night. His eyes had sparkled with warmth, his lips had curved in the sweetest of smiles, and for an instant, she had thought he might kiss her again. If only he had, the evening would have been perfect.

Harriet giggled again, feeling like a schoolgirl infatuated with the most handsome boy in the class. It was silly, of course, to entertain dreams of a future with Lawrence. Even though he seemed to care for her and her family, it was a long way from caring to accepting responsibility for raising five children. Still, Harriet could not forget how wonderful it had felt to be held in his arms, to have his lips on hers. Surely it wasn't wrong to want another kiss. Just one more.

∽

"What's wrong?" Though the evening was cool when Lawrence arrived at the Lazy B, Zach was sitting on the porch, a lantern by his side, apparently waiting for him.

"What made you think something was wrong?"

Lawrence's antennae quivered. There was more here than met the eye. Zach had his hat tipped over his face. That in itself was odd, since the sun had long since set. And then there was his voice. The rancher sounded as if he were struggling to contain mirth. Something was going on, but Lawrence had no idea what it was.

"What made me think something was wrong? How about your note?" Lawrence was tired. That was bad enough, but finding Karl at the Kirk household had made him cranky, and so he laced his words with more sarcasm than he might have ordinarily. "You said you needed to see me and that it was important. What else was I supposed to think?"

Zach rose, pushing his hat back so he could look directly at Lawrence. "You spent too many years as a Ranger, my friend. Not all news is bad."

"Then there hasn't been more rustling?"

"Nope."

"And no one poisoned the well?"

"Not only that, but no more buildings have burned, and no one stole the silver." Zach appeared to be enjoying himself.

"So, why did you want to see me?"

The dark-haired man grinned as he opened the door and strode inside, leaving Lawrence to follow him. When they

324

were both inside, he turned and grinned again. "I'm going to be a father."

"You are?" Lawrence heard the incredulity in his voice. As he had ridden to the ranch, he had imagined half a dozen reasons why Zach might have summoned him. Fatherhood was not one of them.

"That's what Priscilla tells me, and she ought to know."

Zach a father. That was an even better announcement than Sterling's love for Ruth. "Papa Zach. It's got a nice ring to it." Lawrence clapped his friend on the back before wrinkling his nose in feigned concern. "I sure hope your children look like Priscilla. It would be a crying shame to see them saddled with your ugly mug."

"And I thought you were my friend." Undaunted by the teasing, Zach headed toward the kitchen. "Let's have a drink to celebrate. Take a seat." Zach gestured toward the table. "If you thought you were getting whiskey, I'm afraid I'm going to disappoint you. You have your choice of coffee or buttermilk."

Harriet would approve. Lawrence chuckled in amazement that almost every thought led back to her. Even when he'd fancied himself in love with Priscilla, she hadn't dominated his thoughts the way Harriet did. "I'm not disappointed. I'll take the coffee." Perhaps that would clear his head. When Zach poured them each a cup, Lawrence raised his. "Here's to your son . . . or daughter."

An hour and three cups of coffee later, he rose, suddenly aware that he hadn't seen Priscilla. It was a measure of how much he'd changed that he could come to the house he had once associated only with Priscilla and not have his first thoughts be of her.

"Where's the mother-to-be? I want to congratulate her."

"She was called out tonight. Another baby." Zach's pride in his wife's profession was apparent. "The town is growing."

"That's good news. It means they'll continue to need me."

Zach gave him an appraising look. "So, you decided to stay?" When Lawrence nodded, Zach reached for the coffeepot. "That's cause for more celebration."

It was close to midnight before Lawrence left the Lazy B, his fatigue masked by the quantity of coffee he'd consumed. When he reached the main road, he looked both directions. It was a reflex action, the result of his time as a Ranger, when he had learned the importance of being aware of his surroundings. Though Lawrence doubted there was anyone lurking behind a tree, waiting to ambush him on the way back to Ladreville, this was one habit he would not discard.

To his surprise, he saw a rider approaching rapidly from the south. Lawrence reined in Snip, wondering who was out at this hour of the night. The only houses in that direction were Clay's Bar C ranch and the Friedrich farm. Given the rider's speed, it must be Clay, heading into town to see a patient. Lawrence waited. He'd ride with Clay.

"Clay!" he called as the horseman approached. Though it was difficult to be sure in this light, it appeared that the horse was Clay's gray. But instead of waving, the rider hesitated a second, then turned around and began to gallop south. Whoever the rider was, he was not Clay. Lawrence's pulse accelerated as his instincts took over, telling him something was wrong, that these were not the actions of an innocent man. Snip needed no urging. A second later, they were in pursuit. The horseman had no chance. Only very few could outrun Snip, and the fugitive was not one of them.

As he pulled alongside the gray stallion, Lawrence reached

over and grabbed the reins, and as he did, he stared at the rider, astonished. Though he had considered the possibility that the suspicious-acting man might be someone from Ladreville, he was not prepared for his identity.

"Jake! What you are you doing out at this time of the night?" It was difficult to imagine an innocent explanation.

"Nothing. Just taking a ride."

It was a blatant lie. The way Jake refused to meet his eyes told Lawrence that, as did the fact that only a person with something to hide would have fled. "Does Harriet know you're out?"

"She doesn't need to know everything I do."

It was as Lawrence had surmised. Jake had been up to no good. "You want to tell me where you were?"

"Why should I?" His tone was defiant, definitely not the voice of someone taking a harmless midnight ride.

Lawrence kept his own voice even as he said, "You know the answer to that, Jake. I'm the sheriff. It's my job to know what's going on in my town."

"Nothing's going on."

Another lie, although perhaps not a total lie. While it was possible that nothing was going on at this particular moment, Lawrence's instincts told him that something undesirable had indeed happened and that Jake was responsible. He gave the boy a long look before he said, "If that's true, you won't mind paying a visit to the Friedrich farm, will you?" Knowing Jake's dislike of Karl, that was the logical place he would have gone tonight if he were bent on mischief.

"They're asleep."

Lawrence nodded as his suspicions were confirmed. "So you were there. That's the only way you'd know that."

"I didn't say I was there." Jake's voice rose in what years of experience had taught Lawrence was another sign of guilt. "At this time of night, most folks are asleep."

And that, Lawrence knew, was why Jake had chosen this time to be out. Had it not been for Zach's announcement, Lawrence himself would have been asleep, unaware of Jake's presence on this side of the river. "You're not asleep," he pointed out, "and that concerns me. I want to check on the Friedrichs."

"No!" Jake grabbed the reins and tried to wrest them from Lawrence's grip, grunting when he failed. The boy was as guilty as sin.

"What did you do?" He wouldn't ask why, not now. For the moment what was important was learning what had transpired at the Friedrich farm.

Jake stared into the distance, refusing to meet Lawrence's gaze. "Nothing more than he deserved."

A wave of anger rushed through Lawrence. Jake sounded like Thomas Bruckner and the vast majority of culprits he had apprehended. Whatever happened, it was never their fault. Their victims had brought it on themselves, or so the miscreants wanted to believe. Lawrence had thought Jake was different, that he had learned a lesson as he'd worked to pay for the damage he'd inflicted on Karl's buggy. But Lawrence had been wrong. Jake had learned nothing.

When they reached the Friedrich farm, instead of the darkness Jake had predicted, light shone from the barn. A second later, Karl emerged. "You! I knew it was you. When I heard a horse, I came out, but I was too late to catch you." His face contorted with fury, Karl hauled Jake from the horse and began to pummel him. "You miserable cur!" he shouted as his fist connected with Jake's nose. "You've hurt me for the last time!"

Lawrence leapt from Snip and grabbed Karl, dragging him from the boy. "That's enough, Karl. Remember, I'm the sheriff."

"And this ruffian destroyed my barn. Look." Through the open door, Lawrence could see the damage Jake had wrought. Bales of hay were coated with muck; the tack was slit beyond repair; only the animals were unharmed.

"Look at what he did! He's got to pay." Lawrence was surprised that Karl's shouts hadn't wakened his parents. As it was, the horses inside the barn moved restively, and Jake's mount pawed the ground.

"He will pay." Lawrence pulled the handcuffs from his belt and fastened them around Jake's wrists, not bothering to be gentle. Jake didn't deserve gentleness or kindness. He deserved . . . Lawrence wasn't certain what he deserved. What the boy had done was criminal. He'd destroyed Karl's property. But, more than that, he had destroyed Lawrence's faith in him. He'd thought Jake had changed, but he hadn't. The feeling of betrayal that surged through him made Lawrence want to pummel Jake the way Karl had. He'd tried to help, and this was how he was repaid. Bile rose to Lawrence's throat as he considered the possibility that Jake might wind up like Bruckner, a man without a conscience who took what he thought should be his. How would that affect Harriet? That was one thought Lawrence did not want to entertain.

"What are you going to do?" Jake asked when Lawrence had hoisted him back onto the horse and they'd left the Friedrich farm. His tone, Lawrence noted, was less defiant. Unfortunately, it was too late.

"What I should have done the first time you damaged Herr Friedrich's property: put you in jail. We'll see what the judge has to say when he comes through."

"But that won't be for months." There was no doubt about it. Jake was scared. Good. Maybe this time he *would* learn a lesson.

His own anger undiminished, Lawrence glared at the boy. "You should have thought of that before you wrecked the Friedrichs' barn."

🙟

Harriet bolted upright as the sound was repeated, banishing sleep. Why was someone knocking on the door? She fumbled on the table, searching for her spectacles. Once they were in place, she thrust her feet into slippers, reached for her dressing gown, then padded down the stairs.

The knocking continued, and with each rap, Harriet's heart beat faster. Whoever it was, he wasn't going to leave, and that could only mean bad news. With hands that shook so much she could barely strike a match, Harriet lit a lamp before she cracked the door open. Light might not change the news, but at least she could see the messenger.

"Lawrence!" Her heart skipped a beat at his foreboding expression. "What's wrong? Did Thomas escape?" That was the only reason she could imagine Lawrence coming to her house in the middle of the night. If Thomas was loose, he would want to protect her.

Lawrence shook his head as he entered the house. "It's your brother." He closed the door and stood in the hallway, his eyes dark with pain. "Jake's in jail."

"Nonsense. Jake's upstairs asleep."

"I'm afraid not." Lawrence extended his hand as if he wanted to touch her, then withdrew it. "Jake snuck out without your knowing it. There's no easy way to tell you this, Harriet. Your brother destroyed everything in Karl Friedrich's barn. It's at least a hundred dollars of damage."

As her legs threatened to buckle, Harriet leaned back against the wall, trying to understand what Lawrence was saying. The words made sense, and yet she couldn't believe them. "It can't be true." But Lawrence's presence said it was. "I thought Jake was past that sort of behavior."

"So did I, yet the fact remains that he did it. He didn't even show any remorse."

Harriet closed her eyes, wishing this were a nightmare but knowing it wasn't. No matter how much she wanted to pretend otherwise, Lawrence was standing in her house, telling her things she didn't want to hear. She opened her eyes and looked at him. "I don't know what I'm going to do with him." They could move again, though Harriet wasn't certain that would accomplish anything. She had believed that taking Jake away from Fortune and Chet's influence would solve the problem. Obviously it had not. "I just don't know what to do."

Lawrence shook his head slowly. "There's nothing for you to do. Jake has to face the consequences of breaking the law. He's in jail, and he's going to remain there for a good long time."

As Lawrence's words registered, Harriet gripped the door frame to keep her legs from collapsing. This was worse than Fortune. There she had had to deal with rumor, but now Jake was in jail like a common criminal. There had been no lasting consequences when Jake had destroyed Karl's buggy, but this was different. She doubted the townspeople would be as forgiving, when it was clear that Jake had not reformed. "You don't mean that." To her chagrin, Harriet's voice sounded like a croak.

"I most certainly do."

Fear swirled through her at the thought of her brother incarcerated and all that would mean. Unlike Fortune, where the Kirk name served as some protection, the family would be exposed to outright ridicule here. Given the severity of the crime, the townspeople might even decide Harriet was unfit to teach their children. Her contract stipulated that she must conduct herself with dignity and propriety at all times. Some towns, she knew, extended that condition to the teacher's entire family.

Harriet bit her lip, trying not to cry out. "Everyone in town will know. We'll never live it down." She looked up at Lawrence, remembering the warmth she had seen in his eyes, the concern she had heard in his voice. He cared for her; surely he did, and surely he would listen to her now. "Please, Lawrence, don't leave him there."

A flicker of something—could it be remorse?—appeared in his eyes, but Lawrence shook his head. "Whether I jail Jake or not, everyone will know, just as they know what he did to Karl's buggy. This is worse. You don't think Karl will remain silent, do you?"

Recalling Karl's temper and his demands for a severe punishment when Jake destroyed the buggy seats, Harriet started to shake her head, but then she remembered the past few days. "He might, if . . ." She let her words trail off. There was no point in voicing them, not unless she had to. Perhaps Lawrence would reconsider. Perhaps he would realize that jailing Jake would accomplish nothing and that it might hurt the family she had struggled to keep together.

"If what? If you promised to marry Karl?" Lawrence's lip curled in obvious distaste. "I know you love your family, but that's going too far. Jake needs to learn a lesson."

"I wasn't planning to marry Karl, only to ask him—as a friend—to spare us all. Public humiliation is not the answer."

"And covering it up will only encourage Jake's behavior. He has to be punished."

"But not in jail. That won't solve anything."

"Then you tell me what will. Nothing else seems to be working."

Harriet sensed Lawrence's frustration and suspected it was as great—perhaps greater—than hers. He had been the one who'd tried to help Jake by giving him constructive work to do. Lawrence had been reasonable then. Perhaps he would be reasonable now.

"You don't understand. If Jake remains in jail, you'll be punishing all of us. Is that what you intend—for us to be pariahs?"

Lawrence's lips thinned with anger. "Of course not. You're the one who doesn't understand. You won't be shunned because of what Jake has done."

"How do you know? You've never been in this situation." She saw his back stiffen and his lips tighten. In that moment, though they bore no other physical resemblance, he reminded Harriet of Thomas the day she had refused his proposal of marriage. "I thought you were different, but I should have realized you were like the others. You've distanced yourself from your family for so long that you don't know what it's like to love someone. You're heartless, Lawrence Wood. All you care about is the law, not people."

He recoiled as if she'd slapped him, and she saw his mouth move as if he were biting back an angry retort. When he spoke, Lawrence's voice was calm but cold. "Believe what you want. The truth is, you're so intent on controlling everything that you haven't admitted you might not always be right."

Harriet felt the blood drain from her face. "There was no call for that."

"Yes, there was. You need to realize that you can't do everything yourself. I thought you learned that when the school burned, but it seems that I was wrong." Lawrence's eyes blazed with a mixture of anger and sorrow. "I hate to say it, Harriet, but it looks as if you're like Jake, and you just don't learn. That won't continue forever. Eventually you're going to be forced to admit that you don't have all the answers and that you need to rely on someone else."

He was like every man she'd met, turning the tables, trying to blame her for what was wrong. Harriet tipped her head up and glared at Lawrence. "If I did rely on someone else, it would most definitely not be you." She shot the words back at him, then turned toward the door. "If you're willing to destroy my family by keeping Jake in jail, then you're not the person I thought you were. You're not my friend, and you're not welcome here." Harriet opened the door. "Good-bye, Lawrence. I don't want to see you again."

23

"Where's Jake?" Daniel looked around the breakfast table, clearly puzzled by the absence of both his brother and a place setting for him.

This was the question Harriet had dreaded. After Lawrence had left, she had paced the floor, trying to make sense of all that had happened. When she'd failed miserably at that, she had prayed that God would soften Lawrence's heart, that he'd send Jake home. That, too, had failed. There had been no lightning bolts, no prison doors opened in the middle of the night. Her brother remained in Ladreville's one cell.

"Jake did something bad, and he's in jail." By some miracle, Harriet's voice did not break as she pronounced the words.

"He's behind bars?" Daniel appeared more intrigued than surprised.

"Can we go see him?" Like his younger brother, Sam seemed to think this was an adventure. "I never saw anybody in jail."

"When's he gonna come home?" It was Mary who asked the practical question.

"I don't know." That had been one of the things Harriet had pondered during the sleepless night. "The judge will decide."

Mary's face crumpled and tears streamed down her cheeks. "I miss Jake."

"Eat your eggs, sweetie." Ruth gave Harriet a look that telegraphed her displeasure at not having been told earlier as she wrapped her arm around Mary's shoulders. "We'll visit him after breakfast."

Half an hour later the family made their way to the big stone building on Hochstrasse that served as the jail as well as Lawrence's office and home. When they arrived, Harriet insisted that the others remain outside. She wanted a private word with Lawrence and then with Jake. Unfortunately, Ladreville's sheriff was not there.

"He just left," Jake said, making Harriet wonder whether Lawrence had seen her approaching and did not want to meet her. So be it. She had told him she didn't want to see him, and she meant it. But as she had lain awake, Harriet had realized that silence and avoidance might not be the best approach. She should talk to Lawrence again and convince him that he was wrong. But Lawrence, it seemed, did not want to listen to her. She would deal with Jake first.

"Why did you do it?" Harriet tried not to cringe at the sight of her brother behind bars. He looked pitiful this morning, his face and hands unwashed, his hair in dire need of a brush, his clothing wrinkled from being slept in. And then there were the bruises. She could see the impression of a fist on one cheek, and his eye was starting to blacken. Harriet's sympathy faded when Jake's expression remained defiant.

336

"I hate him." Jake spat the words at her. "He's a mean man. I don't want you to marry him."

He was speaking of Karl. Of course, he was. Jake wasn't privy to her dreams; he had no reason to consider Lawrence a potential suitor.

"No one has asked me to marry him," Harriet said shortly.

"But Karl will. I know he will." Jake pounded the thin bedroll. "I don't want you to marry a man like him, and I don't want him to be my father. He's almost as bad as Thomas."

Was this the cause of all that destruction? "Jake, I've told you before that I'm not planning to marry, and even if I did, my husband would not be your father." *My husband*. It was the first time she had voiced those words. How strange they sounded.

"But he'd boss us all around. He already does that. He even bosses you, and I hate that." Jake stood up and clenched the bars. "Promise me you won't marry him."

Harriet's anger at her brother began to recede as she realized that he had been trying to protect her. It was strange to realize that Jake was old enough to think he should take care of her. Perhaps this was Jake's mistaken idea of what being the man of the family meant. Perhaps Lawrence was right when he'd said that her brother wanted to be accepted as an adult. Lawrence might be right about that, but he was wrong in believing that jailing Jake was the way to change his behavior. Surely he could turn the other cheek once more.

Harriet frowned at Jake. "What you did was wrong. I won't reward you by making any promises."

His upper lip quivering, as if he were trying to hold back tears, Jake shouted, "I hate you!"

She had expected that. Harriet reached out to touch his

337

hand, trying not to mind when he snatched his away. "You don't hate me, Jake. You only think you do."

᪄

Harriet tried not to frown at the raindrops that spotted her spectacles. Though she knew that rain was essential—hadn't she spent half an hour explaining its benefits to her pupils this afternoon?—she did not enjoy walking in it. Perhaps she should have gone directly home after school, but she wanted to visit Isabelle. An hour with her friend would boost her spirits. Harriet was counting on it.

As she plodded down Hochstrasse toward the miller's small house, she realized she should have come sooner. The last time she had been here was before "the night," as Harriet referred to Jake's imprisonment. The weeks had passed more quickly than she had expected. Although she had not thought it possible, her brother seemed to have settled into life behind bars. There'd been no more talk of hating her and Karl. Instead, seemingly chastened, Jake had told Harriet he knew he'd done wrong and had agreed to apologize to Karl and his parents. Though the scene had been awkward, with Frau Friedrich keeping a tight grip on her son's arm as if she feared he would try to break into the cell and pummel Jake, Karl had accepted the apology and had resumed his visits to the Kirk house.

He came almost every evening, occasionally bringing his mother. The visits verged on boring, for he spoke of things as mundane as the weather and the crops he planned to plant. The one topic Karl studiously avoided was Jake. That was fine with Harriet. She had no need to relive the embarrassment of seeing her brother in jail, of knowing that the town was

338

talking about him and that several parents had questioned her ability to teach their children. That echo of life in Fortune was painful enough without resurrecting it during Karl's visits.

Harriet still wasn't certain why he came so often. Despite Ruth's comments and Jake's concerns, she did not believe Karl was courting her. He said nothing that could be construed as personal, but the fact that Karl, who had good reason to shun the Kirk family, did not had not gone unnoticed by the town's grapevine. It was, Harriet suspected, the primary reason she had not faced more disapproval, and for that reason she did not discourage Karl's visits.

The biggest surprise was Daniel and Sam. Though their initial reaction had made Harriet fear they would lionize their brother's exploits, they had not. Instead, when they had realized that Jake could not leave the cell to roll a hoop down the street, that he had no toys to while away the day, and that friends were not permitted to visit, they had both become unusually docile, declaring they would not misbehave, because they feared winding up in jail. If that continued, at least one good thing would have resulted from Jake's incarceration.

And, Harriet reminded herself, today's rain meant spring was approaching. Spring had always been her favorite season, a time for delighting in the smell of new grass, the chirps and twitters of baby birds, and the sight of bluebonnets carpeting the countryside. She ought to be happy, and yet she wasn't. Though she could blame it on Jake, her brother's absence was not the cause of Harriet's malaise. As much as it pained her to admit it, the problem was Lawrence. She missed his visits to the schoolhouse, their arguments over books, the quiet comfort of walking down the street, her hand on his arm. She missed him—the old Lawrence. But that Lawrence was gone forever. In his place was the stern stranger who insisted that Jake remain in jail. Now that Harriet no longer had Lawrence's visits to look forward to, her days felt gray, even when the Texas sky was its normal faultless blue.

Harriet collapsed her umbrella as Isabelle ushered her into the house with a warm smile. This was what she needed, time with her friend.

"I'm glad you came." As they took seats at the kitchen table, Isabelle laid her hand on her stomach. "It's difficult for me to get out much. Gunther insists I stay inside when it rains." She wrinkled her nose. "He's worried that I'll slip and fall. And then there are the babies. They seem to take turns sleeping so I can't ever rest."

Though the complaints might be valid, Isabelle did not appear to be suffering. "You look wonderful," Harriet told her. "Your face is glowing, and your eyes—I've seen stars that sparkle less."

"Maybe so, but I'll be glad when I can hold the little darlings in my arms." Isabelle poured a cup of coffee for Harriet, her eyes darkening as she handed it to her. "If I'm overstepping, blame it on friendship, but no one would say you were glowing. What's wrong?"

Harriet debated what to say. She wanted to talk about Lawrence, about the hole their estrangement left in her life, but at the same time she didn't want anyone to know how foolish she had been, believing that the kind, thoughtful Lawrence was the real one. She settled for saying, "It's the rain. I never did like rainy days." That was not a lie. Soggy skirts and boots were no fun, and the mud the younger children invariably dragged into the house only added to her dislike of precipitation.

Isabelle set her cup down and stared at Harriet, her expression filled with skepticism. "I think it's more than that."

That was the problem with friends. They saw too much. Harriet wouldn't mention Lawrence, but she could ask Isabelle about Jake. More than anyone in Ladreville, Isabelle knew what it was like to have a brother in trouble. "I'm concerned about Jake," Harriet admitted. "You may have heard that the judge is scheduled to be here next week. I suppose you'll tell me that worrying doesn't accomplish anything, but I wish I knew what kind of sentence he'll impose."

"Isabelle, everything's fine," Gunther's voice boomed as he opened the door. "The dam will hold." He shook the rain from his clothes, then turned, his face reddening when he saw Harriet.

"*Entschuldigen Sie mich.*" It was a measure of his embarrassment that he had reverted to his native German. "Excuse me, Harriet. I didn't realize Isabelle had a visitor."

"My husband worries about everything," Isabelle said with a fond smile for Gunther. "Every day he worries about me, about our babies. Today he's added the dam, which is perfectly fine, as are the babies and I." She shook her finger at Gunther in playful reproof. "I told you there was no cause to worry, didn't I?"

"You were right," he admitted. "I just wanted you to know. Now I'll leave you alone."

When Gunther returned to the mill, Isabelle smiled. "Even if he does worry, I love him dearly."

And Gunther loved her. Even a blind man would have known that, simply from the way Gunther's voice changed when he spoke to or about his wife. It was difficult to believe he'd courted two other women, including Olga Kaltheimer.

"You need to find a man like Gunther," Isabelle said, placing her hand on her midsection, "someone who will love you, even when you're as big as the mill."

As Lawrence's image flashed before her, Harriet frowned. "I'm more worried about Jake and what the judge will say."

The twinkle in her eyes said Isabelle recognized Harriet's deliberate change of subject and was amused by it. "I can't imagine that the punishment will be serious. Maman heard some of the townspeople say they'd testify on Jake's behalf."

What? Harriet swallowed her coffee so quickly that she began to choke. "Truly?" she asked when she could breathe again. She hadn't been able to ignore the speculative looks she received each time she entered a public building. Church services were the worst. It might have been her imagination, but she felt as if disapproving eyes were boring into her back throughout the sermon.

"Don't misunderstand." Isabelle's brown eyes sobered. "Everyone believes that what Jake did was very wrong, but they think he's paid for his crime. A month in jail when you're Jake's age is an eternity."

"It feels like that to me too." Only a month, but it seemed much longer since her life had changed. While it had once been filled with anticipation, now it seemed empty, devoid of Jake and Lawrence.

"It will get better. I know it." Isabelle reached across the table and laid her hand on Harriet's, squeezing it slightly.

"I wish I shared your optimism."

Lawrence stared at the papers on his desk, laying the judge's telegram on top, trying to ignore the fact that he had a prisoner in his jail. He would be thankful when the judge arrived and he could put the whole incident behind him. Things certainly hadn't turned out the way he'd expected. Instead of telling Harriet he loved her and wanted to court her, Lawrence had wound up angering her.

He leaned back in his chair and propped his feet on the desk. From Harriet's reaction, it appeared that he'd done more than anger her. Though he'd been too tired to recognize it at the time, there had been fear on her face—stark, undeniable terror. It was only afterward, when he'd replayed the scene for what seemed like the hundredth time, that he'd realized what he had seen. If he'd been less tired and frustrated and more aware, he might have acted differently. He couldn't have agreed not to jail Jake, but he might have provided Harriet with some reassurance.

As it was, no matter what Lawrence wished, it appeared he could not undo the damage. Harriet refused to listen to him. This was worse than the time she'd seen him leaving the saloon. Then she treated him like a stranger. Now it was as if he'd become invisible. When they were together, she somehow managed to look right through him, even though her eyes reflected so much pain that he knew her fears had not subsided.

"She's afraid we'll be separated," Jake said one day when Harriet had left. Though Lawrence had asked no questions, not wanting to take advantage of Jake's vulnerability, the boy had begun speaking of his family. "I wasn't supposed to be listening," Jake admitted, "but I heard her and Ruth talking one day. It seems when our parents died, folks in Fortune thought she was too young to care for us. They were going to send each of us to a different family. Harriet must have fought

343

like a cat to stop that." Jake frowned. "And then there was Thomas." Lawrence was tempted to smile at the way Jake spat the name. It appeared he and Harriet's brother shared at least one thing: contempt for Thomas Bruckner.

"Thomas wanted to marry her," Jake said, "but he didn't want us. He said Ruth was old enough to be in charge. Harriet didn't like that."

And now she probably feared that the judge would send Jake away. It was in the man's power. Lawrence knew that, just as he knew he couldn't let it happen. Fortunately, his word as Ladreville's sheriff and a former Ranger would hold weight in the sentence, as would the private, informal conversation he planned to have with the judge. One way or another, Lawrence would ensure that the Kirk family remained together. Then he'd do what he could to rebuild Harriet's trust in him.

"What do you think the judge will say?" Jake asked when Lawrence brought him his midday meal.

"I don't know." Lawrence knew what Jake wanted him to say, but he could guarantee nothing. Drawing up a stool, he reached for his own plate. Other sheriffs might frown on it, but he'd taken to eating one meal a day with his prisoner. For a boy Jake's age to be kept in what was close to solitary confinement had to be difficult. Lawrence would not release him, but there was no statute against a lawman eating with his prisoner, especially when the prisoner had begun to evidence remorse.

As painful as it had been for Jake, it appeared that the stay in jail had changed him. Gone were the defiance and sullen mien. At his own request, Jake spent an hour each day with Sterling, reading the Bible and praying. Though it might have been a ploy for mercy, Sterling believed the changes he and

Lawrence observed were real. While it was true that Jake's feelings toward Karl hadn't softened, the way he acted on those feelings had.

"I wish I hadn't done it." Jake shoveled the stew into his mouth as if he were starving, when it had been only a few hours since he'd eaten a hearty breakfast. "I caused everyone a lot of pain. Harriet, Karl, you."

Lawrence chewed carefully as he tried to find the right words. Though Jake had admitted his wrongdoing and apologized to Karl, this was the first time he'd recognized the pain he had inflicted. It was a major step forward. Sterling would claim that God was softening Jake's heart.

"It's amazing, isn't it, how one act affects so many and how even the simplest thing can have unplanned repercussions?" Lawrence asked as casually as he could. "My mother used to warn my sister and me to be careful what we said and did. She claimed it was like casting a stone into water. The ripples spread across the pond. They even touch the shores."

Jake's eyes darkened. "I didn't mean to do that."

"I know."

❦

"Miss Kirk! Miss Kirk! You've gotta come." Eva burst through the door to the makeshift classroom, her face red with exertion and excitement. Every day since school had moved to the French church hall, she had been the last to arrive back from the midday recess. Though Harriet suspected she knew what delayed Eva, today was her first confirmation. "The garden's sprouted."

Harriet smiled at the knowledge that Eva was inspecting the garden each day. Though she had expected that the rain earlier in the week would hasten the flowers' emergence, Harriet hadn't thought it would be so soon. Today was supposed to be Texas history day, but looking at the children's faces, she knew there was no point in trying to teach this afternoon. All thoughts would be on the germinating seeds.

"All right, children. Let's go to the garden."

"Yeah!" The pupils leapt to their feet.

"It's a miracle." Marie Seurat stared at the tiny shoots. "They were dead, and now they're growing."

"They weren't really dead," Harriet explained. "They were dormant." When the children gave her puzzled looks, she added, "That means sleeping. Now they're awake."

Marie shook her head vehemently. "I still think it's a miracle."

❦

What was a miracle was the judge's decision a week later. When he heard all the evidence, he declared that Jake had spent enough time in jail and that no further punishment was necessary other than restitution. Now Jake was home again, sitting at the kitchen table, waiting for supper as if nothing had happened. But it had, and the younger children stared at him, as if searching for visible signs of his incarceration.

"Are you coming back to school?"

Though Mary posed the question, Jake looked at Harriet before he answered. "I still have work to do," he reminded her. "I need to finish paying for the buggy seats. And then there's the barn. I haven't told the Friedrichs, but I want to paint it when I've paid for the damages."

Harriet wanted to shout with joy at the realization that one of her prayers had been answered. Jake had changed.

The judge had not stipulated anything more than payment for the damage done to the barn, but Jake was volunteering to do more. Her brother was growing up.

Keeping her face as neutral as she could, Harriet said, "You can do lessons at night."

Jake wrinkled his nose. "Aw, Harriet."

Some things would never change.

⁊

Karl looked different tonight. It wasn't simply the fresh haircut or the carefully trimmed beard. Though normally relaxed, tonight he appeared almost ill at ease. Harriet wondered if that was because he knew that Jake was in the house. Karl alone of the people who had stood in Lawrence's office as the judge made his decision had appeared unhappy. Though she suspected his spirits—and perhaps his opinion of Jake—would rise if he knew that her brother planned to do more than replace the contents of the barn, she would say nothing. When and how Karl learned that was up to her brother.

"Sit down, Karl." Harriet motioned him to one of the comfortable chairs, hoping that would ease whatever was bothering him. As usual, as soon as he had knocked on the door, the rest of the family had left. Ruth remained in the far corner of the parlor for propriety's sake, but the younger children fled upstairs.

Karl looked around, as if assuring himself that they would not be overheard, but instead of relaxing, he gripped the chair arms for a moment, then leaned forward slightly, clasping his hands around one knee. It was a gesture Harriet had never seen him make. Something was different, decidedly different, tonight.

347

"You must know that I admire you," Karl said, looking directly at her, his light blue eyes shining with conviction. "You're a strong woman, Harriet. The way you raised your siblings tells me you would be a fine mother. Mutter says you're a fast learner and could be a good cook."

Harriet tried not to frown. Though she hadn't really believed Karl was courting her, his behavior tonight made her wonder if that was the case. But what a strange way to start. Why, it sounded as if he were evaluating her the way he would a hog or a cow he was considering purchasing. Surely that was not the prelude to a declaration of tender feelings. Though Harriet had no way of reading what was inside his heart, Karl's words were not those of a man who cared deeply, and his voice held none of the warmth Gunther's betrayed when he spoke to Isabelle. Harriet was mistaken. She must be.

Karl cleared his throat, then stroked his beard in his habitual gesture. "What I'm trying to say is, I believe we're suited to each other. Will you be my wife?"

For a second Harriet could not speak. Once again she had been wrong. Karl *was* courting her, and now she had to refuse him. If only she'd paid more attention to Ruth and Isabelle, she might have prevented this.

No! she wanted to shriek. *I will not marry you.* But a blunt refusal would hurt Karl's feelings. As she recalled the kindness his family had shown her, Harriet knew she could not hurt Karl. Somehow she had to find a way to preserve his dignity. "I'm sorry, Karl," she said at last. "I'm not ready to marry."

The frown that crossed his face said he hadn't expected her refusal. "Why not?"

So many reasons. I don't love you. You don't love me. We're too different to get along together. I have responsibilities to my family. The determination in Karl's eyes told Harriet he would argue, no matter which of those excuses she cited, and so she seized on the one he could not dispute. "I need to finish my contract."

"Olga Kaltheimer would take over."

How often would she be wrong? Karl could dispute even that reason. "I made a commitment to finish this year," she said, "and I plan to honor that. Besides, I'd like to teach at least one year in the new school." It would be her school, just as the first one had been Sarah's.

"There's more, isn't there?" When Harriet did not reply, Karl said, "If you're worried about your brothers and sisters, there's a place for them on the farm too. If Jake agrees to behave, he can work with the horses. I can teach the younger boys how to raise crops, and the little girl can learn to cook."

Mary. Her name is Mary. If Harriet had had any doubts at the wisdom of refusing Karl's proposal, the way he had referred to her siblings, almost as if he were hiring servants, would have quashed them. "I'm sorry, Karl," she said firmly, "but I cannot marry you."

Though his lips twisted in obvious disapproval, his voice was calm as he said, "I can see that this came as a surprise. I will let you think about my proposal. We will not speak of it for a month. By then you will have had time to reconsider."

Harriet shook her head, not wanting to encourage him. A month, a year, a lifetime. It would make no difference, and it would only be cruel to offer hope when there was none. "I don't need more time." Though it might be harsh, she had to tell him the truth. "I like you, Karl, but I don't love you."

He nodded, as if he had expected that. "I don't need love."

"But I do."

349

24

Harriet turned, startled by the sound of the front door knocker. It was Saturday morning, and for once she was alone in the house, kneading bread dough. Recognizing Harriet's refusal of help as a sign that she needed time to think, Ruth had taken Mary to the mercantile with her, while the younger boys had gone to Herr Goetz's woodworking shop with Jake. Far from being annoyed by the boys' interest, the carpenter had agreed that they could spend Saturday mornings helping him and Jake. Though Harriet suspected the help would involve nothing more than sweeping shavings and cleaning tools, she was grateful for the man's willingness to include them. Lawrence claimed that a masculine influence was important, particularly for boys at what he called an impressionable age. If Herr Goetz could provide a positive example for her brothers, he would have Harriet's deepest gratitude. Perhaps that, as well as Jake's experiences, would keep them safe from temptation.

But it wasn't thoughts of the boys that tumbled through her

brain like water over Gunther's dam. It was worries about her future. Harriet didn't regret refusing Karl's offer of marriage, for she couldn't wed a man she didn't love simply to avoid being alone. What concerned her and what had kept her awake most of the night was the realization that the future she had dreamt of, a future that included a small house of her own and no responsibilities, had lost its appeal. What had once seemed like a blessed respite from the years of raising her siblings now appeared to be nothing more than an existence devoid of everything that made life worth living. Harriet had hoped that the light of day would clear her thoughts, but instead of the silence she craved, she was faced with a visitor.

Hastily she washed the dough from her hands and walked to the door, wondering who it could be. Despite her increasing girth, Isabelle would be at the mercantile. Karl would not return, and it wouldn't be Lawrence. Harriet was certain of that. She opened the door, her eyes widening at the sight of Frau Friedrich.

"May I come in?"

Harriet nodded and ushered the older woman into the house. "Certainly. You're always welcome here."

Frau Friedrich's blue eyes clouded with doubt. "I wasn't sure after what happened last night." As she took the chair Harriet offered, she nodded slowly. "Oh yes, Karl told me you refused his offer of marriage." Frau Friedrich leaned forward. "He doesn't know I'm here. Karl would probably be angry if he knew, but I wanted to see whether you would reconsider. My son may not be as handsome as the mayor and he might not appear exciting, but he's a good man."

"Yes, he is." Harriet would never dispute that. Karl *was* a good man; he simply wasn't the right man for her.

His mother gave her a wistful smile. "Otto and I love you. We often say you're the daughter we prayed for. It simply took God a while to send you to us."

Blinking her eyes to hold back the tears, Harriet nodded, then leaned forward and clasped Frau Friedrich's hand between hers. "I love you too." If she could have chosen her parents, she would have picked Frau and Herr Friedrich. Though not outwardly demonstrative, their love for each other was evidenced in everything they said and did, proof for Harriet that love existed outside the covers of a book. When she'd been with them, she had been able to pretend that she was part of a real family, but now that relationship was in jeopardy. Harriet hated the thought that her unwillingness to marry Karl might estrange her from his parents.

"Then, won't you reconsider? You may not love Karl now, but love can grow." Frau Friedrich smiled again. "I know, because it happened to me. Like many of the marriages in the Old Country, mine was arranged by my parents. Otto and I were practically strangers when we wed, but our parents knew each other and believed it would be a good match." She nodded briskly. "It has been. Our parents planted the seeds, and Otto and I nourished them. It may have started as friendship, but now I love Otto dearly and cannot imagine my life without him."

It was a lovely story. Unfortunately, it would never be hers. Harriet tightened her grip on Frau Friedrich's hand, willing the older woman to understand. "I wish I could say I believed I would learn to love Karl, but I can't. I would not be a good wife for him."

"Don't be hasty, my dear. Marriage is for a lifetime. Take time to think about it. That's all I ask." Frau Friedrich rose and drew on her gloves.

When Karl's mother had left, Harriet returned to the kitchen, wishing she had been able to give the older woman a different answer, knowing she could not. She was in the midst of giving the bread its first kneading when she heard another knock on the door.

"You're still alone." Isabelle looked around as she entered the kitchen. "Good. I hoped I'd beat Ruth and Mary home."

The gleam in her friend's eyes told Harriet this was not a casual visit. "Would you like to sit in the parlor?"

"Oh no." Isabelle pulled out a chair and settled herself by the kitchen table. "I can't stay long. Maman needs me at the store, but I thought you might need a friend."

What Harriet needed was solitude, but that, it appeared, would not happen. "Did Ruth tell you I was baking bread?" she asked, trying to deflate Isabelle's curiosity by reminding her of the time when she'd forgotten the second kneading and the bread had been tough.

Isabelle shook her finger at Harriet. "I know what you're doing, and it won't work." Her expression radiated sympathy as she said, "I heard Karl was here only a short time last night, and Madame Seurat said she saw his mother heading this way this morning. That can mean only one thing."

Harriet tried not to sigh at the evidence that the Ladreville grapevine was alive and healthy. "What it means is that the Friedrichs are my friends," she said with a bright smile.

Isabelle's eyes narrowed. "Then you didn't agree to marry Karl."

There was little point in pretending. "Did you think I would?"

Isabelle shrugged. "I prayed you wouldn't, but I wasn't sure. Some days I don't understand you."

"Some days I don't, either."

Five minutes later, Isabelle had departed, promising to do her best to deflect rumors of Karl's proposal. It might not work, but Harriet wanted to spare the Friedrich family embarrassment.

The bread was kneaded and placed in pans for its final rising when someone knocked on the door. Not again. Had Ladreville's citizens somehow decided that Saturday was the day for visits?

"Pastor Russell." Harriet stared at the tall, thin man, wondering why he had come. When he visited, it was always in the evening. "Is something wrong?" Harriet's heart began to pound at the realization that the minister was Lawrence's closest friend. Had something happened to Lawrence?

Color rose to the minister's cheeks. "No, no, there's nothing wrong. I simply wanted to speak with you."

He might deny it, but something was amiss. The man who was normally self-assured, the same man who had shown no fear when his congregation had turned against him, was decidedly uneasy.

"Come in." Harriet ushered him into the parlor. "How can I help you?" For there was no doubt that Sterling Russell needed assistance. His hazel eyes moved nervously around the room, as if he were seeking something, and she detected a slight tremor in his hands.

Perched on the edge of the chair, Sterling cleared his throat. "I must confess that this is not the way I envisioned this moment. I always thought I'd be addressing an older man, not a young woman."

Though his words formed complete English sentences, they made no sense. "What is it?" Perhaps if she was direct with her question, she would receive a coherent answer.

Sterling cleared his throat again. "It's Ruth. Since your father is no longer alive, I've come to ask your permission to court her. I love Ruth, and I want her to be my wife."

Though his words lacked the eloquence of his sermons, no one could doubt Sterling's sincerity. He loved Harriet's sister. His voice held the same fervency that Frau Friedrich's had when she'd spoken of her beloved Otto, the same warmth Harriet heard whenever Gunther addressed Isabelle. Unlike Karl, who had proposed marriage because his head told him it was a good idea, Sterling's deepest feelings were clearly engaged.

"Does Ruth know how you feel?"

"I'm not certain." Sterling had begun to relax, perhaps realizing that Harriet would not dismiss his suit out of hand. "I have not made a declaration, if that's what you're asking, but I also have not tried to hide my feelings. I don't want her to be shocked when I ask her to marry me. Do I have your permission?"

Ruth, little Ruth, would be a bride. Harriet tried and failed to picture her sister living in the parsonage. She was too young. Harriet shook her head slowly, admitting that at eighteen, Ruth was indeed old enough to marry.

"Why not?"

Harriet blinked at Sterling's question before she realized she had shaken her head and he'd believed that was her answer.

"I want my sister to be happy," she said slowly, remembering Ruth on Christmas Day, how her face had glowed with happiness. That glow had come when Sterling had entered the house. "I believe you'll bring her that happiness." Harriet nodded at Sterling. "You have my permission to court Ruth."

"If you don't get in this buggy of your own volition, I'll drag you into it."

Harriet couldn't help it. She laughed. "In your condition? I think not." Though Isabelle's babies weren't due for another two months, she moved slowly and deliberately, and she was careful not to lift anything heavy, lest she harm the twins. Still grinning, Harriet climbed into the buggy. "What's so urgent?" When she had returned from the midday recess, Eva had delivered a note, saying Isabelle wanted to take her for a ride after school.

She had certainly picked the perfect day. A few lazy cumulus clouds, so white they almost made Harriet's eyes hurt, drifted across the sky. And then there was the sky itself. Though normally a vibrant blue, today it seemed brighter than usual, almost the same shade as Lawrence's eyes. Harriet bit the inside of her cheek, reminding herself there was nothing to be gained by thoughts of Lawrence. "What's going on?" she asked.

"The bluebonnets are in bloom," Isabelle announced as the buggy began to roll forward. "I didn't want you to miss them, so when Priscilla told me about a wonderful spot, I decided we should go there." She guided the horses into the river, the tightening of her grip on the reins and the straight line of her lips telling Harriet she did not enjoy fording water any more than Lawrence. *Stop thinking about Lawrence,* Harriet chided herself. *Stop remembering that he promised to show you the flowers.*

"You can't miss seeing our bluebonnets." When they reached the opposite bank, Isabelle's shoulders relaxed and she smiled again. "I know you said there were bluebonnets in Fortune, but ours are the best in the state."

Though Harriet wondered how Isabelle, who had never lived anywhere else in Texas, was so certain of the local flowers' superiority, she forbore asking. "I've never been this direction," she said as the buggy turned right. The Friedrich farm and Zach's and Clay's ranches were on the south side of the crossing, but Isabelle was headed north.

"This is part of the Lazy B," Isabelle said, referring to Zach's ranch. "Priscilla said she and Zach want to build a new house in the place we're going to. In the meantime, they use it for picnics."

"And they don't mind us coming?"

Isabelle laughed as they turned onto what appeared to be little more than a track. "They're happy to share their flowers with us."

Though something in Isabelle's tone told Harriet she had more on her mind than bluebonnets, she said nothing, knowing her friend would raise the subject when she was ready. Meanwhile, Isabelle's attention was on the horses. Maneuvering carefully, she guided them through a small grove of trees to a clearing.

Although she'd expected bluebonnets, Harriet could only stare at the sight of a meadow so carpeted with flowers that it appeared blue. "This is incredible." She took a deep breath as she admired the flowers. "We had patches of bluebonnets near Fortune, but they were nothing compared to this."

While Isabelle tied the horses to one of the trees, Harriet climbed out of the buggy, then bent down to touch the delicate flowers. Though mostly blue, the tips of the blossoms were white with yellow highlights. "It looks like icing, doesn't it? The flowers could be some kind of sweet—blueberry, I guess—with vanilla icing." As Isabelle chuckled at the image,

Harriet leaned closer, searching for a fragrance. Though the Fortune bluebonnets had had no distinctive perfume, these were so much larger and so much deeper blue that she thought they might possess a fragrance. They did not. Slightly disappointed, Harriet reminded herself that the absence of a scent did not in any way diminish their beauty. "Oh, Isabelle, this is wonderful." She fingered one of the blossoms, reveling in the softness of the petals.

"I know how you love flowers, so I thought you'd enjoy this."

"I do." Harriet stood, gesturing toward the meadow. Perhaps a strong fragrance would have distracted her from the bluebonnets' beauty. Didn't the Bible claim that people were given different talents? Perhaps flowers were like them, some meant to dazzle the eyes, others to tantalize the nose. "There's something magnificent, isn't there, about wildflowers? We do nothing, and yet they're there for us to enjoy."

Isabelle nodded. "They're one of God's gifts to us."

"As are your babies."

Placing her hand on her abdomen, Isabelle smiled. "The twins are kicking. I think that means they're saying amen."

"Just think. Next spring you can bring them here. I can picture them crawling through the flowers. Be careful, though. They'll probably try to eat them." Mary had when she'd been an infant.

"That's what I wanted to talk to you about."

"Your babies eating bluebonnets?"

"No." Isabelle reached for Harriet's hand as they walked toward the center of the meadow, their skirts brushing the flowers, setting off a ripple of blue. "Next spring is what concerns me. Everyone in Ladreville is excited about Ruth and

Sterling's betrothal." Isabelle wrinkled her nose. "Everyone but you. You don't seem happy. Are you displeased by the match?"

"No." How could Isabelle think that? "When Sterling asked permission to court Ruth, I gave it freely. I'll admit I'm thankful they've decided to wait a year, because that will give them a chance to prepare for marriage. It's a major step . . ." Harriet paused before adding, "for all of us."

Isabelle did not appear convinced. "Are you certain you're happy about this?"

Of course she was. A year would give Harriet time to plan the next stage of her life. "Only a selfish ogre would begrudge her sister happiness. I hope I'm not a selfish ogre."

"You're not." Isabelle squeezed Harriet's hand in reassurance. "But something's wrong. The sparkle has left your eyes."

Nonsense. "I must need to clean my spectacles."

Isabelle stopped walking and faced Harriet. "You're trying to distract me, but it won't work." She gave Harriet a long look. "I doubt you're bothered by the fact that Karl hasn't resumed his courtship, so if you're not concerned about Ruth, there's only one reason I can find for your megrims: Lawrence."

"That's preposterous," Harriet sputtered. "Ladreville's mayor has nothing to do with my moods."

A frown greeted her words. "You never were a good liar, Harriet. Your eyes darken when you're fibbing. Don't try to deny it. After all, I know you better than most people in town." Isabelle took a step forward, placing a finger under Harriet's chin and tipping it so that she looked directly into her eyes. "I've tried not to say anything, because I know you don't like people interfering with your life, but I can't let you go on this way. Face it, Harriet. You're miserable without him. Why don't you admit you love the man?"

"Because I don't." Isabelle's frown deepened, leading Harriet to add, "The truth is, I don't know if I'm capable of loving anyone." She hadn't loved Thomas, and she certainly didn't love Karl. As for Lawrence . . .

"*Quelle blague.*" Isabelle shook her head when she remembered that Harriet did not understand French. "What a joke. You're a loving, caring woman. You love your siblings. That's why you'd do anything for them. You care about your pupils, and I don't believe I'm stretching the truth when I say you love me. Why won't you admit you love Lawrence?"

"Because I don't." Dissembling would accomplish nothing. Isabelle was right; she knew Harriet well enough to recognize a lie. "Oh, I may have fancied myself in love at one point, but that was before he showed his true colors and proved that I don't know the least bit about love. Oh, Isabelle, I want to *be loved*, not just love someone, but Lawrence is like all the rest. He thinks only of himself."

Isabelle gasped, clearly shocked by Harriet's accusation. "You're wrong. Lawrence is a good, kind man. He's a lawman, so he has to follow the law, but at the same time, he tries to do what's best for everyone." When Harriet started to protest, Isabelle placed a finger over her lips, stifling her retort. "If you're still angry that he jailed Jake, shame on you. That was Lawrence's job, but he did more than he had to. Your brother is a changed man, and it's because of Lawrence. If you hadn't closed your eyes, you'd see that. You'd also see that he's perfect for you."

"You're wrong."

"No, I'm not. You're just too stubborn to admit it."

ॐ

Lawrence stared out the window. It was a beautiful May day. Though Zach had told him that Clay's father, a Texas old-timer if there ever was one, was predicting heavy rain in the next few days, the sky was devoid of clouds and as deep a blue as Lawrence had ever seen. He wouldn't dispute the old man's prognosticative abilities, but it sure as bluebonnets in April didn't look like rain.

His lips curved in a smile at the thought of his favorite spring flower. Though the bluebonnets had faded as they did each year at this time, Harriet's garden was flourishing, providing beauty for the entire community. Any fears Harriet had once harbored about her contract not being renewed should have been put to rest. The Christmas pageant, the garden and, of course, her response to the school fire had established her as a local heroine. The townspeople could not say enough good things about her. Lawrence didn't disagree.

Harriet was the most fascinating woman he had ever met— and the most frustrating. It appeared that once she made up her mind, nothing would change it. Other than superficially polite greetings when they met in public places, she refused to speak to him. She wouldn't even open the notes he'd sent but returned them without a word. Though Sterling had suggested trying another small gift, Lawrence was unwilling to risk more rejection. Harriet's mind was closed to him.

Each day Lawrence prayed for understanding, but there were no answers. He knew God had brought him to Ladreville for a reason, and as the months had passed, he had believed that reason was to settle down, marry, and raise a family—a ready-made family. He had also believed Harriet was the woman God intended for him. It appeared he was wrong.

"Sheriff Wood." Lawrence turned, surprised by the familiar voice. What was Jake doing in his office? "Er . . . Mayor Wood . . . er . . ." Whatever brought him, it made the boy uncomfortable. Or perhaps Jake's uncharacteristic reticence was the result of his proximity to the jail cell.

"Mr. Wood is fine." Lawrence accompanied his words with a warm smile. "It's good to see you, but shouldn't you be at work?"

Jake shook his head. "Herr Goetz told me it was okay to come. I need to talk to you." Though he did his best to hide it, Harriet's brother sounded as if he were scared.

"Sit down." Lawrence gestured toward the chair that faced away from the cell and took the other one, further blocking the view of the place where Jake had spent a month. "Now, what's on your mind?"

"Will you marry Harriet?"

Lawrence felt his jaw drop with shock. "Did I hear you correctly?" When he'd first thought of marrying Harriet, Lawrence had known that her siblings could be a barrier. Harriet, he knew instinctively, would not consider a man the rest of the family would not accept. Lawrence had hoped that one day they'd give him that acceptance, even if it was grudging, but he'd never dreamt that one of them would approach him. "You want me to marry your sister?"

Though Jake nodded, his blue eyes were clouded with concern, as if he feared Lawrence would refuse. "Yes, sir," he said, his voice shaking ever so slightly. "I talked to the others, and they all agreed. We'll even call you Pa if you like."

Lawrence smelled a rat, and it didn't take a genius to figure out that Karl Friedrich was involved. "What's going on, Jake? I know you don't want a father."

"No, sir, but if we have to have one, you're the one we want." Jake's words confirmed Lawrence's belief that Karl had said or done something to precipitate this unexpected conversation. "You wouldn't boss Harriet around."

"I don't think anyone could boss your sister."

Jake's lips curled in contempt. "He tries, and he'll be worse if she marries him."

It had to be Karl. The grapevine had been silent, but whatever had happened might have been too recent for the town's busybodies to learn of it. A chill snaked through Lawrence as he considered the possibilities. "Has Harriet agreed to marry Mr. Friedrich?"

"No." It was only one word, but the relief it sent through Lawrence was far greater than the simple answer should warrant. Jake clenched his fists and stared at Lawrence. "She won't say anything, but we think he asked her already and plans to ask again. We're afraid she'll give in."

"Your sister is the strongest person I know. She won't capitulate just because someone is persistent."

"Cap . . . ? What does that mean?"

"It's a fancy way of saying 'give in.' Believe me, Harriet won't agree to anything she doesn't want."

"You don't know her the way we do. She might marry him if she thought it was best for us." Leaning forward, as if to emphasize his words, Jake continued. "Harriet's always done that. Looked after us, that is. She didn't have any friends in Fortune because she was so busy taking care of us. The only person who came around was Thomas, but she sent him packing. I heard her tell him she wouldn't marry anyone who wouldn't take good care of us, and he sure wouldn't. He didn't even love her."

Lawrence heard the pain in Jake's voice. "It was nothing personal, Jake. Thomas Bruckner doesn't love anyone but himself."

The boy's face brightened. "You're different. You may not love us, but you care about us. I know you do."

"I do, and I'd like to help you, Jake." Lawrence preferred not to imagine what the Kirk children's lives would be like with Karl Friedrich as their brother-in-law. Though Lawrence had once been reluctant—oh, all right, downright unwilling—to take on a ready-made family, he had gotten past the point of considering Harriet's siblings a nuisance. Unfortunately, he doubted that Karl had changed his mind. "The problem is, there's nothing I can do."

Jake shook his head vehemently. "Yes, there is. You can marry Harriet."

He couldn't let Jake continue with that fantasy. "It wouldn't work. She wouldn't agree. You see, Harriet doesn't love me."

Jake's lips tightened. "She does. I know she does. Just ask her."

And have his heart wrenched from his body and handed back to him on a silver platter like John the Baptist's head? No, thank you. "Jake, I—"

Before Lawrence could finish the sentence, Steven Dunn poked his head through the door. "I'm sorry to interrupt, Sheriff," Ladreville's postmaster said, "but this telegram just came for you. It seems important." He handed the piece of paper to Lawrence, waiting while he read it.

Lawrence frowned. Steven was right. This was important. More than that, it was urgent. Rustlers had struck, and

Golden's sheriff needed his help. With a deep sigh, Lawrence rose. "I'm sorry, Jake. I've got to go. I'll talk to you when I get back." And then he would consider the preposterous, wonderful suggestion that he marry Harriet.

When he returned four days later, the Hill Country was blanketed with the rain Robert Canfield had predicted. Though Lawrence had seen his share of heavy downpours, he'd never seen any like this. Lashed by strong winds, the torrents were so thick that visibility was reduced to mere feet, and the roads were muddy morasses that challenged even Snip. The only good thing Lawrence could say about the rain was that it had slowed the rustlers even more than the posse, aiding in their capture. Now all he wanted was to be home and out of his sodden garments. He'd welcome a hot drink and a warm room to wait out the storm.

"Just a little longer, Snip," Lawrence promised as he cut across Zach's ranch, racing toward the river and home. Half an hour, and they'd be there. But when he reached the river, Lawrence shuddered. The Medina did not want to be crossed. He slowed his horse, staring at the sight of water spilling over the banks, rushing downstream at twice its normal speed. Snip whinnied, sensing Lawrence's fears. A river like this could kill. Man and rider could be swept away in the blink of an eye.

A wise man would turn around and take refuge with Zach. Lawrence had always thought he was a wise man, but something he could not define made him urge Snip forward. He felt the way he had the day the school burned, filled with the certainty that he was needed on the opposite bank.

Help me, God, he prayed silently. *Show me what you need.*

As a feeling of peace settled over him, Lawrence bent

forward and patted Snip. "You can do it," he said, infusing his words with confidence. The horse was a strong swimmer. He'd make it to the other side.

The current was fiercer than Lawrence had thought, buffeting Snip, threatening to knock them both sideways. He bent low, encouraging his stallion, trying desperately to keep his own fears from spooking the horse. "You can do it, Snip. I know you can."

And he did. As the palomino struggled to climb the muddy bank, Lawrence slipped off and guided him to safety. "Good job," he said to the horse. Raising his eyes to the leaden skies, he murmured a prayer of thanks. It was time to learn who needed him.

25

She had never seen rain like this. Two days of heavy downpours had soaked the ground, creating puddles that turned into ponds, leaving Ladreville looking like an inland sea. Then, when everyone had thought the worst was over, the storm had intensified. Now wind lashed the rain, making it virtually impossible to traverse the roads. Harriet had canceled school for fear that a child might slip and be injured, though she doubted anyone would have ventured outdoors, even if she had tried to conduct classes. It appeared that all commerce had been halted, waiting for the storm to subside.

Harriet and her siblings remained at home, clustered around the stove in the parlor, for—despite the calendar's declaration that it was early May—the house was chilled by the days without sun. The boys were playing games, and Ruth was helping Mary piece a quilt for her doll while Harriet read. Or tried to read. She'd already put down the copy of *Vanity Fair*, for it reminded her of the conversations she and Lawrence had had about Thackeray's story. The next book on the stack was the one Lawrence had given her for Christmas. As beautiful as the pictures were, she wouldn't pick up that one, for it held even more memories. The problem was, no matter where Harriet turned, there were memories of Lawrence. She remembered his laughter, his solemn moments, even his anger, but the memory that haunted her was the disappointment she'd seen in his eyes the last time she had snubbed him.

Harriet closed her eyes. It hadn't been disappointment. It had been pain, and she had caused it. She, Harriet Kirk, who taught her pupils to be kind to one another, had been cruel to a man who deserved nothing but her thanks. Isabelle was right. Lawrence had simply been doing his job. The town had hired him to uphold the law, and that was what he'd done. It was only Harriet, afraid of public shame, who hadn't accepted that.

Her fingers touched the picture book Lawrence had given her, savoring the fine leather binding, but the volume she pulled from the table was her Bible. As it fell open to the center, Harriet's eyes lit on the first verse of Psalm 133. "Behold, how good and how pleasant it is for brethren to dwell together in unity." It *had* been good and pleasant when she and Lawrence had been friends, but she had spoiled it. She had been stubborn and headstrong and had refused to forgive him.

The truth was, there was nothing for her to forgive. It was Harriet who needed to ask for forgiveness. She was the one who'd wronged him. Though her last words to Lawrence had been angry, their friendship didn't have to end that way. It wouldn't be easy for her. Harriet knew that. But when he returned, she would apologize and ask his forgiveness for her unkindness. Then perhaps the world would once again be filled with promise.

Harriet laid the Bible back on the table, feeling more at peace than she had since the night she'd sent Lawrence away. Soon it would be all right. She would have her friend back in her life. She started to smile, and then . . .

Rap! Rap! Harriet's hands began to tremble with dread. This was no ordinary knocking. Someone was pounding on the front door, and that could only mean an emergency. Had Lawrence been hurt? Jake had said he'd gone to catch rustlers. Lawrence was a good shot, an excellent shot in fact, but even Rangers were occasionally injured. Or worse. Harriet wouldn't allow herself to consider that possibility.

"I'll go," she told her family as she hurried to the door, flinging it open.

"Gunther!" The man appeared soaked to the skin. Even his hat provided little protection, for water streamed from the brim onto his shoulders. "Come in." Harriet beckoned him inside, her heart beginning to thud at the anguish she saw on his face. "What's wrong?"

Fear shone from Gunther's blue eyes, and his accent was more pronounced than normal as he said, "It's Isabelle. Her time has come."

"But the babies aren't due for another six weeks."

A shudder rippled through him. "They don't seem to know that. Ach, Harriet, you've got to help her. She's been having pains for hours." His face contorted with the memory. "They're getting closer now. You've got to help her," he repeated.

Though Harriet had heard of women having pains that proved to be nothing more than a false alarm, it didn't sound as if that was the case today. Isabelle's travail had begun, and somehow, some way this man thought she could help. "But, Gunther, I know nothing about babies," she protested.

He shook his head. "She wants you by her side. Her mother is gone. They took Eva to Fredericksburg for a few days. Priscilla and Clay are on the other side of the river. No one can cross it now." Harriet nodded, knowing Isabelle's worst fear had come true: the river was impassible when she required Priscilla's care. "Please, Harriet." Gunther gripped her hands, his eyes shining with intensity. "She needs you. I need you. I can't lose her."

"Of course I'll come. But then I want you to go for Madame Seurat." Though she had no experience as a midwife, Madame Seurat had three children of her own. Together, they could help Isabelle, for Gunther, close to paralyzed by the memory of his first wife's death in childbirth, would provide precious little assistance. Grabbing her cloak, Harriet gave Ruth a quick explanation of the situation, ending, "I don't know when I'll be back."

Seconds later, she had climbed into Gunther's wagon, headed toward Hochstrasse. Though she had hoped otherwise, the storm had not diminished. If anything, it had intensified, sending sheets of rain cascading across the street, reducing visibility further, muffling even the sounds of the wagon wheels. Harriet peered into the distance, hating the way the rain spotted her spectacles, making it difficult to see. Not that there would be much to see. Nothing short of an emergency would bring people out in this weather.

She and Gunther had reached the corner of Hochstrasse and were preparing to turn right toward Gunther's house when Harriet blinked, startled by the sight of what appeared to be a horse and rider approaching from the river. Surely no one had attempted a crossing. The Medina had spilled over its banks earlier today, and the current was dangerously swift. Who would have been so foolish as to even approach the river? It must be more bad news.

The rider continued toward Harriet and Gunther, and as he drew closer, Harriet recognized him. "Lawrence!" she cried, her heart filling with joy at the realization that he was back, unharmed. "I'm so glad to see you." She had been wrong. This wasn't bad news. Lawrence was safe, and if anyone could help her, it would be he.

"What are you doing out in this weather?" Lawrence reined Snip in on Harriet's side of the wagon. Though his eyes reflected concern, there was none of the pain she had seen the last time. *Thank you, God.* She wouldn't wait another day. As soon as Isabelle's babies were safely delivered, Harriet would tell Lawrence everything that was in her heart. But first her other friend needed her.

She leaned over the side of the wagon, raising her voice to be heard above the pounding rain. "Isabelle's babies are coming before their time. I don't know anything about babies, and . . ." She darted a look at Gunther, as if to tell Lawrence the prospective father would provide no assistance. "We can't reach Priscilla or Clay, but I need someone who can help Isabelle. Would you bring Madame Seurat? I think Isabelle would be more comfortable with someone who speaks French." And who knew something about childbirth. Harriet did not voice the words, but she suspected Lawrence understood.

"Ja. That would be good."

Though Gunther spoke, Lawrence kept his eyes focused on Harriet, and she saw the lines between them deepen. "What

371

Isabelle needs is a midwife or a doctor." Lowering his voice slightly so that Gunther would not overhear, he added, "Clay said twins can be complicated."

They were being pelted by cold rain, discussing a possible medical crisis. She ought to have been shivering with apprehension, and yet warmth spread through Harriet. It felt so good to be with Lawrence again, working together to solve a problem.

"I won't argue with you, but there's no way either Priscilla or Clay can cross the river. Madame Seurat is the best alternative."

Lawrence shook his head. "Let me be the judge of that." He looked down Rhinestrasse toward the main river crossing. The Medina's overflow had turned the street itself into a small river. "I'll get you the help you and Isabelle need."

Blood drained from Harriet's face as she realized what he was proposing. He couldn't. No one could cross the river when the current was this strong. It would be difficult—perhaps impossible—for anyone, but for someone who feared deep water as Lawrence did, it was unthinkable.

"Please, Lawrence, no."

"Don't be a fool." Gunther's words were harsh. "It's suicide to try to ford the river now."

Harriet clenched her fists as Gunther's words sent images racing through her brain. "You can't do this, Lawrence. Even if you could cross, how could you bring anyone back?"

Lawrence's lips tightened. "We're wasting precious time. I crossed it before, and I can do it again. Snip knows how to swim this river. He can bring Priscilla back. I'll ride her horse." Lawrence gave Harriet a fleeting smile. "Don't worry."

But she would. Of course she would. Until Lawrence was

372

safely back on this bank, she would worry. And pray. *Dear Lord, keep him safe.*

Lawrence leaned forward, murmuring something to his horse, and the two galloped toward the Medina, water splashing each time Snip's hooves hit the ground. When they reached the raging river, the horse hesitated.

"No, Lawrence!" Harriet doubted he heard her shout, for he was a block away. She turned toward Gunther. "We've got to stop him."

It was too late. Snip entered the river and began to swim toward the opposite bank, his rider bent low over his neck. It was slow going, for they had to dodge the branches and logs that were being propelled downstream at a fearsome rate. Harriet winced when one collided with Snip. But then she realized that there was another, greater threat. The river had begun to swirl, creating a series of whirlpools that threatened to drag Lawrence and Snip down. Twice Harriet saw the palomino falter, and she feared he would drown. *Keep them safe*, she prayed. *Let them reach the other side.*

They had reached the middle, the deepest part, when a loud rumbling filled the air. Harriet looked at Gunther, confused. Though it sounded like thunder, she knew it was not. Storms like this brought no thunder.

"*Nein. Gott in Himmel, nein.*" Gunther's eyes widened, and his words were part prayer, part horrified exclamation. "The dam has broken."

It couldn't have. Harriet remembered Gunther entering his kitchen during the last rain, telling Isabelle the dam was fine. Surely he was mistaken. Surely the dam would hold again.

Harriet stared at the spot where Lawrence had been. More

quickly than she had dreamt possible, an enormous surge of water swelled the already overflowing river. Gunther was not mistaken. The dam that powered his mill had crumbled, sending hundreds of thousands of gallons of water downstream at a truly frightening speed. The deluge was sweeping everything away, including the man Harriet loved. *Please, God*, she prayed silently. *Save him. Save Lawrenc*e.

There was no answer, no sound but the roaring river, no sight but raging water that had overflowed the banks and was heading toward her and Gunther. Lawrence was gone.

As the horses began to rear in panic, Gunther tugged the reins and turned the wagon northward toward his home. "There is naught we can do for Lawrence." Sorrow filled Gunther's voice. "Isabelle needs us."

Harriet shuddered, her heart refusing to admit what her brain had registered. It wasn't possible. Lawrence hadn't been taken from her. But he had and in the worst way possible. Oh, Lawrence! She closed her eyes, trying to block out the image of the water closing over his head. How horrible it must have been, knowing he was suffering the same fate as his sister. Surely it was a nightmare. Surely she would soon awaken. But the emptiness deep inside told Harriet this was no nightmare. It was real. What a fool she had been. She had wasted the time she and Lawrence might have had. She had let her pride, her foolish pride, keep them apart, and now it was too late.

Numb with grief, Harriet nodded. Gunther was right. There was nothing they could do here. Nothing she could do would change what had happened. Nothing would bring Lawrence back. But now, somehow, some way she had to help Isabelle.

"Please, God, help me." She murmured the words, praying that the fact that she had spoken them would make a difference.

God had not answered her first prayer. He had not saved Lawrence, but surely he would not let Isabelle and her babies die. Surely he would not let Gunther lose another wife. Taking a deep breath, Harriet resolved to do everything in her power to keep Gunther's family alive.

"I knew you'd come," Isabelle said five minutes later when Harriet entered her bedchamber.

"I'm here, but your husband is heading out again. He's going to bring Madame Seurat."

"But the water . . ."

Harriet gripped Gunther's arm and turned him toward the door. "We need her. And," she added softly, "Isabelle doesn't need to know what has happened." Once the babies were born would be time enough to tell her about the broken dam and Lawrence. "She doesn't need to know, not now." And Harriet did not need to think about all she had lost. There would be time for grieving later.

She studied the woman on the bed. Isabelle's face was paler than normal, her brown eyes two enormous spots in an expanse of white. Lines etched the corners of her mouth, telling Harriet more clearly than words the pain she was experiencing. Though the last thing she wanted to do was laugh, Harriet respected the therapeutic effects of humor. Fisting both hands on her hips, she pretended to glare at her friend. "Your babies sure picked a fine day to be born. I hope you're planning to call them Rain and Drop."

As she had hoped, Isabelle began to chuckle. A second later she grasped her abdomen as a contraction began. "Don't make me laugh," she said when the pain subsided. "It hurts."

But, though Isabelle might claim otherwise, she looked better. A tinge of color had reached her cheeks, and the pain in her eyes had diminished.

"I'm going to boil some water and gather some clean cloths." Harriet gave Isabelle a conspiratorial smile. "I've always heard that's what you need for a birth. I guess you and I are going to figure out what we're supposed to do with them while we wait for Madame Seurat."

"You're doing it again. You're making me laugh." Isabelle's laughter ended abruptly as another contraction seized her. "Oh no! I think they're coming. Do something."

But what? It was one thing to comfort her friend, quite another to deliver two babies. The closest Harriet had come to birth was watching the barn cat have kittens.

"Can't you wait?" Even as she asked the question, Harriet recognized its absurdity.

"No!" Isabelle screamed as another pain rippled through her. "I can't wait."

It had been only a few minutes since Gunther had left, not nearly long enough to have reached Madame Seurat's house, much less bring her back here. There was no choice. *You're going to have to help me, Lord*, Harriet thought as she positioned herself at Isabelle's feet. *Guide me. I can't do this alone.* She closed her eyes for a second, and though her hands continued to tremble, Harriet felt a newfound confidence settle over her when she opened them again. "I see something," she told her friend. "I think it's a head." When Isabelle merely grunted, Harriet continued, "The next pain you feel, push. Push hard."

By the time Gunther arrived with Madame Seurat, Isabelle was cradling both sons in her arms. Though tiny, they had been endowed with powerful lungs and wasted no time in announcing their arrival. While Madame Seurat checked the babies, Harriet wandered around the parlor, passing the time until she could ask Gunther to take her home.

When she spied a Bible sitting on a small table, she picked it up and, as she had only a few hours earlier, opened it at random. This Bible fell open to the New Testament, and a chill ran down Harriet's spine when she read the words of John 15:13. "Greater love hath no man than this, that a man lay down his life for his friends."

How could she have ever doubted Lawrence? There were times when she had believed him to be a taker like Thomas, but she was wrong, so very, very wrong. Lawrence was a giver. Harriet sank into a chair and cradled the Bible between her hands. Now, when it was too late, she recognized the depth of her love for him. Like the first seeds in the children's garden, Harriet's love had sprouted quickly, but then it had appeared to die from an early frost.

Why hadn't she realized that love didn't die? It had merely become dormant. Under the surface it was still alive, waiting for the spring rain to bring it back to life. Tears streamed down Harriet's face as she admitted the truth. It wasn't friendship she felt for Lawrence but love. She loved him, and she knew without a single doubt that he loved her. Though he'd never said the words, Lawrence's actions had proven how much he loved her, for, as the Bible said, he had given his life to help her. There could be no greater love than that.

By evening the rain had ended. The river was still high and would remain so for several days, but the current was slowing. Soon after Harriet returned home, the townspeople emerged from their houses to recount the day's events: the arrival of Isabelle and Gunther's sons and the tragic loss of Ladreville's sheriff and mayor. Finally as night fell, they went back indoors, leaving the streets empty once more.

Harriet stared out the window. Though the rest of her family was upstairs, she was unable to sleep. Each time she closed her eyes, instead of seeing Isabelle and Gunther, their faces wreathed in radiant smiles as they looked at the tiny boys they had named Harry and Joshua, her mind filled with images of Lawrence being swept away. Sterling had told her that God would give her the strength to endure the pain. Perhaps that would be true in time, but tonight her grief was too deep, her emotions too raw, for her to sleep, and so she sat in the parlor, searching for words of comfort in the Book that had guided her before.

Help me bear the pain. Show me what to do. Instead of an answer, Harriet heard the sound of wagon wheels and horses' hooves. That was odd, for few people traversed this block of Rhinestrasse, and never so late. More than a little curious, Harriet peered out the window, trying to see who was coming this direction. The answer surprised her. Though the night was dark, the moon that emerged from the heavy cloud cover was bright enough that Harriet recognized Clay. For some reason the town's physician was on this side of the river and headed her way. He tugged on the reins, stopping the wagon directly in front of the Kirk house.

Why was he here? Harriet hurried outside. "Clay! I didn't expect to see you for a couple days." And she wouldn't have expected him to be driving a wagon. Normally Clay came into town on horseback. It was only when he brought Sarah and little Rob that he drove the buggy. As for the wagon, this was the first time Harriet had seen it here.

"Why did you come?"

Though he nodded solemnly, Harriet thought she saw a note of amusement in Clay's eyes. It must have been her imagination, for there was scant reason for amusement tonight.

"The river dropped faster than I expected," he said, "so I thought I'd check on Isabelle and her babies, but first I have a delivery for you." There it was again, a hint of amusement. This time Clay's lips twitched as if he wanted to laugh. He dismounted, then gestured toward the wagon bed. "Your delivery is here."

A taller woman might have been able to peer inside, but Harriet's less than average height left her staring at the side of the wagon, not its contents.

"Here, let me." Clay placed his hands on her waist and lifted her so she could see inside.

For a second, Harriet stared, not believing her eyes. "Lawrence!" This couldn't be a dream, for her imagination would not have conjured the image of a badly bruised man lying on the wagon floor, his left leg encased in a white plaster cast, his face sporting four large bandages and an even larger smile.

"Oh, Lawrence!" Harriet leaned forward, wanting to touch him, to assure herself that this was no mirage. When he stretched out his hand and clasped hers, Harriet's last doubt vanished. This was a flesh and blood hand, Lawrence's hand. "Thank God. I thought you were . . ."

"Dead." He finished the sentence. "So did I, but God appeared to have other plans for me." Lawrence struggled to a sitting position. "Will you invite me inside?"

"Of course." She held the crutches while Clay helped Lawrence slide out of the wagon. Then, slowly so he would not fall, Harriet and Lawrence walked into her house. "What happened?" she demanded when he was seated on the settee, his leg propped on an ottoman. "How did you survive?"

She lit two more lamps, wanting to banish the darkness, for even though Lawrence sat only a foot away, Harriet's mind was filled with images of him being swept downstream, disappearing into the muddy depths of the Medina.

"I don't really know what happened," Lawrence admitted. "When the dam broke, I was knocked off Snip." His eyes darkened. "I've never felt anything like it. The river was moving faster than I could have imagined. Even though I can swim, there was no way to fight the current, especially with all the water I'd swallowed. Every time I managed to get my head above water, I'd be knocked under again. Each time I thought it was the last, but then I'd bob to the surface, only to be knocked under again."

Harriet shuddered, trying to imagine how frightened he must have been, knowing this was how his sister had died.

"I knew I was drowning." Lawrence confirmed Harriet's thoughts. "There was nothing more I could do. I was so weak that all I could do was take one more breath. Then everything went black. The next thing I knew, I was lying on the other bank of the river." Lawrence's eyes reflected the light of wonder. "I have no idea how I got there. What I learned afterward was that Clay went out in the middle of the storm to check the horses, and he felt an urge to head toward the river. When he got there, he saw Snip. Somehow, Snip managed to swim to shore, and he was standing next to me, keeping watch. It seems he's gotten me out of a tough spot again. Clay might not have found me if it hadn't been for Snip." Though Lawrence's words were matter of fact, the tremor in his voice told Harriet how deeply affected he was by his rescue.

"God sent him."

Lawrence nodded. "Our Lord knew that I had unfinished business. I didn't want to die without telling you how I felt. Harriet, I—"

"No, Lawrence." Harriet held up a hand, asking him to wait. No matter what he wanted to say, she owed him an apology. That was the first part of *her* unfinished business. "I'm the one who was wrong. You were only doing your job when you arrested Jake." She bit her lip as she remembered her harsh words that night and all the times since then when she had rejected Lawrence's overtures.

"Jake deserved to go to jail," Harriet said firmly. "Nothing else was working. If you hadn't insisted, there's no telling what else he might have done. Now he's a changed boy."

A smile crossed Lawrence's lips. "A changed young man." He amended her words.

"You're right. That's another thing I've learned. My siblings are growing up. They won't need me much longer." Though it was painful, though it meant baring her heart, she could not stop now. She owed Lawrence a full explanation. "You were right. I fought that, because I liked being in control. I made all the decisions." Harriet shook her head slowly, her eyes moving from his face to the Bible on the small table. "You know what I learned? I was only deluding myself. I wasn't in control, not ever. It was God who was leading me. He was trying to show me the way, even when I stumbled. Once again you were right. I needed help, and I had to learn to ask for it. When I did, God answered my prayers. He saved you."

Harriet's eyes filled with tears at the realization that not only had she not lost Lawrence, but she had also regained her future. Lawrence claimed that God had more plans for him. Maybe, just maybe, those plans included her.

"Can you forgive me for being so pigheaded?" Harriet asked softly.

His eyes a deeper blue than she had ever seen, Lawrence met her gaze. "Can you forgive me for being so proud? I thought I knew better than everyone, even God. I was the big, strong Ranger. Even though you told me otherwise, I was sure I knew what Isabelle needed today." Lawrence gave his broken leg a wry glance. "Look what that got me. I was also sure about my life. Even when God pointed me in a different direction, I kept going my way." Lawrence shook his head slowly. "I considered myself a good Christian, but—like you—I forgot who was in charge. I hope I never make that mistake again. God gave me a second chance today, and I don't want to waste it."

Harriet nodded as Lawrence's words echoed her thoughts. The psalmist was right. It was pleasant to dwell together in unity. It was even more pleasing to be at peace with the Lord. Whatever God's plans were for her, Harriet would do her best to accept them, for he was the source of all wisdom. She knew that now.

Lawrence reached forward and took her hand in his, his voice husky as he said, "Life is too precious to let another day go by without telling you how I feel. That's why I insisted Clay bring me here tonight. I want you to know what's in my heart."

Raising her hand to his lips, Lawrence pressed a kiss on it. "I love you, Harriet. I know you once said you would not marry for a long time, if ever, but I hope you'll reconsider. Will you be my wife?"

The bubble of happiness that had started deep inside her rose to her throat, and for a second Harriet could not speak. The second's delay was too long, for Lawrence's smile faded. "There have been times when I thought you cared for me. Perhaps I was mistaken."

She was such a fool! Though it had been unintentional, once again she had hurt him. "You were not mistaken, Lawrence," Harriet said firmly. "And you're right that I once feared marriage." She had to make him understand that she was the problem, not him. "I have to admit I was scared when I realized I loved you. You see, I haven't had a lot of experience with love. My parents weren't much of an example, nor were my grandparents. It was only when I came here and saw the Friedrichs and Gunther and Isabelle that I started to realize love is real, not just a story in a book." Lawrence nodded as if he understood.

Tears of happiness filling her eyes, Harriet smiled at the man she loved. "For a while I didn't dare to dream. All I thought about was the present, because I was afraid there would be no future. What would I do when Mary didn't need me anymore? I thought I'd be too old to have a life of my own, and so I tried not to think about it. But then you came into my life, and I began to believe there was more than the present. I started dreaming about a future, and suddenly I knew what I wanted. I wanted marriage and children of my own. I wanted you, Lawrence." Harriet tugged his hand toward her and pressed a kiss on it. "You're the man of my dreams."

Though his cast made it awkward, Lawrence rose and drew Harriet to her feet. Gently, he pulled her into his arms. "Will you marry me?" He repeated the question, his lips only a fraction of an inch from hers.

She could feel the warmth of his breath, smell the sweet, pungent fragrance that was his alone, and hear the urgency of his question. Harriet smiled and looked into the blue eyes of the man she loved so deeply. "Yes, yes, a thousand times yes."

Author's Letter

Dear Reader,

It's always a bittersweet moment when I finish a book. While I'm happy to have the manuscript ready to send to my editor, at the same time I hate to say good-bye to the characters. Reaching the end of *Tomorrow's Garden* was particularly poignant, since it's the final book in the Texas Dreams trilogy, and that meant leaving Ladreville and its inhabitants.

Though it's time to say farewell to Ladreville, it's also a time for new beginnings, namely the start of a new trilogy. I invite you to join me for a series set in my home, Wyoming. In what I've tentatively named the Wyoming Winds trilogy, three sisters find love, adventure, and deeper faith in a territory on the verge of statehood. Faced with everything from stagecoach robberies to blizzards to murder, they learn that only strong women survive on the windswept prairie. The first book will be available in the spring of 2012.

Meanwhile, if this is your first Texas Dreams book, I hope

you'll read the others. *Paper Roses*, the first of the trilogy, tells the story of Sarah's arrival in Ladreville and her rocky road to romance. Though you know that she and Clay have a happy ending, I assure you it wasn't always certain. And, if you were intrigued by Lawrence's infatuation with Priscilla, don't miss *Scattered Petals*, the second in the series. In it you'll learn how they met and how Priscilla, who was looking for adventure, found that love may be the greatest adventure of all. But first she had to surmount almost impossible obstacles.

One of the things I truly enjoy is hearing from readers, and so I encourage you to visit my website (www.amanda cabot.com). It includes an email link, my snail mail address, and information about my books. It also has discussion guides for readers' groups. Please let me know what you've enjoyed about my stories and what you'd like to see next.

Until we meet again, I send you blessings and remind you of Isaiah 12:2: "Behold, God is my salvation; I will trust, and not be afraid: for the Lord Jehovah is my strength and my song; he also is become my salvation."

Amanda Cabot

Acknowledgments

It takes a team of talented, dedicated professionals to turn an author's words into a finished book like the one you're holding. I am blessed to have such a team working on my stories. My publisher's staff is, without exception, a true delight. If I listed everyone at Revell who's helped me along the journey to publication, I'd fill several pages and would still run the risk of missing someone. But I do want to single out two women, without whom the Texas Dreams trilogy would not have been possible.

First, my agent, Joyce Hart. Joyce is a consummate professional who's always provided me with excellent advice. Just as importantly, she believed in these books from the beginning and kept assuring me that she would find the perfect editor for them. She did.

Vicki Crumpton is—at least in my estimation—the perfect editor. Her insights and sense of humor make the dreaded revision process enjoyable, and her confidence in my writing helps me through the inevitable middle-of-the-book slump. She is, quite simply, fabulous.

I am deeply grateful to Joyce, Vicki, and the entire Revell team for their support.

Dreams have always been an important part of **Amanda Cabot's** life. For almost as long as she can remember, she dreamt of being an author. Fortunately for the world, her grade-school attempts as a playwright were not successful, and she turned her attention to writing novels. Her dream of selling a book before her thirtieth birthday came true, and she's been spinning tales ever since. She now has more than twenty-five novels to her credit under a variety of pseudonyms.

Amanda is a member of ACFW, a charter member of Romance Writers of America, and an avid traveler. She married her high school sweetheart, who shares her love of travel and who's driven thousands of miles to help her research her books. A few years ago they fulfilled a longtime dream and are now living in the American West.

MEET AMANDA CABOT AT
www.AmandaCabot.com

Sign up for her newsletter and learn fun
facts about Amanda and her books!

f Amanda Cabot

Don't miss any of the

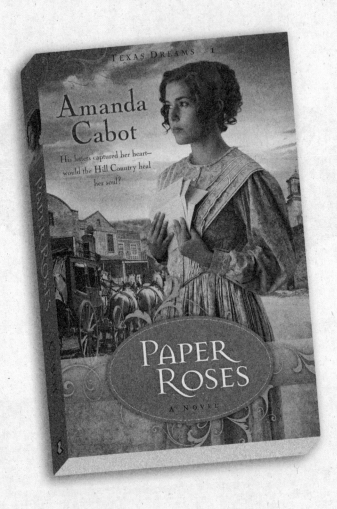

His letters captured her heart—
would the Hill Country heal her soul?

Texas Dreams series!

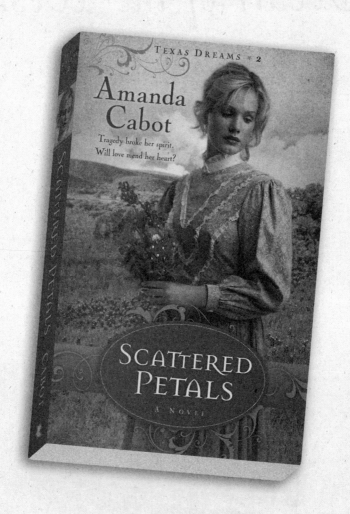

Tragedy broke her spirit.
Will love mend her heart?

Journey into the
Heart of the West

Can a Southern belle tame the heart of a rugged cowboy?

a division of Baker Publishing Group
www.RevellBooks.com

Sweet Romances
That Capture the Heart

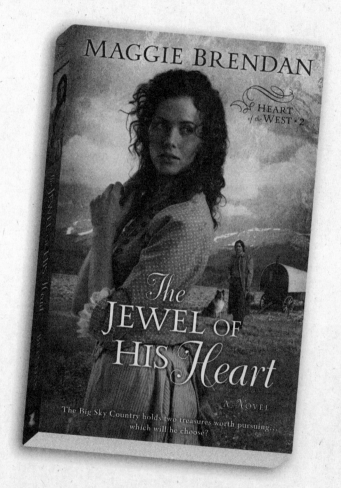

The Big Sky Country holds two treasures worth pursuing . . .
which will he choose?

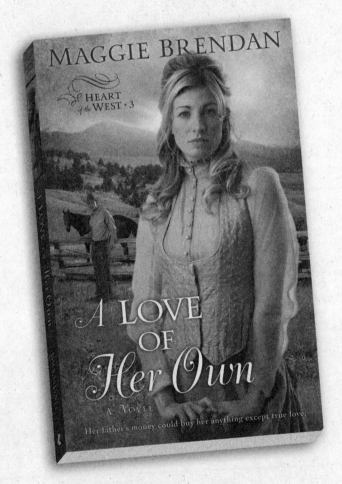

When tragedy strikes, how will Molly McGarvie survive?

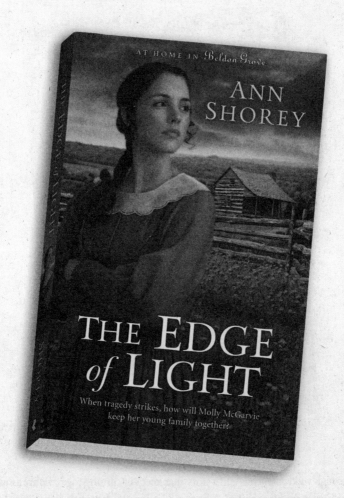

Experience the wonder and hardship of life on the prairie with Molly McGarvie as she fights to survive loss and keep her young family together.

When loss drives them apart, can their faith bring them back together?

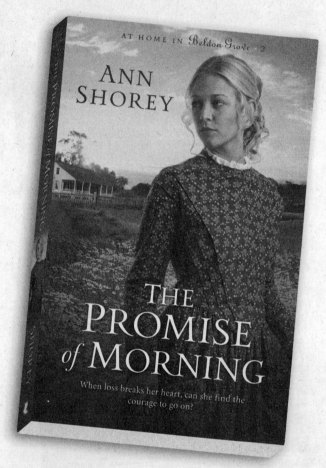

AT HOME IN *Beldon Grove · 2*

ANN SHOREY

THE PROMISE of MORNING

When loss breaks her heart, can she find the courage to go on?

"Through vivid characters and a story that keeps us turning pages, we are assured that God keeps his promises. A fine read."—**Jane Kirkpatrick**, award-winning author of *All Together in One Place* and *A Flickering Light*